Who by Fire,
Who by Blood

11·1·07

To Rosalyne
Berstein

Best
Wishes.

Jon Papernick

Who by Fire, Who by Blood

Jon Papernick

[signature: Jon Papernick]

No. 9 of 1001

The 1001 Book Project
Back Pages Books
Waltham, MA

Exile Editions

Publishers of singular
Fiction, Poetry, Drama, Non-fiction and Graphic Books

2007

Library and Archives Canada Cataloguing in Publication

Papernick, Jon, 1970-
  Who by fire, who by blood / Jon Papernick.

ISBN 978-1-55096-102-7

    I. Title.

PS8581.A6645W46 2007   C813'.6   C2007-904876-5

Design and Composition by Homunculus ReproSet
Typeset in Minion at the Moons of Jupiter Studios
The poem by Yehuda Amichai is originally from the book *Travels*,
  © Exile Editions, 1986
Printed in Canada by Friesens

The publisher would like to acknowledge the financial assistance of
The Canada Council for the Arts, and the Ontario Arts Council–which is
an agency of the Government of Ontario.

 Conseil des Arts   Canada Council
du Canada   for the Arts    ONTARIO ARTS COUNCIL
CONSEIL DES ARTS DE L'ONTARIO

Published in Canada in 2007 by Exile Editions Ltd.
144483 Southgate Road 14
General Delivery
Holstein, Ontario, N0G 2A0
info@exileeditions.com
www.ExileEditions.com

Canadian Sales Distribution:
McArthur & Company
c/o Harper Collins
1995 Markham Road
Toronto, ON M1B 5M8
toll free: 1 800 387 0117

for Eve

וּבְשֶׁקֶט, כְּרוֹפֵא וָאֵם, גָּרְכְנוּ הַיָּמִים מֵעָלַי
וְהֵחֵלּוּ לְהִתְלַחֵשׁ בֵּינֵיהֶם, בְּעֵת הָעֶשֶׂב
כְּבָר שָׁכַב, מִשְׁכָּב בְּרוּחוֹ הַמָּרָה
בְּמַעֲלֵה הַגְּבָעוֹת שֶׁלְּעוֹלָם לֹא אָשׁוּב לִדְרֹךְ בָּהֶן.
יָרֵחַ וְכוֹכָבִים וּמַעֲשִׂים עַתִּיקִים שֶׁל מְבֻגָּרִים
הוּשְׂמוּ בְּאָצְטַבָּה גְּבֹהָה מֵעַל
לְהַשָּׂגַת זְרוֹעוֹתַי;
וְעָמַדְתִּי לַשָּׁוְא מִתַּחַת לַכּוֹנָנִיּוֹת הָאֲסוּרוֹת.
אַךְ כְּבָר אָז הָיִיתִי מְסֻמָּן לִכְלָיָה כְּתַפּוּף
לְקִלּוּף, כְּשׁוֹקוֹלָדָה, כִּרְמֹץ־יָד לְפִצוּץ וָמָוֶת.
כַּף הַכַּתָּנוֹת הֶחֱזִיקָה אוֹתִי הֵיטֵב. שָׁמַי הָיוּ
פְּנִים כַּף־הַיָּד הַמַּחֲזִיקָה, הָרַכָּה, וּבְחוּץ
הָעוֹר הַמְחֻסְפָּס, כּוֹכָבִים קָשִׁים, וְרִידִים בּוֹלְטִים,
קַוֵּי תְעוּפָה, שֵׂעָר שָׁחוֹר, מַסְלוּלֵי פָּנִים
בְּדוּמֵם וּבְמִיַּלֵּל, בְּשָׁחוֹר וּבְנוֹתֵב זֹהַר.
וּבְטֶרֶם הָיִיתִי מַמָּשִׁי וְשׁוֹהֶה כָּאן,
עָמְסוּ כִּתְפֵי הַלֵּב יָגוֹן לֹא לִי
וְרַעֲיוֹנוֹת זָרִים נִכְנְסוּ, עֲצוּרִים
וּלְאַטָּם וּבְגִרְגּוּר עָמֹק, כְּרַכֶּבֶת
לְתוֹךְ הַתַּחֲנָה הַחֲלוּלָה וְהַמַּאֲזִינָה.

The days bent over me quietly, like a doctor
and a mother, and began to whisper together,
while the grass bent, flattened by the bitter wind
on the hills I shall never climb again.
Moon and stars and the ancient deeds of adults
were put high on a shelf
out of my reach;
in vain I stretched up to the forbidden bookshelves.
But even when I was marked for death like an orange
for peeling, like chocolate for breaking, like a hand-grenade
for explosion, the hand of fate held me tight.
My heaven was the soft palm—its outside
coarse skin, hard stars: its protruding veins,
airlines; its black hairs, the trajectory of shells
silent or shining, in darkness or with flares.
And before I was real and here to stay,
my heart shouldered sorrows not my own,
and strange ideas entered me, muffled, slow,
jolting like a train
into a listening, hollow station.

—*Yehuda Amichai*

"... he whose blood is especially warm has the requisite quality to become a brave man. But another whose heart is colder than it should be, is naturally inclined toward cowardice and fear."

—MAIMONIDES

∾ 1 ∽

Matthew Stone opened his eyes and looked down into the street. People in twos and threes moved about languidly in the pale yellow haze as if constrained by a barely discernable gauze. A bus roared past and Stone could see a trail of vapor shimmering in its wake. The whisper of a gentle breeze on his face brought him back to his body, his hard-beating heart, and it convulsed in a sudden discordant two-step that left him gasping for air. He gathered his breath and wondered what it would be like to jump. From the rooftop, looking across the river towards the city and the fading pink sunset, he could see the monolithic Twin Towers and the crenelated spires of the Woolworth Building, all the way to the Chrysler Building halfway up the island, rising like a stainless-steel rocket ship from the dissonant chaos of Midtown. A battered billboard on a facing neighboring building read "COP SHOT REWARD $$$."

He removed his glasses, and Manhattan's jagged skyline smeared before him. Stone closed his eyes and the last rays of sun, red and dull, still managed to penetrate his eyelids. The pigeons cooing on a ledge below sounded almost human, a choir full of sorrow and regret and loss, unintelligible, but almost human.

Stone wore his father's judge's robe again. The sleeves hung beyond his wrist and flapped awkwardly like fins as he sat hunched on a rusty bridge chair with his elbows resting on his knees.

As a boy he used to sneak into the Judge's room, awed by his father's tremendous bulk, and pull the majestic robe from the closet which forever smelled like the stale smoke of Nat Sherman Originals. Matthew would drape the robe over his slight body. He felt like a superhero, like Batman, like the Caped Crusader. Anything was possible.

But that was a long time ago.

Still breathless from the five flights to his roof, he pulled a pack of matches from his pocket and lit a joint. As he inhaled, he felt the heat of the burning tip near his skin, and he was reminded of the old feelings, the need for release.

He dropped a match into the street where a bus rumbled by. He lit another match, held it for a five count, and dropped it. A cluster of pigeons rose into the sky and scattered, a pungent rush of air blowing past on the updraft. A few streets over a car alarm wailed and from an ice cream truck a delicate tune warbled as if being played from underwater.

Stone pulled the robe tight around him, binding his chin for a moment against his chest. He could smell his father now, the stale scent of his tobacco. He felt his father's strong hands on his shoulders, heavy and firm. The hands tightened around his neck, a school ring ice-cold against his skin.

Stone took another drag, and as the smoke filled his lungs he felt his muscles slacken, his blood slowing, his seasick stomach calming.

He thought of his father, who appeared before him, a paragon of scholarly civility, wearing a three-piece suit and half-moon glasses, shaking his head in disapproval.

The sky had turned a murky gray. A single green iridescent feather floated in the air just out of Stone's reach. The wind was picking up when the steel door swung open behind Stone and his roommate Pinky called, "Matty! Phone!"

"Who is it?" he called, but Pinky had already disappeared back down the damp stairwell. *Probably Seligman again,* Stone thought. *He can wait.*

The sky continued to darken, heavy black clouds rolling in high on the wind, as eerie yellow lights came on in the greasy streets between his apartment house and the river. Brooklyn looked somehow more lurid in the gathering dark, its low buildings more shabby, its windows filling with the broken silhouettes of WIC-assisted poor, bent over dinner plates in the blue glare of their televisions; rooftop water tanks formed shapes of smeared darkness against darkness; disembodied renegade shouts filled the air, the streets below burning with anger freed by the falling night. He had heard gunshots the night before, four of them, but no sirens. Manhattan, too, looked different; its jagged spine lit up spasmodically, randomly, lights flaring up the length of the island like torches lit by primitives in another age.

When Stone had first heard Seligman's brassy voice on the line, the valves of his heart had constricted, the familiar baritone so similar to that of his father it had nearly caused Stone to lose consciousness. The dead cannot speak, they cannot, he had thought. His father was dead and buried on the Mount of Olives in Jerusalem. But the voice persisted. "It's me, Uncle Zal."

Stone had not seen him at the funeral and had put the Judge's friend out of his mind, figuring he was afraid to leave the barbed-wire compound of Giv'at Barzel. He had offered his condolences, by telephone, "It is never easy to lose a parent. But your father will be the first in line when Redemption comes."

He had asked Stone where he was saying *Kaddish*. "As the only surviving son, it is your obligation."

His worst fears had been realized. Seligman was an emissary sent by his father from the other world to belittle him, make him feel small, the way the Judge had done his entire life. The finish line was always being extended, just out of his reach. He would never be free.

Now, in the cool air of the rooftop, Stone tried to mouth the words of the *Kaddish*, but they tasted like ash on his tongue, and the pounding subsonic bass beat of a car stereo below caused a vein in his temple to throb. He wrapped the robe tight around him and smelled his father again, the stale smoke of his cigarettes, his sour sweat. A pigeon appeared on the rusted railing before Stone, strutting with avian bravado. He flapped his wings and disappeared into the sky. Stone spread his arms out like wings, the fabric flapping in the wind, and stepped forward to the railing. He looked down and saw a storekeeper rolling closed his heavy steel shutter with a clattering slam. He threw one leg over the railing, feeling dizzy with exhilaration, a vein jumping in his wrist.

"What the fuck?" Pinky called, stepping on to the roof. "Get offa there before anyone sees you. You're lookin' like a fuckin' Dracula."

All Stone had to do was tilt forward and he was gone.

"Answer the phone. I'm not your bitch secretary."

Their living room was stacked almost to the ceiling with cardboard banker's boxes of the Judge's belongings, sent over that day from his Midwood apartment. The boxes were filled mostly with worn books and photographs; his personal papers having been shredded in the early days of his illness. The Judge collected rare books and had catalogued them chronologically from "In the beginning . . ." and his 19th-century reprint of the Gutenberg Bible through to the Spanish Inquisition and the Jewish mystics, to a signed copy of the writings of Ze'ev Jabotinsky, to bound copies of the reviled Oslo Peace Accords.

Stone found the receiver on the floor next to the coffee table, its coiled cord tangled around itself. He picked up the phone and heard the persistent hum of the dial tone.

"Who was it?" Stone asked, untangling the cord mindlessly.

Pinky looked up from a cold plate of leftover chop suey. "Your mom," he said, as if that was the only possible answer despite the fact that Stone had not heard from her since she disappeared nearly 14 years earlier.

Stone went cold and dropped the phone to the floor.

"What did she say?"

"She'll call back," Pinky said.

Pinky had scattered dozens of transparent plastic Bingo chips across the floor: red, orange, yellow, mint, blue, violet and pink discs clung to the floor like tiny puddles of paint. Now that he had gone out for smokes, Stone was alone. *I've got to clean this place up,* he thought. He dragged a heavy box down the long hallway to his room and sat on the floor with it beside his bed.

Stone's room felt empty and bare. He had begun sealing the boxes up before his father had died, emptying the Judge's drawers, book shelves, and closets in an unconscious burst of energy after two days without sleeping. It had felt ghoulish boxing up the Judge's belongings while his heart still beat, but Stone did not know what to do with himself with his father dying in the next room. And now, on the floor of his room, he pulled a wrinkled manila envelope off the top of the box – old black and white photos from the thirties and forties.

"Papa Julius," Stone said aloud.

He was surprised that the Judge had kept pictures of his own father – he rarely spoke of him – and had not seen him, as far as Stone knew, since he had moved uptown to Columbia over forty years earlier. But there was Stone's grandfather, faded against the yellowing photographic paper, smiling, his foot on the running board of a black Oldsmobile. Another shot – under the sign for Ratner's Deli, the Williamsburg Bridge in the background – Julius laughing as he pulled the hat off of Meyer Lansky.

"Meyer Lansky!" Stone said, laughing. He rolled a joint, lit it, and smoked.

There were dozens of photos of Julius Stone from his days with Murder Inc. Stone studied the photos for a long time; his grandfather did not look like a killer. He had intense eyes, sure, but there was a spark in them, as if he were about to tell a joke. Stone was amazed how similar in build he was to his grandfather, the wild-haired killer, one hundred and twenty pounds of dynamite with a short fuse.

Stone found photographs of his father as a child when on Ocean Parkway: his father and poor Aunt Bunny playing on the front lawn, her broad mongoloid face shining beneath a frilled bonnet. Color pictures sent from Florida, of Papa Julius lounging in a chair, straw hat pulled over his eyes. He saw his father as a shirtless, radiant teen, his full head of hair cropped short. He could not imagine that this was actually his father, this smiling teen leaning, carefree, on an oar beside some nameless lake. Stone relit his joint and picked up a copy of his father's *New York Times* obituary that sat on his bedside table. The newsprint felt like dry winter skin against his fingers.

WALTER STONE, 63, YOUNGEST ASS'T D.A. IN NYC; JURYMANDERING JUDGE; PURSUED NAZIS.

Walter Stone, a New York State Supreme Court judge who presided over the controversial Court Street Riot trial and was later forced to resign over improprieties regarding jury selection, died Monday at his home in Brooklyn. He was 63. The cause of death was lung and throat cancer, said his son Matthew Stone.

Mr. Stone became the state's youngest assistant district attorney in 1957, at the age of 22. He doggedly prosecuted organized crime figures, including street gangs in the Hell's Kitchen neighborhood of Manhattan after two children were killed in gang-related violence, and after the theft of priceless jewels from the Museum of Natural History. He was widely noted as a forceful proponent of law and order during the mayoralty of Robert F. Wagner.

Mr. Stone left the District Attorney's office in 1965 to join the army during the Vietnam War. He served in the Judge Advocate General's Corps, assigned to the 25th Infantry Division from 1966-1968. He was awarded a Bronze Star Medal for Meritorious Service.

In 1970, he was appointed to the criminal branch of the King's County Supreme Court, where he served until stepping down from the bench amidst controversy in 1992.

Downtown Brooklyn exploded into riots and looting after an ultra-Orthodox Jewish man ran over a nine-year-old Arab-American boy on the district's main shopping thoroughfare, Atlantic Avenue. In the wake of the riots, an Orthodox Jewish man, Isaac Brilliant, was charged with killing a Palestinian immigrant. Mr. Stone's impartiality was questioned after he allowed a member of the jury who was admittedly sympathetic to Mr. Brilliant, and his fate, to stay on after he became aware of his sympathies.

"Walter felt embarrassed, humiliated, he was never the same again," New York State Supreme Court Justice Leonard Samuel said, referring to Mr. Stone's resignation.

Born in 1935 in Brownsville, Brooklyn, the son of alleged mobster and Murder Incorporated trigger man, Julius Stone, Mr. Stone enrolled in Columbia College at the age of 15 after graduating at the top of his class at Brooklyn Technical High School. He completed Columbia Law School at the age of 20 and was admitted to the bar in 1955. Mr. Stone worked for the firm Golden-Solomon until he was hired by the District Attorney's office.

A proud Zionist, Mr. Stone was a member of the Betar Youth group, co-founder and chairman of the Eretz Fund, and later served as an advisor to the Israeli Supreme Court, helping to extradite and prosecute suspected Nazi war criminals, most notably John Demjanjuk, thought to be the infamous Ivan the Terrible at the Treblinka death camp. Demjanjuk was extradited to Israel in 1986 and sentenced to death.

Controversy continued to follow Mr. Stone, however. In 1993, the Sixth Circuit Court of Appeals in Cincinnati,

finding that former Cleveland auto-
worker, John Demjanjuk, was not Ivan
the Terrible, quashed its order to extradite Mr. Demjanjuk, and the Israeli
Supreme Court rescinded its earlier
judgment and returned him to the United
States, citing ". . . misconduct on the part
of over-zealous prosecutors."

Mr. Stone faded from the public eye,
dividing his time in recent years between
Jerusalem and Brooklyn. He died in his
home in Midwood after a long illness.
Mr. Stone is survived by his one son,
Matthew Stone.

Matthew continued unpacking 13 volumes of Rashi's
Torah commentary, smelled the pages and ran his fingers
over the Hebrew words that his father had read. More religious books: *Tanach*, bound in green leather, *Gemarah*, and
the *Shulchan Aruch*, Joseph Caro's code of Jewish law.

Stone dragged a second box into his room and found a
photograph of himself at the age of seven frowning as he
stood before Rachel's Tomb in Bethlehem.

Stone's first trip to Israel at the age of seven was a disaster.
He and his father woke early to the blazing white sun of July,
ate a breakfast of cucumber and yogurt, and drove up and
down along Israel's roads and highways – from the Upper
Galilee to the hills of Judea and Samaria to the Negev, stop-

ping here and there along the way. They visited countless tiny pine forests, planted by North American and European Jews; the trunks barely thicker than Matthew's wrists, and Matthew wondered aloud why Christmas trees were being planted by Jews in Israel.

They would walk for hours at a time beneath the sharp sun, passing below the new red-roofed settlements perched on the hills above, gnarled olive groves, shepherds and their mangy flocks, Matthew protected only by his sopping baseball cap. The balls of his feet had hurt, so he walked on his heels through the Hebron casbah until his father told him to stop being a fool. He realized if he swung his arms as he walked, he could move faster, projected forward by the force of his swinging. He paddled through the air to Efrat and Bethlehem, all the way to the small stone dome of Rachel's Tomb, where his father had stunned him with a backhand across the mouth.

"Rachel was one of our matriarchs," he said, followed by a story of the biblical Rachel and Jacob. Matthew's father had never hit him before and he could think of nothing but the stinging pain, but he managed to hold back his tears. Whenever they stopped, there was always a story, and Matthew would flush and sweat as his father rolled out names and dates and places, spellbound by his own storytelling. Matthew, however, was confused. These people seemed so distant, alien, practically of another world. He could not understand why his father was so excited.

When they visited the Old City and the Western Wall, Stone felt like the sun was sitting directly upon his head, like a weight. He wanted a drink of water – his mouth felt dry, his tongue thick – but his father seemed to be lost in prayer, solemnly swaying before the bright bricks of the Wall. Matthew found a cool, dark tunnel and entered it with the sensation of swimming in an icy pool. The darkness coated him, chilled the silver beads of sweat on his skin and propelled him towards the light. He emerged from the tunnel in a narrow stone street, crowded with shops and battered storefronts. He heard the guttural calls of Arabic being spoken for the first time, and saw a boy his age rush past with a huge pallet of steaming pita bread balanced on his head. Matthew followed the boy for as long as he could, up and down the winding streets through the falling shafts of light, until he lost the boy in the crowd. He saw Arab men wearing *keffiyahs*, who he figured must be wealthy sultans or sheiks and imagined their palaces, hidden away somewhere in the labyrinthine city. He passed butcher shops with rows of sleepy sheep heads lined up like bowling balls in the windows. He saw men smoking water pipes and playing backgammon and laughing at low wooden tables. He saw a crippled man begging for money, his left foot bulbous with gangrene, veiled women moving swiftly like ghosts and a hunched man dragging a wood coffin by a frayed rope. Matthew felt as if he had been transported to another planet as the faces whirled around him, and the smells of spices filled his nose. It was only when he saw a solitary Orthodox Jew emerge from a hidden alley that he was reminded that he was alone in the heart of the twisting city and that his father was still praying at the Wall.

The Judge found him hours later, filthy and dehydrated, passed out on the stones along the Via Dolorosa. He remembered the Judge silently picking him up and throwing him over his shoulder. He awoke later in Hadassah Hospital, on

Mount Scopus, horrified to find he was hooked up to tubes and machines, his father leaning against the window ledge like Herzl at Basel, a curl of blue cigarette smoke rising above his head.

The flight home passed in silence. The Judge sat across the aisle from Matthew, his head buried in a book.

⟡

Later, close to eleven o' clock, Stone awoke from a restless sleep in which he dreamed the earth had opened up and swallowed his father, leaving no trace that he had ever existed. He then realized that if his father had never existed, neither had he – and he felt the ground shake beneath his feet.

Pinky called him to dinner, "Hey, Fucka. Let's eat."

Among the boxes and empty Chinese food containers Pinky said, "Let me buy you a drink, roomie. To celebrate your new digs."

"It's late," Stone said.

"What are you, afraid?"

"I want to be alone."

"Come off it, you can jerk off later."

Stone wanted so badly to say something sharp and biting but could only think, *I don't even like you that much. It's just you're the only one left.*

All of Stone's childhood friends had gone. Danny Green was in med school in Baltimore; Alan Grinstein, Harvard Law; Alvin Essrog, Stanford Law; Jay Coopersmith, head chef in Amsterdam; Mickey Zin was married; Ami Alf-asi, dead nearly two years in the Security Zone in Lebanon –

buried on Mount Herzl in Jerusalem. Even his ex-girlfriends were long gone, beyond his radar. Most were married, as far as he knew. But it didn't matter anyway.

Only Pinky, Michael Pinsky, the schmuck who dropped out of 12th grade to try out for the Yankees, who got scabies from a prostitute in Paterson, who believed that Jack Ruby was a great American Jew, only Pinky remained. He had always been in the thrall of Julius Stone, and, Matthew figured he kept up his end of the friendship to be close to the grandson of the great gangster.

"I don't feel like going out."

After Pinky had gone again, Stone stood in the dim yellow light of his living room, shivering still, face to face with the black and white photo of the stern-eyed Jabotinsky, his round steel-rimmed glasses seemingly a part of his sallow face – polyglot, fluent in eight languages, writer and translator of Dante and Poe, a lawyer by training, a journalist, creator of the first Jewish army since the time of the Romans, and above all the most eloquently forceful voice in Zionism. Jabotinsky stared stolidly ahead. Stone knew that his father had loved this man more than he had ever loved his only son, and it was Stone's fault. If only he had cared about Israel, studied at Columbia, dated even one Jewish woman. "Stop looking at me!" Stone shouted. He moved to take down the picture of Jabotinsky, but looking into his cold eyes, so much like the eyes of his father, he left the picture where it was.

He sat staring at the remainder of the boxes that, for the moment, seemed as mysterious as the pyramids of Egypt. Stone closed his eyes and thought, An entire life in 36 boxes. Two inches in *Who's Who in America*, a third of a page obituary in the *Times*, an op-ed article supporting the "Jury-mandering Judge." An accomplished life, Stone thought, but incomplete. The Judge never even finished reading volume two of Edward Gibbon's *The Decline and Fall of the Roman Empire*.

Matthew felt such resentment that his father would call him home from his studies, refusing to check himself into a hospital, that they spent weeks in silent stalemate, Matthew sleeping on the couch and muddling through his thesis while his father, stubborn and cold, lay in bed reading in silence, attended to by a gleaming Trinidadian nurse. Neither Matthew nor his father, it seemed, realized that the Judge was actually going to die.

The last days were bad. He had called a locksmith, and set up an alarm system after firing the Judge's nurse when, upon returning from a walk to clear his head, he had found a bearded yeshiva student in his father's study, searching through the nearly emptied filing cabinets, looking for God-knows-what. Matthew then sequestered himself inside his father's apartment, alone with the Judge and ample amounts of morphine.

For the first time in his life, Matthew had his father to himself. He had wet his blackened lips every ten minutes with a cloth, given him pills, set his morphine drip, bathed him, but the stubborn Judge gave nothing back. Even pale and faded, his father struck Matthew as awesome, frightening. His will was radiant. It was as if he thought he had a cold and would be back on his feet again in no time. Lying in bed with his half-moon reading glasses perched on the end of his nose, more out of habit than anything, the Judge tried to read, a book propped on a pillow before him. Then one morning, it seemed with the swiftness of a sudden summer storm, they both realized he was going to die. The Judge faded in and out of consciousness, muttering the words of the *Sh'ma* and "God Bless America," languages mixing and blending. In the half-dark, his voice destroyed by the cancer, the Judge had called out the Aramaic words of the *Kaddish*, enunciating every syllable of the ancient recitation, with crystalline clarity, before quickly slipping back into delirium.

The Judge called out the names Daddy, Bunny, Abi, and Matthew. He called out the name Henry, more insistently than the others. But Matthew knew of no one by the name of Henry, and he imagined that Henry was one of his mis-carried brothers, flushed down the drain before he could ever feel the pain of living; a brother who never had the chance to disappoint.

Matthew could no longer understand what the Judge was trying to say, as if he had already passed over into the world to come and was speaking its timeless language. He muttered "Seligman" in his sleep and had woken, repeating the name, "Seligman. Seligman," and then in the same breath, "Henry." When Matthew had asked, "Who is Henry?" the Judge mumbled some words. Matthew could only make out "the numbers."

He had asked, "What numbers?"

"Which— Which—" the Judge had said with difficulty, and Matthew realized to his horror that even now, with com-munication so tenuous between them, the Judge was cor-recting his grammar. He dabbed water on his father's lips and the Judge had said, "Seligman. Seligman."

The day he died, the Judge had, with monumental effort, motioned to a thick book on his bedside table that he had been reading. Matthew had propped it on the pillow for him and opened it at random for the Judge. The Judge moaned. Wrong page. Matthew flipped to another page and then another, until finally the Judge stopped moaning. He was calm and though his eyes were glassy, Matthew could see his father's eyes moving across the page.

Later, when his father died, Stone lifted the heavy, rare edition from the Judge's chest. It was open to page 1613, the section discussing the succession of Greek Emperors of Constantinople. The words at the top of the second paragraph were underlined in red and Matthew froze in place. He read aloud to himself as if the words had to be spoken to be understood. *After the decease of his father, the inheritance of the Roman world devolved to Justinian II; and the name of a triumphant lawgiver was dishonored by the vices of a boy.*

☙ 2 ❧

The sky was a bright Dodger blue, and the glare of the piercing sun was sharp and pricked Stone's retinas like needles. He sat beneath the tall pillar of the Prison Ship Martyr's Monument feeding scraps of week-old bread to a cluster of pigeons. The idea of sitting directly atop a crypt that held the remains of eleven thousand anonymous prisoners from the Revolutionary War galvanized some triumphal life-force within Stone, made him feel a small temporary victory over the ever-lurking Angel of Death. He saw a red kite flying high against the pure blue sky like a blood streak, and Stone found that the longer he looked at the sky the less intense its glare became. He heard the homeboys from the Walt Whitman Houses down below the trees playing basketball and cursing.

"The prodigal son returns," a voice to Stone's left said.

When Stone raised his head, the afternoon sun blurred his vision. He could see the outline of a man, standing casually with his hands in his pockets. "Mind if I join you?"

"It's a free country," Stone said.

The man sat down and for a moment. They were both silent. Stone noticed that the man was humming a jaunty, familiar tune under his breath, but he could not place it.

"I used to race pigeons when I was a kid," the stranger said at last. "Look," he said, pointing to a blue-gray pigeon strutting towards Stone, who simply shrugged his shoulders. "Look at the neck, that iridescent green patch, it's like emerald, then azure, the way it catches the light. There's nothing like it in nature."

"Is that true?" Stone said.

"I like to think so," the man said.

The man was ten or fifteen years older than Stone and of a trim, sturdy build – he must have been an athlete once. He had an olive complexion and a dark circular birthmark high on his right cheek. He wore a neat goatee. Stone noticed that his nose seemed to have been broken numerous times. His eyes were small and brown and intense. He held Stone's gaze in his for a long time.

"Happy Birthday," the man said, forcing a smile that made the skin around his eyes crinkle like paper.

"Do I know you?" Stone asked. "Who are you?"

"A friend."

"Right," Stone said bitingly. "A stranger is just a friend you've never met."

"I'm not a stranger," the man said.

"Who are you?"

"I'm Larry," the man said, rising slowly with his hand extended.

Stone jumped to his feet so the pigeons scattered. He had just reached the edge of the grass when the man called flatly, "What a day for a birthday."

Stone stopped short. He felt a chill tingle along his skin. A breeze blew through a nearby ailanthus tree, rustling its leaves.

"Surely your father talked to you about the massacre at the Munich Olympics – about how the unthinkable happened again in Germany."

"What do you know about my father?"

"I'm sorry for your loss," the man said, approaching. He neither smiled nor frowned when he reached Stone, his face inscrutable, blank. But there was something in the way he moved, a simple gesture he made, tilting his neck to one side as if he were working out a crick, that brought him into focus for Stone. He had seen him before, at his father's funeral, high up on the Mount of Olives, bent over a tripod and telephoto lens. He was too far away to make out his features, but the way he kept stretching out his neck served as his signature. Stone knew that no two people moved the same way, their movements and gestures as individual as the lacy patterns of a newly fallen snowflake.

"It must be difficult," the man said, and then, "I lost my old man a few years back. Cancer."

They were both silent for a moment. Stone noticed the pigeons had returned. He threw them a last scrap of bread from his pocket and they dove in with a rush.

"It's a shame," the man said, shaking his head.

The sun had moved around in the sky so it was directly in his eyes. "What were you doing at my father's funeral?"

He tilted his head to the left and then to the right as if to acknowledge Stone's suspicion. "I'm an interested party, that's all."

"Interested in what? Misery? Plain human misery, or that pile-on of misery that only the black-hatted Orthos can serve up on their holy soil?"

"It wasn't fair," the man said.

"Fuck no, it wasn't fair!" Stone shouted. "It was a god-damned circus. Every time I took the *kippah* off, one of them made me put it back on, like Pin the Tail on the Donkey, it was absurd. Another tore the pocket on my suit jacket and told me as the son I had to rend my clothes as a sign of mourning. And then demanding, *demanding* I say this and that in Hebrew as he was lowered into the ground. It didn't matter that I didn't understand a word. And then there was the journalist, sticking his microphone in my face, asking what I thought about Ras al Amud and Abu Dis."

"I'm sorry," the man said.

"I didn't even know what he was talking about. So he kept on saying Ras al Amud, Abu Dis, Ras al Amud, Abu Dis, as if I were an idiot, as if repetition would make me understand what he was talking about."

"They are Arab neighborhoods in Jerusalem," the man interjected.

"That still doesn't explain what you were doing there."

"You and your father didn't get along."

"If this is some sort of interview just stop now."

"I hated my old man," the stranger said. "He used to hit me with a belt when I was a kid. If I struck out in baseball, if I came in second, if I got a B in school, out came the belt. Strict immigrant father trying to make it in America through his son. I prayed for him to die, prayed for it as I lay in bed at night. What did I know? Then one day he was gone – but you're never rid of him. He's always there, an indelible print that you can't wash off."

"Did you know my father?" Stone asked, then changing his tone, "Did you know him?"

"I know about him. I know his life, the milestones and the minutiae, the facts of his life, his accomplishments and failures. I know him academically, the way you know Whitman, intimate yet distant, the only way that a man can truly know another man dispassionately."

"Whitman . . ." Stone began.

"I know you were halfway through your graduate thesis on the universal spiritualism of Walt Whitman's work before your breakdown. I know of your predilection for self-mutilation, burning in particular. I know of your failed relationships and of Fairuza Freij . . ."

"Fairuza?" Stone said.

"You don't want to talk about her?"

"No. I don't."

"I figured you wouldn't."

"Who are you?" Stone said, reaching for breath.

And as if he had been waiting for just the right moment, he flipped from his pocket a small white business card and handed it to Stone. In the top right corner it read "Federal Bureau of Investigations." Below, centered in capital letters, "Larry Zohar – Special Agent, Joint Terrorism Task Force."

"What do you want?"

"I only want to talk."

The sweat on Stone's fingertips dampened the corner of the card. "Aren't we talking now," Stone said, "or do you want to make it official?"

Stone noticed that the red kite was stuck in the ailanthus tree, tangled in its smooth-edged leaves. He heard a child crying down the slope. A man wearing a straw hat rode past on a bicycle, pulling a wooden cart that was brightly painted with the words "Ice and Fruit."

"You understand history, you're well read, educated, aware. You know the old cliché that those who forget history are doomed to repeat it. There really is something to that. You were born the day eleven Israeli athletes were murdered at the Olympic Village in Munich. A violent welcome to the world. Of course you don't remember, but you were told later, you were told how your father spent the entire day watching Peter Jennings report for ABC – and it wasn't until the next day when all the hostages were dead that he came to see you resting in the incubator."

Stone felt his eyes filling with tears, and Zohar's expression finally changed into something short of a smile.

"You didn't know," he said, "I'm sorry."

"You're lying."

"That would explain a lot, wouldn't it?"

"It's not true."

"Who can deny it?"

"It's not true," Stone said again.

"I'm not trying to put the squeeze on you. I'm just putting things in context, so you'll understand what we're dealing with. I'm not trying to hurt you. You're going to have to trust me."

"Why?" Stone said.

"Because people's lives are at stake."

"C'mon," Stone said, laughing for the first time. "This is a joke."

"Your grandfather, Julius Stone . . ." Zohar continued.

"Oh, so this is what it's all about."

"It goes way back," Zohar said. "Your grandfather and Meyer Lansky regularily contributed large sums of money to the World Zionist Organization – money that was funneled directly to the Irgun, money that paid for the bombing of the King David Hotel."

"Listen," Stone said, "I only met the man once, and that was just before he died, so whatever he did in his twisted life has nothing to do with me. My father upheld the law, fought against organized crime. He was a lawyer and a judge. He didn't even see Julius, he was so ashamed of him. He hated him."

"Just like you hate your father?"

"I'm not talking about him."

"I just want to ask you a few questions about the Judge."

"Listen. Fuck off, okay. I'll never tell you a word about him. This is the last thing I'm going to say to you."

❧

When his father was selected to judge the Court Street Riot trial, during his junior year of high school, Matthew was unimpressed – his father's accomplishments had long ceased to mean anything to him, seemed to only draw the Judge farther away. He became even more silent and introspective, rarely uttering a word. He locked himself in his study for hours at a time and fell asleep at his desk. The life the Judge was living, immersed to the eyeballs in legal texts and documents, seemed to Matthew to be antithetical to life. No wonder his mother ran off. Matthew thought his father was selfish, self-absorbed, and dull. He felt abandoned by both parents. He went to Coney Island and walked in the shallows of the shore every night that September. As the trial came closer and protests became louder, calling for the Judge's ouster, Matthew hid from reporters and sometimes stayed out all night with one of the girls impressed by his new-found celebrity. One thing that Matthew remembered clearly was that he hadn't cared who had died and who had killed during the riot. He felt almost as if bloodshed in the streets of New York was a matter of course.

Seeing his father on the nightly news, Matthew realized that the Judge did not belong to him, but to the state, the public, the media – that he was his father in name only. It was ridiculous to think that this man, larger than life, and vibrant on television, was the same silent, moody grouch who holed up in his study as if it were a defensive bunker. But Matthew missed his brooding presence at home and he went to the King's County Supreme Court building in downtown Brooklyn. The honorable Walter J. Stone sat at the front of the courtroom beneath the engraved words

LET JUSTICE BE DONE
THOUGH THE HEAVENS FALL

his half-moon glasses pushed down on his nose. He spoke with a firm tone, questioning both lawyers at length. This was the man Matthew knew, who had been absent around the house for so many months. He spoke with force and confidence and authority. He spoke like a father, at least the only father Matthew had ever known. He felt the absurd realization, sitting there in the courtroom, that the Judge was father to all those people present – no wonder he had no time or tenderness for Stone.

He could see the defendant, Isaac Brilliant, thin and wiry in his black suit, slouched in a chair beside his lawyer. Matthew did not remember the jury or the makeup of the spectators, but he did remember the exhausted *New York Times* reporter who slumped next to him, doodling in his notebook, again and again, over the words that would eventually make up his lead paragraph in the next day's paper. Quoting from Oliver Wendell Holmes, the words read "The world's great men have not commonly been great scholars, nor its great scholars great men."

Not long after, when the selection of jurors exploded into a full-scale controversy and the word "jurymandering" entered the New York lexicon, Matthew felt that his father had gotten what he deserved for his icy arrogance, overriding the challenge to the jury choice of the defense. It was the first time in his life that Matthew had seen his father wounded, truly battered by a world that he strode through like a giant, brushing aside problems with ease. The Judge was questioned numerous times by the District Attorney's office, walking the humiliating media gauntlet, passing signs that read "Blood is on your hands," and "Bassam didn't do it," as the clutch of TV cameras pressed in on him. The Judge was composed and stoic as he walked, but Matthew realized that he had clearly lost control of his personal narrative, this carefully constructed mystique smashed to pieces, when he heard the young television reporters begin each day's coverage with ". . . son of notorious gangster Julius Stone . . ." It was then that Matthew finally allowed himself to feel sympathy for his father. Papa Julius had laid these minefields long ago and only now was the Judge picking his way through them.

A man and a woman from the District Attorney's office rang his doorbell at home one night after dinner. They both showed their D.A.'s badges and asked Matthew if he could answer some questions. The questions related mostly to the Judge's character, and they were general questions that he finessed with ease – he said nothing while he seemed to be saying something. The woman, who Matthew had noticed had enormous, firm breasts and an achingly long, white neck, asked point-blank, "Did your father, Walter Stone, knowingly approve, as a member of the jury at the trial of Isaac Brilliant versus the State of New York, a man he knew would not be able to fairly render a decision considering the facts presented to him?"

"I don't know," Matthew said flippantly.

"Is that your answer?" the woman asked.

"Yes," Matthew said. "I don't know."

"Can you repeat that, please?" the man said, taking notes. "Did your father, Judge Walter Stone, knowingly approve . . ."

"I don't know."

"Thank you," the woman said. "Thank you very much."

The Judge walked in the front door as the pair from the D.A.'s office was leaving.

"What are you doing in my home?" the Judge said to the man as he fiddled with his briefcase.

"Just asking a few questions. We're leaving now, Judge Stone."

He stepped up close to the man and said, "Get out of my house." Then, turning to the woman, he added, "This is my private home. If you want to speak with me, you know where to find me, but leave my family out of this." He spoke calmly, in a measured tone that belied his obvious irritation. "Now," he said. "Goodbye."

When they were gone, Matthew sat frightened at the foot of the stairs. He could feel his innards steel themselves, hardened with fear. The Judge lit a cigarette and held the smoke a long time before expelling it into the air. "What did they ask you?" the Judge said, turning to face Matthew.

Matthew told his father everything that he remembered, and as he did so he watched the Judge's face to make sure he did not slip up. His face still betrayed no emotion but he knew that the Judge was calculating the consequences in his mind.

"Is that all?" the Judge said, a long gray ash hanging precariously at the end of his cigarette.

"They asked if you knowingly approved a juror who would not be able to render a fair decision."

"What did you tell them?"

The ash fell to the floor.

"I said, 'I don't know.'"

"*I don't know?*" the Judge said, his voice rising. "When the District Attorney's office asked you if your father knowingly approved a juror who was dishonest and corrupt, your only answer was 'I don't know.' What is the matter with you, Matthew? Don't you have a brain in your head?"

"Dad, you don't understand."

"Matthew," the Judge said, cutting him short. "I don't think you understand how serious this is. You're graduating high school soon – you're going to be a man. You have to know these things."

After a moment, Matthew said, "I made a bad choice."

"Blood is not a choice, Matthew – yet somehow, somehow you managed to circumvent thousands of years of genetics, biology, and history in one fell swoop." And now, turning away and speaking as much to himself as his son, he said, "He's a modern miracle, a revolutionary wonder. He stormed the Bastille and brought down the *Ancien Régime*."

"I made a mistake," Stone pleaded.

"Matthew. Have you ever read a play called *Othello* by a man named William Shakespeare who had the answer to everything? I suggest you read it. Particularly Act II, Scene III, lines 281-284."

"I made a mistake," Matthew sobbed.

"No mistakes," the Judge said, walking towards the open door of his study. "There can be no mistakes."

ꙮ 3 ꙭ

It was a cool September evening, with a soft breeze off the river. Stone and Pinky walked in silence past the tangle of graffiti tags on the wall of their apartment building. Pinky's shadow bounced jauntily ahead of Stone's, his head briefly blackening the carelessly scrawled words "Brovaz 'n Strenf." Three young black men hung out in front of the Tip-Top Deli and Grocery, crowding the payphone, waiting for it to ring. Pinky muttered under his breath, "I'm getting some smokes." And then inside the deli, "Don't they got phones at home?"

They passed a vacant lot and then a small set-back storefront "Brotherhood Ministries" church where one of the Reverend Randall Roebling Nation's preachers could easily be heard shouted "Jeeeesus!" from a basement pulpit. "Jesus gonna bring ya on home . . ."

"This Jesus guy, he don't know shit." Pinky said, laughing.

"Nation's a fool," Stone said.

Stone could still hear the parishioners clapping their hands and stamping their feet when he and Pinky reached the overpass of the Brooklyn-Queens Expressway two blocks away. A livery cab drove past honking its horn, a Puerto Rican flag waving from its antenna.

Under the damp belly of the BQE they walked alongside a rusted chain-link fence with the flow of traffic, then turned left at Washington and stepped out from underneath the BQE into a street that looked like the last battlefield of the Industrial Revolution. Forklifts were parked in a crazy array on the sidewalks, some with their silver prongs still raised. Twisted metal lay hunched in piles against the ancient, graffitied warehouses. An oil drum burned on the corner. Somewhere in the distance the ice cream truck passed by, playing its mournful song.

"How did you find this place?" asked Stone.

"I found it, is how I found it."

All Stone could see was a burnt and boarded-up red brick building with smashed windows shining jaggedly on the top floors. A small stairway lit by a single bare bulb led to a basement. A stenciled sign on the door said "Hit sign. Win suit." Music played from behind a steel door.

Stone started to backpedal away, with his hands in his pockets.

"It's not the way it looks," Pinky said. "It's like a speakeasy or something. Think of Big Julie in the old days."

Stone turned back to the overpass, where he saw, through the sparks of the oil drum fire, dressed in black, three figures moving quickly out from under the shadow of the BQE, their hats propped on their heads like smokestacks. He heard garbled mutters of Yiddish.

"They're like rats," Pinky said. "They're everywhere, I'm telling you. Now let me buy you a drink."

The Catbird Seat was no more than a redecorated fall-out shelter in the basement of an abandoned bottling plant, torched by arsonists in the Seventies. The brick walls had been painted a vivid purple and gold. Violent-looking abstract paintings hung too high on walls, punctuated by candelabrum fashioned from parts of industrial machinery

"I'll get you a beer," Pinky said, lighting a cigarette.

Stone couldn't stop thinking about those three men in black, who appeared like ghosts from under the BQE. He had fooled himself into thinking that he had moved to another planet, a planet of graffiti, dice games and urban decay, a block where the words "Jesus" or "motherfucker" sprung from people's lips and never "*Baruch Hashem*, the Judge's son!" But he realized, the farther he got from Mid-wood, the closer he got to the ultra-Orthodox of Williamsburg. He popped two antacids into his mouth.

Pinky lingered at the bar. He leaned close to the red-haired bartender and whispered something that would be drowned out by the music. Stone couldn't understand what any woman would find in Pinky with his satiny Adidas soccer shirt tucked in to his beltless black jeans, his white running shoes that reminded Stone of pillows or clouds, the thick silver chain and *mezuzah* around his neck, the way he wore his hair brushed forward on his head. Pinky spoke of his long eyelashes and his brown puppyish eyes, how no woman could resist. But Stone had heard Pinky talk nonsense about a country house in the Hamptons and a job at Goldman Sachs; one only needed to see his graffiti-covered apartment and unmade futon to figure out that Pinky was a fraud, who bounced from job to job and made his money God-knows-how. Pinky had a six-foot-high stack of VCRs in his room, still in their factory wrapping, and a box of Rolex watches under his bed that must have been hot to touch. When Stone pressed, Pinky said they were his "tips," from work.

Pinky disappeared behind a mustard-yellow velvet curtain at the end of the bar and returned a moment later calling Stone after him. "Need an invitation?" he gestured with a glass of beer, spilling some on his shirt.

Stone pushed aside the curtain and took the beer from Pinky as he entered the low tin-ceilinged room, stained blue with cigarette smoke. A group of shabbily dressed students sat laughing around a long table beneath an antique billboard that read "Astral Oil: Safe and Best." One of the students had thick sideburns down to his chin and shaped like the state of California. Another wore an army jacket with "Crass" written in black marker on the back. A girl with blond pigtails and glitter on her cheeks laughed. The room was dimly lit by candlelight. Stone took a seat at a small table nearby, and noticed in the flickering yellow light the drawn faces of the students. He wondered what they could possibly be laughing at. "A Great Industrial City," another vintage sign read, and Stone imagined that they were the great industrial workers worn down by coal dust, asbestos, ashes and gas.

Before the Judge had died, Stone had been constantly terrified of death; healthy people, who lived and laughed and made things happen, just disappeared in the blink of an eye; a professor of Stone's had died suddenly of a stomach aneurysm while driving his car; a television star had dropped dead of a heart attack on the set of his show; a former girl-friend's mother complained in French of a headache and then never woke up. Stone realized that with death hiding stealthily in the shadows, ready to strike at its convenience, that it was best to go out and meet death on his own terms.

"Take a drink already," Pinky said. "To life."

Stone took a drink of his beer and made a sour face.

"Drink up, you're depressing me."

"What would it matter if I wasn't here?"

"Are you talking about killing yourself?"

"I'm talking about the difference between being and not being."

"Whoa, you're blowing my mind," Pinky said.

Stone took another gulp from his glass. "You know he died – just like that. The Judge. His heartbeat was replaced by a rattle in his throat. You know the death rattle is real. And then the rattle stopped. You look and he looks the same, the eyes maybe, but he's not in there. Where does he go?" Stone said. "Where does he go?"

"Take a drink already, you're giving me the death rattle," Pinky said.

"Tastes funny."

"You taste funny."

"No, really," Stone said. "This doesn't taste right."

"Maybe it's the taps," Pinky said, lighting a cigarette. He blew a perfect O into the air and stuck his index finger into it. "Relax. I brought you here for a reason. Look around. Art students. They're easy." He blew another O and suggestively pierced it with his finger, raised his eyebrows and gestured to the table behind him.

Stone took a sniff of his beer and pushed it away.

"What? I bought it for you," Pinky said. "I'm only trying to poison you." And he took a long drink from his pint glass.

Stone drank.

The Catbird Seat was crowded with black-dressed hipsters and art students by the time Stone's third beer arrived. He called Pinky "Camerado" and hovered above his glass, like a bumblebee pollinating a flower, to avoid spilling.

"You feel good?" Pinky said, laughing.

Stone did feel good.

"Tequila," Pinky said.

Stone didn't understand what he meant. He could see in the light of the guttering candle tiny black hairs on the bridge of Pinky's nose, and the ripe pinkness of his tongue when he spoke.

"In the beer," Pinky said. "What did you think, I pissed in it? Go talk to someone, already. We can't be Frick and Frack all night." Pinky grabbed his beer and stood up. "Check out Fuck Mouth over there," Pinky said, pointing towards a woman with red bee-stung lips.

The dark flickering room pulsed like a heartbeat, bodies pressed so closely together Stone could barely tell one from the other. Every mouth seemed to burn like an orange star as cigarettes were drawn and then exhaled.

Later, a song by Nico carried out from the darkness, an acoustic song, sad and beautiful, the simple strumming of the guitar, her voice breaking and dropping, that accent, low and full of disappointment, then rising with hope through the strings.

A tall skinny girl in a red wool hat and dark sunglasses mouthed the words. Points of reddish hair poked severely out of the bottom of her hat against her pale cheeks. She was almost flat-chested, wearing loose black peasant pants and a ripped green cardigan. Stone thought she looked like a boyish elf when she sucked her cheeks in to draw on her cigarette.

The girl seemed to be dancing almost without moving. Stone knew her eyes were closed behind her dark glasses, but she was singing to him.

"Don't look so sad," she said.

He had thought he was smiling but when he caught a glimpse of himself in the mirrored pillar he saw that his eyes were ringed in black and his mouth was down-turned.

"I'm *Sarah*. Spelled S-a-i-r-a," she said brightly. "I'm depressed too."

"Matthew."

"You look so wan. Are you an artist?"

"No."

"You look like an Egon Scheile self-portrait. There's such humanity, beauty, and nobility in your eyes. I'll bet you hear that all the time." She ran her tongue over her teeth displacing a piece of lime pulp. "Let's talk," she added, swaying slightly. She looked at her watch and said, "Midnight. Don't you think midnight is such a sad hour?"

Stone noticed that the clock above the bar read 2:45.

And then he noticed Zohar, wearing a suit and tie, pull aside the velvet curtains, and enter the smoke of the Catbird Seat, a figure so out of place that the hipsters and students spun their heads in a comic double-take, cleared a path for him, and resumed drinking.

"I gotta go," Stone said.

Stone staggered into the street where he had seen the three shadowy men stepping out from under the overpass and turned left and headed towards the river and the Navy Yards; the city was lit up beyond. He heard his feet echoing off the factory walls and imagined the second set of feet pursuing him to be those of Zohar. He felt a paranoid chill on the back of his neck, and stepped quietly, so he could not hear the ghost of his footsteps.

A loud *pop-pop* from inside a building jolted Stone. He read the building's sign, "Crown of Solomon Talmudical Academy." A faint light burned behind grated windows and Stone jumped in the air to see inside. Propelled by drink he felt light as he jumped, but the windows were too high. Stone found an empty can, and stood shakily on his toes on top of the can. The frosted windows prevented him from seeing clearly, but he did see what he thought were several shaded figures moving quickly about.

Stone reached his apartment building, which looked more like a by-the-hour motel than a residence. A monstrous marquee that appeared to be made of aluminum siding and faded driftwood hung above the entrance, suspended by two steel chains. The building had once been a dance hall before it was condemned, gutted and then resurrected.

The Judge had never had a parking ticket. Matthew inherited his father's ten-year-old Volvo, and it was parked on the wrong side of the street. Besides worrying about being ticketed, Stone had seen kids playing stickball dangerously close to his father's car the day before.

Stone started the engine and turned right onto Washington, and the green ailanthus and sycamore trees flanking the street seemed to crowd him. On his right, he passed the abandoned Graham Home for Old Ladies, its windows shuttered like coins on the eyes of the dead, and then the skeletal jungle gym in an empty playground. He pressed his foot to the gas and passed under the giant cruciform shadow bleeding from the roof of Christ: Light of the World Church, and narrowly beat the red light at Lafayette.

"Roar, lion, roar. Awake the echoes of the Hudson Valley," Stone sang. He noticed a car shadowing him.

"Fight on to victory evermore while the sons of Knicker-bocker rally around Columbia, Columbia."

The red neon hands of the clock atop the golden domed Williamsburg Savings Bank Tower read 3:20.

"Shouting her name forever, roar, lion, roar."

He raced along Clinton at sixty, seventy, eighty miles an hour, right down the middle of the broad, wide avenue, passing 19th-century mansions and brownstones, when a man stumbled into the street.

Stone hit the breaks hard with both feet, spun, and tore through a cast iron fence and a flower garden, coming to a stop against a brick wall.

ᵔ 4 ᵔ

Stone's vertebrae felt like they had been knocked out of place by a hammer. It hurt his neck to turn, but he slowly eased his head from left to right until the pain blunted and moved into his shoulders. *Blood,* Stone thought, noticing the stain on his pillow. *Did I really crash my father's car?* He ran his fingers over his face and felt a small dry cut on his forehead, no bigger than a paper clip.

A horrifying thought occurred to Stone. *Zohar.* Had Zohar helped him out of his car, unlocked the door for him and dumped him into his bed? He remembered the snapping back and forth of his head, and the seat belt restraining him, he remembered crashing through the fence, tearing it from its century-old moorings, driving home, his fender dragging sparks against the road.

But Zohar had been there. Stone could hear the homeboys from the Walt Whitman Houses noisily playing dice in the street outside his bedroom window. The late morning sun cast curlicued shadows of the wrought-iron window bars in the shape of a bass clef against his closet door. Stone lay numb beneath his sheets, trying to piece together the night before, the accident, but he kept hearing Zohar warning, "Steady, steady," like a Little League coach. His throat was parched. When he swallowed he heard what sounded like tiny bones cracking deep inside his ears.

The dice clattering against the sidewalk reminded Stone of the sound of earth being shoveled into his father's grave.

Stone padded into the kitchen to get a drink of water. He turned on the faucet and, sensing something was wrong, he turned around.

"Pinky! Get up!" Stone called. "Where's the boxes?"

A mug shot of a young Sinatra torn from a magazine was tacked to Pinky's closed bedroom door.

"Get up," Stone shouted. "The boxes are missing."

Stone felt his father slipping away – his last chance to understand the Judge hidden within the books he had read. Stone had consoled himself after his father died with the fact that he still possessed the Judge's most precious books, books that had shaped his mind, framed his being. Stone had planned to read the words his father had read, his eyes following the same paths, his fingers turning those pages that still smelled of the Judge's Nat Sherman tobacco. He wondered if these words would touch him the same way they touched his father. It wasn't a Columbia education, but it was the education of a Columbia man; the books closest to his heart. The Judge had read these books right up until his last breath and guarded them like gold.

The History of Nations – all sixty-eight volumes, reprinted from the London edition, encapsulating the histories of all nations from Greece to Rome to Persia to Palestine; from the beginning of time to the late nineteenth century, in the United States, Canada – his father had bought these as a student and read them all.

More histories: Josephus, Churchill, Thucydides, Gibbon, a three-volume set of the *History of the Jews in Russia and Poland*. Biographies of Montefiore, Jabotinsky, all the prime ministers of Israel, Kafka, Lincoln, Hitler, Stalin, Machiavelli's *Prince*, the pages edged in gold leaf, Clauswitz's *On War* in the original German; a signed, personalized copy of Hannah Arendt's *Eichmann in Jerusalem*.

These were all lost to Stone and with them went part of his father. Stone had hoped to read the poetry of Ibn Gavirol, the tales of Nachman of Bratzlav, the works of Maimonides, the Harvard classics, all forty-two volumes, Faulkner's novels, Tolstoy, Dostoevsky, Shakespeare, the Greek tragedies – all rare or first editions in English.

Pinky sauntered out of his room, shirtless, wearing only a pair of boxer shorts and his thick gold chain.

"Where's the boxes?"

"Call the cops," Stone said, putting his mouth to the faucet. The water tasted bitter and metallic and it hurt his neck craning under the tap.

They could hear the homeboys shouting and laughing in the street.

"I know who did it," Pinky said. "On the stoop. If you'll excuse the expression, those African-American princes. "

"What are you talking about?"

"You'll never understand," Pinky said, sadly.

That was when Stone noticed the red wool hat hanging on the back of the door. The door was unlocked. Stone clicked the lock on the door back and forth, emphasizing to Pinky that the door had not been locked. *Click-Click-Click.*

"Was someone here last night?" Stone said.

"Naaah," Pinky said.

"The door was unlocked."

"No, it wasn't," Pinky said. "It was locked, see." And he bounded over to the door, fumbling with the lock. "See, it's locked."

"My father's boxes are gone," Stone said, squeezing the hat in his fist and dropping it on the floor.

"Don't worry. We'll find them," Pinky said.

Stone weighed in his mind the possibility that Zohar had taken the boxes against the possibility that the home-boys in front of the apartment had taken his father's books. But the balance shifted towards a third possibility, and that was Pinky. He knew now that he had made a mistake moving in with him – all the old feelings of anger and humiliation flooded back to him, obscuring the good times, the times when they had laughed and raised hell back in high school. But that was a long time ago, and Stone was an orphan now, with nothing remaining of his father except those books.

"We should call the cops," Stone said.

"Fucking cops," Pinky said, and went into his room. He came out a moment later, pulling on a pair of pants.

"What are you doing? Stone said.

"Going out."

"Can I come with you?" Stone said. He figured if Pinky stole the boxes, it would be best to stick near him. Stone paused before speaking, and he realized that he meant exactly what he said, though Pinky's company would be cold comfort. "It's lonely here."

"You wanna come to work with me, pal?"

"I do. If that's okay," Stone said, swallowing. "Staying home is no good for me right now."

"Yeah, okay. But we're taking your wheels."

Stone wondered for a moment if his car would even work, but he realized that the Judge's Volvo had been through worse; the dent on the hood from a previous crash had been there for years without affecting the drive.

"All right," Stone said. "But what about the boxes?"

"Let me talk to the homeboys, see what I can do."

The homeboys didn't look up from their game when Pinky and Stone walked out into the blinding sunlight. Stone's eyes burned. His car was parked across the street and, as he had imagined, a ticket was folded under his windshield wiper.

"Hey, get the fuck away from there," Pinky shouted, as he stepped into the street. A skinny black kid was busy screwing the gas cap onto Stone's car. "I got it," Pinky said, holding Stone back with an outstretched arm. "Yo! Whassup, blood?"

"What the fuck? You're not my blood."

"What are you doing with my homey's car?"

"Nothing."

"Come on, Pinky. Forget it."

"This is his father's car, his father died last month and now you come over here and fuck with the fucking car. I should bash your fucking brains in, you fucking fuck."

The kid was no older than 16. "Hey, Fab," he called across the street. "These guys messin' with me."

In no time the dice-playing homeboys were in Pinky's face saying, "What the fuck?" with him saying, "What the fuck?" right back to them, practically nose to nose.

Stone stepped back, took a deep breath and shouted, "Stop!"

Pinky and the homeboys disengaged and Stone absently, as if he were floating, moved between them. His head ached terribly. The sun was blinding. "It's all right," Stone said. "It's okay. Now, what's going on?"

One of the dice players stepped forward, grimaced at Pinky and said, "My boy here just stashin' his weed, that's all. Know what I'm sayin'? Cops and shit."

"Take it out," Pinky said.

"Is that fair?" Stone said.

"Naw my ride," one of the homeboys slurred.

"Take it out," Pinky repeated.

"Awright," the kid in the basketball shirt said. "Shit."

"Give us a dime," Pinky said.

"A fucking dime? Why? This bullshit."

"Rent."

"Aw shit."

One of the homeboys laughed. "He got you. You been busted, son."

"You cold," the kid said, slipping Pinky a dime bag.

After they left, Stone turned to Pinky. "What the hell was that?"

Pinky took the keys and they got in the car. "They took the boxes. They would have never given the weed if they hadn't done some other fucked-up shit." Pinky pulled out of the spot and floored the gas, screeching onto Myrtle Avenue. He tossed Stone the bag of marijuana. "Roll up a fat one."

They raced along Myrtle Avenue, stopping short for red lights, passing the park and the hopeless brown brick towers of the Whitman Houses. Pinky turned left at Flatbush Avenue and gunned the engine through downtown Brooklyn. Stone lit the joint and took a hit.

"This is oregano, tough guy."

"Bullshit," Pinky said, letting go of the steering wheel. "Shit. Shit."

They drove along streets that Stone had never seen before; poor streets with stunted trees, standing naked, brownstones crumbling from age and neglect. A clutch of Puerto Ricans sat on milk crates flipping cards onto the sidewalk.

Pinky pulled the car over on a bleak one-way street where cars sat double-parked and a hydrant leaked water onto the littered street. "Back in a minute," Pinky said, closing the door. He crossed the tilted slate sidewalk and walked up the steps of a brownstone that had been stripped of its façade. The walls were gray and rutted with rusted ribs of iron showing through. Pinky disappeared through a battered green door.

Stone sat in the passenger seat staring out the window. A group of pigeons rose from the roof of a building across the street. They seemed to make a pattern against the sky that Stone could not decipher, shifting and turning, and finally breaking up into smaller groups and landing on an adjacent rooftop.

Pinky slipped back into the driver's seat and started the car.

"That's it?"

"That's it," Pinky said with a smile.

"What did you do?" Stone asked, as the car screeched out of the spot. He thought he saw a pale face at the window of the denuded brownstone. "Nothing," Pinky said. "That's the beauty of the thing."

They stopped at several more places, each stop more bleak and depressing than the last. Stone imagined the pigeons were following, and each time they stopped, he tried to count and catalog them. The birds all looked alike to Stone, and he was sure it was always the same flock.

Pinky drove with one hand on the steering wheel, the other, a tightly curled fist, held a cigarette which he smoked with intensity and portent, his brow furrowed in deep concentration as he inhaled the blue-gray smoke. They passed one of R.R. Nation's storefront "Brotherhood" ministries, a sign emblazoned with the words "Trust Nation. He will lead you!" blurred past, replaced in the passenger window by an auto body repair shop, a ramshackled bodega that accepted food stamps, a vacant lot, and an endless vista of treeless urban blight. Stone slipped deeper and deeper into himself.

His father had tried to drill into him the ideals that his own hero Jabotinsky had preached: the concept of *Hadar* – beauty, respect, self-esteem, politeness, faithfulness. Stone displayed none of these qualities. He had willfully made himself ugly in the eyes of the Judge. He had spent his life ignoring the wisdom of his father, chasing after sexual disasters, the sinking lifeboat of hopeless relationships, cheap marijuana highs and empty ideas that toyed with unpractical revolution. He believed in nothing. He was nothing. And sitting in the passenger seat of his father's car, with Pinky at the wheel running red lights and cursing, he realized that he was in danger of becoming less than nothing, an absolute unexalted negative clinging to this world simply through the vagaries of biology and a deep-seated stubbornness.

"I want to go home," Stone said at last.

"Home?" Pinky said, as if trying to unravel a riddle.

"I want to go home."

Pinky licked his fingers and brushed his hair forward with his left hand. "You got a date?"

"No."

"You got to be someplace?"

"No."

"I thought so."

Pinky parked the car on a side street and they walked a few blocks in silence. Stone had no idea where they were, but the simple act of walking propelled him forward and shook him somewhat from his lethargy. The air in the car had been close and smelled heavily of the Judge and his odors – the interior had long been stained a pale amber color by the Judge's cigarettes. A breeze blew past and Stone thought that he could detect a hint of ocean salt in the air.

"Where are we going?" he asked.

"Enough already," Pinky said. "We're here."

They stood before an old art deco movie marquee, its chrome oxidized and stripping in places; a three-story tower rising from the top. Stone deciphered in the burnt out remnants the word *"Palatial,"* once arranged vertically in neon bulbs. The title of a long-forgotten movie from the late '70s clung stubbornly beneath the words "elc me to t e alat al."

Layer upon layer of movie posters covered over with handbills, advertisements and announcements had been peeled away from the wall at a corner, revealing burnished chrome beneath the phone-book-thick agglomeration of glue and paper.

The windows had long been smashed and the booth, behind the bronze cage, was filled with assorted detritus including a haphazard pile of plush velvet chairs, torn across the seat by age and vandalism. The door, by contrast, was new and was the type one might find on a suburban home with its raised moldings, mail slot and knocker. Pinky knocked twice on the door, and it opened after a moment.

He shook hands with an unshaven man who must have weighed 350 pounds; his head was shaped like a warhead and his tiny eyes looked cruel.

"He's here to play?" the man asked Pinky, with a lumbering Russian accent.

"No. He's with me."

Stone noticed that the lobby was stripped and bare and that a clutch of middle-aged women, dressed in gaudy housedresses, pressed forward towards the candy counter. A sign read "Oasis Bingo – Cards, Daubers, Chips, Waiters, Cushions, etc." alongside a list of prices.

"What is this?" Stone said.

"I'm here to make sure no one cheats."

They passed through a curtain into the auditorium. And the first thing Stone noticed was an oppressive wall of cigarette smoke. The noxious fumes filled Stone's lungs and weighted him down. His eyes burned.

"B-12," he heard a gruff voice mutter through a microphone which echoed through the hall. "B-12 vitamins. Take dem every day." A false ceiling hung dangerously low; banks of fluorescent tubes lit the room with a greenish glow. Stone was shocked to see that in this vast theater, with its original seats plucked from the gently sloping floor, that folding card table after card table had been set up to accommodate what must have been at least 400 people.

"N-41," the caller said. "Fwoaty one. A year that will live in infamy." He coughed rudely into the microphone.

Stone could see dozens of heads bob up and down in sync. They sat waiting for the caller to pull another number, necks bent back like supplicants, then heads dropping like Christians at prayer.

"I-30," the voice on the stage called. "Dat's a toity."

Stone followed Pinky as he wound his way slowly about the rows of tables. He walked with more of a swagger than usual past the people; they were mostly women, white and Hispanic and something that Stone could not determine. They looked to Stone like grown-up parochial-school drop-outs. Many of the women were old enough to be grandmothers, and some wore nets binding back their hair, cinching cheap dye jobs that burned fluorescent under the greenish light.

"N-Fawty Tree."

Stone caught up with Pinky. "What's going on?"

"I am their worst nightmare." He pulled Stone close to him. Stone smelled a strong musky odor emanating from Pinky's body. "Half the players are addicted to the fuckin' game – welfare cases, unemployed, drips and losers, it's gambling for the lower classes. A quick fix."

"O-61. Maris 61 in 61," the caller said.

"Like going to the racetrack," Pinky continued. "Except there's no bookies and no ponies. But it's serious shit. They cheat, bring in forged cards, they're out." Pinky shot a sharp glance at a woman who sat before a half dozen cards. A plastic troll sat at the head of her card. "On average, I would say they drop over 50 bucks a pop in here."

"O-75," the caller grumbled.

"Bingo! Oh my God. Bingo!" A woman moved with a speed and dexterity that belied her bulky form. A collective groan rose from the room as the woman made her way to the front to verify her card. A woman in a "Heavenly Mother of God" T-shirt ripped up her cards, threw the pieces in the air and muttered, "Shit on a stick." Stone noticed that a woman wept quietly before a spread of cards. A man in a ski jacket called out, "I ga a goo one," but nobody listened.

"Awright, awright," the caller said. "Let's play Blackout Bingo. Winner gets the big payout. Mawk ya cawds caeful now."

The crowd buzzed with anticipation, a raucous chatter bouncing off the chrome and ebony walls that still held their original beauty.

"Awright boys and goils. Eyes down," and there was instant silence; the God of the Bingo Hall had spoken.

The next game began with an increased intensity. Stone could sense a collective desperation; muttered Hail Marys and curses floating through the air. Pinky moved with a martial precision through the tables.

"G-33. Toity-tree RPM."

A woman with crossed fingers scanned the array of cards before her and slammed her hand onto the table.

"B-5. Still alive."

In the taut silence of the room between calls, Stone realized that these sad people with flattened spirits had prematurely gone to their graves, a walking death that was more impulse than desire, their lives flaming out beneath the low fluorescent sky. He found the room spinning, slowly at first, then faster as the caller barked out letter-number combinations with a mystical inscrutability as if the correct combination would solve some eternal riddle. Rows of lights glittered above the tables like precious gems, and Stone wanted to go to them, but could not, suspended as he was in a gathering darkness.

⊂✴⊃

"Get up," Pinky said, shaking Stone.

He lay on the cool floor of the Bingo Hall, eyes fixed at a distant point. And as Pinky's face came back into focus, he realized he must have passed out. The game continued. The caller matter-of-factly said, "B-8. Don't be late."

"What the fuck," Pinky said.

"How does it happen that someone can just disappear?"

"What are you talking about?"

"Someone who was alive and walked the earth – loved, hated, hoped – gone, like that?"

A woman leaned in and asked if she should get a cup of water.

"Nothing but dust," Stone said. The woman rolled her eyes and went away.

"What's your problem?" Pinky said. "I'm working."

"I don't know," Stone said.

Pinky pulled Stone to his feet. He could see the overhang of a balcony beyond Pinky's shoulder pushing closer like the prow of a mighty ship. In the darkness he thought there was the outline of figures moving about behind the brass railing of the balcony. He saw a glinting, as if someone's glasses had caught a snatch of light in its lenses.

"You OK to drive?"

"I-17. Sexy and 17," the caller continued.

"I think so," Stone said. Pinky smacked Stone repeatedly on his cheeks until they were pink and tingling.

"Good," Pinky said, handing Stone the car keys. "Get the fuck out of here."

When Stone arrived back at his apartment, the homeboys were still playing dice against the outside of his bedroom wall. A tall homeboy, with a shaved head and sunglasses perched backwards on his clean scalp, tossed the dice. The dice bounced off the wall and landed at Stone's feet. He picked them up and held them. They were warm in his hands. The corners of one of the dice had been rounded by the sidewalk.

"Give 'em here," one of them called.

"Did you see anyone come out of this apartment last night with a bunch of boxes?" The voice did not sound like Stone's.

"Maybe I did, maybe I didn't," the tall one said.

"Gimme the fuckin' dice, cracker barrel."

Stone tossed him the dice and the game continued. The tall shaven one took the glasses off the back of his head and placed them over his eyes. "Maybe I seen something. It'll cost you."

"How much?"

"A 'c'."

Stone didn't have the money on him, so he stumbled to an ATM around the corner, returning with five crisp $20 bills. The homeboy snatched them and put the money in the front of his pants.

"Well?" Stone said.

"They was two of 'em."

"And? What did they look like?"

"Ah 'on know. All white folks look the same to me."

∞ 5 ∞

Doctor Ghazi took Stone's pulse, blood pressure, and temperature, pressed the cool disc of his stethoscope to his chest and back and asked if Stone was a smoker. Stone lied, "No."

He eyed the curved scar on Stone's bicep suspiciously.

"Your pressure is good. 128 over 75. You say you blacked out?"

"I think so."

"You had a fever and chills?"

"Yes."

"Everything seems normal now. Did you eat today?"

"No."

"Is that usual?"

"I eat a little bit," Stone said.

"Protein?" the doctor asked, peeling back Stone's eyelid and flashing a small pen light into his iris. He felt his pupil dilate, a dull ache flooding back through his retina, with a quick chain reaction causing his temples to pulse like a second heartbeat.

"I don't feel like eating," Stone said. "Food is dead."

"But a necessary evil," the doctor said as he pressied a wooden tongue depressor on Stone's tongue. "To sustain life. Has anything traumatic happened in your life recently?"

"No," Stone said.

The doctor asked him to step up on a scale, and as the counterweight found its center he asked Stone to stand up straight.

"You say you have lost seventeen pounds," the doctor said. "Your ribs are showing."

"I have to reach my fighting weight," Stone joked.

The doctor frowned. "I have a lot of patients in the waiting room right now. I'm asking you to answer a few simple questions. Give me one word to describe how you feel."

"Melancholia, malaise, desolation, disconsolation. Most days I don't feel like getting out of bed."

"Mr. Stone," the doctor said, "I think you are depressed."

"It's possible," Stone said.

"Those scars on your arm. Are they new?"

"No," Stone said.

"Are there others?"

Stone knew Dr. Ghazi would never understand. He shook his head.

"Thoughts of suicide?"

"Yes."

"Have you ever considered any sort of medication?"

Stone was silent. The thought of the Judge and the morphine drip flashed into his mind.

"Mr. Stone?"

"That was my father."

Doctor Ghazi looked away absently. "Let me just check your insurance, and I'll be right back."

Stone sat perched on the edge of the doctor's table, wearing a thin paper gown. He felt insignificant, his body like a plucked bird, like some depilated mammal waiting to be snatched in predatory jaws. The flickering fluorescents lent his skin a dull greenish hue and his eyes wandered about the bare room. Stone's eyes finally set on the glossy anatomical chart pinned on the wall to his left, the gaudy horror-show of the human anatomy. He saw a man's round head flayed on one side, exposing incessant multiplying networks of blue veins rising from the thick cords of the neck to its delicate tributaries in the face and skull. The man wore a peaceful expression as if he were taking a nap and that it was a simple matter of course that he would be skinned in his sleep. Stone saw the pink fibrous muscles and tendons, a rich garnet cord twisting up through the neck into the jaw. His eyes drifted down to the digestive system and the variegated shades of brick, rose, and scarlet, the nut-brown liver, the warm pink of the smooth stomach, tight as the skin of a newborn, the intestines coiled like sleeping nudes. He saw flaming valves and tubes that he could not name and the layered walls of the stomach in cross-section, piled high like the silty deposits of an archaeological dig. It seemed to Stone that every color of the spectrum was contained within the human body. His face was pressed close to the chart, straining to read the names of the blue and purple valves within the pumping heart, when he heard a voice behind him.

"Careful, you'll catch a draft." Stone heard the door close and turned to find Zohar standing before him dressed in his standard suit and tie. Stone gathered the paper gown behind him in an attempt to cover his exposed bottom.

"What are you doing here?"

"You called me," Zohar said.

When Stone had returned to his empty apartment earlier that day, the enormity of his loss struck him anew, as if he had lost his father's books all over again. He had pulled Zohar's card out of his wallet and dialed the number. He hung up when the voice mail came on, and called the doctor instead.

"I thought you'd want to talk somewhere in private."

"The doctor's coming right back. You shouldn't be here. Get out," Stone said, trying to cover himself. "I didn't call you."

"Oh, Matthew," Zohar said in a pitying voice. "You called me at exactly 1:16."

"Forget it," Stone said. "I made a mistake. How did you find me here?"

"Trust me, you're not that hard to track down," Zohar said.

"The doctor's coming right back."

"Let's talk."

"No."

"That's right, who gives a damn about the world. You and your problems are the only things that matter."

"My father's books are missing."

"I know."

"Do you know who took them?"

Zohar smiled, pulled a pack of gum out of his pocket, and offered Stone a piece. "Relax," Zohar said, popping a piece in his mouth. "I'll only be a minute or two."

Stone was momentarily disarmed by Zohar snapping bubbles like a kid in the schoolyard and said, "Okay," looking towards the door.

"Does the name Avraham Grunhut mean anything to you?"

"Sure," Stone said. "He was a rabbi."

"And . . . ?"

"That's it," Stone said.

"And he's dead," Zohar said.

"If you know all this, then why are you asking me?" Stone felt a sudden chill as the air vent hummed and cool air blew onto the back of his neck.

"He was assassinated," Zohar continued.

"If you want to call it that."

"He was a controversial religious leader," Zohar said. "He was an important figure in many circles."

"Fine," Stone said. "But, what does this have to do with my father's missing books?"

"You didn't think much of him." Zohar ignored Stone.

"He was a religious fanatic."

"Who was friends with your father."

"Maybe you'd better leave," Stone said, "The doctor wants to take my blood."

Zohar blew a large pink bubble, held it for a few seconds, and then snapped it back into his mouth. He smelled of cinnamon. Zohar did not look away, and his expression never changed. "So Grunhut was murdered by who?"

"You know this," Stone said, "so why are you wasting your time? He was killed by a Palestinian terrorist – a bullet in the back of his head." Stone glanced towards the anatomical chart and imagined the bullet smashing through the cranial vault, shock waves radiating through his muscular and nervous systems as the pinprick of eternity closed up around Grunhut and his rapidly ebbing life.

"That's the common belief," Zohar said.

"What do you mean?"

"Yes, they arrested a Palestinian, put him on trial, and convicted him, but he wasn't the killer, wasn't even involved. He had gotten himself in trouble in other ways so the killing was pinned to him to avoid reprisals and to close the book."

Stone reached for a wooden tongue depressor on the counter, and began breaking pieces off.

"What about Zalman Seligman? Does that name mean anything to you?"

Stone continued snapping the tongue depressor, breaking it into smaller and smaller pieces.

"Another rabbi – also connected to your father and with the Eretz Fund, the foundation that Grunhut and your father co-founded."

There was a knock and Doctor Ghazi opened the door. He stood in his long white doctor's coat uncomprehendingly staring at Zohar. "Sir . . ." he began.

"I'm with the insurance company," Zohar said. "Make sure to check his neck. He was in a car accident."

"You can't stay here, I've got to do Mr. Stone's blood work."

"Just make sure you check his cervical spine." Zohar said authoritatively. "I think he's knocked C3 and C4 out of place."

Zohar nodded his head and dropped his gum in the garbage can. Halfway out the door he turned and looked directly at Stone, his small brown eyes glittering. "You can reach me at my 24-hour number if you remember anything. And," he added, "leave a message this time."

Doctor Ghazi closed the door and Zohar was gone.

When Stone stepped out into the street, he nearly walked into the chest of a giant dressed in the style of the ultra-Orthodox, in a dark rumpled suit and standard white shirt that smelled like it hadn't been washed in days.

"Hey," Stone said. "Watch it."

But the man did not move. He must have been six-foot three or four and blocked Stone's way with his massive body.

"Your friend left without you," the man said, with the slow cadence of someone not accustomed speaking much.

"He's not my friend," Stone said. He looked up to see the bearded man nodding his head.

"Rav Seligman wants to see you."

"Seligman," Stone said.

"Rav Seligman wants to see you," the man repeated.

"No, thank you." Stone glanced at his watch and he realized he was going to be late for his first class. "I'm in a hurry."

"He said he was," the man paused, searching for the correct word, "delighted to see you're interested."

"Interested in what?"

"He said he was delighted," the man repeated.

Stone's stomach tensed and he took a deep breath.

"He said to give you this." The man slipped a round Bingo chip into his hand, turned his back on Stone as if he were programmed to do nothing more, and walked away.

⌾ 6 ⌾

The medication the doctor had prescribed to Stone did nothing but make him thirsty. When he arrived home after class, he did not notice the living room was piled high with his father's boxes, stacked exactly as they had been before they were stolen. He had walked past them, the way one might walk past a gnarled tree or a graffiti-tagged mailbox, part of the urban landscape, barely registering in his brain. It was only after he had tilted his head under the sink that he realized the books had returned.

"Pinky!" he called, but Pinky was not at home, and his disheveled room, full of his own misbegotten merchandise, provided no answers. Stone rushed around the apartment with renewed energy, opening cabinets, pulling out the garbage can, rifling through his closets. It took him a few moments to gather himself, until he knew what to do next.

He hurried into the street in search of the homeboys, but they were not playing dice in front of the building; the barbershop around the corner where they had their heads shaved every week was empty. A young child sat on the sidewalk banging on a garbage-can lid. For a moment, Stone wanted to ask him if he had seen who returned the boxes, but a long string of snot hanging from the child's nose told him not to bother. Stone looked around, as if through some secret power he would be able to see the repentant thieves. If he looked hard enough, he would catch a glimpse of their vapor trails shimmering like diamonds in the sun.

A long black car pulled up at the curb in front of the Brotherhood Ministry, and Stone watched as two stylish black men stepped out – they were tall and broad – shouldered and could have been former college football players. The setting sun cast a pinkish glow over the street, and the two men, from a distance seemed to be moving in slow motion, as if grooving to their own private soundtrack. One of the men opened the passenger door, and out gracefully stepped the Reverend Randall Roebling Nation, dressed immaculately in a dark blue pinstripe suit, his hair gleaming in the afternoon light. Stone was overcome by pure hatred; this was the man who had singled out his father as a villainous *cause célèbre,* who had fanned the flames with his rhetoric and had drawn the national media to Brooklyn. In a moment, he had disappeared into the ministry and Stone stood alone in the street. He suddenly realized that he had better get back home before something happened to his father's books again.

Stone felt humbled beneath the boxes that were piled unbelievably high – halfway to the ceiling, some eight or nine feet in the air. He pulled over a kitchen chair and began, gingerly, to lower the uppermost boxes to the floor. He did this until there was almost no room to walk in the living room. The first box seemed to open with a sigh, as if the books were glad to have been returned. They lay stacked in the piles, exactly the way Stone had packed them. As he pulled the books out of the boxes, he realized how dusty they were, how quickly his fingers blackened. He had not dusted while caring for the Judge, and the caustic, particulated Brooklyn air made it difficult to keep anything clean without significant labor. He opened the second and third boxes, washing his hands of grime after each carton. A yellowed, torn envelope with Israeli postage, addressed to Walter J. Stone fell out of one of the books; it had been folded as a bookmark. The return address was from Abba Eban at the Ministry of Foreign Affairs. The envelope was empty. Stone soon noticed the dust on many of the book jackets had been smudged, indicating that someone had been through them. He unpacked nearly half the boxes with an incredible burst of energy, and with each book, each familiar title, something whispered inside him.

The Judge was calling him through these books. He was gone, but his eyes had tracked these pages, his mind had been shaped by the words written before him. Stone found a leather-bound copy of *The Thousand and One Nights*; Churchill's *History of the English Peoples*; Rashi's commentaries; a massive book on the origins of the Spanish Inquisition; religious texts; legal texts; all of William Faulkner's novels; two books on the Gematria; the complete works of G.K. Chesterton; a silk-bound copy of *Othello*, with a tasseled bookmark that tickled Stone's wrist.

And with each book, Stone felt like he was unearthing his father, communing with his father in a way they never had in life. He picked up the *Othello*, and turned to the pages his father had cited all those years ago. He read, *Reputation, reputation, reputation / O, I have lost my reputation / I have*

lost the immortal part of myself, and what remains is bes-
tial.

His father was speaking to him through his books, and now Stone understood the enormity of his betrayal. He had been instrumental in destroying his father's carefully constructed reputation. He was guilty, there could be no doubt. Proof of Stone's disgrace lay before him and condemned him. Stone determined that he could make good on his sins, and that he would read all his father's books, and piece him back together like a child's jigsaw puzzle, solve the mystery of the man he could not please.

Stone found a package of his father's cigarettes in one of the boxes. He opened the flat cardboard pack and placed a Nat Sherman between his lips. The smoke curled in the air and danced before him, spinning up into the light and dissipating. His muscles burned, his neck ached. Books lay everywhere. Stone could smell the musty pages, the dried-out glue from the binding, the formaldehyde. He picked up a copy of *The Power Elite* that had been written by one of the Judge's teachers while he was at Columbia. It was signed, "To Walter, Prestige is the shadow of money and power. Best of luck." It was signed in faded blue ink. He was reaching for another pile of books when the phone rang.

"Hello, Matthew."

"Yes."

"It's me."

And after all that time, over half his life since he had last spoken to her, she offered up only the simple moniker, *me,* not Mom, or mother, but, *me,* as if she were a friend returning his call after a weekend vacation, because no one forgets his mother, no matter how long it has been, no matter how hard he tries to bury the memory of the woman who first broke his heart.

"Matthew. You have no idea how sorry I am."

Stone dragged on his father's cigarette. His blood seemed to have stopped flowing, to have gelatinized in his veins. He blew a crooked smoke ring into the air.

"I don't blame you for hating me, but I'm asking you to give me a chance to explain."

Stone's smoke rings died with his cigarette. He found the last remnants of his pot in a small plastic bag balled up next to the empty Chinese food containers, dumped it into a Zig-Zag and rolled it, one-handed, into a tight joint. He took a long drag on the joint and held the smoke in his lungs until they started to burn.

"Are you going to say something?" the voice on the other end of the phone said in a near monotone. The voice was older, worn down, tired perhaps.

"Are you?" Stone replied at last.

"Things must be hard for you right now."

"No shit," Stone said.

"I just want you to know, you are not alone."

He tried to picture her in his mind, but he could not; colors he could see – red, blue, black, abstractions of feeling – but no clear image of his mother.

"I'm sorry."

"About what? That my father's dead? Or that you ran out on me when I was 12 with no explanation, nothing?"

"It was the hardest thing I ever had to do."

Stone almost laughed, "Your career sure didn't suffer."

She had disappeared from Stone's home, his life, but not from life, the life out there; he read about her periodically in

the Arts section of the *Times* touting one of the most important American figurative painters of the second half of the
20th century. She had last appeared in the paper three years
earlier when the National Gallery in Washington had purchased her work for its permanent collection.

"I would have taken you with me."

"That's easy to say now," Stone replied. "What about my
father? You'd just take me like a piece of luggage?"

"Screw him! I should have done it," she said.

"What about me? What if I didn't want to?"

"You still think your father was Mr. Clean, shiny head
and all, because he was a judge."

"He didn't do anything wrong."

"Listen Matthew, I don't want to fight. I want to come
see you."

"Does it ever matter what I want?" Stone said, turning
over a fortune in his hand that read "You are lucky boy/ girl."

"It's too late."

"Matthew, it's Rosh HaShana, a new year. Give your
mother the chance for a new start."

He did not remember his mother celebrating Rosh
HaShana, as a matter of fact the High Holidays were always
a bone of contention between her and the Judge.

"Wait a second," Stone suddenly realized. "How did you
get my number after all this time? I just moved in here."

"What's important is I'm coming to see you," she said
over his words. "You have to say yes or I'm coming anyway."

The line went dead.

"Fuck," he shouted.

Stone felt his stomach rising with his words and he
rushed to the bathroom. Catching a glimpse of himself in

the mirror as he passed, he noticed the filmy sickness in his eyes, the revolting sallowness of his skin, his spiny hair that hadn't been washed in days. He tried to vomit, but could not, forcing his toothbrush into his parched throat. It only made him gag. He saw himself in the mirror again, saliva hanging in strings from his chin. He sat swaying on the toilet seat for a moment, and knew that the only thing inside him was bile and vomit kicking to be released and he curled his head into his hands. The lights were too bright when he raised his head, squinting. "Hello!" he called out. But no one answered, just the honking of a horn in the street. "Go to hell then!" He sat down in the cool bathtub, rolled a towel between his neck and the tile wall and smoked a cigarette. He unbuttoned his pants, pulled aside the zipper and found the pale winter white of his upper thigh. It had been a long time, but the skin called to him now. He took a deep drag on the cigarette, the tip, a bright orange star. His hand shook as he maneuvered the cigarette towards his thigh. An old purple scar, in the shape of the letter C seemed to smile at him, beckoning. He felt the hair burn first, then the skin. He felt his blood begin to calm, soon, he closed his eyes.

A memory appeared in Stone's mind, brightly colored and crystal clear. He was five or six, and his mother had taken him to the Brooklyn Botanic Garden to stroll through the greenery. They walked through the Rock Garden, the Children's Garden, the flaming purple Bluebell Wood and through the entire cross-section of the Native Flora Garden where they stopped along a ledge of limestone.

"Here is the Bladdernut tree, and there the Butternut and the Angelica tree." She told him those trees grew best in highly alkaline conditions such as are found in limestone areas.

Matthew gripped his mother's hand, feeling some importance in her words, but not understanding their meaning.

His mother had said, "If you can name it, you own it. It becomes part of your life, part of your world forever. Nobody can take that knowledge away from you. If you don't have a name for something, how do you think about it, talk about it? How can you paint something and make it yours if you don't know what it is you are trying to paint?"

"What's that?" he said pointing into the middle distance.

"Slippery Elm."

"Yuck," Matthew had said.

In the Herb Garden she had pointed out *conium maculatum*, which was poison. "Stay away from Hemlock."

Later she pointed out Lavender, Rosemary, Mint and Thyme and explained their various healing qualities.

"Time?"

"*Thymus Vulgaris*. It means 'courage' in Greek."

"Courage," Matthew said, rolling the word around his mouth like a cat's purr. "It smells good."

On their way home, Matthew had pointed to a tall, leafy tree, its graceful leaves palm-like, almost tropical, swaying languidly in the spring breeze.

"What's that?"

"That's an Ailanthus tree."

Matthew was disappointed. "Why would they call it that?"

"It means Tree of Heaven."

"Really?"

"Really," his mother said. "I read about it as a little girl. *A Tree Grows in Brooklyn.*"

"Can I climb it?"

"Climb it? No."

"Why not?" He had stamped his feet and raised his voice in bitter objection; it was still an effective technique back then. "Please, please. I want to climb the Tree of Heaven."

The bark was smooth and she had to boost Matthew up to the first branch so he could climb to the yawning Y of the next branch. The leaves were smooth and tear-shaped, tapering out in the end to a fine point. He could see the roofs of houses and the tops of cars passing by. His mother looked small, childlike standing below, her face etched with worry. The canopy was fuller above him and he wanted to climb where the leaves were thickest; beyond was heaven after all.

"Don't go any farther," his mother called from below.

"One more branch."

"No. Come down right now."

Matthew had made the move to climb further up the tree when his foot slipped against the smooth bark and he tumbled to the ground below, hitting his head on the recoil.

"Oh, my God! Matthew! Are you all right?" his mother had screamed out. She placed her hands under his head and kissed his forehead.

"Are you all right?"

He pulled himself to his feet. "I'm fine," Matthew had said, more embarrassed than hurt; he had taken worse in the schoolyard. He was a big boy, after all, and he had climbed the Tree of Heaven.

"Are you sure?" His mother pressed the back of her hand to his forehead. "Do you need to go to the hospital?"

"I wanna go home."

"Are you sure?" She stared hard into his eyes. "You know I love you and wouldn't want anything bad to happen to you."

"Yeah, I know."

"Okay. Let's don't tell your father about this. It will be our little secret. Deal?" And she extended her trembling hand to shake.

"Take me to McDonald's?"

"Deal."

Stone wondered now, as his head throbbed in the bathtub, if that simple deception was the beginning of a life of betrayal towards his father, its consequences echoing to this very day.

If you can name it, you own it. If you can name it, it is yours forever.

◌ 7 ◌

Stone emerged from the subway across from the courthouse and made a sharp right turn toward Brooklyn Heights. He walked in silence towards the law offices of Holland and Mckim, a bright sun burning above. How strange, Stone thought, he had never imagined when his father was on the bench, all-powerful and impregnable, that one day he would return to hear the reading of his will. Stone stopped cold amid a rushing crowd of office workers and looked at his watch. He was over an hour early.

He had attended high school a few streets over, at Beecher Academy, established after the Civil War by Henry Ward Beecher as an institution of higher learning, "founded upon the principles of abolitionism, liberalism, and faith." Beecher Academy had almost gone broke throughout the '60s and '70s, as enrollment dropped, and drugs found their way into the classrooms. Students graduating with inflated grades and poor skills became known as Beecher Bums, fit only to work in the service industry or, at best, to join the white-collar assembly line of corporate America. Infusions of private money, particularly from local Jews of Brooklyn

Heights turned Beecher around during the '80s, and by the end of the decade it was one of the top-rated independent schools in the Tri-State area, boasting a 99-percent graduation rate and acceptance at all of the top schools across the country. After his mother left, the Judge had chosen Beecher because of its proximity to the courthouse and its graduates' high acceptance rate at Ivy League schools. Stone decided to walk the few blocks to the imposing Tudor Gothic structure. The Beecher Academy's maroon and white flag hung limply on its pole beside a dispirited-looking Stars and Stripes. Stone stood before the intricately designed iron fence, beneath the brick brownstone façade covered in flowing ivy and thought back to the day that his life changed, the day of the Court Street Riot.

It was Friday afternoon, in early September of Stone's sophomore year. He had been dozing through math class when an increasing density of sirens in the streets aroused him as they filled the air layer upon layer.

Court Street was burning. A fire truck at the entrance to Joralemon Street blocked traffic, and a man was calling out instructions through a megaphone. Molotov cocktails were flying from the sidewalk in front of Borough Hall. A man had been killed. An Arab. Smashed in the head with a piece of brick.

Within minutes, the storefront shutters all along nearby Atlantic Avenue clanged shut and dozens of Arabs charged towards the medical supply shop whose name had been emblazoned across the back of the truck, shouting, "Kill Jews."

They threw rocks and bottles, smashing windows and scattering pedestrians, pulling the teaching skeleton into the street and burning it in effigy.

Though Stone did not know it at the time, he would soon learn that Menachem Wuensch, an Orthodox Jew, driving a truck for Court Street Medical Supplies, had run over and killed a nine-year-old Arab boy as he sped down Atlantic Avenue. Wuensch, afraid to get out of his truck in the heart of Brooklyn's Arab shopping district, rolled down his window, saw the boy's broken body, and drove off.

The riot became a media sensation, another link in the narrative of Brooklyn's racial strife. Only this time the spin was new; African-Americans were not at the boiling center. The oldest conflict in the world, as old as Isaac and Ishmael, played out on Brooklyn's mean streets, and the media descended hungrily.

In the end, one Arab man had been killed, almost a dozen injured and several shops had been damaged in the rioting.

A twenty-two-year-old yeshiva student, named Isaac Brilliant, who worked as a part-time stock boy at the medical supply shop, was charged with aggravated assault and the murder of Nasser Al-Bassam, a sixty-three-year-old Palestinian-born shopkeeper who died a week later of his injuries.

The case went before the Supreme Court of the State of New York. Stone's father was to preside.

The *New York Post* wasted no time in splashing its front cover with outrageous headlines alluding to Walter Stone's Zionist past during the Six Day War. "Will Judge Stone Pals Again?" appeared on the cover the day Walter Stone was announced as presiding judge. A twenty-year-old photo-graph of Judge Stone embracing the recently assassinated Rabbi Avraham Grunhut made the front page the following day. "Blood Brothers?" appeared with the sub-headline, "What do these two have in common?"

Grunhut had been shot two years earlier by a Jordanian who was angered by Grunhut's belief that Arabs should be transported out of the Land of Israel.

The flamboyant Reverend Randall Roebling Nation, a preacher who claimed to have been ordained at the age of eight, took up the fight with his daily soapbox orations: "The elucidation of the struggle is coming to a head; the judges will be judged and the people will have justice, freedom and liberty at last!"

Stone knew that Nation, with his tailored suits and gold jewelry, was full of wind, politicking simply to get his face in the papers. Every day before the courthouse, he took aim at the Judge, shouting "I beseech you all to listen to R.R. Nation, as Nation speaks God's truth. Judge Stone is a crim-inal, a crook and a thief, and if he is not punished in this life, God will punish him in the next."

And even as Brooklyn's Arab community protested Wal-ter Stone's selection, picketing outside the Supreme Court building, the Judge said nothing. A spokesman stated, "The Judge's record speaks for itself."

Matthew became a quasi-celebrity; at school, people he had never even spoken to asked him whether Brilliant was guilty or not, and some wondered if the Judge would go easy on a *landsman*. At a party one girl flirtaciously asked him if it was true that Grunhut had performed Matthew's *bris*.

Matthew heard nothing from his father who had receded into his study with his law books for days on end, only leaving to dump his full ashtray into the toilet.

By the time the case came to trial, Matthew noticed that he had developed constant canker sores in his mouth; he found it difficult to speak, his mouth felt like a piece of tenderized meat, some days he didn't even want to leave his room. He gargled salt water, apple cider vinegar, peroxide, but nothing helped.

One evening, his mouth on fire, sucking on ice cubes to numb the pain, Matthew knocked on his father's study door. "I want to go to the Emergency Room," Matthew said standing before the closed door.

"Fine," his father said after a moment.

Matthew remained at the door, his fist poised to knock again.

"I said 'fine.'"

That night, Matthew burned himself for the first time. He realized as he stood, match in hand in his bathroom, that in the entire universe he truly only had control over his own body, and he felt an unbelievable release when he realized that he could cause pain whenever he wanted, and remove it just as easily.

"Murder Inc. Kin To Rule" was headlined the day of the trial, and the story was picked up by the national media. The trial had all the makings of a Movie of the Week, said a Los Angeles columnist, and had joked that Marlon Brando from *Apocalypse Now* should play Judge Walter Stone.

The Judge broke his silence the day before the trial was to begin. Appearing on the front steps of the Supreme Court, wearing his gray three-piece suit and a pair of half-moon glasses, he read from a prepared statement: "I am addressing the spurious canard that appeared in this morning's paper in relation to my father. What my father may or may not have done before I was born holds no bearing on today's proceedings and I expect to hear nothing more on this matter."

The jury was comprised of seven women and five men, three of whom were African-Americans, four Hispanic, four Whites and one Korean-American. There was one Jew in the jury, Emile Alacalai, a teacher from Sheepshead Bay, who wore thick tortoiseshell glasses and had terrible dandruff.

Brilliant, flanked by his lawyer and the court bailiff, wore a black suit, white shirt and a black silken *kippah* on his head. He smiled from behind his beard and nodded his head confidently at the court assembly, as if he knew all along he would soon be free.

When friends and family members attesting to the character of Al-Bassam were cross-examined by Brilliant's lawyer, the courtroom buzzed. "Is it not true that Mr. Al-Bassam, a fervent Muslim, has three times made the *Haj*, the pilgrimage to Mecca . . ."

"The question is not relevant," the prosecutor interjected.

Judge Stone flatly said, "Answer the question."

Later when Brilliant's lawyer said, "Mr. Al-Bassam left the Samarian town of Tulkarm in June of 1967. Local records show that he had a daughter killed two years earlier in what is known as an honor killing . . ."

"Objection!" The prosecutor said. "That question is inflammatory and improper."

"The question is allowed," Judge Stone answered.

When Brilliant took the stand he was unable to explain that the bloodstains on his shirt came by self-defense. When grilled by the prosecution, he claimed he was attacked by a vicious Nasser Al-Bassam, whom he identified in a photograph as the man who he had tried to stop from throwing a garbage can through a plate-glass window. Brilliant then claimed Al-Bassam had turned his fury on him.

"Considering the victim's chronic epilepsy," the prosecuting attorney directed toward the jury, "where convulsing seizures strike in moments of exertion and stress, it is most unlikely, almost impossible, to consider that Mr. Al-Bassam, a very careful man, who did not drive, in fact was so impaired by his condition that he was capable of posing a threat toward Mr. Brilliant. In addition, witnesses at the scene claim Mr. Al-Bassam was turned away from Mr. Brilliant when he received the deadly blow to the back of his head."

Judge Stone commenced his charge to the jury after lunch. Quoting Gibbon, the Judge said, "'In every deed of mischief he had a heart to resolve, a head to contrive, and a hand to execute.' Here we are absent the heart and the head, so I ask you, is there an act of mischief, a crime?" Without using his notes he spoke at length into the early evening, revisiting the facts, explaining the nuances and minutiae of the law until the jury retired to deliberate.

The jury reached a decision shortly before midnight. The press was confident that the verdict would be Guilty of Murder.

"Not So Brilliant Verdict" the headline read the next morning after rioting broke out in front of the court house a second time. Brilliant was found not guilty of murder but guilty of the lesser charge of aggravated assault.

Stone was sweating heavily as he entered the glowing lime-stone building through a heavy wrought-iron gate woven with delicate vines and arabesques. And as he stood waiting for the elevator before a great hall – a marble and gold tem-ple to banking and commerce, Stone felt as if he had stepped back in time.

C.T. Holland rose from his desk to greet Stone, wearing a midnight-blue pinstriped suit, his hand extended.

"Matthew. Charles Taylor Holland." His eyes were a pale silvery blue behind round rimless glasses. He seemed to have no eyebrows. Stone shook his hand and felt blue-blooded vigor pulsing in his touch.

"Have a seat," the lawyer said. A pair of stuffed leather and mahogany chairs faced his desk. Stone sat and had to look up to the lawyer who reclined in a swiveling leather chair. He was about fifty-years old and wore his hair slicked hard against his scalp like a helmet.

"My condolences," Holland said, leaning forward in his chair. "I was fortunate to have gotten to know Walter very well during his time on the bench. He was a good friend and a very fair judge." He spoke in a flat, dry tone free of any accent or affectation.

"Was he fair?" Stone asked provocatively.

Holland blanched slightly then said, "You tell me." He paused. "Since you are the only beneficiary to your father's last will and testament, we can begin. Now bear in mind it may take a few months for the will to clear probate, how-ever what we are going to read today, assuming no unex-pected bumps in the road, is his legal will."

Stone nodded his head and noticed with some irony that a Yale Law degree hung framed on the wall behind Holland. He slid some documents across his gleaming desk and Stone picked them up and absentmindedly flipped through the pages.

"Most of this page is standard boiler-plate stuff – name, Walter Joseph Stone, domicile, etcetera, revoking all previous wills and codicils. It states a beneficiary must survive the deceased by at least thirty days." He paused, "On what day did your father die?"

Stone told him.

"Now, we have debts, expenses, taxes. You needn't worry about that. As the executor, I'll see to it that his debts and funeral expenses are taken care of. These expenses will be subtracted from the estate."

He spoke clinically and matter-of-factly as if he were discussing a car warranty or baseball trade and not the remnants of a man's life.

"After your father liquidated his home on Ocean Parkway, he lived a pretty spartan life in a rented two-bedroom apartment in Midwood. As a result, his personal effects are few. They devolve to you, Matthew Stone, his only heir." Holland pointed to a few single-spaced columns near the bottom of the page. "This means you get his books, clothing, furniture, photographs, jewelry – basically whatever was in his apartment at the time of his decease. You also receive ownership of his 1989 Volvo."

Holland did not look up at Stone as he spoke.

"This other item does not really concern you, however, I should note that there is also a property on Henry Street that your father co-owned with Zalman Seligman.

And by right of survivorship, Zalman Seligman becomes the owner."

"What does that mean?" Stone said.

"Basically, it means that your father was a landlord, and now Zalman Seligman becomes the sole landlord. Trust me, you don't want to deal with that kind of headache in New York City."

Holland tapped impatiently on his desk as if he were anxious to move on.

"And now your father's foundation that he chaired – the Eretz Fund with assets exceeding 45 million dollars," Holland said, rolling a pencil between his fingers as he puzzled over the text.

"Forty-five million dollars," Stone said, shocked. "That's a lot of money!"

"It's not all liquid. This includes property holdings, annuities and other appreciated assets. This is a 501c3, not-for-profit organization, as registered with the Internal Revenue Service. Most of the monies are restricted funds, designated for existing projects. Basically what this means is that the Eretz Fund raises and distributes funds to programs it supports, and it enjoys the tax benefits that come along with being registered as a 501c3. Are you following?" the lawyer asked.

Stone nodded his head.

"It also says that in the event of the Chair's decease, the beneficiary becomes president of the foundation. This means you."

"Me?" Stone said.

"There is a stipulation here," Holland said, pointing with the end of his pencil, "that you are to be the *de jure* chairperson of the Eretz Fund. However in the event that you are unable to participate, the foundation will continue to function as is, meaning it will continue to operate, supporting the same programs that presently enjoy its support."

"Do you have a list of the groups he was funding?"

Holland nodded his head.

"All foundations are required to file 990 tax forms with the IRS. This is how we keep track of the money and how it is allocated." Holland scanned a page from his files with his pale eyes. "There's Project Natan, which supports the absorption of recent Russian immigrants to Israel; there's Etz Haim, a group that plants trees throughout Israel; the Trumpeldor Museum at Tel Hai; Ghetto Fighter's House Holocaust Museum; Yad Vashem in Jerusalem; Hebrew University in Jerusalem; Bar Ilan University; there's a grant supporting American-Jewish students studying a year in Israel; there's the American Friends of the Crown of Solomon. They have something to do with purchasing properties in Jerusalem."

Stone interrupted, "Does it say where in Jerusalem?"

"No," Holland said. "It doesn't."

Holland turned back a page and cleared his throat. "There is also the Bensonhurst Benevolent Fund."

"Bensonhurst," Stone said.

"Yes," Holland said.

"That doesn't make any sense."

"It's written right here in front of me," Holland said. "These are unrestricted monies that support various afterschool programs, sports teams, neighborhood watches, etcetera, with the remaining monies collecting interest for future use."

Stone had never heard of such a fund. He had always known that his father had been a supporter of Israel, but Brooklyn, and a non-Jewish neighborhood, did not make any sense to him.

"Where does the money come from?" Stone asked.

"A charitable Bingo operation called Oasis Bingo. The money is paid out to those community groups. Any of the remaining monies are unrestricted in use."

"And who controls that money?" Stone said.

"Why, you do," Holland said. "With the rest of the board of directors." Holland looked impatiently at Stone, signaling he was ready to move on.

"Who's on the board?"

"You are, in place of your father, along with Abe Greiner and Zalman Seligman."

Holland paused. "But, there is a bit of a problem. Perhaps I have overlooked something, but I can't find the Benson-hurst Fund bank account numbers among your father's papers. But, don't worry they'll turn up before long. Your father was too careful to misplace something like this."

The lawyer's eyes were firmly set on Stone. "Shall we continue?" he asked.

Stone closed his eyes and he became aware of a vague masculine smell in the room that he could not place.

"Okay," Stone said at last.

"Now the issue of the Trust Agreement," the lawyer said, flipping back a page. "This is an agreement between the Creator, your father, and yourself, the Beneficiary. It is a standard, revocable Trust Agreement with one special proviso. It says here that the Creator bequeaths a one-thousand dollar monthly allowance to the Beneficiary until the Beneficiary achieves something measurable: completion of a law degree; medical degree; Ph.D; attainment of a full-time tenure track lecturer position at a private or public university, excluding community college and trade school; publication of a full-length book with a reputed university or trade publisher; invention or trademarking of a product that is not commercial in its usage and significantly benefits Mankind; making *aliyah* and dwelling in Israel eight months out of the year for no less than three years; marriage to a woman whose lineage through to her grandparents is Jewish. The remainder of the assets will be paid in a lump sum to the Beneficiary upon meeting with one or more of the provisions."

"Am I supposed to feel some sort of gratitude for this?" Stone asked.

"There's more," Holland said flatly.

Stone moved forward in his seat to avoid the glinting lenses.

"Failure to achieve any of these provisions within five years after the decease of the Creator voids the Trust Agreement between the Creator and Beneficiary. All remaining assets and fiduciary concerns will be transferred into the accounts of the Eretz Fund."

"Well, that's bullshit." Stone said, pounding his hand on the lawyer's desk. "He's just trying to hold power over me for as long as he can so I can never escape him."

"This is not such an unusual way to devise a residuary estate . . ." Holland interrupted.

"It's sick, sadistic," Stone said.

"If you can live without the money," Holland added, "you can wash your hands of it and walk away. The fund will run itself. You're a free man."

8

When he had finished unpacking his father's books, Stone sat down with an open copy of Aeschylus. He had decided with trepidation and a stubborn sense of resignation to read all of the Judge's books starting with the letter A. He soon realized that his father had made marginal notes in many of the books, his script curling out with the same confident tone that the Judge had spoken with "This is hypocrisy," triple underlined; "Check your facts," written in red; "Smilansky agrees," with an uncharacteristic happy face. These books spoke to Stone, and he heard whispers rising from the pages.

A book by Henry Ward Beecher was of particular interest to Stone, considering he had studied at the school the preacher had founded near the end of his life. A quote was underlined by the Judge referencing the Sharp repeater rifles shipped to Kansas abolitionists in crates labeled "Bibles": "There is more moral power in one of these than in one hundred Bibles."

Later, amongst the growing chaos around him, Stone realized that he needed shelves to hold his father's books.

He walked towards Atlantic Avenue and its stretch of antique shops in search of something sturdy, made of old hard wood.

September burned in all its blue-skied glory; sharp shards of sun careening off car windows as they passed, blinding Stone with its white light. He smelled incense and burning meat and looked up and realized he was standing in front of a mosque. Three or four men, wearing *jalabiyas* and *kufis* on their head, bearded but clean-shaven on their upper lip in the Islamist style, stood talking in Arabic. One bareheaded man in sandals was handing out fliers as Stone passed. He didn't mean to take the flier, but somehow the man had managed to slip it into Stone's hand. There was a crude drawing in the shape of Israel, covered entirely with the colors of the Palestinian flag. It read, "Rally for Palestine!" Stone noticed that the date was the anniversary of the Court Street Riot. There was a list of Arab dignitaries from the West Bank and Gaza and other parts of the Arab world. Stone knew some of their names. He tore up the flier when he noticed that the master of ceremonies was to be Randall Roebling Nation.

He walked on, passing shops called the Fertile Crescent, Dar-es-Salaam Books, Treasure Islam, Zawadi Gift Shop, and stopped before an antique shop called Second Chance Antiques & Collectibles, and pulled the door open, finding himself in a vacuum of silence. Atlantic Avenue, with its sirens and horns blaring, was gone. The shop had broad-slatted wood floors, grooved and unfinished, such as one might find in a country barn. Tables and chairs sat piled on top of each other as far as the eye could see. The ceiling fan turned slowly, pushing dust motes on its currents.

"Hello," Stone called out. He could hear his own footsteps echoing as he passed under an iron bedframe, balanced across two stacks of wooden tables; he felt like he was walking through the ribs of death. "Hello," he called again.

A sign on the far wall read "Wanted to Buy – Antique Furniture, Old Photographs & Prints, Books & Letters, Silver & Jewelry, Oriental Rugs. *ENTIRE E$TATE$ PUR-CHA$ED.*"

It was then that Stone fully realized that these haunted remnants were the belongings of people gone from this world. He dropped down into a rocking chair and rocked with a morbid curiosity; the flesh dies, but the property lives on. That is our legacy. Stone retained his father's books, but they were not silent like an armchair or sideboard, they continued to speak, all Stone had to do was listen.

Back in the burning street a car horn honked.

"Hey. Wake up," a voice called.

Stone rubbed his shaven face, and moved on with head down.

"Matty! I'm talking to you. Get in."

Seligman's face was at the passenger window of a black sports utility vehicle that crept along slowly beside him.

"What are you doing here?" Stone replied.

"The question is, what are you doing here with the Mohammedans?"

"Walking."

"Get in." The car came to a stop and so did Stone.

"Are you following me?"

"I own some property around the corner."

Seligman looked the way he always had, with his gray trimmed beard, knitted *kippah* on his head, aviator glasses obscuring his eyes. His face was bright and alive. He had not aged a day since Stone had last seen him.

"Get in. You want to talk?"

Stone climbed into the back seat.

"Don't mind him," Seligman said. "He's just my golem. Moshe," he said, gesturing to the giant at the steering wheel, "drive us around the block."

The side and back windows had been blacked out and Stone could feel the frigid air-conditioning against his bare arms. Seligman turned his head, but did not look at Stone, addressing him from a 90-degree angle. He had a wooden toothpick jammed in his mouth.

"We were delighted to see you at the gaming hall. After you ran off from Giv'at Barzel, I figured . . ."

"If it's the account numbers you are interested in, I don't have them."

Seligman turned his head finally to look at Stone. He wore a hurt expression on his face. "Kid, I have known you since before you were born. Your father and I, we go a long way back. You know that. He was one of the smartest men I have ever known. We grew up together, we studied together . . ."

"Worked together," Stone said.

"You want to talk about your father's business, we'll save that for another time. Yes, we worked together. But, I'm not talking about that right now. You're his only son. I'm talking about *rachmones.*"

"What do you mean?"

"Compassion, Matthew. I know it is not easy for you to be alone now. And I know that you and your father did not always see eye to eye."

A memory burst into Stone's mind in a sudden flash, dredged out of his subconscious by the presence of Seligman. It was after Matthew's Bar Mitzvah, and the Judge, proud perhaps for the first time had gathered Matthew up in his massive arms and whispered, "*Yashir Koach.* Today you're a man." Later the Judge had taken Matthew to a meeting hall crowded with men and boys as the guest speaker, Rabbi Seligman, gesticulated with clenched fists from a podium, shouting to the fired-up crowd. Stone remembered the absurd rhyming title of the speech, "Ishmael in *Eretz Yisrael.*" He told his father that the speech made him nervous and that he never wanted to go to a talk like that ever again.

"He's gone," Stone said.

"I know," Seligman said, putting a hand on Stone's hand.

The car turned a corner and Stone could see a group of school children crossing the street, bright colored backpacks clinging to their backs.

"What are you going to do Matthew? You don't need to hang out with the Arabs, you see where that got you."

He was talking about Fairuza.

"I've tried to take care of you for your father. If only you had stayed at Giv'at Barzel . . ."

"Look," Stone said. "I didn't want to stay on some settlement in the middle of nowhere."

"Okay," Seligman said. "I understand. But you don't need to be alone now. It is the penitential month of Elul. The new year is upon us. Tomorrow is Rosh HaShana. Come pray with me."

"I don't believe in that stuff."

"Okay. I understand. Belief is a constant struggle for most. But, you should not be alone. Come with me. You'll sit, you'll listen. You'll be with Jews instead of wandering the streets."

"I don't know."

"Your father would want you should be with family. And every Jew is family. Think about it," Seligman said. "You know Beit Avraham? On Ocean Parkway near Avenue X? First thing, Matthew. Don't be late."

❧ 9 ❧

In the dim light of his bedroom Stone sensed a dark presence crowding him, a spatial dislocation, a disorienting wrench in the darkness. He flicked on his bedside lamp. A large wood-framed canvas was stretched across the entire width of his bed. He sat up facing his mother's handiwork: a pencil sketch of a human form curled in a fetal position, filled in here and there with bright yellows and oranges and reds. Only the face reflected the human palette, with its shades of beige, burnt ochre and brown. The face was a mask of agony, twisted in pain, the brow furrowed intensely, the jaw set hard. It was an old face, worn down by hardship and loss. The hair looked to Stone like spikes of flame; vigorous reds and oranges burning like tangled barbs of fire. For a moment he thought this was a portrait of his grandfather, Papa Julius, returning in death to the womb.

Matthew had met Papa Julius once, in Miami, not long before his mother disappeared. After a fight with the Judge, his mother had packed a suitcase and flown to Florida with Matthew. He remembered thinking she was taking him to Disney World to ride the Matterhorn, and that the Judge would meet them there. Instead, they had arrived to Julius' humid apartment, thick with the smell of illness, where he lived alone overlooking a verdant golf course. His mother shook Papa Julius' hand and Matthew noticed she was trembling as she said, "Nice to meet you, Mr. Stone."

"Don't charm me, Abi. You got me."

Matthew was surprised to see that his grandfather was so frail and so small; his thick hair had gone white, his bare feet were purple, and he wore a pair of striped pajamas, the sleeves rolled up. Matthew could see a tattoo of a pair of dice creeping out of the sleeve onto his forearm. At first Matthew was afraid, seeing this little man walk towards him, cognac glass in hand.

"How ya doin' there, Dodger?" Papa Julius said, and splashed the drink in his face. But it was a trick glass, something found at a joke shop, and Papa Julius was laughing as the golden liquid swirled around beneath its clear concave top. "You gotta be quick," Papa Julius said, shaking Matthew's hand. "Hey kid, nice to meet you. I'm your grandpa."

Even at that age Matthew could see the resemblance, the same wild hair, the wiry frame. He thought his grandfather looked kind, like someone he'd throw a baseball around with all afternoon.

And his mother had said, "Okay Matty, go watch TV. I'm going to paint your grandfather."

Matthew remembered falling asleep, and then waking up to the sound of his grandfather coughing in the living room, a thick phlegmy wheezing hack, that rose from somewhere deep inside his small frame. It was nighttime and he sounded to Matthew like he was dying. And he was. Matthew never saw his grandfather again but he did see the painting, years later on a break from college, at Abigail Shnitzer's first showing at the Whitney, entitled *American Portraits at the End of a Gun*, which included John Hinckley Jr., Bobby Seale, Bernard Goetz, and the "Son of Sam" killer, David Berkowitz.

In the painting, Papa Julius sat back on a tattered blue couch, arms spread wide on the high back, his wrinkled face worn from a lifetime of violence, his pajama shirt open at the neck. He looked sly, streetwise, as if he was calculating his next move, which happened to be against Death. There was pathos, humanity, even humor in the portrait, as he stared down his final adversary. His mother had captured something so elemental in Julius that Matthew had stood for a long time before the painting of his grandfather feeling that his entire history had been smeared across that canvas.

The portrait now in front of Stone sent a chill through him; the similitude was approximate enough, except that the figure in the painting lay twisted in the position he had woken in. The light sting in his nostrils told him that his mother has used oils.

A stabbing pain shot across his chest. *Is she planning on hanging this in the MoMa beside a pair of my soiled underwear?* He went to the bathroom, turned on the sink and doused his face with cool water. *How could she just show up after all this time and paint me, as if I were nothing more than an extension of her egotistic desires?* The water swirled down the drain, clear and crystalline. Stone raised his eyes hesitantly to the mirror for the first time and noticed a tiny post-it note stuck on the corner of the glass like an afterthought. It read, in Pinky's manic scrawl, "Couldn't wake U. At the Catbird Seat w/ your Moms."

A siren shrilled in the street outside and Stone raced back into his room, water dripping from his face, his heart still pounding. He could feel his blood charging through his veins and his breath quickening. He tried to catch his breath – holding it – then expelling it quickly – then holding it again and expelling – something short of asthmatic. Then he saw something he could not comprehend, something completely beyond his sphere of understanding, something that froze him in place and knocked the breath out of him like a punch in the gut.

His father's judges' robe was spread on the floor haphazardly beneath his mother's canvas, spattered here and there with phlegmy dots and splotches of her paints. The pattern on the robe seemed almost calculated the more Stone stared at the damp pinpoints arranged like an astrological chart of the sky.

The Catbird Seat was quiet when Stone entered. The front room was empty and the abstract paintings on the wall looked hostile, forbidding.

Stone pulled back the velvet curtains and entered the next room. Standing at the entryway, he shuddered to see Pinky hunched close to his mother, leaning in boozily as he spoke. Stone stood for a moment watching his mother, cool, impassive. She brought a drink to her lips. She was dressed in black and muted grays in the Banana Republic style with its timeless lines, its clean cut, eschewing fads and trends. She looked to Stone like the consummate New Yorker, urbane, cynical, confident; and it suddenly struck Stone that perhaps she had never even left New York, that she had been living across the river all this time, painting her pictures while Stone struggled to keep himself together.

Pinky wagged a finger at her, too close to her face, and she lightly pushed it aside. Stone held his breath and listened. Her voice was flat, flinty, absent of affect. He could not make out the words, only the voice. He could hear no maternal compassion and he momentarily held the forbidding thought that he had wished his mother dead instead of the Judge.

"There he is," Pinky said. "Come on. Sit down."

His mother raised her eyes, but they were black pools, showing nothing. Not even a smile. Stone's face burned. He sat down.

"Hello," she said.

"Hi."

"Look. She's gotten younger, while we've gotten older," Pinky mused.

"Michael, why don't you go bring us drinks. Give us a minute to talk."

"Sure. G and t?"

The room was dark, and in the flickering candlelight his mother's face looked hard. She was still pretty, though her skin was tanned and worn. It was still the same face he had known as a child.

"You look good," she said at last.

"You painted me," Stone said.

"I'm sorry," she said. "We tried to wake you, but you wouldn't move."

"I've been a bit depressed. I don't expect you to understand."

"Matthew, I can't pretend to understand. But painting you allowed me to get inside you, understand you. I'm sorry. It wasn't fair."

"If you name something, you own it?" Stone said. "You don't have that right. It's been so long."

"I know, Matthew."

Pinky returned with the drinks and drifted off again.

Abi stared at Stone with those black eyes, betraying nothing. He noticed that she had stray gray hairs in her shoulder-length hair that had once been as black as newly poured tar.

"I don't blame you for hating me," Abi said. "But I'm not a villain. I just want you to understand that I always loved you, and I hurt every day that I didn't see you. I'm your mother, Matthew, and you are my only son. How do you think it feels?"

"I'm not going to feel sorry for you."

"I don't want you to. I just want to explain. Maybe we can salvage something."

"Why? So you can paint me and add me to your rogues' gallery?"

"Fuck the painting," she said, raising her voice for the first time. "I'll throw it out. I'll get rid of it. I was afraid to see you after all this time. The painting gave me the chance to get to know you a bit first. That's all. You are in a lot of pain."

He nodded his head.

"So am I. It was the hardest thing I ever had to do. Leaving you."

"Then why did you do it? For years I kept expecting you to walk through the door any minute."

"You were young."

"It was so sudden. There and gone."

"No, it wasn't, Matthew."

Stone noticed a vein trembling in her neck.

"It had been happening for years."

The gin burned in Stone's sinuses. Pinky had the bartender pour it strong, nearly absent of tonic. "Why didn't you at least call me, tell me you were okay?"

"That wasn't fair."

"Why?"

"Him."

"Why?"

"You know what kind of man he was."

"What do you mean?"

Abi brought the drink to her mouth. Her fingernails were short and cracked with black residue under the nails.

"I was afraid of you becoming like him."

"A Jewish mother who doesn't want her son to become a lawyer, a judge?"

"Not that, Matthew," she said. "He was a very willful man, very powerful. He had strong ideas about how the world should be."

"What's wrong with that?"

She reached a hand out, but Stone let the hand remain in the center of the table, beside a perspiring ring of gin.

"I would have taken you with me."

"So it's all about you. What about my father's feelings?"

"Matthew, I was afraid for you. Getting involved in his business." She paused. "I tried once. When we went down to Florida. But he found us and brought us home. I don't know how he did it. He hadn't spoken to Julius in years. How could he have suspected?"

"You just wanted the painting."

"I did want the painting. Very much. But I also wanted to start a new life with you."

"Bullshit."

"Matthew, he said he'd kill me if I tried again."

"And you believed him?"

Abi paused again, finished her drink. Now she seemed to be having difficulty gathering her words. The vein jumped in her neck. Her voice wavered, no longer the confident, flat tone.

"The year I left, I sent you a birthday card, a Chagall painting of a mother and child. I'm sure you never got it. Because, a couple weeks after I sent it, I was out in San Francisco, staying with friends from graduate school. One of your father's associates, some Midwood low-life, showed up at the apartment where I was staying and said that if I ever tried to contact you again, he would shoot me in the back of the head and throw me in the Bay. And he put the gun to the back of my skull. I still feel it. And he meant it, Matthew. I had never been so scared in my life, not for me, but for you, because I was beyond helping you. I had to leave you on your own with him and you would have to fend for yourself."

"So you are some sort of tragic heroine. Is that the way you imagine it?"

"That's not what I'm saying."

"Do you know what it was like growing up, learning about your mother through the newspaper and through her paintings? Every time your paintings turned up in a gallery I went, half-hoping to see you, but knowing that you would not be there when I went. I wanted to see if there was a sense of sadness in your paintings, something that showed me that you cared, that you had lost something precious, something to explain what could never be explained." Stone gestured to the waitress with two fingers. "You ran out on me, and your career took off, and now you want me to forgive you."

"Matthew, please."

"I'm going to the bathroom."

When Stone returned, he downed his drink and raised his arm to order another. He saw a brief twinge of concern flash across Abi's face, but she stopped herself. She knew she had no right. Pinky lit a cigarette and offered one to Stone. He was only accustomed to smoking the Judge's stray Nat Shermans, an act of internal self-immolation that had likely given the Judge the cancer that had killed him. He took Pinky's filterless Kool, drew on the cigarette and breathed in deeply. He felt some long-lost, childish satisfaction that he had been denied, dragging on Pinky's coffin nail before his silent mother. But she did not, could not react. For the first time, Stone was able to observe Abi objectively, not as a mother, but as a woman. He noticed that her lips were full and pink and that her thin neck was long and slender. Her small breasts looked sporty, firm, despite the onset of middle-age. Her eyes sat narrow and sharp, black as licorice candy. Stone could imagine someone falling in love with her, her movements graceful, unstudied, smooth. But, could he imagine his mother loving anyone in return?

"What kind of pictures do you paint?" Pinky asked.

"People mostly. I'm interested in delving into the mystery of what it means to be human. There are a lot of secrets that people hold inside that reveal themselves in different ways. Have you heard the saying that people are born with a face they are given, but they end up with the face they deserve?"

"That's some deep shit."

"Basically. It's the essence of what I am trying to do with my art."

"Paint me," Pinky said suddenly, flexing a muscle.

"I could paint you," she said, narrowing her eyes further. "You might be surprised with what I see."

"What do you see?" he said, reaching for the sunglasses propped on Abi's head and putting them on.

"What I see now is not what I see after I paint you."

Stone finished his drink and crunched on a mouthful of ice. He felt a tight ball of belligerence gathering in his hot belly.

"Did you remarry? Have kids? Run out on them too?"

Abi did not flinch.

"Snap," Pinky said.

"Am I keeping you from some art opening in some podunk town somewhere?"

"No," Abi said. "This is where I want to be."

"It's too late," Stone said, standing up. "I'm going home."

Stone moved down the length of the bar, putting distance between him and Abi, drinking as he went. He imagined her eyes on him as he found himself at the end of the long mahogany bar, before a frosted mirror. He tried to find his image reflecting back, but he could not find himself in the crowd of drunken bodies.

Saira sidled up beside him.

"Hey, stranger. What happened to you?"

Stone had trouble placing her for a moment. She wore a Sun Studio T-shirt and a red skirt over a pair of worn blue jeans.

"You come here often?" Stone offered lamely.

"I live here," she said, laughing. Her translucent skin seemed to support her statement.

"Good for you. Can I buy you a drink?"

"That's the least you can do," she said, leaning in. Her cheeks were flushed and her skin a pale, pasty white.

He fumbled in his pocket and threw some balled-up bills onto the bar top. "What are you drinking?"

"Anything. Doesn't matter."

"My thoughts exactly."

"By the way, your friend is *faux*."

"My friend's a foe?" Stone said.

"He's ersatz, you know? Like a watch you'd buy on Canal Street."

"Sure," Stone said.

They clinked glasses and drank.

"Let's go," Pinky said several drinks later. He steered Stone away before he had a chance to say goodbye. "Stay away from her. She's the original cold-ass Mary."

Stone's feet felt as if they were a mile away, his head light and heavy at the same time. His mother blurred in and out of his vision as if seen through the filthy peephole on the front of his apartment door.

"Where is she?" Stone flailed.

"I'm here," Abi said. She was a smear of black against the oil-drum fire.

"I wanna hug," Stone slurred. "Just one hug."

"For godsake, hug the kid already," Pinky said, maneuvering Stone forward.

His mother held him in his arms and he could feel his cheek against her. Her heart beat quickly through her light jacket.

"It's all right," she said softly. "It's going to be all right."

A livery cab passed and honked its horn.

"*Puta*," Pinky muttered.

"What was that?" Stone said.

"Just a taxi."

"I wanna hug you."

"You are," she said softly.

"I am."

"Oh, Matthew, I'm terrified to death for you."

☙ 10 ❧

The synagogue was a large red-brick, square building, several stories high, adorned with golden hued Hebrew and English letters:

CONGREGATION BEIT AVRAHAM
FOUNDED 1920

The building was set back from Ocean Parkway and separated by a small service road on which cars were parked and children played. Small groups of men and their wives gathered in the warm sunshine as Stone tottered across the street. Most of the men were dressed in black. Some were dressed in white.

Abi had woken early to catch the train from Grand Central to White Plains and had shaken Stone awake asking if he would join her at his uncle's for Rosh HaShana. His head felt shattered, broken, and he had pulled the covers over himself, telling her flatly he wasn't going. After she had left, Stone splashed water on his face, dressed, and still a little drunk, drove to Ocean Parkway.

Stone was not surprised to see Seligman, wearing his ever-present aviator glasses, holding court to a group of younger men, who wore knitted *kippahs* on their heads, the young men eagerly listening to his words.

"Come here, *bubee*," Seligman said, waving at Stone. "You're just in time."

The sun was so bright that Stone's eyes, narrowed to slits, gave him the sense of a warm halo-like glow around Seligman. His gold wedding band caught a flash of sun.

"So glad you could make it," Seligman added, pulling Stone into an embrace. He smelled like fresh laundry and the beginnings of perspiration. "I assume you walked," he smiled. "Since it's a holy day. You know, many consider Rosh HaShana to be the anniversary of the Creation of the world."

Stone was silent, his mouth coated in a thick pasty film.

"Not just that," Seligman added. Stone could see Seligman's eyes through the tinted glasses. "But a chance to start over . . ."

"*L'Shana Tova Tikateivu*, Rabbi Seligman." A young yeshiva student pumped Seligman's hand and turned to Matthew.

"This is Matthew Stone."

"The Judge's son?" the student said, wide-eyed. "They should have hung Demjanjuk when they had the chance. Honored to meet you," he said, taking Matthew's hand and shaking it adamantly. "Be inscribed in the Book of Life for a good year."

"Same to you," Stone said. The student walked away and was immediately replaced by three or four other yeshiva students wishing Seligman well. Two were very thin and one was very fat. All of them wore knitted *kippahs* and were dressed in identical black suits with white shirts.

"*Shana Tova,*" the first one said to Seligman. "Welcome to *Galut.*"

"Next year in Jerusalem," another student said, laughing. "Or *Gan Eden.*"

The third student added, "*Baruch Hashem.*" And they all laughed again.

Stone stepped to move outside of the circle, but Seligman's firm hand squeezed Stone's shoulder. "Stay with me."

Seligman whispered something into the ear of one of the students, a final word at the end of an embrace.

"No problem," one of the boys said, and wished Stone and Seligman "*Shana Tova*" again.

Seligman put his hand on Stone's shoulder and he could feel the warmth through his suit. He felt strangely comforted by the hand as it guided him towards the stairs leading inside. "We'll talk more later," Seligman whispered in Stone's ear. "The service is starting." They passed two black police officers manning the door and Seligman shook his head.

The sanctuary was larger than Stone had expected it to be, with a balcony on three sides where the women sat. The ceiling was very high, scooped out like the dome of the sky. Light shone in from small windows and filtered down onto the front rows with a distilled radiance that Stone understood to be appropriate for a holy place. Seligman led Stone down the center aisle to a reserved seat near the front, just to the right of the *bima* and the ark, both of which were covered with a pure white fabric. Hundreds of voices buzzed in Stone's ears all at once. He felt a paranoid suspicion that he was being watched. Perhaps Zohar was somewhere in the crowd, blending in with the suits. He looked around, just as a man was sneezing into a handkerchief. Zohar was nowhere to be seen. If the eyes were staring at anyone, it was at Seligman, the eminent head rabbi of Giv'at Barzel in far-off Samaria.

It had been so long since Stone had been in a synagogue – he had had a small service for his father at the burial chapel – that he felt like he didn't belong, like an intruder crashing a private ceremony. Stone saw smiling men dressed all in white, or in their finest dark suits, draping their flowing *tallit* over their bodies.

"Here's your *machzor*," Seligman said, handing Stone a thick prayer book that smelled of formaldehyde. "There is an English translation on the left."

"Should I be wearing . . . ?" Stone indicated Seligman's prayer shawl. Most of the men around them wore long flowing *tallit* over their shoulders.

"Are you married?"

"No."

"Then, no." Seligman chucked him softly on the shoulder as if to say, "One day."

He opened the book and read the written dedication, "A gift to Cong. Beit Avraham in memory of Ephraim Glatzer." Stone wondered if Ephraim Glatzer too had an unfinished story crying out to be completed.

The rabbi appeared before them, followed by the cantor, both dressed in white. The cantor began to sing in Hebrew and the congregation rose as one, Stone a second behind the crowd, his hangover slowing him, as if caught in a molasses haze.

"Just follow along," Seligman said, pointing to the place in the prayer book. The Hebrew lettering on the right side of the page looked like the blackened bones of the dead.

Now his mind turned to his Bar Mitzvah lessons that he took in the musty basement of an ancient rabbi who spat phlegm into a handkerchief and praised Matthew for his beautiful singing voice. He was a survivor from Bergen-Belsen and his skin was thin and pale, like wax paper. Stone did not dare defy a man of his condition and years. It seemed he had spent much of his life treading the dreamy line between the living and the dead, that with him, being on a first name basis with the Angel of Death needed only a small push to reach the other side, so Stone paid attention and learned the words. It was easy memorization and he managed the Torah portion without too much difficulty.

And so it was that on the day of his Bar Mitzvah, he shone, made his father proud. But Stone felt like little more than a trained seal clapping his flippers, he had been so grudging in participation in the empty ritual (the memorized words meant nothing) that he did not speak to his father for weeks after his Bar Mitzvah.

He thought of the pigeons, lightly singing beneath the eaves of his apartment's roof and thought, *Their prayers have as much strength as these.* But Seligman sang along in a firm voice, his Adam's apple jumping in his throat. What did he see that Stone could not? The prayer ended and Stone was about to sit back down when the congregation began singing again. This went on for about 20 minutes, alternately standing, sitting, standing again. He only recognized the tune for the *Sh'ma* from his childhood but could not figure out what being mumbled by the congregation. It seemed that different men mumbled different words. They swayed back and forth in their prayers, seemingly lost only to return in sync with the rest of the congregation.

Seligman, too, swayed seductively with eyes closed, his lips speaking the ages-old prayers faster than he could get them out. Stone watched the powerful Seligman, a supplicant, burning with an obsessive flame that he could not understand. All of his intelligence and knowledge turned inward, all of his energy directed towards an absent God. This was more alien to Stone than anything he had encountered in all his years at school. His mind had been trained in the art of reason, conquering the unknowable, cynicism penetrating any lie. He knew God was a construct, created by man to explain the manifold mysteries of the universe, a character out of an ancient book read into existence by sheer repetition.

Seligman leaned in close to Stone and whispered, "You may want to join in." He pointed to the page in the prayer book. "You are in mourning, aren't you?"

The *Kaddish*, the ancient prayer of sanctification, lay on the page in its strangely rhythmic transliteration. It had been his father's wish, and he had denied him that. Perhaps it was Stone's headache or his exhaustion but the italicized words seemed frayed at the edges, blurry, impossible to read, like an ancient tablet rubbed out by the sands of time.

"I can't," Stone said. He decided to engage with the text, follow the words, root out the meaning, like an academic exercise.

The voices rose again in song. This time the reverberation of their many voices hummed off the walls and domed ceiling, running up and down his spine like a chill.

"*Avinu Malkeinu*," Seligman whispered, pointing to the left side of the page.

"Our Father, our King," Stone read, recognizing the tune. He read the words and saw the contradictions of an accepting father, a loving father and that of a stern, demanding, unforgiving father. He thought of the Judge and his cruel unblinking blue eyes as he lay on his death bed.

Seligman continued to sing along. His voice robust and full, he leaned close singing the simple chorus, his mouth articulating for Stone to join in, insisting he join in. And he sang out tentatively as the prayer came to an end "Our Father our King, hear our voices!"

A moment later, the worshippers stood again – this time, though, buzzing in expectation as the Torah scroll was taken down from the ark. For the first time, Stone noticed the flickering red eternal light burning above the ark, winking at him like an ever-seeing eye. The rabbi made his rounds – up and down the aisles, with the Torah hefted high onto his shoulders. Men reached out with their prayer books, kissed them and touched them to the passing Torah. The Torah reached Stone, and Seligman touched his *tallit* to it.

"This is the Torah portion," Seligman said. "Follow the story in English," he added, sounding to Stone like an old teacher easing his students into work. Several men were called up to the *bima* to join in with the reading. The first man's voice was high and nasal and his Hebrew, sharp and jagged, in contrast to the flowing voice of the cantor.

Stone read ahead, of the birth of Isaac, to the aged Sarah and Abraham – and of the exile of his half-brother Ishmael. The story fascinated him, as he read on about God calling out to Abraham demanding he sacrifice his son. And the fanatic Abraham, who had circumcised himself at the age of ninety-nine, unquestioningly accepting God's request, taking his beloved son to the land of Moriah to sacrifice as a burnt offering. As Stone read, he felt the tiny hairs on the back of his neck electrified, as if someone were standing over him, breathing lightly at his back. He imagined young Isaac bound on the altar and the profound humiliation and fear and worthlessness he must have felt when he weakly asked his father, "Where is the lamb for the burnt offering?" And Abraham lied, and told his son that God would provide a lamb just as he unsheathed a knife and pressed the blade to his son's throat. And the angel of the Lord called out from Heaven to Abraham, "Lay not thy hand upon the boy . . . For now I know thou art a God-fearing man."

Stone imagined Isaac's permanent anxiety and distrust and guilt, his feelings of failure and disgrace before his awesome father, bound on the altar beneath the bright blade. Stone finally understood why the Jews, descended from the patriarch Isaac, were such a neurotic people born from this frightening act of faith, a psychological wrecking ball that echoed through the millennia.

Seligman cleared his throat and coughed, and Stone saw dust motes descending on the shafts of sunlight. A sorrowful moan cried out from the center of the sanctuary. A dark bearded man who wore off-white canvas tennis shoes, his *tallit* casually draped over his head, raised a twisted ram's horn in the air, his hand halfway up the shining shaft, as he blew three blasts followed quickly by shorter staccato blasts. There was something primal and ancient in these cries, and Stone felt his blood stir, his heartbeat quicken. He wanted to cry out, he wanted to run, he wanted to close his eyes and drink in every sound. The blasting of the *shofar* was both beautiful and horrifying.

"Got your attention," Seligman whispered. Stone nodded his head in assent. "It's your wake-up call," Seligman added, as the last long note sounded, filling the sanctuary with its mournful cry. The Torah was returned to the ark, and the rabbi stepped up to the *bima* to give his sermon. His voice sounded so different in English than it had in Hebrew that Stone had to look twice to make sure it was the same person speaking. The rabbi's accent had a strong local flavor and it was clear to Stone that he had likely lived his entire life not far from Beit Avraham and Ocean Parkway.

"Last Rosh HaShana, I spoke about the murder of Moshe and Devorah Blickstein, and their infant Rivka, former congregants who were gunned down as they drove from their home in Giv'at Barzel toward Jerusalem to celebrate the new year. Their first *yahrzeit* passed this week – and was marked in Israel by stone throwing, a stabbing, and an attempted suicide bombing perpetrated by their 'neighbors,' strangers in the Land of Israel, descendants of the ancient Canaanites who cry 'occupation' while plotting to push the Jews into the sea. I said last year that we would not stand silent on the graves of fellow Jews. I said that we were on the threshold of Redemption and the new Kingdom of Israel. And we have not stood silent. The reclamation of the land of Judea, Samaria, Gaza, and Jerusalem has continued. Fourteen new communities have been established, the outpost community of Rivkia, commanding the hilltop above the spot where the Blicksteins were killed, is a living testament and an affirmation that we will not stand silent when Jewish blood is shed.

Looking back through the prism of time, we see that Jews have always been abundant upon the land. God promised the land to Abraham and to his descendants, and that they would be as multiple as the stars in heaven. It was the Almighty who chose from all the nations the Jews as His Chosen People – and in return for observing His laws and statutes as given at Mount Sinai, we were given *Eretz Yisrael,* decreed *Eretz Yisrael* as our home in perpetuity. Today we stand on the threshold of Redemption as Hellenists and Socialists and every other kind of abomination including the Sons of Ishmael sit in the seat of government in Jerusalem, negotiating 'peace' accords, engaging in a 'process' to return the land to our sworn historical enemy. They come under many names: the Amorites, the Canaanites, the Hittites, the Jebusites, the Philistines, and now, the 'Palestinians,' though it is a known fact that the 'Palestinian people' is a fiction created in the second half of this century by politicians, revolutionaries, and murderers. The sages said, 'Great is peace, for God's name is peace.' But what kind of peace is contingent upon the wholesale destruction of the Land of Israel? We will not stand silent upon the graves of Jews killed for living on their land. The 'government' that sits in the Knesset is bankrupt, foggy-headed, and a danger to the future of Israel. The prime minister says that peace is at hand as terrorists blow up our children in the streets. The prime minister says there will be a Palestinian state while their children learn hatred in their schools and their clerics preach hatred from the loud speakers of their mosques. The prime minister turns a deaf ear to the murderous mantra, 'With blood and spirit we shall redeem you, Palestine.' Their fantasy maps of a future state cover all the Land of Israel, from Metulla to Eilat. This peace is Chamberlain's 'peace in our time.' This is not peace. This is suicide. It seems in the face of this bitter reality to be so simple, logical – our universal right to defend ourselves against our enemy who has sworn our destruction. It is written in Deuteronomy, 'When you go forth against your enemies – confront them as enemies. Just as they show you no mercy, so you should show them no mercy.' Strangely, through the looking glass of modern Israel, we are seen as zealots, villains, bent on bloodshed and destruction, though our ethical foundations are built upon the word of God and his Commandments. We agree – to kill innocent people is evil, though sometimes we must kill to protect our land. Our enemies kill innocent people in the name and service of some dark God. It is written in Isaiah, 'Woe unto them that call evil good, and good evil.' We will not stand silent upon the graves of Jews as the secular government of Jerusalem fans the flames of our enemies' hatred, showing eagerness and weakness to make peace at any cost, the way a school child bribes a bully with his milk money. As we all know too painfully, he always comes back for more. We must speak out. We must act. We are on the threshold of Redemption. The Temple of Israel is poised in the heavens, waiting to descend. The Kingdom of Israel lies before us, this Rosh HaShana, as we mark the first *yahrzeit* of the martyred Blickstein family. As Jews, we must continue steadfastly to honor God's Commandments and covenants. Every Rosh HaShana, as self-reflection, penitence, *teshuvah* fill our very souls, we read of the story of the Binding of Isaac, the *Akeda*, a story which tells of our father Abraham and his willingness to sacrifice his beloved son Isaac. It was Abraham's act of faith over five thousand years ago that bound the Jewish people forever to God and God to the Jewish people. The Lord said, 'Because thou hast not withheld thy son, thine only son, that in blessing I will bless thee.' Today, in a reversal of that act of faith, the secular government is sacrificing Jewish children upon the altar of peace and in return for that sacrifice, giving away land that God granted us to bloody-handed murderers. There are nabobs and naysayers who claim that we do not want peace – that we want to live behind our fences and walls in a perpetual never-ending garrison state. That could not be farther from the truth. We want peace. It is the Arab who does not want peace. So we must stand strong in the face of our enemies. It is our duty and obligation to history to fight those who seek our destruction. We have a blood-tie to the land and cannot give up one grain of sand, one blade of grass, as we stand on the threshold of Redemption. The secular government seeks instant Redemption in the eyes of the world, like an unpopular child giving away its toys in return for friendship. But this sort of capitulation will ultimately bring tragedy and death not seen since the dark days of Auschwitz. Instant peace is an illusion, a mirage shimmering on the desert sands. True peace and true redemption will only come with *teshuva*, penitence – a return to God and his Commandments. Rosh HaShana is a day of judgment, and God will look back on our deeds of the past year, at those who have misbehaved and those who lived by His Commandments. And He will decide who will be inscribed in the Book of Life for another year and who will be burned into the Book of Death. A year ago, it was the secular government who condemned the young Blickstein family to the Book of Death, righteous Jews just twenty-six years old living on our God-given land. It is our duty to do all we can to assure that Jews can live in peace and protection in *Eretz Yisrael* and continue to populate the land and flourish like we have since the days of the Patriarchs. This is the time of year to ask God for forgiveness, to atone for sins of the past and to look towards a bright shining future in which all Jews will live in peace in the Kingdom of Israel."

The rabbi's booming sermon ended and the congregants slipped quickly into another prayer. Seligman looked towards Stone for a moment and smiled wryly. Repeating the liturgy had been a challenge for Stone, the words sticking in his throat, but the sermon hit Stone like a hammer. It wasn't so much that he believed what Rabbi Greiner was saying, it was just that Stone knew Moe Blickstein, had gone to middle school with him, remembered later hearing that he was moving to Israel, his picture in a local paper. What did anyone care whether Moe Blickstein, whose ill-timed jokes made him a laughing stock in the schoolyard, moved to Israel? Now he was dead. Now he was a martyr and Stone saw the worshippers wiping tears from their cloudy eyes.

Stone had long suspected that being dead got you farther in life than being alive. Moe Blickstein had died because he had lived on disputed land in a violent neighborhood. But was that enough to have made his life worth living? Stone imagined moving to the South Bronx or Brownsville, dodging bullets among the wrecked lives of blacks and Puerto Ricans. Would his life matter if he were to die on those mean streets? No. Stone knew there was something else. Blickstein's death was tied to a long litany of historic tragedy reaching back thousands of years – he had become part of the continuum, part of the long Jewish narrative of heroism in the face of tragedy.

The sanctuary was silent now, the congregants lost in silent meditation. The streaming shafts of light suddenly seemed too bright for Stone and he closed his eyes. The murdered Moe Blickstein appeared before him, his bearded face broken, shattered by gunmen's bullets, his skin grayish-green, his eyes a cold silver. His jaw was thick, his cracked lips, purple. He was trying to speak out but he could not. "What is it?" Stone asked, as a pale grave worm slithered from Moe Blickstein's nostril. "What's in your mouth?" Moe Blickstein coughed and vomited out dirt and dust and sand. "The Land of Israel," he said and laughed before disappearing. Stone heard a man fart several rows back, breaking the silence of the sanctuary. He felt a cold rivulet of sweat drip down his arm. To his right, Seligman was praying, eyes closed, oblivious. Stone wanted to reach out, touch him, feel the warmth of another person, clear his mind of the awful vision. He was afraid Blickstein would return to exact some sort of revenge on him for some long-forgotten slight. Stone closed his eyes again but this time the darkness, suffused with sunlight, was golden.

Later, Seligman leaned close to Stone and whispered, "Pay attention to this one. It's an ancient poem by Rabbi Amnon of Mainz. This is the big prayer. It's magnificent."

The congregation took up a plaintive sing-song and Stone followed along in his *machzor*. The words immediately frightened Stone as no other words had before – apocalyptic, horrifying, cruel, violent – and speaking directly to him. The eerie chanting and rhythm sounded like a judgment upon him alone.

We shall ascribe holiness to this day.
For it is awesome and terrible.
Your kingship is exalted upon it.
Your throne is established in mercy.
You are enthroned upon it in truth.
In truth You are the judge,
The exhorter, the all-knowing, the witness,
He who inscribes and seals,
Remembering all that is forgotten.
You open the book of remembrance
Which proclaims itself,
And the seal of each person is there.
The great shofar is sounded,
A still small voice is heard.
The angels are dismayed,
They are seized by fear and trembling
As they proclaim: Behold the Day of Judgment!
For all the hosts of heaven are brought for judgment.
They shall not be guiltless in Your eyes
And all creatures shall parade before You as a troop.
As a shepherd herds his flock,
Causing his sheep to pass beneath his staff,
So do You cause to pass, count, and record,
Visiting the souls of all living,
Decreeing the length of their days,
Inscribing their judgment.
On Rosh HaShana it is inscribed,
And on Yom Kippur it is sealed.

Stone's father appeared radiant before him, wearing an immaculate white robe. He sat high above, his shining gavel held aloft in the air. His eyes were cruel, indifferent, chastising his son for not following his commandments. And from his heavenly bench, he pronounced with terrifying clarity:

How many shall pass away and how many shall be born,
Who shall live and who shall die,
Who shall reach the end of his days and who shall not,
Who shall perish by water and who by fire,
Who by sword and who by wild beast,
Who by famine and who by thirst,
Who by earthquake and who by plague,
Who by strangulation and who by stoning,
Who shall have rest and who shall wander,
Who shall be at peace and who shall be pursued,
Who shall be at rest and who shall be tormented,
Who shall be exalted and who shall be humbled,
Who shall become rich and who shall suffer penury,
But repentance, prayer and righteousness avert the
  severe decree.

As Stone stared at the *machzor* before him, he realized he was guilty and would have to pay. Seligman leaned close and whispered in Stone's ear, "Are you all right?"

"I don't know."

"The *Unetanah Tokef* can be quite powerful." He pulled away, leaving Stone's ear feeling hot and humid. He felt his stomach boiling, the acid creeping sourly up his esophagus which felt thick and raw, swollen as if a hand were reaching up and out of his belly. He sat down in a chilled sweat and remained sitting through the reprise of *Avinu Malkeinu* and the *Kaddish*.

The blast of the *shofar* roused Stone and the room was alive with shifting bodies and the voice of a man calling out the order of the *shofar*. "*Tekiah, teruah-shevarim, tekiah . . .*"

Afterwards, out in the street, in the sunshine, strangers, people he had never seen before, wished Stone well, wished him a "*Shana Tova*," and their eyes, kind and sincere in a way that almost frightened Stone, made him realize that he was being accepted because he was a Jew and that he was not alone. He sat on a low wall, neck bent, head down between his knees while Seligman greeted the congregants. They had practically lined up to get a word with him. "Rav Seligman, we're so honored. Thank you for blessing us with your presence," etcetera. And they would kiss his cheek. He conferred privately with each one, whispering intimate wisdom into each of their ears.

"Matty," Seligman said, approaching after a few minutes. "Are you all right?"

"Headache," Stone said to the pavement below.

"It's an intense service. It can be difficult to face. Reflective. A time to look back on our lives and make changes." He paused and then said, "Like a New Year's resolution."

"They're useless," Stone said. "Empty resolutions."

Seligman sat on the wall beside Stone.

"Yes, they are useless. And that is what's wrong with the secular world. Nobody's watching over you. Without God, man is nothing but impulse and energy bouncing from whim to whim. But if you speak to God, he listens."

"I don't feel well," Stone said, raising his head.

He was surprised to see Seligman was smiling broadly. "And whose fault is that? Did God tell you to go drinking all night long? You smell like a Bowery bum."

Embarrassed, Stone offered, "Maybe I'm dying."

"Ha!" Seligman said. "Not so fast. No Jew dies between Rosh HaShana and Yom Kippur – not while the Book of Judgment is open."

"Do you really believe that?"

"Talk to me next week – if you're still alive."

"It's not funny."

"You're not dying. You've just got a hangover for the ages," Seligman said, ruffling Stone's hair with his rough hand. "That's what people do in the secular world, a world with no sense of proper values. Do you want to live like the goyim, drinking and rutting like a beast? I understand you have lost your father. But you are not alone in the world. We can help you."

"How?"

"There are means built right into your own culture to help you release the pressure stored up inside. Why do you think the Jews have survived so long?" Seligman paused as a fire engine raced down Ocean Parkway. "Your father was very proud of you," Seligman said. "It wasn't easy for Walter. He kept so much bottled up."

"What else?" Stone pressed.

"Matthew, you were his only son. He loved you, you have to know that."

Stone looked skeptically at Seligman.

"You can trust me, Matthew. Your father and I were as close as brothers. He spoke about you all the time. He had such hopes."

"And I disappointed him."

Seligman stood up, straightened his suit, and said, "No, no. Not at all. Come on. Let's go to lunch. We'll be late."

"No, no. I don't feel well. And I need a shower."

"Come to lunch, kid. You'll wash your face in the sink. The walk will do you good."

"No."

"Maimonides says it is a *mitzvah* to celebrate and eat together."

"I'm not hungry."

"Eat. Don't eat. But, come to lunch and be among your people, your family. You'll see that you never have to be alone in the world."

ꙩ 11 ꙩ

They walked in near silence from the synagogue. Seligman seemed lost in thought or in prayer. He took long healthy strides and Stone had to push himself to keep up.

"I wanted to talk to you about the account numbers," Stone said.

Seligman raised his head. "Not now Matthew. Not on the New Year." And then Seligman added firmly, "and not in the street."

The Rosh HaShana meal was well underway when Seligman and Stone arrived at a white brick house just off one of the lettered avenues that bisected Ocean Parkway, not unlike the one that Stone had lived in as a child. Now they were late for lunch and Stone was faint from hunger.

"Finally, Zalman arrives!" a bearded man at the head of the long luncheon table called out ebulliently. "We were placing our bets about who would arrive first – you, or the Messiah."

"You know," Seligman said, matter-of-factly, "the Messiah will only come when Jerusalem is a Jewish city again."

"Meanwhile, we eat," the man said, laughing.

A ceiling fan rattled quietly above the long dining-room table that was covered with an off-white lace tablecloth, stained here and there with pinkish glyphs and splotches, suggesting that Elijah's cup had overflowed many a shaky-handed time. A wooden hutch stood to one side of the table piled high with plates, saucers, and teacups. A honey cake overly sprinkled with confectioner's sugar and several other desserts languished in the sunlight and the stunted breeze of the dining room's only window. The wall to Stone's left was tightly filled with framed sepia-toned photographs of Old World Jews – staring stunned and stilted – perhaps sensing the coming disaster. These were family photographs as there was an eerie resemblance in the facial structure and the eyes of these unsmiling Jews to the loud man at the end of the table.

About fifteen people of all ages sat around the long table, eating turkey and brisket, gelfilte fish and cucumber salad, *tzimmes* and candied yams. A glazed round challah sat at each end of the table beside small pots of honey and fans of sliced apple.

"Take a seat. Eat. Eat!" an older woman seated next to the bearded man said.

"I want to introduce you all to Matthew Stone," Seligman said. "He's family."

"Is this Walter's kid?" the man said, chewing a mouthful of brisket.

Stone smiled weakly and nodded.

"Truth?" the man said, sizing up Stone.

Seligman nodded.

"You don't say. Walter's son," the man said. "Then it will be a sweet year."

A girl around Stone's age across the table smiled, her large brown eyes bright and welcoming. Three yeshiva students wearing matching white shirts and knitted *kippahs* nodded matter-of-factly. The older woman who had beckoned Stone to eat reached out her arms and raised her eyes to the heavens. She muttered a prayer. It was as if he were given an instant line of credit solely because he was Walter Stone's son.

"Matthew, I'm only going to say it once – so pay attention," Seligman said, gesturing to the bearded man. "This is, uh," and he paused in jest, finger extended, pretending he had forgotten the host's name.

"Dovid Grunhut," the man said, laughing. "You'd better keep an eye on your uncle. He knows more than he lets on."

Seligman laughed and extended his hand, moving it counter-clockwise around the table as he spoke.

"Esther." And the older woman smiled again. "Yossi, Dov, Natan, Meir, Malka, Gabby." Seligman stopped again. There was an empty high chair next to the brown-eyed girl who Stone was introduced to as Gabby. "Where's Arieh?" Seligman said.

"Napping," Yossi said. "I'm ready to crash too."

Stone noticed that Gabby's big brown eyes, warm under long lashes, were firmly focused on him. They were the kind of eyes that made Stone feel like he was the only person in the room and that they shared an intimate secret. She had tiny freckles on her cheeks and nose with skin a tanned, burnished golden brown. Stone thought she was adorable but looked away, following Seligman's introductions.

"This is Dr. Cohen," Seligman said, gesturing to the thin elderly man sitting beside Stone at the head opposite Dovid. "Matthew, you know who you are. I'm Zalman Seligman."

"The revered Rabbi Seligman. Huzzah!" Dovid Grunhut called out, laughing again. "But seriously. We are honored to have you here in Brooklyn this Rosh HaShana. I know you have traveled far to share this *simcha* with us."

"*Baruch Hashem!*" someone called out from the near side of the table.

After Seligman finished the introductions, he went to wash his hands in the kitchen. Stone served himself some brisket and challah. His stomach felt scraped out.

"Nachmanides says 'Do not abandon the land to any other nation,'" Dovid Grunhut said, picking up their broken strand of conversation.

"That is absolutely correct," someone to Stone's right agreed. "And that is exactly what Rabbi Greiner was saying in today's sermon. That we have been commanded not to surrender a single inch of the Jewish land. To do so would be—"

"Catastrophic," the elderly Dr. Cohen interrupted. "I was a young man in Germany and bit by bit Germany grew; the Sudetenland, the Anschlus. It's true that the German thunder rolled slowly at first, as Heinrich Heine warned. But he also said that you will know that the German thunder has hit its mark when you hear a crash like nothing has ever crashed in the history of the world." He paused for a moment and took a sip of wine. His white hair was immaculately combed back beneath a blue and white knitted *kippah*, his blue eyes pale. "We were warned. The world was warned. Heine wrote his prophetic essay on Germany in 1834, a full one hundred years before the Nazi war machine rolled. Germany's intentions were no secret."

Dr. Cohen's eyes filled with tears.

"Irving," Seligman said, drying his hands on his pants as he sat back down. "We endured. We are living in the Land of Israel while Hitler burns in Gehenna."

"Piss on Hitler," Dov said. An arrogant, angry expression remained after he had spoken.

"Listen," Dr. Cohen said.

"We understand," a disembodied voice said at the other end of the table.

"No, you don't understand," the frail Dr. Cohen insisted, pounding his fist on the table. "It's happening again. Amalek is gathering strength."

Though this talk seemed half-mad to Stone, he envied their conviction, the fact that there was something in the world to care about and to fight for.

"You've all heard of the Amalekites, that ancient tribe who tried to destroy us at the Exodus, and you all know that Amalek reappears every generation, to bring us low, to fight us, to destroy us all. Nazi Germany was the ideological bastard child of Amalek, so were the Tsarists, the Spaniards, the Romans, and the list goes on throughout history—"

"We're ready to defend ourselves," Dov said. His jaw was firm as he recited, "From Dan to Beersheva, from Gilad to the sea, there is not one spot of our land that was not redeemed by blood."

"Yes, yes," Dr. Cohen said dismissively. "And even in poverty, a Jew is a prince, and you were created the son of a king—"

"But Jewish blood—" Dov interrupted.

"Crowned with David's crown," Dr. Cohen continued bitterly.

Esther broke in, "I've seen Amalek, Doctor. We've all seen Amalek. He killed my husband. This family is on a first name basis with Amalek."

The first glass of sweet wine went directly to Stone's head. He felt a humming in his temples and a light burn in his belly. The hair of the dog did its trick as Stone settled into a mellow buzz. The brisket was overcooked and almost cold, the glazed challah was sweet and filled with raisins. Stone tried to inconspicuously pick them out with his fork.

"I don't like raisins either."

The conversation melted away and he caught Gabby smiling at him.

"I pick them out, too," she said, gesturing with her silver-ringed fingers. She half-closed her eyes and bit her lower lip. "I taught Arieh how to flick them at his grandfather."

"That's not nice," Stone said, feeling a charge in her words.

"Neither is his grandfather," she laughed, gesturing to Dovid Grunhut, who was loudly declaiming in Yiddish, dominating his interlocutor, Dr. Cohen. "He thinks he's the boss of the table."

"It's true, isn't it?" Stone said cautiously.

"Half of what he says is wind. He talks more than he listens. He hasn't been to Israel in three years and he's an expert on all things Israeli. Meanwhile, I just got back two weeks ago." She paused and shouted the last part loud enough for the whole table to hear. "And I can tell you all what's really happening."

The baby was crying in another room.

"Aw Gabby, you did it again," Malka said. "You're so noisy."

"Somebody check on Arieh," Dovid said. "He's crying."

"I know he's crying," Malka said, throwing her napkin onto the table and pushing back her chair.

"Ask him what he's crying about," Dovid called.

"He's hungry," Seligman said.

"Then feed him, Malka," Dovid said.

"I'm going, okay?" Malka said. She was short with thick shoulders and large matronly breasts, several months pregnant, and wore a constant look of irritation on her face. Her mouth twisted into a bitter, shriveled pucker as her blue floor-length skirt caught on her chair.

"Ask a man to know what a baby wants." Gabby mischievously smiled at Stone. "He probably pooped himself."

"Gabby, not at the table," Esther said.

"Not back from Israel two weeks and your head is already in the toilet," Dovid said, smiling but stern.

Dr. Cohen cleared his throat. "We were talking about 1938 and the historical parallels—"

"He pooped!" Malka said, bursting back into the room, flustered, her hair tied back with an elastic.

"Thank you for the announcement," Dovid said. "I've lost my appetite."

"I love my uncle," Gabby said to Stone. Her eyes focused on Stone's face. "We're just playing. He's a big bear, that's all."

"Look, Irving, we're closer to Redemption now then we are to a repeat of 1938," Dovid said.

"The difference between then and now," Seligman added, "we've got the hammer. We've got the bomb. He who has the bomb has the land."

It was Yossi's turn to speak. "And he who has the land – all of it – gets *Moshiach* and the Heavenly Kingdom."

Stone finished a second large cup of wine feeling flushed and happy and leaned forward. Gabby did the same, as if on cue, and he could see that her breasts were large and firm. She wore a silver necklace with a greenish blue Roman glass pendant. It looked like a drop of sea water. The buzz in his head told him to speak, and he said, "We might as well nuke them now and get it over with."

"What?" Dr. Cohen said, indignantly, his blue eyes hard and cold.

Seligman apologized on Stone's behalf and explained that Stone had gone to a fancy private university and was simply being ironic.

"Irony is nothing more than half-educated sarcasm. Childish," Dr. Cohen said, turning away.

"That was funny," Gabby said, ignoring Dr. Cohen's rebuke. "You're trouble, aren't you?"

"I'm drunk," Stone said.

"You haven't eaten."

"I don't eat anymore," Stone joked, picking up a pale piece of brisket in his fingers. "I can never find anything I like to eat."

"You need someone who knows how to cook."

"Do you know how?" Stone said, suggestively.

"Maybe." And her cheeks burst into the biggest dimpled smile Stone had ever seen. "I'm sorry about your dad." She paused, and her voice softened. It was full of tenderness and warmth. "It must be hard."

"It is," Stone said.

Gabby looked on patiently, a tiny crease forming between her eyes and even in stillness her face was vivid, alive, animated.

"Where's the bathroom?" Stone said, after a moment.

"Down the hall," she said, softly.

The harsh bathroom light was as sharp as an interrogation lamp. He stared at his face in the mirror. He looked like a drunk, his lips ringed in a burgundy crust from the wine, his matted hair, unshaven face, and eyeballs that looked swollen as pickled eggs. He turned on the sink and ran some cool water over his skin, splashing some on his hair as well. He rinsed his mouth out with a smear of toothpaste. *Amalek*, he thought.

He met Fairuza Freij one night at a teahouse off of Nahalat Shiva in Jerusalem. She was sitting with a group of students, noisy Israelis, from the Hebrew University. Stone had noticed that as they smoked and laughed with a heightened sense of youthful drama, waving their arms and touching each other for punctuation, Fairuza sat quietly at the edge of the circle, absorbed in a water-damaged copy of *Light in August*. He felt an immediate desire to talk to her. He didn't know she was an Arab; she was dark and pretty, like so many Israelis, that exotic mix of history and geography compressed into a seemingly impossible genetic mix that was so startling in comparison to the doughy American Jews Stone had grown up with.

"Hi," he had said, simple as that, and they were talking. They walked through the streets of the Old City, and found themselves on a rooftop facing the Dome of the Rock. With his fingers lightly breezing the small of her back she had said she was from Beit Jala – and that was how Stone discovered she was an Arab. And in the same way that Faulkner's Joe Christmas was neither black nor white, he was guilty of being both, Fairuza was guilty of being neither Jewish nor Muslim, but somehow suffering the slings of each.

Looking back now, Stone didn't think he could call it love, but the six months he spent with Fairuza, in bed in his tiny apartment, sitting in the cafés in the German Colony discussing art and literature, attending lectures at the University, wandering the length of the country on week-ends, had been the only time Stone had been happy since he was a very small child. He felt as if a glowing bubble had descended to protect them from earthly concerns.

The Judge was coming to visit, and Stone decided it was time to tell him about Fairuza. It wasn't that he expected him to be pleased or that he wanted his blessing, he simply felt that the Judge should know about his girlfriend before he met her.

"What kind of name is Fairuza?" the Judge had said over the telephone, the day before he was to arrive.

"It's a name," Stone said idiotically.

He could already sense disapproval in his father's voice. "I know it's a name. What kind?" There was silence on the line and for a moment Stone was worried that his father had hung up on him.

"Matthew. I'm coming to get you, to take you home."

"What?"

"Tell me you are joking, that this is some stupid adolescent joke."

"It's not."

"You never miss a single opportunity – I'm coming to get you."

"Why?" Stone said, suddenly brazen. "I love her. I don't give a shit what you say." Stone was astounded by his own words, as if his convictions were solidified simply by vocalizing them.

"A Muslim?"

"She's not Muslim," Stone said, realizing now that nothing he could say could ever mitigate the unalterable fact that Fairuza was an Arab. "She's Christian," Stone said.

"You are unbelievable," the Judge said. "You are doing this just to spite me, to humiliate me. Matthew, I swear to God that in all my life in which I have worked harder than any man, you are my only failure. What are you going to do, marry her? Have babies with Amalek?"

It was the first time he had ever heard that word.

"I don't know."

"I'm coming to get you. You'd better kiss her goodbye now because tomorrow you're flying back to New York with me."

Stone had gone to meet Fairuza at a coffee shop on Azza Street. His bags were already packed and he had figured it would be best to keep it short. "I'm leaving," he would say, "Business back home." She would have to accept the fact that he was going back to America – he was clear to her that he would leave one day – and Stone had never even met her family, so she must have realized as well that they did not have a future. Sitting in the coffee shop, sipping his bitter Turkish coffee, Stone felt more and more anger towards Fairuza, who was already twenty minutes late. She was ashamed of him, she kept him secret from her family. Stone had been willing to introduce her to the Judge, and had been prepared to do just that despite the Judge's close-mindedness. But now, Stone saw the whole truth. She was ashamed of him! He was simply something to play with and throw away. *Bitch,* Stone thought. *Where is she?*

When Fairuza arrived, almost 40 minutes late, her face was thin and drawn, worry welling up in her eyes; her expression seemed to say "bad news." But, she couldn't possibly have known, they had just the week before arranged a trip to Eilat for the weekend. She sat across from him, looking sorry and sad. Stone seethed. He had drank three cups of coffee as he waited.

"There was a bombing near Sheik Jarrah – the bus had to detour."

"Fine," Stone said. He was now fully aware of her Arabic pronunciation, the way she said 'bombing,' emphasizing the second 'b.'

"We have to talk," she said

"I know," Stone said, steeling himself. He felt like his father, hard, brave, tough, uncompromising. He would do it now.

"Matthew," she said softly. "I'm late."

"Listen, Fai," Stone cut in, about to say "things just aren't working out," but she continued, "I missed my period. I, I missed it."

❧

He opened the medicine cabinet. It was full to bursting with pill canisters and half-crushed tubes. He found Esther's heart pills, some Valium, and a long-expired antibiotic. He had never tried pills before. There were others, too – anti-depressants, sleeping pills, a canister filled with black-striped yellow capsules, buzzing like bumblebees, "Take me! Take me!" He found some aspirin at last and dumped a couple into his hand. He shook several pills at random from the canisters into his shaking hands, and in the sparkling sterility of the bathroom his left hand felt both surprisingly heavy and terribly light.

He could hear Dovid's raised voice in the dining room, brow-beating the humorless Dr. Cohen, and the sound of silverware clinking against plates. He lifted the toilet seat, threw the pills in, and counted seconds as his bladder emptied.

There was a knock at the bathroom door and Stone, still holding his penis in his hand, jumped back in surprise.

"A minute," he called, in a voice that sounded staged, suspicious.

"Matty, are you all right?" It was Gabby.

"Do you want to know the truth?" he said, zipping up and flushing.

"Open the door."

"Hold on." He capped the pill bottles, threw them back into their approximate places, and slammed the cabinet shut. His face stared back from the mirror, crooked, exhausted, but handsome, he saw now. He smiled a rakish smile unlocking the bathroom door, swinging it open casually. The warm smell of brisket filled his nostrils.

Gabby stood in the half-dark of the hallway, wearing a fitted black skirt that showed the full curve of her body. She was Stone's height in her platform heels and her face was full of freckled concern. One of her incisors sat twisted adorably sideways between a row of straight, white teeth.

"What's the matter?" she said, leaning close enough that Stone could smell her scent.

"Too much wine. You know, everything's hilarious, and then suddenly you just get sad."

"I shouldn't have mentioned your father."

"No," Stone said, "it's not that."

"Gabby, what are you two doing back there? It's time for dessert," Dovid called from the dining room.

"Coming, all right?" She turned to Stone, squinting. "You'll eat some dessert at least?"

"Did you make it?" Stone said.

"I bought it," she said, laughing.

"Then I might just try it."

When Gabby spoke, she leaned close enough to Stone that he could feel her movements mirrored within him. Her arm raised in a sweet gesture offering dessert sent a warm glow up the rungs of his ribs as if guitar strings were being strummed inside. Her hip tilted in his direction, set an instantaneous fire in his groin. He felt her without touching her, some sort of charged electrical caress that he had always associated with new love.

"Are you nervous?"

"A little," Stone said. "I think the wine may be wearing off."

"Beware, the Manishevitz hangover," she said, laughing.

"Does that amuse you?"

She smiled broadly and led him back to the dining room. Dr. Cohen was finishing his Jeremiad on the fate of the Jews, a piece of honey cake crumbling between thumb and forefinger.

"If you look at the level of anti-Semitism today compared to then, you will see that precious little has changed. Wake up, Jews!"

Arieh started crying again in the bedroom, harsh and high-pitched like a siren.

"At least someone is listening to Dr. Cohen," Gabby said, laughing aloud.

"God in Heaven, see what he wants," Dovid said. "Feed the boy, he must be hungry."

Stone sat back in his seat beside Seligman, Gabby poised and beautiful across the table. "Are you all right?" Seligman asked quietly.

Dov crossed his arms, frowned and whispered something to the other student.

"Just too much wine."

"Well, watch yourself. You were gone a long time."

"Maybe you have made a *shiduch*, Zalman," Dovid said.

"That would please his father," Seligman said.

Stone felt color flush his cheeks, but Gabby just twisted her face comically and then set her eyes back on Stone.

"Did you hear that, Irving?" Dovid said. "There's a Jew who did all he could to hasten Redemption and hold back the flood tide that you speak of."

"I knew the man," he said, in a sepulchral voice.

"The Judge worked tirelessly, raising capital for the Eretz Fund, building communities throughout Israel, Kiryat Arba, Gush Etzion. You've been to Silwan, you've been to Har Homa. Where were they ten years ago? One day all of Israel will be Jewish."

"And what then?" Dr. Cohen said. "We are sitting ducks waiting to be gassed."

"We must carry on," Seligman said. "If it is written 'catastrophe,' then catastrophe. But it will bring the Jews closer to Redemption."

"Hey, Gab. You believe in Redemption, don't you?" Dov called across the table.

She ignored him.

"Of course she does," Yossi said. "Gabby's Gabby."

"Thank you for your kind response," Dov said, glaring sidelong at Gabby.

She leaned forward towards Stone. "Ignore him. He's a child."

"And what of Walter's initiative to construct a new neighborhood in south Jerusalem?"

"Near Wallajeh village? That's just a dream," Dr. Cohen said.

"Nearly 2,000 dunams of land have been purchased from the Arab squatters."

"He's right," a voice down the table intervened. "The neighborhood will be able to absorb nearly 50,000 Jewish residents, connecting *Yerushalayim* in an unbroken chain to Gush Etzion."

"What's going to happen with the Eretz Fund now that Walter, bless his name, is gone?" a voice asked from the far end of the table.

"Yeah," Yossi chimed. "Are you going to take over Matthew?"

"He's still in mourning," Dovid Grunhut said. "Leave him alone."

"The *shloshim* ended over a week ago," the disembodied voice called. "Should we wait until his *Yahrtzeit*?"

"Okay, yes, it's getting late," Seligman said. "We should *bentsch*."

"Hold on, Zalman," a man in his fifties, who Stone had heard but not seen, said, as he leaned back boyishly in his chair. He turned his face to Stone and addressed him directly. "I knew the Judge well." The man wore his rust-colored beard close-cropped and had tiny black eyes set far back in his sockets.

"Eli, listen," Seligman said. "He's not ready to talk about him."

"It's all right," Stone said.

"Just a story," Eli said, "about a great intellect, lawmaker and Jew."

"Here, here," Dovid said, clinking his glass with a dessert fork.

"He straddled the secular and Jewish worlds with the ease of a statesman. Now you all know," he said, leaning forward in his chair, his large fingers tapping softly on the table, "there are many myths surrounding Walter Stone – some are true and some not."

Stone felt eager anticipation flash through his innards, the way he remembered feeling before leaping off the high-diving board at camp. Gabby seemed to be hanging anxiously on Eli's words too.

"I was a young yeshiva student, 1968 – a million years ago, after the great victory in the Six Day War. And I remember the excitement at the time, returning for the first time to the land of our forefathers; Hebron, *Beit Lechem, Shchem.* Praying in those places was intoxicating, like being in the center of a whirlwind.

"The first time praying at the Kotel was like," and Dovid paused and chuckled, "the first time." At that, Esther stood up and went to the kitchen.

"Anyway, *Pesach,* 1968," Eli continued, "Rav Grunhut, may his memory be blessed, rented the Park Hotel in downtown Hebron for us to celebrate the Passover. Surrounded by thousands of Arabs, mind you. But we were there, on our land, at long last, *Baruch Hashem*. The Israeli government wasn't happy with the idea of Jews moving into the heart of Judea and Samaria, where all the Arabs were living. And they wanted us out. But the army did nothing as we moved in. The living conditions were terrible. Our first step to re-demption consisted of sleeping in sleeping bags on the concrete floor, and cooking with old army gas stoves that stank of kerosene. We had nothing and the government wanted us out. But Rav Grunhut said we were staying until the Messiah came.

"So, one day, a couple of trucks arrive. A man steps out of one of the trucks with a big, fat perfecto between his teeth – he's tall and rugged and bald and embraces Rav Grunhut. He was so handsome, fit like a marine and at the time, before I knew who he was, I remember thinking that it looked like he was cut out of stone. It was Walter. Just arrived back from Vietnam, it turns out. He and Rav Grunhut visited for hours. There are rumors the government is going to throw us out by force, and we're thinking that Walter might be an emissary from Jerusalem, negotiating some kind of deal to withdraw. Next thing you know, they are unloading the trucks with all of the Rav's belongings, everything he has in the world. There are beds, proper stoves and refrigerators for the rest of us. We're staying.

"Later, they went for a walk, both he and Rav Grunhut carrying Uzis at the ready. Remember, Jews had been mas-sacred there in 1929 and 1936, before being evacuated. Myself and a couple of other students join them as they move through the dusty cinder-block streets. Walter knows some Arabic and he is translating what the Arabs shout as we pass. Nasty stuff. We arrive outside the city on the jagged rocky slopes, overlooking Hebron. And the Judge and the Rav walk ahead and kneel and touch the earth, as if surveying the land. And I'd swear I saw tears in the Judge's eyes.

"Two years later, the city of Kiryat Arba is established right on that spot where they knelt. Rows and rows of Jewish houses, springing out of the land, and watchtowers rising to assure that a massacre will never happen again. Today Kiryat Arba thrives and Jews still live in Hebron."

"They were quite a team, Walter and my brother," Dovid said. "You could always count on the Judge to get things done. He was the pragmatist. Isn't that right, Irving?"

"Yes, that's right," Dr. Cohen said, wiping his thin lips with a napkin.

Stone sipped his wine and looked at Gabby. Her eyes were fixed on him as if she were searching for Walter within Stone's meager frame.

"Now, I can tell you, that is true, because I was there," Eli continued, "but there are other stories that are apocryphal that I would be willing to bet are true as well. I came to know Walter and he was capable of the most amazing things."

"I beg you, Eli, it's nearly three o'clock," Seligman said. "Perhaps you can save the tribute for another time. I'd like to take a nap before going back to *shul*."

"Go on," Gabby said, "I want to hear more about the heroic Walter Stone."

"I'll keep it short, Zalman."

"Give us the *Reader's Digest* version, *al regel achat*," Dovid said.

"Okay," Eli said, straightening his *kippah.* "Moshe Dayan was Minister of Defense at the time and ran Judea and Samaria with an iron fist and he was not happy. But he was in the hospital, practically paralyzed with broken ribs. Walter pays a visit to him. He's about 35 years old, charismatic, and an important face of civility for the movement. You'll excuse me, Dovid, but a lot of people thought that your brother was a madman, a fanatic and wouldn't touch him with a ten-foot pole. Walter, he spoke perfect Hebrew, like a poet, like a philosopher. He was at home in the halls of power and he got what he wanted. He went to see the Old Man at his home in the Negev. He visited every member of the Israeli cabinet at their homes, pleading his case. Not long after, the cabinet voted to allow us to stay in Hebron. The first permanent community re-established in Judea and Samaria, the first step towards redeeming the Land of Israel. And do you know why Walter was able to have the ear of the Israeli cabinet? Given the opportunity to change hearts and minds, and push the vote through—"

"All right," Seligman said, standing up and stretching his back. "We don't need the whole megillah. Let's *bentsch.*"

"Awww!" Gabby said.

The table slipped quickly into prayer, Seligman swaying back and forth beside Stone, singing in his robust off-key tenor. *Why did he stop him there?* Stone thought.

The story of his father filled him with horror and intense shame. Stone knew who lived at Kiryat Arba – the settlement it seemed his father was instrumental in founding – fanatics, radicals, murderers, the Brooklyn-born doctor, Baruch Goldstein, had lived there until he massacred dozens of Palestinians with his army-issued machine gun while they prayed at the Tomb of the Patriarchs. And there were others too, splashed across newspaper headlines, who had rampaged through the Hebron casbah, looting and firing their guns like Wild West outlaws.

But Stone's incipient shame was quickly overwhelmed by a burning pride for his father, for his accomplishments. This was a man who had made a difference. He had left his mark on the world, while Stone drifted, maundering around like a corpse. It was clear that these people loved the Judge in a way that Stone had never loved his father, or been loved by him.

⍥ 12 ⍥

The lonely tomblike halls of the Brooklyn Museum echoed with the sound of Abi's footsteps, mismatched with the slow, reluctant steps of Stone, several feet behind.

"I'm glad you decided to put down your books for a few minutes."

"I like reading," Stone said. In fact, he had remained holed up in his bedroom, draped in the Judge's robe, poring through his father's books ever since he had returned from lunch at Esther Grunhut's. He had just found a copy of Jabotinsky's novel *Samson* at the bottom of a tall pile when Abi, back from White Plains, interrupted, "Did you stay home the whole time?" The translation was archaic, tin-eared, laughable. Stone was about to toss the book aside to answer his mother when he noticed that the book was signed, but not to his father, who would have only been five years old at the time. The inscription read:

"To Julius,
The Movement appreciates your support and friendship.
Hazak v'Ematz
Ze'ev Jabotinsky
August 1, 1940, Brooklyn"

"You can't stay home like a hermit," she had said.

"Is that how you explain your whole life?" Stone responded. "Run away to the great adventure."

"Matthew, try and be civil. You can't beat me up forever."

"Is that the rule?" Stone said. "I didn't know."

"Matthew, your anger is getting redundant. Are you ready to move on? People get sick that way, holding onto every insult, every slight."

"What you did was more than just a slight."

"Okay," she said, crossing her arms. "Let's have it out right here, right now. Because I want to get this over with now so we can move on. Matty, are we going to get along or not?" Her voice echoed off the high ceilings, and Stone noticed for the first time that his mother was shorter than him, her high boots deceptively hidden by the hem of her pants. When she had left, she had been a good three or four inches taller than him, now it was the other way around. Her hair was tied back youthfully, and her sharp black eyes were full of light. There was a robust certainty in her voice that made Stone realize she would go on with or without him, just as she had done before.

He stared at her in amazement for a moment and then uttered a quiet "Yes." The mummies and sarcophagi bore silent witness, the decorated tombs of long-dead kings, lying mute around them.

"Where did you go," Stone said, "when you left?"

His voice was solicitous, so Abi relaxed and tossed her head back. "Where didn't I go? Sometimes I feel like the original Wandering Jewess. I was out West, in San Francisco, painted indigents in the Mission District, went to Seattle,

Portland, Kansas City, if you can believe that, taught at the University of Chicago, up and down the East Coast as well. Basically, you follow your subject wherever that may be."

"Sounds convenient."

"No. It was lonely a lot of the time."

They stopped before a papyrus rendering of Nefertiti, her right arm raised before her.

"What do you think?" he said. "How's the execution?"

Abi laughed. "It's like she's been run over with a steamroller. The ancients hadn't figured out the third dimension yet."

A group of public school children entered the hall, led by their harried teacher, a rail-thin middle-aged black woman with a nearly shaved head. The children may have been third or fourth graders, and their dark faces turned in every direction, their feet poised to follow their impulses.

"Children!" the teacher shouted in a voice that sounded like God, echoing in the hall. "Can we all say 'pharaoh'?"

"Pharaoh," they responded weakly.

"Let's get out of here," Abi said.

They climbed up two flights of stairs, passing a couple on the way down, and Abi's voice was lost in the echo chamber of the stairwell. They found themselves in the cool air of a sculpture gallery; half-nude bodies, unashamed, frozen in time.

"There won't be any schoolkids up here," Abi said. "That doesn't fit in with the public-school curriculum."

Stone felt breathless from the climb; he leaned on the muscular arm of a bronze Rodin.

"Why don't you go back to school?" Abi said at last.

"School?"

"You haven't finished your Master's."

"Don't remind me."

"Why don't you do it? It's still September. I'm sure you can make just a few calls and be readmitted to finish your coursework."

"No," Stone said. "I'm not going back to Connecticut."

"Are you just going to stay in Brooklyn?"

"Maybe," Stone said. He thought of Gabby from the luncheon the day before, her smile, the curved shape of her body, the possibility in her eyes. "Yeah, I'm staying in Brooklyn."

"There's so much despair. Everywhere you turn there is filth, graffiti, gangs hanging out on the street, food stamps and WIC advertised in the windows of all the grocery stores. Do you want to become one of those people? Do you want to be part of this poor world?"

"I already am."

"You should finish your degree."

"I'm not going back there."

"Why not?"

Stone was silent for a moment. They passed into the next gallery: European paintings and sculpture.

"I had a breakdown," he answered quietly. "I didn't want get out of bed. I didn't want to live."

"Matthew," she said softly. "That was a long time ago."

"How do you know?"

Abi seemed momentarily stunned; she had been caught. "I'm your mother, Matthew. Of course I knew. Did you think that I'd let you go that easily?"

"You knew?"

"Yes."

"What else did you know?"

"Matthew, don't."

"Did you know that I burned myself? Did you know that I would put quarters, dimes, nickels, it didn't matter, in the oven, turned to broil, and then pressed them to my skin?"

"I know you haven't been happy, and it killed me because I couldn't do anything."

"Why not?" Stone shouted, his voice echoing through the hall.

"Matthew."

Stone shivered in the frigid gallery.

"Are you cold? Do you want my sweater?"

Abi lifted the charcoal gray V-neck over her head and handed it to Stone. Her skin was clear and pure. The sweater smelled of her scent, something clean, indescribable, a scent that Stone had not smelled since he was a child. He pulled the sweater on; he had tears in his eyes.

"When I got a call that he was sick, that he wanted me to come back to Brooklyn, I was actually happy, relieved, thankful that I had the excuse I was looking for to not finish my work. It was bullshit anyway. Who needs another Master's thesis?"

They stopped before a stormy, tumultuous landscape, the sky lit bright behind its veil of darkness.

"I couldn't do it. I would have failed if I hadn't been called. I had prayed for something drastic, some change that would save me, and it was the Judge. I didn't know he was going to die. Who would have thought that he would actually die?"

"But he's gone now," Abi said. "Why don't you do yourself the honor of finishing what you started?"

"It's useless," Stone said. Dead faces peered gloomily down from the walls, their gilt frames contrasting with their pale skin.

"Why?"

"Another academic thesis. Who needs it?"

"A lot of people."

"Oh, please. Name one."

"Matthew. Don't be so hard on yourself. You chose to stay for grad school."

"What else would I have done? When the Judge was 26 he was already working at the DA's office. Even Papa Julius was famous in his own way."

"Matthew, it's not about fame."

"It's not! Do you think I don't know that one of your paintings is hanging in the next gallery? Tell me it's not about fame now."

"He was critical of me as well, diminishing my accomplishments as if only he was permitted to succeed. You had to grow up with that."

"If it wasn't Columbia, it wasn't good enough. I could never win."

"You went to a very fine school."

Stone knew now that no matter how hard his mother tried, whatever she attempted to do to make up for all of those lost years, it was too late, the damage had been done. Her leaving him alone with the Judge at the age of 12 was a permanent nullifying act that made any attempt to reconcile useless.

"Promise me you'll stop abusing yourself. I'm worried about you."

"Good," Stone said, stalking off. "Worry."

Abi found him a few minutes later, sitting on a bench before a large painting of a roiling Niagara Falls, the green-black water luminescent, the world falling away, tumbling in swirling waves into a ghostly, rising mist.

"Mind if I sit?"

Stone shook his head. The elemental power of the painting had his heart beating hard in his chest, the thumping audible in his inner ear. He could hear the water too, deafening as it crashed to the bottom, a constant, never-ending roar that filled the entire room.

"That's Mignot. Niagara. A view from the American side."

"It's incredible," Stone said, not taking his eyes off the painting.

"It's one of my favorite paintings," Abi said. "Look how life is infused into every square inch of the painting, every brushstroke."

"It looks like a photograph."

"It's more than just that. He's telling us something about ourselves that can't be said in words. It's something you feel."

"Yes," Stone said.

"This is the power of the act of creation. That's why I paint. I create something that tells the truth that can't be told in any other way."

"Look at it," Stone said. "So powerful."

"It's frightening," Abi said.

"Could you imagine riding over the edge, crashing to the bottom and surviving?"

"No," Abi said. "It's impossible."

"No it's not. People have survived."

"A few."

"Imagine how that feels? It would be like witnessing the Big Bang or the Ice Age first-hand. Survive that, and anything is possible."

❧

The next day, Stone found himself sitting across from Seligman at a faded Formica table at Schochner's Glatt Kosher Diner, a converted mobile home anchored on blocks beneath the hum of the BQE in the Williamsburg neighborhood. The sounds of Yiddish and English mingled in the greasy air. Four broad-backed men in matching suits sat hunched on low stools at the counter eating lunch. The air was thick and humid with the smell of overcooked meat. He noticed that at three of the tables, men gesticulated and held court with mouths full of food. The dim brown light illuminated very little, and Stone was glad for that.

"You've got to eat something," Seligman said, "especially with a fast day coming up."

"I'm not hungry," Stone said.

"You fast on Yom Kippur, not before," Seligman joked. "If you do, all bets are off."

Stone puzzled over the mackled letters of the grimy cardstock menu, stripped of its jaundiced lamination. He ordered kasha and varnishkas, and a cucumber and vinegar salad.

"Okay," Seligman said, taking a sip of his tea, "that's something."

"Why didn't you come yourself?" Stone asked. "Why did you send him?" he said, nodding his head in the direction of hulking Moshe, standing sentry at the door, his *tzitzes* hanging sloppily from his shirt.

"I apologize," Seligman said. "I had already ordered when I realized you lived nearby. My apologies. My blood sugar gets low and I don't think straight."

"You could have called first," Stone said.

"Listen, he's harmless. He didn't strong-arm you, did he?"

"No," Stone said. "He made me sit in the back. He kept his hat on the passenger seat."

"Well. Moshe's Moshe. What can I say, you're here."

Stone closed his eyes and heard the drone of the highway outside and the clinking of silverware against Schochner's chipped plates and dishes.

"Your mother came back. She's staying with you?"

"For now," Stone said.

"Hmmf," Seligman said. "Well, it's a Commandment of God to honor your parents." He ran his thick hand over the silver scruff of his beard. "Have you said *Kaddish* for your father yet?"

"No," Stone said.

"Listen, I'm not being a *Yiddishe* Mama here. It is a son's obligation. But there's more to it, Matthew. This could help you move on, get on with life again."

"I'm tired of death."

"You have to understand the *Kaddish* is not about death. In fact, it's a celebration of life and the glory of God."

"God," Stone said, doubtfully.

"Whatever you want to call that entity that gives and takes life," Seligman said. "I know you and your father did not always see eye to eye. He could be a hard man, but he was your father and you owe it to him to honor his memory, to say *Kaddish* for him. Is this some sort of petty liberal revenge, Matthew? Is this some sort of childish fantasy? Look, I'm trying to help you out here—"

"He was always judging," Stone said.

"Listen, there's only one true judge and when you buried your father and then the prayer *Baruch Dayan Ha'Emet* was recited, you were blessing the one true judge. And who was that?"

Stone hadn't said that prayer either.

"Play along with me, Matthew, you're not an idiot. It's God, and He's the only one who judges. Think about that while the Book of Judgment is still open. Yom Kippur is in less than a week."

"I'll think about it," Stone said.

"Good," Seligman said, "There's a *shul* right near your apartment, so no excuses."

Stone shrugged his shoulders.

"I know what you're thinking," Seligman said.

"What's that?"

"You're thinking this is all nonsense. That you've buried your father and that's that. But a son's obligation to his father never ends."

"I could never please him."

"Matthew, I know as well as anyone that Walter could be a sonofabitch. I've known him over 40 years."

Stone was silent as Seligman took a bite of his food.

"Have you heard of Eliezer Ben-Yehuda?"

"Of course," Stone said.

"Well, there was another sonofabitch, of course depending on your point of view," Seligman said. "The father of modern Hebrew, the language of the Torah. Hebrew would not be a living language in *Eretz Yisrael* today if it wasn't for him and his determination. But Ben-Yehuda was not much of a father, unless of course you consider his great dictionary a child, and his flesh and blood son, a Petri dish in a lab."

Seligman paused and ran his fingers over his trimmed silver beard. "You think you had it bad? You think your father was hard on you? Think about the son of the great lexographer, Ben-Zion Ben-Yehuda, the first Zionist baby, the first child in modern history to grow up speaking only Hebrew. Can you imagine what that felt like? Can you imagine speaking a language that only your mother and father could understand? Remember, Hebrew had not been spoken outside the synagogue in nearly 2000 years. So, Ben-Yehuda, driven by his passion to renew the language after all those centuries lost in the diaspora, took extreme care, almost to the point of mania, so that his son would only hear, and consequently speak, the Hebrew language. He would not let his son hear foreign languages, so where could he go? Nobody was speaking Hebrew then. He wouldn't even let his son listen to the sound of chirping birds, or the barking of dogs, or the crow of a rooster, since they too communicated with foreign languages. Well, it wasn't Hebrew, that was the point. One day when Ben-Zion was still a small child, about four or five years old, his father was away, and his mother, frustrated by the crying child who would still not speak, slipped into her native Russian and began to sing lullabies to the boy. Can you guess what happened?"

Stone thought of his father walking through the front door as the District Attorney's office was concluding its interview. "Ben-Yehuda came home."

"That's right. Ben-Yehuda came home early, heard his wife, who had broken her pact to speak only Hebrew, speaking Russian to their son. Well, the shock of Ben-Yehuda's anger had several effects; one was that the boy, as if woken from a daze, spoke at last, his lips unclamped, free to speak the words that had been forced upon him; and second, well, let's just say it's not a coincidence that he made his name as an adult as Ittamar Ben-Avi and not Ben-Yehuda."

"That's a terrible story," Stone said.

"Matthew, it's a beautiful story. Hebrew exists today because of that man. His son, he lived, he had a life, and he died, like the rest of us. But, Hebrew remains a living language."

"Why are you telling me this?"

"Because, your father did not want that to happen with you. Yes, of course he wanted you to follow in his footsteps, to be his spiritual heir, but he knew the dangers and he did not want to force anything upon you, because he knew that would ultimately push you further away. But, he always thought you would come around eventually. Only he died too soon."

"My father thought I was worthless."

"No he didn't. He loved you."

"How could he have? I was constantly in disgrace. Do you know how badly I wanted to please him? It's just that for some reason, I couldn't do it. Like every step I had to climb to reach him was two or three times as high as it should have been, and every commandment he made, I broke. I defied him at every opportunity."

"Matthew," Seligman said. "That's your secret. But the Gates of Repentance are open now. You can change all that."

"I was alone with him when he died, just the two of us."

Seligman interrupted hastily, "You don't need to—"

"He tried to tell me something in his shattered voice that had instilled fear in me for so long. But I couldn't understand him and he knew it and rebuked me with the last of his energy. And when he died, I stood over him for a long time, almost triumphantly staring into his face, at his body, a skeleton really, and I felt that his domination of me had finally ended. All the guilt feelings I carried constantly would fall away, and I would be free. But I can still feel him calling out to me."

"Eat something," Seligman said. "I understand that death raises a lot of complex emotions."

"He's still such a giant."

Seligman offered Stone a tissue and said, "Matthew, eat something."

He shoveled a few forkfuls of food into his mouth. "I want to talk to you about the account numbers."

"Yes," Seligman said.

"I don't have them."

"You don't have them?"

"He never told them to me."

"Are you sure?"

"Positive," Stone said.

Seligman wiped his brow with a napkin. "You know we shared a property on Henry Street; an old brownstone built after the Civil War. We rented it out for years, and for a while Walter had an office there away from the bustle of the courthouse. But it is starting to crumble. The foundations need to be reinforced, the roof leaks. I'm afraid it may be condemned for destruction if we don't make the repairs soon."

"And you need the money to do it."

"Old houses can be very expensive to fix. Walter always controlled the account. He was here in New York, I was in Israel. It made sense."

"And now that he's gone?"

"His wish was to repair the house on Henry Street. To turn it into a historic museum dedicated to American Jewish lawmakers. Louis Brandeis, Frankfurter, Cardozo and the like."

"What about the Bensonhurst Benevolent Fund?"

Seligman leaned forward, "Yes."

"Isn't that money supposed to be used for the benefit of Bensonhurst and the surrounding area? Henry Street is in the Heights."

"How much do you think a few ping-pong tables and park benches cost? There's money left over."

"That doesn't sound right," Stone said.

"We are not required by law to use all of the money for the stated purpose. Certain amounts can be diverted. This was your father's wish."

Stone scooped out a mouthful of the limp cucumber salad. Seligman looked on and smiled, and through his tinted aviator glasses, Stone saw his eyes and what he imagined to be kindness.

"You and Gabby had a lot to talk about," Seligman began after Stone had eaten a few mouthfuls of his kasha.

"My father would have been proud," Stone said sarcastically.

"So you didn't like her. You live your own life. There's a chicken for every hen. She liked you though."

"She did?" Stone said.

"She's a lovely, vivacious girl – and smart. She has just moved back to do her Master's. She's sharp, irreverent – drives her parents crazy. You'd like her."

"I do like her."

"Good."

"Why are you so interested in taking care of my love-life?" Stone asked.

"A good woman can do a lot to heal a damaged spirit."

"Did she say something to you?"

"I'm not saying a word."

Stone imagined Gabby across the table from him in place of Seligman, and even in the dingy light she shone, her smile bursting into bloom, her eyes electric under long lashes. He felt a sudden ache for her full breasts, her freck-led neck, her bronzed summer skin – he tasted the salt on her neck and heard her breath escape her in whorls of pleasure.

Seligman held his cell phone out to Stone, "Call her."

"I can make my own date," Stone said.

"Call her." He began dialing. "She's staying with her aunt, who you know, so – Hello, Esther? Zalman. Where's the *vildechaya*?" He paused and raised his eyebrows. "Put her on."

❧ 13 ❧

"Matthew, I'm so glad you could come," Esther Grunhut said, unsmilingly. "Gabby will be ready in a moment."

Esther Grunhut's house seemed to have been transformed since the day of the luncheon, absent of conversation, laughter, and the smell of food cooking. The silence was disturbing to Stone. The black and white pictures on the walls no longer cried out their stories; they sat mutely, their subjects as alienated from this world as Stone was from theirs. As if reading his mind Esther said, "Life goes on," and shuffled off into the kitchen. She seemed to wear the permanent countenance of the widow; the face of a woman too familiar with death and the shadowy emptiness left behind.

"I'll call her," Esther said, after a moment. "Gabby! Hurry up!"

"I'm on the phone," she called.

"You're friend is waiting."

"Okay!"

Stone felt the nervous flutter of wings in his belly, the anxious tickle of doubt humming through his innards.

Gabby appeared a few moments later. "Hi," she said. Stone returned the greeting and then there was a long pause. She wore a flowing black skirt, fitted at the hips, that still managed to show the curve of her thighs, her ass, and Stone noticed that her shoulders were broad and strong beneath her striped shirt. He could hear the sad, doubtful sigh that preceded her words and time seemed to slow down. "Matty?"

"Yeah," Stone said.

"This is awkward," she said, "And I hate to do this, but something's happened." Stone was silent as she searched for the right words. "Remember Dov from Rosh HaShana?" Stone nodded – he had been the surly yeshiva student – Stone had instantly disliked him. "Something terrible has happened and he's in the hospital. I don't want to spoil our date but I have to go. I'll only be an hour." She paused again and Stone felt the thrill of her smile breaking across her face. "I don't mean to be presumptuous, but you'll come with me, right?"

"Sure," Stone said.

"Great," she smiled. "And then we'll go out."

She had a freshly scrubbed scent, as if she had just stepped out of the bath, and a snatch of late afternoon light fell across her face, giving her skin the burnished texture of polished gold.

"Shall we go?" she said and laughed. "Shall? I'm not Jane Austen. Are you ready?"

"I'm ready."

"Be back later!" she called to her Aunt Esther in a voice that broke. She was adorable.

"Not too late, huh?" Esther called back.

"Bye!"

"Okay!"

Stone instinctively held his breath as the automatic doors of the hospital slid open, the drifting motes and ions of renegade staphylococcus, influenza, and E. coli kept momentarily at bay. He knew that the last gasping death-rattle breath of the recently deceased still stalked the shining halls of the hospital, and that he would have to be careful to avoid inhaling their final atomized remnants.

Gabby had been silent in the car on the way over, biting her lower lip nervously. She smiled at him and then apologized. "It's not like me to be so quiet. Why do you think they call me Gabby?"

"It's okay," Stone said, releasing his breath.

"We'll just stay a few minutes," she said. "And then we'll do something fun. Something unbelievably fun."

The sound of Gabby's platform heels clacked and echoed through the antiseptic hallways. They passed a man moaning on a gurney. There was blood on the floor beneath him. Stone pointed to a framed landscape drawing hanging on the opposite wall – his attempt to divert her attention.

"It's all right," Gabby said. "This is nothing. Have you ever been in Hadassah Hospital after a suicide bombing?"

"No," Stone said.

The elevator left them off at a crossroads of identical hallways, across from the nurse's station. Gabby asked directions to Dov's room.

"Lucky boy, nearly burn to deat'," the shiny faced Jamaican nurse said, pointing to her left.

They found Yossi and a friend arguing outside of Dov's room. They both wore baseball caps and had *tzitzes* hanging from their shirts. The friend had a soft doughy paunch and wore a thin beard that barely covered his cheeks.

"This is fucked-up shit," the friend said.

"Be cool," Yossi said. "We'll take care of it."

"Who's going to call his mother?" the friend said, his voice rising to a frantic pitch.

"Aren't you?"

"I thought you were!"

Gabby called out to her cousin and the two stopped arguing.

"Hey, Gab," Yossi said flatly, "you had better say a *Mish-ebe'rach*."

"What happened?" she said, biting her lip. Her eyes were glassy.

"Some *schvartz* sprayed him with lighter fluid and set him on fire," the doughy friend said, stepping close to Gabby. "You don't want to go in there. It's pretty ugly." He spoke as if he had been appointed captain of the tragedy and that he knew what was best for Gabby.

She turned to Yossi, "What happened?"

The friend persisted and it became clear to Stone that he was set on impressing Gabby. He gestured theatrically with his hands, out of sync with the words he was saying, as if he were trying to channel drama through his very gestures. "We'll find who did this," he said in a voice full of bravado. "And we'll deal with him. In the meantime, all you should do is pray for a *refuah shlema*."

Stone caught a glint of light playing in Gabby's eyes, as if she would laugh out loud, the way mourners tend to, unable to contain their emotions in their rightful compartments.

"Why don't you call his mother in Israel?" Gabby said. "And tell her what happened."

Stone followed Gabby into the room, leaving Yossi and his friend in the hall. Gabby took a deep breath, and Stone saw her chest rise and fall. It was a semi-private room, and the curtains were drawn tight on the left side where a television blared. A cloying antiseptic smell hung in the air; the whir of machines hummed. Five yeshiva *bochers* stood silently around Dov's bed. Stone wondered if they were praying. Two wore Yankees caps, the others knitted *kippahs*. They were all dressed in slacks and nondescript button-up shirts with fringed *tzitzes* hanging out. Through the small square of window Stone could see the austere pillar of the Prison Ship Martyr's Monument rising in the distance. It wasn't until they approached the bed that the group realized that Gabby and Stone were behind them.

"He's out," one of them said.

"How long?" Gabby asked.

"Since we got here."

"How bad is it?"

"Bad."

Dov lay still on his back, tubes and wires strung between his body and the humming machines. His face and neck and hands were loosely bandaged, leaving small slits for his eyes, nose, and mouth. He looked to Stone like the Invisible Man. He felt compelled to look beneath those bandages, pull back the loose fabric and see the contours of his burned skin. Stone stared into the darkened holes of the swaddling.

Gabby leaned forward over the bed and Stone felt the warmth of her presence dissipate; she had been standing that close.

She whispered, "Dov. Dov, it's me. Gabby."

"He can't hear you," one of the yeshiva *bochers* said in an unregulated voice. "They've drugged him up."

"It's me, Gabby. Dov? I'm going to touch your face now." She had the ability to be caring without being matronly. The timbre of her voice was cool, confident, sexy without being gauche. Her words were never a come-on, but Stone felt a tidal wave rise within him whenever she spoke.

She leaned close and whispered something Stone could not hear.

"Somebody do something," someone said.

"What do you want me to do? Petition to Hashem directly?"

"It wouldn't hurt."

Yossi came back in the room. "Avi, there's a cop outside wants to talk to anyone who was there."

"Aw," Avi said.

"Go on."

"Shit."

They all ignored Stone, as if he was not even present, but he understood it to be part of the selfish tunnel vision of grief. He was glad to have the opportunity to observe Gabby among others, to read her gestures, to follow her movements with his eyes and not have to engage these strangers in conversation.

"He was just coming back from the *beis*."

"Then what happened?"

"Ask Avi."

"Avi's a schmuck for letting this happen."

"That's enough," Gabby said. "Arguing isn't going to help Dov now."

"I can't believe it," one of the *kippha* wearers said. "Three years in the IDF and nothing, not a scratch. All those years driving the back roads of *Yehuda v'Shomron* and nothing. Come to New York – and this." Stone noticed that his face was sharp and arrogant and rat-like. "This is what happens when Jews are in *Galut*. This is exactly what happens."

"Bad things happen everywhere," Gabby said.

"Yes," the rat-face said, "but in Israel, it is credit towards Redemption. Here it's pfff, nothing, a Hollywood movie to eat and throw away."

"Dov will be all right," another said.

"We have to liquidate the Diaspora, before the Diaspora liquidates us," the rat-face continued. "Whenever a Jew is violated, it is an assault on all of us."

"That's true," a voice said, "*Baruch Hashem.*"

Stone thought they were under the sway of a dangerous delusion and looked to Gabby for acknowledgement.

"Who knows," she said. "Maybe this happened for a reason."

"*Heshbon nefesh,*" one of them said. It was the first time he had spoken. He was the shortest of the group and wore his hair cropped short in the military style. He spoke with a Hebrew accent. "Accounting of the soul."

"What?" the rat-face said.

"Maybe he was not so good this year. Maybe he was not a good Jew."

"I should punch you in the face," one said, and the rat-face restrained him. "Who invited you here anyway?"

"For that he has to die?" Yossi said, his voice cracking. "Dov makes a few mistakes. He's human. For that he has to die?" He was on the verge of tears.

"He's not going to die," Gabby said, soothing her cousin. "Nobody dies while the Book of Judgment is open."

⚜

The sun was setting as Stone and Gabby arrived at the Fulton Landing, just in time to see a tense wedding party dressed stiffly in full regalia, mock smile, and pose at the photographers insistent commands, shrilly barked with all the decorum of a middle-school gym teacher. The party looked miserable. Gabby quipped, "And they wonder why I'm not married."

"Tempting though, isn't it?" Stone said

"Very," Gabby laughed, as she strolled along the wooden boards towards the water's edge.

"That would make your uncle happy," Stone said.

"Shh . . . it's our secret," she said, laughing again. Gabby leaned against the low metal barrier on which the lines of a Walt Whitman poem were cut out along the entire length of the fence. *"And you that shall cross from shore to shore years hence are more to me, and more in my meditations than you might suppose."* She gripped tightly with her hands and leaned out as far as she could, "Look." She slid aside and Stone leaned out, looking past the hulking mass of a dormant warehouse, towards the southwest and the setting sun. The brackish smell of the East River assaulted Stone's nose as he leaned out, his thighs pressed against the hard, cold steel.

"See her?" Gabby asked. And now Stone could see in the distance, crowned with the pink and orange nimbus of the setting sun, the Statue of Liberty, arm raised proudly in the air.

"Still there," Stone said.

"She's beautiful," Gabby said. "Look at how strong she is standing sentry at the mouth of the harbor."

"I think I'm in love," Stone said.

"Can you be serious?!" Gabby said brightly. "This is my favorite spot in the city. It's so tied up in poetry, literally. Emma Lazarus, Whitman, Hart Crane and his bridge," she said, gesturing to her right where the Brooklyn Bridge stood, its massive stone base rising out of the East River, not a hundred yards away.

"You read Hart Crane?" Stone said with surprise.

"Do you think I only read Torah?"

"No," he said, "but nobody reads Crane anymore."

A dipping cormorant wheeled across the sky, giving the illusion of strumming across the bridge's mighty cables. Stone felt a soft breeze on his face.

"So, I'm nobody," Gabby said, turning to face Stone, her brow furrowed slightly. She crossed her arms on her chest and leaned closer. Stone felt as if she were trying to read something in his eyes, to divine some mystery, some truth that Stone was withholding.

"You're not alone," Stone said at last, "I love Crane as well." The sun was sinking quickly in the distance over New Jersey, then the bursting palette of colors faded in an instant leaving the city across the river cold, hard and steely, its towers flat and monolithic against the graying sky. Manhattan seemed close enough to touch, the Twin Towers rising above the jumbled chaos of Lower Manhattan looking like the tablets of the original Law – austere, forbidding and awesome – especially in close proximity; the many lights in their narrow casements burned against the coming darkness.

Gabby turned away as she dug into her canvas bag on the ground beside her. Stone saw the buttons of her spine pressed against the light material of her shirt, her firm calves straining as she reached. A moment later she produced a large zip-lock bag that seemed to be full of old scraps of bread. "Matty," she said. And now, for the first time her smile was shy, hesitant – absolutely adorable. "I hope you don't think this is stupid but—"

A tug boat passing by blew its horn. Stone was suddenly aware of the sound of waves lapping beneath them. "After lunch the other day, I thought maybe you'd come back later—" She paused. "It's my favorite Jewish custom, and after meeting you on Rosh HaShana, I know this sounds girlish or silly, but I wanted to share this with you. You've heard of *Tashlich*? It's fun, really and it's supposed to be done after services on Rosh HaShana, but I waited. I thought it would be fun to do it with you."

"Remind me again, what's *Tashlich*?" Stone asked.

"Time to cast away your sins," she said, laughing lightly as she opened the bag. "Throw them all away. Let the river carry your guilt and vices of the past year away."

"In there?" Stone pinched his nose. "Were your sins so bad that you have to drown them in *that*?"

"Be serious," Gabby said, her voice cracking.

"I am being serious. I can't picture you doing anything wrong. You're perfect."

"I'm trouble and you're a liar."

"What?" Stone said.

"You know I'm not perfect." They were both quiet for a moment and Stone could see Gabby's chest rise and fall, her broad square shoulders lift and then drop with her exhale.

"If you want to know the whole truth," Gabby started at the same moment that Stone said, "So, do I throw myself in first?"

"No, of course not," she laughed. Then she reached into her bag and pulled out a heel of hardened challah. "For ordinary sins," she said, holding the challah out to Stone.

"I think I'll need something stronger than that."

"Take a piece," she said.

He tore off a corner of the glazed loaf. "What is a regular sin?"

"Small stuff, like letting a door slam in someone's face, cutting off a car in traffic, not phoning someone back."

"Leaving the toilet seat up?" Stone asked.

"That's two pieces, at least," she said, laughing. Stone noticed that she had moved closer to him but there was nothing forward in her actions; they were simply occupying the same space, moving in sync as if their very heartbeats beat together.

"Now hold the challah in the air."

"Do we have to say a prayer?" Stone wondered.

"You can, but I just fire away." With that, she drew back her arm and threw the challah out into the river. Stone did the same.

"You're strong," he said.

"*I am woman, hear me roar!*" Gabby sang, and tossed another piece of challah out into the darkened waters. After a few minutes of tossing increasingly smaller pieces of challah, Stone said, "You're going to blow out your arm. Haven't you covered everything?"

"No," and she continued tossing the bread. She had such a look of concentration on her face that Stone could not help but conclude that Gabby actually was dredging up every transgression that she could recall and tossing them ceremoniously into the East River. Stone's mind had emptied as he tossed the bread into the rippling water. He had thought only of Gabby and the swift motion of her arm, followed by a slight breathy gasp, and he wondered what sins she was drowning in the murky waters. Stone was aware of the lights running along the taut cables of the Brooklyn Bridge; they hung in the sky like a low-lying constellation.

"Done," Gabby said at last, smiling. A thin film of perspiration shone on her forehead; she wiped it away casually with the back of her hand.

"What's next?" Stone asked.

"Rye bread," Gabby said, reaching into her bag and producing two fossilized pieces of bread.

"I suppose I'm expected to say something wry," Stone said.

"You could do that, but bad puns are the worst sin of all and can't ever be cast away. It's a personality flaw."

"Got it," Stone said. She reached for Stone's hand, pried back his fingers and placed the bread into his palm. It was the first time he had felt her skin and it was like an affirmation of Stone's entire life. She held the bread in the air; Stone did the same.

"This is for the sin of *lashon harah* – the sin of gossip, slander, speaking badly of others."

Stone had no doubt in his mind that he had committed *lashon harah* against his father in every way imaginable. Stone had not gossiped about the Judge, but he had entertained Zohar's suppositions without defending his father, who for once was unable to defend himself. He had allowed his mother to tar him with the same brush as Julius, suggesting violence and coercion. It did not matter in the end what his father had done wrong in his life, it was Stone's job now to uphold his name, respect his name, carry his flame. Stone tore off a piece of bread and threw it into the river. He had slandered his father both through words and deeds — his very way of life was slanderous to his father's name. He threw another piece of bread into the river. And he had slandered his father through omission before his community, by refusing to say *Kaddish*, to honor his name the way sons had done for their fathers for thousands of years. It was a sin of stubbornness, arrogance, and youthful determination, that he was somehow bigger than history, family, wrenched from the continuum of blood ties that reached back through the years to the original flame of life. But Stone was facing up to his sins now and with every piece of bread that sunk under the diamond-black water, a small piece of the old Stone drowned as well; and he felt the dualistic joy of both killing himself and going on. He threw the last scrap of bread far out into the water and felt a pop in his shoulder that sent a tremor down the length of his arm and into his fingertips.

Gabby stared at him, her eyes wide. Stone noticed that a few couples had gathered not far beyond them; they too had a look of fear, concern, confusion on their faces. Stone ignored them and looked into Gabby's face. Her expression had altered her face to the degree that her freckles seemed to have shifted place and settled on a different part of her cheeks.

"You were shouting," Gabby said, "and I tried to stop you and you just looked through me like I wasn't there."

"No," Stone said, feeling a sudden chill.

"Do you want to leave?"

"No, no," Stone said, "what's next? Worshipping false idols?"

"I think we should leave," Gabby said, "and get something to eat."

"No," Stone pleaded. "I want to stay."

She smiled and put her hand on his for a moment. "You sure you're all right?"

"Sure I'm sure."

"Then, that's good enough for me," Gabby said, digging into her bag. "Are you ready for sins of the heart?"

"Oh no!" Stone said, grabbing his chest and mock collapsing.

"Get up, this is fun," she said, and handed him a thick slice of whole wheat bread.

"What's this?"

"It's good for the heart," Gabby said, laughing. "Really, this is when you make up for all the hearts you've broken in the past year."

"Hearts?" Stone said.

"I'm a heartbreaker," Gabby said. "Didn't you know I'm supposed to have three children by now, halfway to a first set of twins?"

"You're a rebel."

"You make it sound so sinister."

"Isn't it?"

"No," Gabby said, stamping her foot on the ground. "I love my culture, my traditions, I love Israel; the trees, the flowers, the way the land dips in a dried-out wadi, the sound of a shepherd's bell, how the moon seems so close enough to touch. I love the silence of the desert, and I love the sonic boom of an F-18 bursting in the sky. And I love the road up to Jerusalem, how the Heavenly and the earthly seem to merge as one. I love everything so much that sometimes I ache inside. I don't know what to do with it all."

Stone thought of Fairuza, whose heart he knew he had broken and how once on a walk along the Old City ramparts she had broken down in tears at the sight of a border guard down below checking an Arab man's ID card.

"They're as bad as those fucking Orthodox at Gilo, with their checkpoints outside my village. I hate them, I hate this world, I hate this country, I hate this time. But I love this city. I love it. I feel like hugging the city and kissing its stones beneath my feet."

Stone held her.

After a moment she said, "Sometimes, I wish I were a giant who could carry Jerusalem away."

"Where to," Stone said.

"Maybe the moon."

Gabby continued and Stone was stunned by the contrast between her and Fairuza. "But I love this world as well; shopping in SoHo, the galleries and museums. I love the opportunities for education. I couldn't get an Ivy League education in Israel. I love both worlds and I don't think I should have to choose one over the other. I'm a citizen of Israel, and a citizen of the United States. What could be better?"

"And the broken hearts," Stone prodded, "here or there?"

She tossed a piece of bread into the water, and he saw Fairuza's image briefly flicker on the waves.

"What about the hospital? I saw how Yossi's friend looked at you."

"It doesn't matter."

"Does that mean yes?"

"It doesn't mean anything."

"Are you sure?"

Gabby paused and they listened to each other's silence and the sounds of the evening for a moment. "I've known him since I was four or five," Gabby said at last. "We were kids together."

"Dov?" Stone asked, remembering Gabby leaning close and whispering to him with an intimacy that belied simple friendship.

"Yes. Dov."

"You hurt him?" Stone asked.

"I don't want to talk about it. Not now." Again they were silent. The sound of the lapping water reminded Stone that he was thirsty and that his mouth was dry.

Gabby faced Stone and smiled. "Well it's Elul, the month of penitence. What about you, heartbreaker?"

"No," Stone said, "nobody. It's been a hard year."

"Oh, I'm sorry," Gabby said, her face softening. "I forgot."

"It's all right." They cast the bread piece by piece, alternately throwing and punting dry scraps into the dark water. Gabby kicked with a natural athleticism, sending the bread in high arcs into the air. Her silver rings flashed on her fingers as she threw. "Goodbye, heartache," Gabby said with a final toss, "good riddance." They worked their way through the rest of their sins as a chill came up from the river. A smudge of moon appeared like a thumbprint on the screen of the sky and disappeared just as quickly behind a bank of drifting clouds. Gabby held a piece of honey cake in her hands, her fingers dusted with a spray of confectioner's sugar. "And finally," she said, holding the cake in the air, "Gluttony."

"That sounds Christian to me," Stone said.

"Well obviously you've never seen me eat," Gabby said, laughing. She tore off a piece.

"If you were such a glutton, would you throw away a piece of cake?"

"Good point," Gabby said.

"Are you hungry?"

"Always."

"Then let's eat."

"What about this?" she said, the honey cake in her palm.

"Leave it for the birds," Stone said.

They found a restaurant up in Brooklyn Heights around the corner from Beecher Academy. Stone told Gabby that he had graduated from Beecher, and she laughed as if she thought Stone were making a joke. They sat by a high plate-glass window with a view of the street. There were two small candles on the table. Gabby ordered a plate of pasta with tomato sauce and no meat, and a glass of red wine.

"No meat?" Stone questioned. "Vegetarian?" Everyone he knew at Wesleyan was a vegetarian, or a vegan, or worse.

"Are you kidding?" Gabby said, gnashing her teeth with carnivorous furiosity. "Kosher." And she shrugged her shoulders.

"But you'll eat in a non-kosher restaurant."

"I'm kosher," Gabby said. "Not crazy."

The wine arrived and they clicked glasses and drank. Stone felt warm inside.

"*Ata medaber Ivrit?*" Gabby leaned forward and asked in a perfect Hebrew accent. "Do you speak Hebrew?"

"*K'tzat,*" Stone said.

"*Yofi,*" and she began to speak with the quick confident cadence of a native Sabra.

Stone knew any response would be babbled nonsense, so he raised his hands palms-out, a gesture of capitulation and said, "I guess I missed that class." He placed a candle in the palm of his hand.

Gabby said something else in Hebrew that Stone did not understand and then said, "It can be hard if you're not around it all the time."

"What's it like?" Stone said. "Living there, and here?"

Her face brightened. "Israel's my home. I grew up there. I was educated there, but I was born here. I have family here, we are back and forth all the time; it sometimes seems like Israel is just across the country, in another time zone, not across the world. But I still get excited when an American wins a medal in the Olympics, and I still refer to the president as our president."

"Sounds dizzying," Stone said. He dipped his fingers into the hot wax.

"It's not bad, really. To have two places in the world where you can kick up your feet and feel comfortable."

"What's it like there?" Stone said, flattening a ball of wax between his fingers. He pressed it to the table and worked it with his fingernail.

"You've been to Israel."

"No," Stone said. "To live in a settlement."

"I hate that word," Gabby said. "I can't help but picture Conestoga wagons and Indians and Little House on the

Prairie. It's a town, Matty, just like any other town. We have shops and restaurants and a movie theater."

The waitress brought their food, and Gabby spun a bale of spaghetti onto her fork. "Okay, not good restaurants. I'll give you that." And she filled her mouth with the steaming pasta. "Now this is good."

Stone felt an impulse to ask her about the Arabs, the violence, but he did not want to bring down the mood. Gabby continued, "What do you do you in Brooklyn? See friends, go out, eat, sleep. That's life. We do the same back home – go for walks in the hills, have campfires, sing. It's not different than living here in Brooklyn, except more pure, I guess. There are olive trees and sheep and a big blue sky that sits so low, you'd swear you could touch it."

"Sounds nice," Stone said.

"It is."

"Look," Stone said, sliding the wax disk towards Gabby. "A happy face."

"I saw your father on his last trip to Israel."

"You did?" He took a sip of wine, and another. Gabby bit her lower lip softly, as if she had thought about mentioning his father for a long time and now wished that she hadn't.

"On Tu B'Shvat. Before he got sick."

"You knew him?" Stone said, failing to hide his surprise.

"Of course," Gabby said. "He was good friends with my uncle, his memory be blessed, and my father and of course Zalman. I'd see him two or three times a year." Stone went pale. His father had kept so much from him; she may as well have been speaking about someone else's father.

"Are you all right?" Gabby asked.

"Yes," Stone said absently. "He never mentioned you."

"Oh," Gabby laughed. "I'm just a kid to him, his best friend's niece. I would still be a kid in his eyes no matter what. But, he was always polite, unflappable, confident. He was doing such important things for Israel. He was amazing, his tireless energy, his commitment, but he always took the time to sit and talk with me."

"That doesn't sound like my father."

Gabby waved a finger at him , saying, "Remember *lashon harah*."

"I'm serious," Stone said.

"So am I. We talked for long time about graduate school and how I wanted to study international relations. I had been thinking about going to Hebrew University, and he suggested Columbia. And I guess he convinced me."

"He can be very convincing," Stone said.

"That," Gabby said, "does not sound very convincing."

"We had a difficult relationship."

"Yeah, I guess parents can be difficult," she said. "But he spoke about you a lot."

"He did?"

"Yeah," she said. "Of course. 'My son Matthew won a medal for his swim team; my son Matthew wrote a poem and was sent a glowing rejection letter from the *Paris Review*; my son Matthew is studying Aramaic; my son Matthew won a scholarship to Columbia.' He spoke about you all the time. And even as a teenager, I knew that one day we would be friends."

"Friends?" Stone said, swallowing hard.

"Okay, more than friends." And she winked at him.

Stone felt a confluence of joy and hatred at this revelation. But what harm was done, really? His father had lied to

Gabby, speaking of his own accomplishments as his son's. The Judge had won a medal for his swim team at Brooklyn Tech, when he had a hairline fracture in his tibia. The Judge had received a two-page rejection letter from George Plimpton himself asking to send more poems. The Judge had studied Aramaic and mastered it in two years. And Stone hadn't even been accepted by Columbia as a freshman. Stone's budding relationship with Gabby was predicated on a lie. She had fallen for his father and his accomplishments. Or, perhaps unwittingly or not, the Judge had planted the seeds for this relationship long before he died. Was this a gift from the other world? Stone wondered. At that moment, beneath the dim light of the restaurant, with Gabby flushed from drink, her breath quickened from the telling of tales, Stone didn't care. He wanted Gabby and he would tell her so.

"I want to kiss you," Stone said.

"In time," Gabby said, leaning forward. "When it is right."

"Okay," Stone said, slipping back in his chair. "I'm not so great."

"Shh," Gabby said, holding a finger up to her lips. "You should look happy. I like you a lot. This doesn't happen very often."

Stone smiled. This was the greatest gift his father had ever given him.

14

Half-dressed and disheveled, Stone opened the door to find Moshe, hulking in the doorframe. He was dressed in a black suit with a white shirt, and the broad-brimmed hat that had occupied the passenger seat of his car now sat cocked on his cinder-block head. "Come say *Kaddish*. Rav Seligman sent me. Get dressed," Moshe said, peering into the apartment. "C'mon, say *Kaddish* for your father."

"Who is it," Abi called.

"Not for you," Stone answered.

"You're a Jew?" Moshe asked flatly. Stone nodded his head. "Say *Kaddish*."

He dressed and as they left the apartment in silence, Abi appeared at the door, calling after Stone, "Where are you going?"

"Out."

They crossed Myrtle Avenue, dodging a bus and continued past the tangled vacant lot where the rusted hull of a car sat, overrun by weeds and vines. A small metal sign on the fence warned of rat poison. Another, perched above a crumbling brick wall read, "Listen to R.R. Nation."

They descended the slope towards the BQE in silence, Moshe several paces ahead of Stone. He noticed that one of the heels of Moshe's scuffed leather shoes was two or three inches higher than the other. Stone felt as if he were sleep-walking, too tired to concentrate, his thoughts on Gabby and the night before.

Moshe crossed during a break in the traffic and did not wait for Stone, who was held back by a row of cars driving abreast, one of them blasting its horn. The echo was deafening. They arrived at a decrepit brick warehouse across from the Catbird Seat which looked unassuming and nondescript in the daylight, marked only by the sign "Hit Sign. Win Suit." The street was a dead-end which ran up against the locked gates of the Navy Yard. Four or five cars were parked up on the sidewalk. Moshe climbed the concrete steps and rang a small buzzer. After a moment a face appeared at the caged window set high on the iron door. The door opened. "You're late."

Moshe pointed with his thumb at Stone. He noticed that the thumbnail was black and battered. They stood in a bare, high-ceilinged room with concrete floors and bare bulbs burning at the end of naked wires. Stone followed them up a flight of stairs, past a religious seminary on the second floor where ultra-Orthodox men in black swayed over their prayer books, to the third floor, and along a narrow hallway to a small room. Stone noted the red light burning above; the eternal lamp, and then the ark and the *bima*.

The room was not illuminated with the magisterial glow that Stone was used to when he had attended synagogue; the sanctifying quality of light he had always associated with what was considered to be a holy place. There were less than twenty worshippers, and the room smelled close and stale. A few men turned their heads and one nodded when Stone entered. Moshe handed him a prayer book and wordlessly pointed to a corresponding page in his own. He followed along silently, observing the congregants in their prayers. Several seemed to shift and shake involuntarily as if they had left their bodies open to the fickle whims of the universe. Their movements did not correspond with anything Stone was used to seeing in his world. One of the worshippers briefly raised his voice higher than the others, his muttered prayer echoing off the low ceiling.

Stone thought he recognized the young Israeli that he had seen in Dov's hospital room, but his face was obscured by the shoulder of another man. He was whispering to the man next to him, who in turn whispered something to the one behind him. A young man with a wide *tallit* thrown over his shoulder ascended the low *bima* and began to read the Torah. Stone turned to find the pages in English, but there were none.

Stone's mind drifted to Gabby and the soft smell of her skin, her easy laugh. She loved him, Stone realized, and she had loved him for a long time, for years in fact. Did it matter that her love was misplaced, that he was not who she thought he was? Perhaps he could become that man after all.

He wished he could feel the warmth and intimacy that these worshippers felt; something to grasp onto in the darkness, but Stone was ever the rationalist, puzzling over the binding of the book, checking inside for a publication date.

Moshe leaned over towards Stone; his breath was otherworldly. Streams of sweat ran down his face. "The *Kaddish*," he said, turning the pages of Stone's book.

And there were the Aramaic words before him laid out like tiny prehistoric fossils on the face of the page. "*Yitgadal v'yitkadash sh'may raba.*" And though he could not understand them, Stone read the words easily – a distant memory instantly recalled. "*B'alma dee v'ra che-rutay v'yamlich mal'chutay . . .*" And as he read the words in lock-step with the voices of the worshippers it became clear to Stone that there was something he could do to mitigate his father's disappointment in his son, and that the Judge had been waiting for these words to be recited in the same way that a flower waits for the spring rains to fall. Stone knew that by reciting the words repeated by generations and generations, he was not alone but part of an inexorable narrative bound by history, grief, and the belief that life is bigger than petty concerns. Stone knew with absolute certainty that his father heard these words, these purifying words, and that Gabby was a gift in exchange for Stone's uttering of them.

The morning sunshine was bright in his eyes when he stepped into the street. He felt some elemental release at having said the *Kaddish*, freed from his father's critical gaze. He had done what was expected. He had cleared the slate for Gabby and for the rest of his life, and he felt he was finally ready to join the world of the living.

A car door opened in front of Stone, blocking his way. Without looking up he stepped around the door, but then heard, "Get in."

It was Zohar.

He sat in the driver's seat of his car, sunglasses obscuring his eyes. "Get in, I said."

"I'm busy," Stone said, walking away.

"Get in," he repeated, starting his engine. "Or I'll have to take you in on suspicion."

Stone froze. "You can't do that."

"I can," Zohar said. "Get in the car, now."

Stone's neck felt hot.

"Let's go for a drive."

Stone slid into the car. "Are you going to arrest me if I don't put on my seat belt?" The car smelled of stale coffee. The relaxed confidence Zohar had carried on their previous meetings was gone. He stepped hard on the gas and the car jolted.

"Where have you been?" Stone said. "I missed you."

Zohar burned. He did not answer.

After driving in silence for a few hundred yards Zohar parked in a gravel drive, before a set of locked gates and the forbidding ghost town structures and smokestacks of the abandoned Navy Yard.

"What were you doing in there?" Zohar asked, his jaw set hard.

"Saying *Kaddish* for my father," Stone said. "How did you find me?"

"Is there any reason you chose a synagogue hidden away in an abandoned warehouse to say *Kaddish* for your father?"

"It's near my apartment."

"Yeah, it's near your apartment."

"I said *Kaddish* for my father, that's it. Can you take me home now?"

"You don't want to get mixed up with them."

"Who?" Stone said.

"Matthew. Don't play dumb. I'm serious. Tell me what else you saw in there. Hear anything interesting?"

"What the fuck are you talking about?"

"Rabbi Seligman. Gabby Grunhut. That crew of yeshiva boys; the one in the hospital."

Stone thought of Gabby the night before, standing by the shimmering waters of the East River and how at peace he had felt. "Gabby?" Stone said.

"You know who her uncle was."

"Enough with the family histories, okay? I have to go to the bathroom."

"And I'm sure your asthma medication is at home as well."

"Fine," Stone said. "Hurry up."

"Did anyone whisper anything to you? Pass you a note? Did anyone tell you anything?"

"No," Stone said. "I was just saying *Kaddish* for my dad. I'm sure you understand."

"I understand," Zohar said. "I just want to make sure you understand."

"Understand what?" He heard the blast of a ship's horn as it moved up the river.

"Do you know about the killing on Atlantic Avenue last week? The execution?"

"I saw the newspaper," Stone said, his bladder pressing uncomfortably against his belly. "I have to go to the bathroom." Stone reached for the door handle but Zohar's hand came down on his.

"Listen. He was a wealthy businessman involved in buying properties in Jerusalem, Jaffa, and Nazareth."

"What about him?"

"Last month in Jersey City another wealthy Arab businessman, Salmeh Gheith, you might have heard of him, a real-estate developer, he was assassinated. Execution-style. Bullet in the back of the head."

"Why are you telling me this?"

"I just got back from the Detroit field office. They're investigating a murder, an execution in Dearborn, a wealthy Arab involved in real estate. Do you see the connection?"

"Three murders."

"Three executions. Same entry point, same caliber bullet. Same M.O. across the board."

"So," Stone said. "What's the point?"

"The point is, we have the killer's car – a rental. Found it outside a motel. We searched the trunk and we found blasting caps, detonators, and a hundred thousand dollars cash. Why do you think he had that?"

"I give up."

"Because something bigger, much bigger, is going on."

"If something's going on," Stone said, "arrest them and leave me out of this."

"It's not a crime until it happens. I'm not going to arrest them on a traffic violation. Why do you think the killer had detonators and blasting caps in the trunk of his car? How do you think Dov Wexler blew his face off yesterday morning?" Zohar paused and looked Stone in the eyes. "Should I arrest you, huh? Is something going on you haven't told me about?"

"I have to pee," Stone said.

"Hold it in," Zohar said. "I know you were at the hospital visiting with Dov Wexler yesterday afternoon."

"You don't understand. It's all a big misunderstanding."

"No. You listen. The killers are traveling back and forth, beneath the radar, because of their dual citizenship. Wexler is part of that crew."

"Oh, shut up."

"I thought you'd be more helpful, considering your relationship with your father."

Stone reached for the door.

"Avraham Grunhut was killed with a bullet in the back of his head. The wrong man was charged and put away. Who do you think killed Grunhut?"

"I give up," Stone said.

"I'll tell you what," Zohar said, starting the car. "We'll go for a drive, talk. And if things work out, I'll take you for a piss at the Waldorf Astoria. How does that sound?"

They drove along the edge of the Navy Yard, the Manhattan skyline coming in and out of view. They passed a pack of Hasidic men, dressed in black, crossing the street: a murder of crows. Zohar sang out something in Hebrew that Stone did not understand.

"Your father and Avraham Grunhut co-founded the Eretz Fund with Zalman Seligman; Seligman running the Israeli operations, your father and Grunhut sharing control in New York. I believe that Grunhut was assassinated because of financial issues, control issues, issues of money and the joint account." They were moving quickly along the highway now, bumping over potholes, the jagged spine of the island still in view.

"Everybody knows who killed Grunhut."

Zohar ignored him. "Why do you think Seligman is courting you like a debutante."

Stone did not answer.

"The bank account. He needs the account numbers that only your father had, and he thinks you have them. You don't have them, do you?"

"How do you know?"

"Your father would never have trusted you with them."

The city was behind them now and Zohar drove with the flow of traffic, his hands loose on the wheel. "I don't know what you know, but I do know they're after you."

"What do you do – tap their phones, spy on them in the shower?" Stone said in disgust.

They drove in silence for a few minutes. Finally Zohar said, "Listen, Matthew, I'll be honest with you. I need you. I need you to help me break the case before something catastrophic happens. There are no phone records. There's no paper trail. All the information must be passed by word of mouth. Zalman Seligman has made six trips between Ben Gurion and Kennedy in the last six months – each trip lasting less than forty-eight hours. This is a man who doesn't speak freely. This is a tight knit group of fanatics. I've got to disrupt them, find out what they're up to, and I need you to be my eyes and ears."

They pulled off the highway and drove under the rusted elevated train tracks, arriving at a scene of utter desolation and poverty. Stone saw burned-out buildings and overrun vacant lots piled high with garbage and refuse, the austere prison-block apartments of city housing in the near distance. He saw a lone spike-collared dog shitting in the street, and a group of blacks drinking cans of malt liquor on the corner, violent rap music screaming from a ghetto blaster.

"Where are we?" Stone asked.

"Brownsville," Zohar said, smiling. "Go on, take a pee." He gestured broadly with his hands. Stone felt his heart accelerate. "Or are you afraid to get out of the car?" Zohar turned off the engine.

"I'm not afraid," Stone said. Zohar opened the passenger door. A young mother walked past, berating her screaming toddler, who was pushing her own carriage full of loaded grocery bags. She smacked the child on the back of the head. "Go ahead. I'll wait for you."

The group had noticed Zohar's car and a couple of the homeboys walked in their direction, their pants hanging low on their hips, the crotches nearly reaching the ground. One of them wore a Crawfords baseball cap on his head and the another a nylon du-rag. They walked with nearly identical slow limping swaggers, cocky strutting steps that were full of violence and the promise of more. Stone could see something tucked in the waistband of the one in the baseball cap – it came into view briefly and disappeared as his open shirt flapped closed against his chest.

"Let's go," Stone said.

"Hang on," Zohar said. "Just a couple of gang-bangers."

"Yo," the first one said, sliding up along the hood of the car on his rear and landing before Stone and his open door. "Dat's a phat ride and shit," he said, laughing and looking into the car. He had the moronic laugh of someone who laughed at other people's misfortune.

The one wearing the Crawfords hat thumped his palms against the roof of the car and leaned in towards Stone. He had two gold teeth and a bubblegum pink scar running from his left ear to the corner of his mouth. His friend stood behind him, arms crossed.

"You ain't be lunchin' – is you?"

"No," Stone said, shaking his head. Zohar said nothing.

"Hey, bruh," Gold Tooth called to his friend, "he swellin'?"

"Ah don' know what he be doin'."

"What you want? French fries? Hamburger Helper?"

Stone shook his head.

"You in da jungle now. Can't nobody read yo' fuckin' mine." His face was close to Stone's. "You a chaser?"

Stone was silent.

"C'mon, snowflake. You been had enough time. What you want? This ain't no Zulu shit. We got cakes, candy, caps, hard ball, hard line, hard rock, jellybeans, kangaroo, parlay, pebbles, white tornado, sight-ball, seven-up. How much you want? A biscuit? A onion? A doub? Double up? Two for nine? A pee wee? A piece? A one-tissue box?"

"I don't know," Stone said.

"You don't know?" The dealer said.

"You got five motherfucking seconds to make up yo fuckin' mine fore I blow yo fuckin' head off."

Zohar whispered, "You'd better say something."

"Whatchyou fuckin' say, cracker?"

"He said, we're lost," Stone said.

"Naw! You shittin' me. Get out of the fuckin' car." He reached in, popped open Stone's seat belt and pulled him out by the neck. He arched him back against the curve of the car's roof. The homeboy's eyes were red, his pupils the size of dimes. His gold tooth shone. Any second, Zohar would flash his badge and it would all be over.

"You ain't come into my 'hood an' fuck wit' me and my homey."

"'At's right," the one with the du-rag said. His head was as slick as a condom. "You up in his grill now fo' sho."

"I rip you up," the one with the gold tooth said. "Got dat?"

He reached into his waistband and pulled out a bright silver pistol; there were two pale scars on his abdomen indicating a bullet's entry. "You got a wallet?" The brim of his Crawfords hat pressed against Stone's forehead.

"He'll hit you back later," the one with the du-rag said, laughing. "On the first."

Stone felt Gold Tooth reach into his pocket, his rough hand grazing his balls. He had never faced a man at gunpoint before, and felt in the intensity of the situation, something similar to what he had felt in synagogue saying the *Kaddish*: absolute clarity.

"Ooh, you got the dragon," Gold Tooth said, leaning in close to Stone. He licked his dry lips. "You brush yo teef today?"

The one with the du-rag went through his wallet.

"What you got?"

"Nottin. Fi' dolla," the du-rag responded. "Where your chingy hid?" he said to Stone, his breath hot and yeasty. He pulled Stone's pockets inside out and ran his fingers through the top of Stone's socks.

Where was Zohar? Stone wondered. He was about to call out when he felt the tip of the pistol against his temple.

"Mister 9. say I'm not playing. Where the Benjamins? What the hook gonna be?"

"That's it," Stone said. "I don't have anything else."

"Shee-it. You trippin', man," the du-rag said. "You hook up my boy or he bust a cap fo' sho."

The sun was suddenly hot, the roof of the car burning against Stone's back. The sky was a buffed powder blue. A 747 circled out over the Rockaways. Stone wished he was on the plane.

"Where you get them hot kicks?" the du-rag said, pointing at Stone's black leather shoes.

"Dem brogans?"

Stone nodded his head.

"Yeah, dey hot," Gold Tooth said, stuffing the empty wallet back into Stone's pants. He nodded his head and said, "Uhn huh."

The du-rag knelt down, untied Stone's shoes and pulled them off.

"Now you run like a black man." They pointed in the direction of the vacant lot and the projects rising in the distance. A fire burned somewhere and Stone could hear a distant siren getting farther away. Gold Tooth held the pistol to the back of Stone's head. "Come on," he prodded with the barrel. "Move."

"In my socks?"

"Move, motherfucker."

"Make this whiteboy dance."

"A'ight."

At last Zohar appeared, popping out from inside the car. "Leave him alone."

Gold Tooth lowered his pistol.

"You and your shit, Mr. Mike. The jay on they way?"

"Just leave him alone."

"Yo, dogg," Gold Tooth said in Stone's ear. "You lucky your friend in thur hooked up."

"Let's bolt, G."

"Better not check you later," the du-rag said, slapping Stone across the side of the head, and sauntering off.

"What was that? Why? Why?" Stone screamed. "They almost shot me!"

"That is violence," Zohar said, starting the car. "The real thing, fuelled by anger, hatred and ignorance. Do you want to see a hundred times worse?"

"No."

"Then trust me."

"Why should I trust you?"

"Because I am right."

Zohar pulled over on the side of a busy thoroughfare, the elevated train rumbling above, leaving Brownsville and its filth for another world, it seemed. Stone was shaking.

"Let's talk," Zohar said.

"Have you ever had a gun to your head?" Stone said.

"I've been through a lot worse. Now, let's talk."

Stone was silent.

"Do you want me to drop you off with those gang-bangers back there?"

"Very funny."

"I'm serious, Matthew. Now let's talk. You're going to answer a few questions, or we are going to go for a drive around the block. Do you know where we are?" Zohar asked.

"No."

"This is where it all began," Zohar said. "Well, not quite. Let me start at the beginning. I want you to listen."

Stone opened his window a crack, and a gust of air blew in.

"Your grandfather, Julius Stone arrived at Ellis Island with his mother and his three sisters in the fall of 1913 at the age of five. His first image of America, after days of seasickness below the deck of *The Excelsior*, was of Lady Liberty holding aloft a shining sword. This is a story he liked to tell with a laugh – it's on record on his FBI files. You can check them if you want. He must have never forgotten that sword, carried that image of America in his mind all through his formative years that were filled with so much violence.

"He was practically an orphan.

"His father, a sickly Berlin tobacconist, had become ill on the ship, contracted pneumonia and died on Hoffman Island in Lower New York Bay. So he was the man of the family, even as a child.

"Julius, his mother, and his three older sisters moved to the teeming slums of Brownsville, Brooklyn not far from here. At the age of seven Julius descended from his crowded wooden tenement flat into the streets. And that is where he spent most of the next twenty years. Now this is long before the blacks moved in. But Brownsville, with its poor immigrant population, was always a tough place.

"He was a small kid, with hair thick and wiry like a shoeshine brush, who grew no taller than 5 foot 5, and had to learn young how to defend himself. At the age of nine he beat up a Pole from East New York who was trying to steal the scrap metal he had gathered that day from the Canarsie dumps. Later, caught stealing a necklace from a Pitkin Avenue jeweler, young Julius grabbed the startled jeweler by the throat and said, "It's for my mother." He was a funny kid. His police records are on file at Police Plaza if you are interested.

"Julius was arrested more than half-a-dozen times for theft, assault, and burglary by the time of his Bar Mitzvah. His mother must have said, "Go to school, learn something." Instead he was sent to a reformatory upstate, where he spent the next two years.

"Prohibition had gone into effect during his time away, and Julius quickly found work, first watering down illicit whiskey, and later delivering alcohol to speakeasies throughout Brooklyn. From Bedford Nest to Oetjen's all the way to the Bossert Hotel in Brooklyn Heights, he was known affectionately as 'Big Julie.' After making his rounds, he would head towards the waters of Brooklyn's south shore, or desolate Breezy Point in the Rockaways, sometimes going out as far as Montauk at the end of Long Island on his nightly liquor runs. He didn't know who he worked for, but there was always work, and his mother either never asked where the money came from or didn't care.

"You know your grandfather was a killer, Matthew."

Stone nodded his head.

"It was on a moonless night off the coast of Jamaica Bay, when Big Julie was said to have killed his first man, a Cuban who had tried to take his cash without making delivery. The Cuban was found strangled by a makeshift garrote, fashioned from a piece of scrap metal. Strangulation became his trademark, and Julius was only seventeen years old. Growth potential, with an endless ceiling," Zohar laughed.

"Anyway, he was a local boy, who the Brownsville crew had heard of and seen jauntily strolling beneath the El, at the intersection of Saratoga and Livonia. That's where we are right now, Matthew. He was a lean and hard boy, small enough to slip under anyone's radar, who had eyes like coals, like death, that didn't give you anything – a perfect killer.

"From the front stoop of Midnight Rose's, the local candy store and hangout, one of Arnold Rothstein's men called out from beneath his hat, 'Hey kid! Whyn'tcha work for us?'

"Julius didn't know it then, but he had been working for Rothstein the whole time.

"He was tied up with Murder Inc. from the start; now it was just a matter of joining the team. Bootlegging, murder, and execution were his marketable skills.

"Throughout the rest of Prohibition and into the darkest days of the Depression, Julius continued to work, collecting taxes from union leaders, killing over a dozen enemies of the Syndicate. Never a fingerprint. Never a witness. He was so good that nobody could ever pick him up. And he was small and affable with a good sense of humor, and people began to think these stories about Julius were just that, stories. Of course these stories were told by men who later on ended up dead.

"And then suddenly, after a decade of murder and bloodshed in which he routinely carried $10,000 in his pocket, Julius decides it's time to settle down, find a wife. Start a regular life. So he married, moved to Ocean Parkway, opened a tavern on Avenue U and had two kids, Walter and Bunny. They joked at the Bureau that Bunny and her Downs was punishment enough for his crimes.

"Anyway, Lepke and Gurrah were in hiding, Dewey and his men were chasing down anyone connected with Murder Inc., looking to indict, and your grandfather just slipped out the way he came, in complete silence. He must have hidden out in Florida while your father was growing up; sending money on the sly to pay for the house and the kids.

"Julius took one more shot at the big money. Now, this story is more rumor than fact, but it's a nice bridge between his life of crime and his life in real estate, and it explains how he became so wealthy.

"The Sixth Avenue El was torn down in 1938, and the street was widened to become the Avenue of the Americas. Julius returned to his original staple that made him his first dollar: scrap metal. Julius took the profits from the Sixth Avenue El, which it was rumored had been sold to Japan for their war effort, and reinvented himself as a legitimate businessman selling real estate in Florida and the south, far from the eyes of his enemies.

"But your grandfather could not stay away from the action for long, and he began, like his friend Meyer Lansky, to contribute large portions of his profits to the Irgun, the militant wing of Jabotinsky's Revisionist Movement, via the guise of the World Zionist Organization; a legitimate structured outlet for his life-long blood lust. In the years preceding Israel's creation, Julius helped arm the Irgun, helping to send over two dozen shipments of weapons from New York to Tel Aviv. It was a long way from Pitkin Avenue, but Julius was sending the same message that he sent to the Pole who tried to steal his scrap metal as a kid: don't fuck with a Jew. After celebrating your father's 13th birthday, Julius signed your father up to join Betar. I've got the papers back at Federal Plaza. You know your father was skinny, bookish, and small for his age, even smaller than Julius had been when he was picking scrap metal as a child in Brownsville. Julius had thought that Betar would toughen Walter up, make him a man. Walter was sent to train in the summers at paramilitary training camps in the Catskill Mountains, where he met the young Avraham Grunhut.

"The rest is history, but you know he grew to the height of 6 foot 3, nearly a whole foot taller than his father, as if through sheer force of will. Walter had remolded himself not in the image of his father, but in the image of some fierce Germanic god. And as if to punctuate their differences, Walter was completely bald by his early 20s, his head massive and majestic, like that of a marble statue."

"I know who my grandfather was," Stone said, "and I know that my father was nothing like him."

Zohar smiled, and his eyes seemed to say that he knew something more. Zohar fixed his eyes on Stone and held him in his gaze.

Finally Stone said, "They were polar opposites – night and day, one was a criminal, the other, a judge. He's clean!" Stone almost pleaded. "He's clean."

Zohar dropped a manila envelope into Stone's lap. "Open it."

"My father was ashamed of Julius and he spent his life distancing himself from that legacy."

"Open it," Zohar prodded.

The envelope was thick and Stone could feel its bulk against his lap.

"Open it."

"They barely knew each other . . ."

"Open it."

Finally, Stone relented, peeling back the worn tab.

"Look inside."

Stone dumped the envelope out into his lap. Photographs, dozens of them, stared at him. Zohar reached across to Stone and propped up a photo against the dashboard.

"This is Miami, January 1972, again in the summer of 1974, here, 1977." Zohar spread the photos across the dashboard. "Here in Brooklyn, Sheepshead Bay, 1975. The upstairs room at Gage and Tollner 1974, 1973, 1976, again

1973 – Christmas, this time. They go all the way back to the 1950s, when your father was in law school."

"What is this?" Stone said, knowing how foolish he sounded. "It can't be."

"It is, Matthew. Look. Here's Julius. You can see him through his living-room window, just before he died, days before he died. See how the Judge is holding him up? Do you see the intimacy in the gesture?"

"How?" Stone whispered.

"Do think the FBI takes their eyes off a man like Julius Stone when he is living right out in the open, for all to see?"

"Well, why didn't you arrest him?"

"He was squared with us."

"What do you mean?"

"Names," Zohar said. "Lots of them. But we still kept an eye on him. Old habits. You know what I mean?"

"My father," Stone gasped.

"I'll be frank with you Matthew. Your father lied to you. He kept you from your grandfather, so you would never know him. Why? Maybe he thought he was protecting you. Maybe something more sinister – I don't know. Whichever way you look at it, your father lied to you, deceived you, right up until the end. Your father started the Eretz Fund with your grandfather's money, and never let you in on it. Never shared the secret. Why do think that was?"

"Fuck you," Stone said.

"Because he didn't trust you, because he didn't trust Abi Stone, formerly Abi Schnitzer, the artist, Barnard girl, free spirit, because he didn't trust that her son, someone born of her, could be trusted. He didn't trust that you were his."

"I was," Stone said. "He was my father."

"Yes. He was. But he doubted for a long time. The American Association of Blood Banks shows in their records that three times, between 1974 and 1977, Walter Stone submitted the old serological blood tests to determine paternity – of course this was before DNA testing and was not 100 percent accurate. And despite the fact that all three tests came back over 93 percent probability of his paternity, he must have had the devil of doubt whispering in his ear right until the end. What else can explain the Judge being such a cold, distant father?"

For a moment, Stone thought about Fairuza and the plaintive expression on her face when she told Stone she was late, and how cold he had been, leaving her alone in that café off of Azza Street, her head slumped into her gasping chest. He had never once thought about what might have become of her from that missed period.

Stone pounded his fist on the dashboard and shouted something incoherent even to his own ears.

Zohar looked on with curiosity.

"I believe these killings that are happening now are tied directly to your father and the Eretz Fund and link all the way back to Julius Stone and his financial support for the bombing of the King David Hotel. All signs point to the fact that the killing is setting the stage for something much larger that I'm afraid is going to happen soon. I need your help."

"What?" Stone said. "To expose my father to the world as a criminal and murderer?"

"To save lives."

"You want me to tear down my father's legacy as a lawmaker and a scholar."

"He destroyed his legacy all by himself with his indiscretions during the Court Street Riot trial. He showed his true colors there."

"Dying once wasn't enough?"

"Do you think he thought twice before having Grunhut killed or the others?"

"I don't believe you. You've got bad information. Everything you say is a lie."

"Do these photos lie?" Zohar said, sliding them gingerly back into the envelope. "I understand that it's hard believing your father and grandfather were both violent, bloodthirsty men. You don't have to be that way. Put an end to this."

"How?" Stone said, knowing now that he could never again betray his father, even if it meant a thousand or a million lives.

"Wear a wire."

"A fucking wire?"

"Zalman Seligman wants those numbers from you. Find out why. And stay close to Gabby and her crew of yeshiva boys."

"Gabby! Why me?"

"I'll be honest. There are no other informant candidates, and you are practically on the inside, given entree not by ideology, which is assumed, but by birth."

"An informant."

"You'll be a hero. I promise," Zohar said. His eyes took on a filmy glazed look, betraying emotion for the first time. "This is something really important, Matthew."

"All right," Stone said at last. "I'll do it. I'll fucking do it."

"Good," Zohar said. "I'll find you tomorrow and have you fitted for a body recorder."

ᵔ 15 ᵕ

When Stone returned home he called Gabby.

"She's in the city," Esther said in a thin, distant voice. "At school."

Stone went to the bathroom, looked at his face in the mirror, his pale skin, his tired eyes. Exhausted, worn out, still shaking, he slammed the bathroom door hard, rattling the wood frame.

"What's the matter?" Abi called from the living room. He hadn't seen her when he came in.

"Nothing. I'm going to shower and sleep."

"Don't you have to teach today?"

"No," he said in an irritable voice.

She was outside the bathroom door now. "Matthew. I'm going out, okay? Maybe later we'll have dinner? I'm buying."

"Maybe," he said.

"Don't sleep too long."

The hands on his watch showed 4:15 when he woke up, refreshed in the peach-colored light. He jumped out of bed and called Gabby again.

"Gabby there?"

"Still at school."

"Tell her I called," Stone said, and hung up the phone.

He dressed, full of restless energy, and paced back and forth in his room wishing Gabby was home. The sun still shone outside his window and he felt the sudden desire to walk, it didn't matter where.

The homeboys in front of the building laughed when Stone emerged.

"She went thataway if you wanna know."

"Thanks," Stone said, turning his back to Myrtle Avenue.

"Tell your moms I wanna date her, know what I'm saying?"

"Yeah, she a doll."

Stone's ears burned all the way up the street until he turned right at the co-op, the homeboys out of earshot.

He walked up tree-lined Clinton Avenue and passed the mansions of the Pratt children, tripping on a root that had pushed up the slate sidewalk.

DeKalb Avenue was a different world – just two blocks away from Myrtle Avenue and its barbershops and fried chicken houses, dice games and drug deals – lined with newly renovated brownstones, chic restaurants, shops selling African crafts and clothing, a black SoHo running from Washington to the park. Stone had seen a film crew on an adjacent street the week earlier filming one of Hollywood's black stars sitting pensively on a stoop. The air felt fresher here, the greenery more full. Students laughed in front of the coffee shop, singing along to an acoustic guitar. He peered in shop windows and stopped at a newsstand to check the Yankees score; they had won again. A new restaurant had opened across the street called The Long Dream. Stone had not noticed it before. Young black professionals and artists sat out on a patio drinking beer and eating before the chocolate façade of a newly renovated brownstone. He entered the low wrought-iron gate and stood for a moment, stunned before the high-glass window with the newly painted phrase "Words Can Be Weapons Against Injustice."

At a small table near the window he saw Abi sitting, sunglasses on, a strand of her hair fallen to the side of her face. She gestured passionately, wildly almost, talking to someone who Stone could only see from behind. He knew right away it was Zohar; his squared shoulders, cropped close at the neck, the subtle tilt of his head.

How had Zohar found his mother, or is that how she found Stone after all this time? Zohar had recruited Abi to inform on the informant. Did that mean that all her apologies, heartfelt declarations meant nothing? Had she been working for Zohar all along, or had she simply been waiting for the Judge to die so she could crawl back into his life and claim the mantle of loving parent?

❧

Gabby met him on the dark porch. She smelled clean and her skin glowed as if she had just stepped out of the shower. She wore her hair in a ponytail, showing more of her neck than he had seen previously. She wore a fitted charcoal gray sweater, and a tight-fitting black stretch skirt with sporty red stripes down each side. "You look great," Stone said.

"You think?" she said, spinning a quick turn in leather boots that raised her up almost two inches. "My friend

Sassona made these," she said, pinching out the sweater and skirt with her fingers. "You've heard of Sassona Ivri?"

"No," Stone said.

"She's cool," Gabby said, "She makes everything in her apartment by hand, and now you see Hollywood stars and models wearing her clothes. She's always going to Paris and Milan to be with the beautiful people. Not bad for an Orthodox girl from Midwood." She laughed.

"She can do that?" Stone said

"Matty!" she shouted, playfully hitting him on the shoulder. "Of course she can. Just not on Shabbat."

"I didn't know," Stone said, throwing his hands up in the air.

"We're more than just baby-making machines," she said, turning and pulling open the screen door. She called inside, "Be back later."

"I know that," Stone said, stepping onto the flagstone walkway. "I just didn't know an Orthodox girl could be so modern."

"Such things are permitted," Gabby said in a solemn tone, before breaking out in laughter.

"Hey," Stone said. "I missed you today."

Gabby looked surprised. "Really?"

"You have no idea."

As they reached the sidewalk, she briefly pressed herself close to Stone and he trembled. He could feel the warmth of her breasts despite the cool air that descended with nightfall. They crossed the busy thoroughfare of Ocean Parkway, racing breathlessly against oncoming traffic. Horns blared as they reached the grassy island separating the two sides of Ocean Parkway. Two disheveled-looking men playing chess on a nearby park bench shook their heads with disapproval.

"Let's stroll," Stone said in an English accent.

"Yes, let's," Gabby said. "Which way?"

"That way," Stone said, pointing toward Coney Island and the ocean. The sun had already moved far to the west, burning pink and orange and red over New Jersey, leaving the sky before them a dark, inky blue. Stone thought he saw a star appear in the sky. They strolled along the tree-lined path, beneath the turning leaves, as the street lamps belatedly flickered on. They passed a group of yesh-iva boys arrayed in a circle on the service road, kicking a pink ball in the air, a couple pushing a double baby carriage passed by speaking Hebrew. The street was alive with people, Jews mostly, enjoying a last taste of late summer, and Stone stopped before a crowd that jostled and pushed and noisily clambered to get a better view of a young boy, no older than six, playing chess against a bearded man in a black suit. They could barely see through the shifting bodies. Gabby stood on her tiptoes, but she could not see. They found a nearby lamppost and Stone offered to hoist Gabby up the pole. "No," she said. "You go."

A pale light fell over the game, and Stone could make out the look of concentration on the man's face. The boy was expressionless – he had the broad-faced look of a simpleton. He wore a blue satin *kippah* on his head.

"I'll bet you $10 on the boy," Gabby called. He moved automatically, seemingly without thought, while the man puzzled and pondered every move in apparent agony.

"I'm with you," Stone said, sliding down the pole. His hands smelled bitter and metallic, so he wiped them on his pants.

"Amazing," Gabby said. "He's just a schoolboy. Second grade. He hasn't lost a game yet."

"So you were trying to hustle me," Stone said.

"If you don't tell, I won't tell," she said, smiling.

"Tell who?" Stone said.

"The Royal Who. They can't handle the truth."

"Hey. How was school today?" Stone continued after a moment. "Do you know the words to *Roar, Lion* yet?"

"I've been studying," Gabby said.

"So serious," Stone said, prodding her.

"Okay, so one day you'll teach me."

They stopped before a red light. He wanted to kiss Gabby. He turned his face towards her and she softly said, "Not here." She squeezed his hand reassuringly.

"So, how was school?" Stone repeated.

"You wouldn't believe it," Gabby said. "Daoud is at it again."

Edwin Daoud had written a number of provocative books on imperialism, Palestinian self-determination, and cultural criticism, and had taught at Columbia for a number of years. "He was out on the steps of Low Library again, spreading his hateful propaganda. You should have seen the crowd gathered. There were over 100 people – and some TV stations as well. You know Daoud, right?"

"My father withdrew his alumni pledge when he was hired," Stone said.

Gabby smiled and then frowned. "He was going on about the Israelis and how they were demographically taking over East Jerusalem. Ras-al-amud, Abu Dis, Silwan – as if only Arabs were permitted to live on that land. And you should have heard the crowd cheer when he said that the

Israeli occupation is being funded by money from the United States and how Columbia should divest its money from Israel the way that it did in South Africa in the 1980s. And he shouted out, 'No to Apartheid. No to Israeli Occupation!' And it made me so sad, the way the crowd joined in, pumping their fists as if they were rallying at Nuremberg. It's all just an excuse for anti-Semitism." Gabby paused, as an ambulance raced passed with its siren blaring. "And you know what is ironic about the whole thing? He stood on the stairs of the Low Library beneath the statue of Athena, Goddess of Wisdom, crying academic freedom, as if that is the highest virtue, ignoring the fact that just last year he was filmed throwing rocks with a bunch of teenagers in the Security Zone in Lebanon. That's terrorism! He promotes violence and hatred against Jews, and Columbia is a private institution and he's using that platform as his own personal soapbox." Gabby paused, she had been shouting. "I'm sorry. It just makes me so mad. I thought I was getting away from all that, coming back to New York. I'm so tired of politics."

"Then, why are you studying politics?"

"That's me. Full of contradictions. Who knows. Maybe I'll join the State Department one day. That's one way to shut down jerks like Daoud. And he grew up in London, anyway. Why doesn't he mind his own business?"

"I've got an idea," Stone said.

"What's that?"

"Let's put a curse on him."

"A curse?"

"Yeah," Stone said. "A curse that he'll die of cancer and leave everybody alone."

"Cancer," Gabby said quietly. "Cancer's terrible."

"I know," Stone said.

"I'm sorry," Gabby said. Then after a moment, "a curse it is." She closed her eyes and muttered some words that Stone did not understand. Her eyelids glittered under the street lights. Stone was falling in love with Gabby – with her, life was interesting and hopeful; without her he was bored, terrified and ashamed. She seemed to glow under the street-lamp, radiating her own light, awesome and sensual. He felt a voyeuristic sense that he was staring into her soul, and that she had left it open for him like a flower in the spring. He wanted to tell her that he wanted to be with her all the time and that it hurt when she was not around. "That should do it," she said after a moment, opening her wide eyes.

"What was that?"

"I have secret powers," Gabby laughed.

"Seriously," Stone said. "That wasn't Hebrew."

"All the best curses are in Yiddish."

"What does it mean?"

"It loses meaning in translation – but it should be enough to keep Daoud down for a while. At least to miss that rally."

"The Rally for Palestine," Stone said. "In Brooklyn."

"Protesting is so juvenile," Gabby said. "It's such a band-wagon mentality. And anyway, you can't change God's will."

They walked on, passing synagogues and yeshivas on both sides of the street, their lights burning against the dark-ness. In the sky above, a few meager clouds shifted, phos-phorescent in the moonlight. Stone could see the flashing beacon lights of a 747 making its turn over the Rockaways in preparation for its landing at Kennedy Airport.

"Have you ever been to Brownsville?"

"Are you crazy?" Gabby said.

"Maybe a little," he said. "It's no worse than the West Bank, or Gaza."

"Matthew. It's a lot worse. Judea and Samaria are very safe. We have our own army to look out for us."

"Jews used to live in Brownsville," Stone continued. "I was out there today."

"I'd rather you didn't tell me that."

They were both silent.

"I mean, I'd rather you didn't go. I'd worry."

"Okay. I won't go. Deal," he extended his hand.

She shook it. "Deal."

"Hey, you're putting me to work," Stone said after a minute. "A lot of walking."

"I'm not easy," Gabby said, a slight bead of perspiration forming on her forehead. "I love to walk."

"'I too walked the streets,'" Stone sang in a stage voice, "'Brooklyn of ample hills was mine.'"

"Whitman," Gabby said. "The first true American poet."

"Yeah," Stone said, pleased. "He was a sexually omnivorous person. He would go with men, women, trees, a lamppost – it didn't matter to him. He was just a big, lusty bear who loved the world so much that he had to fuck everything."

"Matty!" Gabby said, doubling over in laughter. "Do a lamppost?"

"Why not? His writing was all about sex. What does this sound like to you? 'Stand up tall masts of Manahatta! Stand up, beautiful hills of Brooklyn!' Listen to how sensual and erotic this is."

"He's using metaphors to glorify the city of New York," Gabby said.

"No," Stone said. "The tall masts and the ample hills are obviously a phallus and breasts, ample, bosomy breasts."

Gabby laughed again, touching Stone lightly on the arm. "You're crazy," she said. "Funny. But, crazy."

"Isn't all poetry, in one way or another about sex? Are you going to tell me that the *Song of Songs* is just a lyric poem? It is the ultimate manual on how a man and woman should make love."

"I'll bet you're a real Casanova."

"Maybe," Stone said.

"I'll bet you've been around the block once or twice. Been with a lot of women."

"Some."

"Some?" Gabby said. "More than three? Less than 10? What is 'some' supposed to mean?"

"Some means some. Look it up."

"And where am I supposed to look this up? *Great Lovers of the History of the World?* And I suppose I will find a picture of you and your harem." They both laughed.

After a moment she said, "Hey, does this happen often? What we are doing?"

"What are we doing?" Stone said.

"You know," Gabby said.

Stone looked into her eyes with astonishment. "No. No, this doesn't happen often."

"People don't understand me." Gabby said. "They want to classify me and put me in a box. But I am trouble," she said. "So look out."

"I'm looking," Stone said.

"I'm sure they were all beautiful, skinny. Tell me about them."

"I don't know," Stone said.

"What? You don't remember? Come on. You can remember the women you've been with."

"Of course I remember."

"Tell me about them. I want to know."

Stone told her about several, going back to his junior year in high school. He told her about Emmanuelle, the Acadian from Mechanic Falls, Maine, who had been his girl-friend at Wesleyan until he had had his breakdown.

"Well, she sounds beautiful," Gabby said, interrupting.

They passed under a highway overpass, the sound of car engines forcing Gabby to shout her last words.

Pigeons sat huddled in the dark above, their heads nestled into their wings. Stone was overcome by the smell of exhaust fumes, and he was quiet.

"Well, I know you've been with shiksas, but what about the rest of the United Nations? Have you been with a black girl, Chinese, Mexican?"

For a moment Stone thought about Fairuza, her dark eyes, her skin that seemed electric to the touch. He would never tell Gabby about Fairuza. She was something to be erased and forgotten.

"No," Stone said, thinking Gabby would be his first Jew.

"Forget it. I'm just bugging you," she said, pulling him close, hip to hip, and kissed him softly on the lips. They were far enough from home now. Stone pulled her closer and emitted a small sigh into her ear, something so personal and private that Gabby responded by saying, "It's all right. Look, we all have pasts."

They walked on. "Listen, it's not easy being me."

"It's not easy for anyone," Stone said.

"Expectations," Gabby said. "So many expectations. I went to yeshiva, took care of the house, did the army. I'm supposed to be made of steel and silk like some ideological Frankenstein."

"You were in the army?"

"Believe it or not, I was a drill sergeant, a *mefakedet*."

"Were you a good shot?"

"I was expected to be the best."

"I understand expectations," Stone said. "Too well."

"Yeah, well I'm bad news. I make people angry. I disappoint them."

Stone thought that Gabby could have been talking about his own life, and he felt comforted.

"Are you talking about Dov?"

"Not just Dov."

They reached another iron overpass. The subway clattered noisily past, wheels *click-click-clicking* as they faded down the track.

The smell of salt air was strong now as they approached the ocean, and something in the brackish air made Stone feel sentimental, wistful; he desired Gabby in a way he had not desired anyone in a long time. He needed to do something to further bridge that gap of intimacy, something beyond the physical, stripped bare to the soul. Stone could only think to ask, "Hey. What's your middle name?"

A middle name was usually a guarded secret, and discovering that secret would open other doors that led deeper.

"Gavriella," she said. "Gabby comes from my middle name."

"Really," Stone said, realizing the absurdity of such a question on a second date. "What's your first name?"

"If I tell you, I'll have to kill you," Gabby said, aiming her fingers like a pistol.

"It's worth it. Shoot away."

"*Pow*," she said, and Stone clutched his heart.

"Geula Gavriella Grunhut. My parents are in love with the letter G."

Stone laughed. "It's a pretty name."

"How would you feel walking around with a name like 'Redemption' for the rest of your life? Like some sort of advertisement. Anyway, I think we should all get the name we deserve."

"I agree," Stone said, approaching the boardwalk. The ocean shimmered beyond.

"So, what's your middle name?"

"Guess."

"Is it Jewish?"

"Maybe."

"Give me a clue."

"Okay. Yes."

"Moses."

"No."

"Israel?"

"No."

"Come on," Gabby said, stamping her foot on the ground. "What is it?"

Stone mimed a zipper being zipped across his mouth.

"Okay. How about Methusaleh? Zerubavel? Nechemiah? Shemaryahu?"

"It's Ze'ev," Stone said finally. "But I never use it."

"Wolf," Gabby said. "Are you a wolf in sheep's clothing?"

"Ha-ha," Stone said.

"It's a nice name. Like Jabotinsky."

"Oh, he was a fascist," Stone said. "Who would want to be named after someone who admired Mussolini?"

"And Matthew," Gabby said. "All Matthews are perfect?"

They stood in the dark of the boardwalk in silence. Russian couples strolled past, their sonorous words floating on the air like bubbles. Stone took a deep breath of the revitalizing ocean air. He felt clean and pure and despite his exhaustion from walking, he felt his energy return in a burst. Gabby shuffled her feet playfully over the crackling sand scattered about on the deck. The bright lights of the Wonder Wheel beckoned.

"Should we?" Stone asked.

Coney Island glittered like cheap jewelry in the distance and Stone wanted to run there with Gabby and lose himself in laughter and joy and silliness.

"I should get home," Gabby said. "My aunt probably thinks I'm out robbing banks."

They found a taxi on Surf Avenue that smelled like rancid cooking oil and raced down Ocean Parkway with the windows rolled down. On her aunt's porch, Gabby thanked Stone for a fun walk, and he leaned in to kiss her. She backed away. "My aunt has more eyes than the Angel of Death. She's probably watching us now."

Stone could not hide his disappointment.

"Anyway," she added, "my breath smells like onions."

"That's okay," Stone said.

They were silent for a moment. A moth flickered about beneath the porch light.

"Do you have plans for the break fast?"

"No," Stone said.

"See you then for the break fast?"

"Do I have to eat?" Stone prodded. He did not want the night to end.

"Gabby!" Esther called from inside. "You're letting bugs in."

"I gotta go," Gabby said, and disappeared inside, leaving Stone alone on the porch with the tangled moths flickering in the light.

✎ 16 ✎

Abi had set up one of her canvases in the center of the living room, a pencil sketch of Pinky filled in here and there in dull blacks and grays. The unread Sunday *New York Times* was spread out beneath, and a pair of halogen lamps cast their white light on the new canvas.

Stone found her on the floor of his bedroom, beside a tall pile of books.

"What are you doing?"

"You have some really interesting books here. *The Artists of Terezin*. It's amazing that people could create art so full of life when they were so close to death."

"Put that down."

"What?" Abi said, looking up. She wore a pair of black thick-framed oval-shaped glasses. "Oh, I'm sorry," she said absently. "I thought you'd be back sooner."

His father's judge's robe hung on a wire hanger on the back of his open closet door. Smears of Abi's oil paint remained on the fabric.

"What are you looking for?"

"Nothing. I just got tired of waiting for you," she said picking up another book.

"Stop it. They are my books. Put it down."

She put the book down.

"I saw you today. With Zohar."

"Zohar?" she said. "What is that supposed to mean?"

Her eyebrows crinkled with confusion. She took off her reading glasses. Her eyes said nothing.

"Don't lie to me. I saw you at The Long Dream, talking to Zohar. I saw it with my own eyes."

"Who is Zohar? What are you talking about? I don't know anyone named Zohar. So just relax. I was there with an art dealer, Miloscz. An old friend."

Stone went cold. How could she lie to his face like that? Her gaze rested on one of his father's books, an old yellowing hardcover. Stone leapt over and picked it up.

"Did he tell you to look in here for something?"

"I don't know what you're talking about."

"Zohar sent you to spy on me."

"Enough with Zohar already. You're tired, Matthew. You need sleep."

"Why? So you can look through all my father's books and find . . . whatever you're looking for?"

"I'm not looking for anything," she said, pulling herself to her feet. "I think you should see a doctor."

"I have," Stone said. He let out a dull cry of raw emotion, something short of a scream.

"What's his number? I'm calling him right now."

"This is my room. These are my books."

"Matthew. They are only books."

"They were my father's books."

"Is this what it is all about?"

"You degrade his memory. He wouldn't want you touching his books. He left them for me."

"Quiet," Abi said. "You're shouting."

"What did Zohar tell you?"

"Nothing."

"So it was him."

"No, no. I've never heard of Zohar. Matthew, you've got to believe me. I don't know anything."

She moved forward in a gesture that Stone knew meant she wanted to comfort him.

"Get away," he said, pushing her back.

Abi stood firm. Her eyes smoldered. She picked up a well-worn paperback and slapped her hand against it. "This is just junk, Matthew, detritus from a misguided life. It's all garbage."

"No it's not. I'm beginning to understand him at last."

"There's nothing worth understanding. Sure, he was sophistication and veneer on the outside, but he was pathological, bloodthirsty, just like Julius."

"Give me that back," he said, grabbing for the paperback in her hand. She was quick, and pulled it away. Stone felt his anger surge.

The book was called *Hidden Worlds: Gematria and Its Secrets.* "What can you learn from this mystical mumbo jumbo? That the world is going to end on such and such a date or that two plus two is actually five? It's garbage, Matthew."

He grabbed the book from her hand. She was breathing heavily now, her passion flared, she hated the Judge that much.

"You'd just throw all this away."

"Yes. I would. In a second. It's time to move on, you have a whole life to live."

"This is my life."

"Oh, Matthew. If you must, then honor your father. But don't mistake that honor for becoming your father."

"I want you out of my apartment."

"What?"

"Get out. Now."

"Matthew. You don't understand. You're sick. You need someone to look after you."

"For the first time in a long time I don't feel sick. When I read these books I feel like I'm getting stronger all the time."

"You're sick. You're depressed."

"You need me to be weak so you can save me and bury your guilt."

"Maybe you're right," she cried.

"I'll call you a car service."

"No, Matthew."

They heard the heavy steel door swing open and Pinky's feet on the wooden floors. He must have been regarding the painting of him, because he was silent for a moment, then called out "What's up?"

Stone felt a measure of relief at the interruption; the exchange with his mother left him feeling dirty, debased. Abi followed Stone into the living room. Pinky's shirt was open at the front and he breathed heavily as if he had been running. He tossed Stone two pairs of stereo headphones, still in their factory wrapping.

"A gift," he laughed. "One for each head."

Stone and Abi were silent.

"What's the matter?"

"My son's kicking me out," Abi said after a moment.

"What?" Pinky said, turning to Stone. "You're joking, right?"

"No," Abi said. "He thinks I'm spying on him."

"Enough," Stone said.

"Let me get this straight. You don't want your mom to stay here because, because what?"

"Stay out of this."

"No. I'm not going to stay out of this while you disrespect your mother."

He had moved around behind Abi and had placed his hand lightly on her hip. Stone understood that his mother was still an object of sexual desire, despite the creases in her skin, the gray in her hair.

"Anyway," Pinky said, "my name is on the lease, so what I say goes. Got it?"

"Michael, you don't have to," Abi said.

"What do you want from me?" Stone said. "I don't need you. It's too late."

Pinky still held Abi by the waist. She did not try to turn away.

"Matthew. You need help."

Stone did not answer right away.

"What do you think you can do for me?"

Abi's eyes filled with tears. "I don't know."

"This is all about you," Stone said, bending to pick up the phone. "I'm calling you a car."

Pinky grabbed the receiver from Stone's hand. "Put it down," he said, though he held it now.

"Okay, you don't want your mom to stay with you. But that's your opinion, your decision. But, I live here too and I say if she wants to stay, she can stay in my room. I'll stay on the couch."

"What?" Stone cried. "Are you crazy?"

"She's not moving in, right?"

"Just a few more days," Abi said.

"Oh, this is crazy," Stone said.

"I'll make it up to you. Just give me a chance."

"I've given you a chance. And you chose Zohar."

"Who's Zohar?" Pinky asked.

"Nobody," they both answered.

"Matthew, please."

"What can I say – it's his choice," Stone said, feeling betrayed, impotent, child-like. He burned with anger. He wanted to hurt Pinky, but did not know how.

"Relax, buddy. It's your mom."

"Shut up," Stone said.

"Hey, give me a few minutes to clean up my room for you. Why don't you go out and grab a drink?"

"Thank you, Michael. You know what, I'll stay with friends in Manhattan tonight and come back in the morning."

Pinky bounded into his room calling Stone after him.

Abi brushed the hair from her face and stood before Stone. He brooded silently with arms crossed.

"What have you got to say?"

"Nothing," she said, swallowing hard.

"Then get out."

"Let's get started," Pinky called from his room. "Come on."

"Goodnight," Abi said.

"Goodbye," Stone replied.

Pinky's bedroom was even larger than Stone's with the same high ceilings and tall windows. He had a wooden loft built into the corner, under which he stored his "merchandise." A pair of stained futons lay supine on the floor, sunken in the middle from the dead weight of sleep. Newspapers, magazines, socks, dirty T-shirts, mugs, plates, peanut shells, coffee grounds, computer parts, nails and screws were scattered about. Stone noticed there was not a single book in his room. Boxes were piled haphazardly, and they crowded the center of the room – it had been a busy month for Pinky.

"Help me move this shit."

Pinky pushed a stack of boxes out of the way; the top box toppled to the ground and smashed.

"Shit."

"How many VCRs do you need?"

"I don't keep them, I sell them, buttfuck."

Stone opened his mouth to reprimand Pinky about letting his mother stay, but Pinky cut him off, "Shut up, shut up, shut up, shut up."

Stone dragged boxes to the corner with a sense of resignation and doom. Now, Stone realized, he truly hated his mother; there was nothing noble or magnanimous about her; her ambition, her desire to absolve herself had taken over every human instinct. Stone leaned over and dragged a large box. It was larger than the other boxes and packed tightly with the care Stone imagined one would give to precious cargo.

"What are you doing?"

"I'm opening it."

"Why?"

"Because," Stone said defiantly. He tore away at the crates with a rusted hammer, and noticed on the packaging, the unmistakable stencil print of Hebrew lettering.

"What are you, stealing Torahs now?"

"What the fuck are you talking about," Pinky said.

"Look."

"I don't know what this is."

"Well, how did you get it?"

"The same way I got all this stuff. Tips. I work hard, I take a little something for myself."

"Let's open it," Stone said. "Maybe it's kosher wine."

"Maybe you're kosher wine," Pinky said, pushing Stone back from the box and hunching low to see it. He stared at it in silence for a moment, as if trying to place a vaguely familiar face. He pulled back the heavy cardboard and rummaged through package after package of bath salts from the Dead Sea. He reached down and found something hard.

"What is this?" Pinky said, clearing away the packages of salt. He pulled out a small steel drum.

"Open it."

Inside they found a white powdery material, with a slight acrid smell.

"Drugs?" Stone said.

Pinky had already dipped his finger into the powder and was tasting it. "Pthew," he spat. "That's not drugs. It some kind explosive or something."

Stone felt like he was suffocating. "Where did you get it? You can't keep this stuff lying around. This isn't like stealing a black and white television. Somebody's going to be looking for this."

"No shit," Pinky screamed. "No shit!" And for the first time since high school, Stone saw Pinky lose his composure. He paced back and forth across the floor. The canister sat open before Stone. He had the urge to dip his hand into the canister. Such power, Stone thought.

"Shit, shit, shit, shit, shit, shit, shit. What do we do? What do we do? I'm in deep shit. What do we do?"

"You're on your own," Stone said.

"No. You've got to help me. Please," Pinky pleaded. "Please." His voice cracked.

"Well, you've got to return it."

"Yes," Pinky said. "Yes. Say it was all a big mistake. I didn't mean to."

"Do you know who you stole it from?"

"You've got to come with me. I can't go alone. Just come with me. I'll do all the talking."

"I don't want to get mixed up in your trouble."

Stone heard footsteps above the ceiling, a chair being dragged.

"Come on."

"Do you know who took my father's boxes?"

"Oh, shit."

"Do you?"

"I'm in deep shit."

"Is that a yes or do you want to go alone?"

"Okay. Okay, I know who took the boxes. I brought you out to the bar, got you drunk and left the door unlocked, okay? But they're back now, just like they said, no harm done, right?"

"Did they pay you?"

"Yes."

"It's mine," Stone said.

"Fine. Now are we going?"

They passed under the BQE, Pinky struggling with the crates. Stone insisted he carry the packages of mineral salt as well, since they had been stolen along with the canisters. The air was cool, but Stone felt warm. He felt a determination inside him he had not felt before, and though he didn't know what might happen, he was overcome with expectation. Pinky walked in silence with an even step, turning around periodically to make sure that Stone was still behind him. They passed the Catbird Seat and turned right at the warehouse, descending a gradual sloping ramp, stopping before a small door that faced the haunted Navy Yard. Black clouds hung low in the sky obliterating Manhattan from view. Pinky rapped on the door with the back of his hand. A tug moaned rudely out in the river.

"Are you sure this is the right place?"

"Of course it is, asshole."

After a moment they heard the lock being unlatched from the inside, steel sliding against steel. Sweat ran down the back of Pinky's neck. The door opened, and Moshe, ripe from the effort of exertion, led them in stilted silence to a small anteroom where Gabby's cousin Yossi sat with three or four other young men, hunched intensely around a small table. They looked up in anticipation as Pinky approached them. He cradled the boxes in his arms and swayed slightly. It was as cold as a refrigerator in the room. Maps plastered the walls; tiny colored pushpins marking points like a constellation of stars. A figure stepped out of the shadows and said, "Thank you for bringing him, Matthew."

Stone's eyes adjusted to the murky light, and a familiar-looking man stood before him.

"You've done a *mitzvah*," he said. "Now go home and get some sleep."

"But—" Pinky said.

"Quiet, *gonif*," one of the men at the end of the table said.

Pinky placed the box on the floor and stepped forward. "It, it was a mistake. I didn't know. I'm sorry."

"Enough, *gonif*."

"Matthew," the man said stepping forward and extending his hand to shake. "Thank you, Matthew. Good night."

The hand was cool and smooth. The man smiled arrogantly and winked. It was Isaac Brilliant, the yeshiva student who had been on trial for murder after the Court Street Riot. He held Stone's hand for an uncomfortably long time and seemed to be searching for something in Stone's eyes, as if the Judge who had saved him resided somewhere behind.

"It was a mistake," Pinky wailed. "I didn't mean nothing."

Brilliant put his hand on Stone's shoulder to lead him out.

"Matty, do something," Pinky called. "Do something!"

Brilliant put a finger to Stone's lip, but he hadn't been planning on saying anything for a cool sense of calm had descended on him, like that which he felt when saying the *Kaddish*, he realized that he had ignored the ruthless whispers of his blood for a long time, and it had cost him his health, his vitality, and his desire to live. He felt the desire to laugh and call out in triumph, "*Heshbon nefesh* – Accounting of the soul."

"Matty, please, please," Pinky called.

Brilliant raised his voice like a seasoned orator and called out as he led Stone from the room, "When a man commits the same offense twice, it seems to him that it has become permissible. But it is a worse sin to steal from man than from God."

Stone could hear Pinky crying in the other room, begging, "I'll make it up to you. I'll pay you back for what I took. Matty, help!"

As Stone was led to the steel door by Brilliant, he heard someone say, "A dead man owes nothing to anyone."

"Thank you again, Matthew," Brilliant said, unlatching the door. "See you in the morning for *Kaddish*." And he kissed Stone softly on the cheek.

❧ 17 ❧

It had rained overnight. The late summer storm had filled the gutters with refuse and waste. Candy wrappers, newspapers, cigarette packs, used condoms lay dispirited on the sides of the road, waterlogged and pale. The smell of human compost, dog shit and birdlime, revivified by the storm, filled the air. It seemed to Stone that giant ferns, their razor-sharp fanlike fronds, reaching aggressively over the top of the wire fence of the vacant lot, had grown overnight – a verdant green jungle amidst the blighted landscape. A car sizzled passed on the slick road, sounding like bacon frying on a greased skillet. Pinky had not returned to the apartment, and Stone had slept well. The sky was gray and the air was cool, a sharp hint of autumn pricking against his exposed skin.

Stone was not surprised when Zohar appeared from beneath the overpass of the BQE. His suit was rumpled and looked as if he had slept in it.

"Good morning," Zohar said. "I've got your body recorder." He held a small package in his hand and smiled reassuringly.

Stone did not respond.

"What's the matter?" Zohar said.

"I'm going to say *Kaddish* for my father."

"Matthew, a major terrorist attack is going to occur here in New York."

"How do you know? How can you be so sure?"

"I have evidence."

"Then make an arrest and leave me alone."

"The evidence is incomplete."

"Your evidence, if you can call it that, points ultimately to my father. And you want me to wear a wire and testify before some grand jury in open court in defiance of my own blood?"

"Matthew, what happened? What did they say to you?"

"I checked you out yesterday afternoon, after you dropped me off. They have more than just porn on library computers."

Zohar crossed his arms.

"Golden Gloves boxer," Stone said. "15-3 record. Good, but not good enough," he taunted.

"Good for you, Matthew."

A passing car hit a deep pothole, its hubcap spinning off and rolling to Zohar's feet. He picked it up and tossed it aside.

"Full scholarship to NYU, law degree before training at the Academy at Quantico, Virginia where you finished near the top of your class. Near," Stone said.

"Matthew, enough. Are you going to wear the recorder?"

Stone noticed that Zohar had the piercing eyes of a fanatic, the dogged tenacity of a man who needed to succeed to justify his existence.

"I'm not finished."

Zohar crossed his arms.

"You were a member of the Joint Terrorism Task Force in New York when the World Trade Center was bombed by Muslim extremists. Correct?"

"Yes, Matthew," Zohar said flatly.

"Are you sure? Because I found an article in a local Jewish newspaper dating from several months after the bombing in which they interviewed you and you said that though it seemed to be the work of Muslim extremists, you believe that certain Jewish groups were planning parallel attacks meant to be obscured by the Muslim ones."

Stone pulled a folded piece of paper out of his pocket and read:

"Q: Are you saying that Jews were behind the bombing of the Towers?"

"A: I'm saying that I won't rule anything out and we can't lose sight of the fact that underground Jewish terrorist organizations are operating in America."

Stone looked up. He could not read Zohar's face.

"You said that," Stone said, taking a breath.

"Yes."

"What are you, some kind of self-loathing anti-Semite?"

"Have you ever heard the saying, 'No good work goes unpunished?' Going back to Hoover, the FBI is very uncomfortable with its agents thinking too far out of the box. An agent is supposed to think by the book."

"You were fired."

"A minor indiscretion. I wasn't even censured. I was just transferred to headquarters in Washington. Then to Salt Lake City of all places."

"You deserved it."

"I'm a good agent, Matthew. I was the one who solved the case of the Mormon church bombings. It was a clan of polygamists who had broken away from the church and were striking out at the elders. I need to be at the center of the storm so they moved me back to New York."

"The Anti-Defamation League has a file on you."

"Quite the scholar, Matthew."

"They questioned you, asking you to prove your claim that organized Jewish terror groups were operating on a large-scale in America, and you said you would not compromise your sources. What sources?" Stone shouted. "Do you consider me a source?"

"Jews are not exempt simply because they are Jews."

"What's next?" Stone said. "Are you going to prove that Manhattan housewives are involved in the blood libel?"

Zohar looked impatiently at his watch. "The service has started."

"You need me to be an informant."

"Semantics, Matthew. I say hero."

"Why should I believe in you?"

"Just appeal to your sense of reason."

Stone was silent a moment. He recalled the DA's visit to his house back in high school, the woman's long white neck, the flat persistent questions, almost robotic in their tenor, his ignorance. And he remembered the Judge's fury, the anger and bitter disappointment. He would not make that mistake again.

"I can't wear a wire," Stone said.

They stood in silence as a phalanx of taxis whooshed past. Zohar tilted his neck again. "Sore?" Stone asked.

"It acts up sometimes."

"I have to go say *Kaddish*. I'm late."

"Listen, Matthew. If it is money you're concerned with, I can see about a small fee for your services. $5,000 for starters?"

"I can't wear a wire," Stone said, and he left Zohar standing on the damp cement, kicking a broken bottle into the street.

Stone rang the bell and he was buzzed in. The air was cooler inside than out, and he shivered slightly upon entering. The stairway before him wound its way up to the synagogue; another dark staircase, lit only by a dim bare bulb led downwards to the basement where he had been with Pinky the night before.

Moshe met him at the doorway and patted him down. His hands were rough and as they ran up and down the inside of his thighs, Stone realized that he was lucky that he had not taken the wire to pacify Zohar.

The service was already underway, and about two dozen men swayed in silent prayer. Stone took his place and picked up a prayer book. He recognized several of the men from last time and a few man turned their heads and nodded silently at Stone. The prayers continued in Hebrew and Stone was quickly lost. He felt moisture at his ear, a humid breath, hot, gamey, whispering.

"Excuse me," Stone said, loud enough that a man in front of him wearing a white knitted *kippah* spun his head around so that his *kippah* flipped on its side, clinging to his head by a small silver clip. The man at Stone's ear was slim and tall, his lips were thick and his eyes, large and watery.

"Matthew Stone?"

"Yes."

The man took Stone's hand and shook it in his, and then shuffled down the aisle to return to his prayers.

Before Stone had a chance to gather himself, another man appeared at his ear. Stone recognized him from the night before in the basement. His pale skin showed acne scars and uneven patches of sparse black hair sprouting from his Adam's apple and cheeks.

"*Kol ha kavod*," the man whispered, squeezed Stone's elbow and returned to his prayers.

Stone followed in the prayer book as best he could and muttered the liturgy under his breath. The words meant nothing to him, but his voice, joined with the voices of the others, rose in confidence as he read. He stood to recite the Mourner's *Kaddish*, as a whispering filled his head. But no one was at his ear this time. It was the voices of the dead calling to him. The Judge was there and so was Pinky and the voices of others gone from this world. He heard Pinky call out to him to remember him while he recited *Kaddish*. Even with his eyes closed the room was filled with brightness, sharp unbearable white, and the Judge, his voice strong and clear, rose above that of Pinky's, "You owe nothing to that *gonif* motherfucker."

Stone suddenly stirred as if he had been woken from a dream and said aloud the name Walter Joseph Stone.

When the service was over, he returned home to find Abi's unfinished portrait of Pinky propped against the brick living-room wall. Pinky stared back from the canvas, his dark hooded eyes lowered to slits. He had been mugging for sure, but Stone saw in those eyes a humanity he had not seen in Pinky since they were children in the schoolyard.

Stone remembered the fear he had seen in those eyes the night before, something animal, beyond words or understanding. He had cried out for Stone's help and Matthew had turned his back. And staring into the face of the unfinished painting, with the tight ropes of muscle running up his neck, his gritted teeth, Stone briefly imagined Pinky's soul separating from his broken body, its gray tattered form taking flight, but no, he knew that Pinky was dead and that nothing would come of that, except perhaps for this painting, *Still Life with Street-Hood at the Dead End of the 20th Century.* Stone vomited and held it in his closed fist. He stumbled to the bathroom, closed the door, leaned over the bowl. He had led Pinky to his death, and strangely, he was glad of it.

The direct route to repentance lay beyond the synagogue now – in those pages. He realized that his guilt fell away as he came closer to his father. He wore the Judge's robe, draped lightly over his skin, and as he read, he felt the unusual sensation of channeling the very spirit of his father. The Judge had marked some books with a severe ferocity, underlining, circling, even rewriting phrases that displeased him. His marginal notes snaked down both sides of many pages, his spidery script screaming above the typeset text. Stone read with a burning stomach, his mind purged. He discovered, as he read, that his father had been tracking the pattern of victimization that brought tragedy and ruin to the Jews throughout their tortured history. And as he read, he realized that his father was prescribing solutions posthumously to the tragic events that had already occurred; a savior out of step and out of time.

His father had found a way to avert the Exile; the last stand at Masada would never have occurred; Bar Kochba's rebellion would have succeeded; the Spanish Inquisition; Chmielnitzky; the pogroms beyond the Pale; the Holocaust especially, occurring as it did right in the middle of modern 20th-century Europe; all could have been avoided. The Jews may have been minorities, but they were large minorities with untapped potential, unharnessed power spent waiting for the Messiah to save them.

The Judge had reserved unusual scorn for the early Zionists who tried to compromise with the Arabs and with the British. In a book in which the essayist Ahad Ha'am had written that 19th-century Palestine was in fact not empty but populated with indigenous Arabs, the Judge had written in red "We Were the Victims." Beside a passage about Chaim Weizmann and his philosophy of havlaga or restraint against the British, the Judge had written one word, "Lapdog."

Stone discovered vociferous agreement with the words Yosef Weitz wrote in 1940, that there was no room in Palestine for both the Jews and the Arabs and that they should be transferred out of the country so that millions of Jews could be absorbed. There was similar agreement with the words of Menachem Begin and Ze'ev Jabotinsky.

When Stone stopped to rest his eyes, his thoughts drifted to Gabby. And with his heart racing in his chest from the thrill of reclaiming his father's thoughts, paired with the image of Gabby's curved form, he felt an incredible surge of sexual desire. Twice he picked up a telephone to dial her number. Stone loved Gabby, but at that moment among the books, empowered by the Judge's knowledge, he wanted her to be his whore, he wanted her to do things to him that she had never done before. But he knew that he loved her because she was different from the other women he had known, and that her liberation only went so far, but paradoxically that made him want to do those things to her even more.

Abi appeared in Stone's doorframe; he had not heard her come in.

"Hi," she said. "You don't look well."

Abi was dressed all in black – dull leather shoes with thick soles, form-fitting pants, a light sweater, even her black hair was held back with a black elastic. But she was not in mourning, she wore the costume of the Manhattanite, the artist eschewing color only when it came to their own lives. Stone thought of the painting, the child in Pinky's gangster eyes.

"Get rid of the painting."

"What?" she said. "I want Michael to see it."

"He's gone."

"He'll see it later. I'm not done yet."

Stone felt a band of irritation tighten around his neck. "You're invading my life."

"No, Matthew."

"I don't want you here. Just leave me alone so I can live my life."

Abi seemed to hear him. She nodded her head. "My friend Judy, I stayed at her loft, she agrees. Yes, it's going to be hard to re-form a relationship with you after all this time, but I can't force it or I risk driving you away. Is that it? Am I driving you away?"

Stone was silent. The books called to him, his father whispering from the pages.

"Because I want to have a relationship with you, an adult relationship, based on respect. And I would never intrude."

"Mom," Stone said. "That's it."

"I'm embarrassed," she said, twisting her mouth. "All these years I've thought about how I could make it up to you, be a good mother, and I guess I lost sight of the fact that you are an independent human being. You have to let me into your life."

Stone was silent.

"Can we try?"

"When are you leaving?"

"Let me finish the painting."

"I'm going out," he said, gathering up a pile of books in his hands.

His watch showed 3:30 when he arrived at the Brooklyn Heights Promenade. Glowing gray clouds hung low in the sky, glimmering with moisture; the tops of Manhattan's skyscrapers lost within their vaporous shroud. People milled about on the deck of the promenade, talking, laughing, taking in the view of Manhattan and the harbor. Stone felt as if he were winding his way through a bed of tombstones, careful not to touch anyone in the crowd as he passed. He carried three of his father's books under his arm and was lucky to find a spot on a bench with a view of the ships moving below. He took a breath of the thick air and opened one of the books near the middle. After a few minutes of feverish reading, he heard his name being called from behind. "Matty, is that you?"

Stone ignored the beckoning voice, as he was just entering the Old City of Jerusalem in June 1967 with Yitzhak Rabin and Moshe Dayan leading the way through the narrow streets.

"Matt Stone?"

A hand fell lightly on his shoulder and Stone looked up to see Mickey Zin smiling over him. Stone had not seen him since his wedding three years earlier and had been embarrassed that he'd never bought him a gift.

"Mickey, how are you?"

Mickey's sharp face had filled out. He looked bloated. He wore a light beige windbreaker over a sport shirt and a pair of beige chinos, and penny loafers. "I'm great. Married life is married life." He blinked his eyes rapidly as he spoke as if there were some deep inner irritation he was trying to shake.

"Hey, I heard your father died. I'm sorry. You all right?"

"It's hard," Stone said.

Mickey sat down beside Stone and stared blankly into the distance. "You weren't that close with him, were you?"

"We became closer towards the end," Stone said, realizing that he knew his father better now that he was dead. A giant steamer moved slowly out in the distance. Gulls circled in the sky above.

"I'm glad," Mickey said. They sat in silence for a minute. His expression hinted there was something on his mind. Finally he said, "How's your mother? Ever hear from her?"

"She died."

"What?" Mickey said, his voice cracking. "When?"

Stone was amazed at how upset Mickey looked. His eyes were filled with tears. He felt a strange desire to comfort Mickey, but realized he was weeping over a mirage.

"Not long ago."

"Oh my God. And you never got to see her again."

"We spoke," Stone said.

"It's terrible, terrible. It's a tragedy. I just lost my grandfather and, God forbid – at least I still have both parents."

"You're very lucky," Stone said.

"I am lucky," Mickey said, brightening. "I have a loving wife, a healthy child, a job I love." Mickey paused, embarrassed, "but this is not about me. It must be hard with the High Holidays and all."

"Maybe my penitence is that I should be alone."

"Come on, Matty. Don't give me that. No one should be alone. Hey, we would have you over for the break fast, but we're going to Rachel's parents in Great Neck. We'd love to have you over for dinner sometime. Is there anything you don't eat?"

The books in his lap pressed hard against his thighs, and Stone grew impatient. A breeze blew open the paperback entitled *Hidden Worlds*. The word BINGO was written in blue ink in his father's careful hand on the inside cover.

"Listen, Rachel and I are flying to Israel next Tuesday. We're just going for a week. We'd love to have you over for dinner when we get back."

"All right," Stone said.

Mickey pulled a scrap of paper from his wallet and scratched out his phone number.

"Are you staying in Brooklyn for good?"

Stone ran his fingers over the word BINGO.

"It's nice to see you," Mickey said, slapping the books on Stone's lap, so the paperback shut. He grabbed Stone by the sleeve and pulled him close. Mickey smelled of laundry soap and breath mints.

Why would the Judge write the word BINGO inside a book on Gematria?

It started to rain softly, a light atomized mist, lending a greenish underwater feel to the promenade. The smell of motor oil and gas fumes from the highway stung Stone's nostrils. He felt a nervous burst of tension behind him, as he realized that people were pulling on jackets and hurrying to gather their things before the rain began in earnest. He slipped the books under his shirt, the paperback cool against his hard-beating heart.

"Listen, I should head out," Mickey said. A drop of rain rested on his eyelash like a shred of diamond.

"All right," Stone said.

"Call me," Mickey said. He stood up and extended his hand to shake, but then thought better of the gesture and leaned in to hug Stone.

"We'll eat. We'll talk."

"Okay."

"Great to see you again."

⊙⊱⊰⊙

Stone drove towards the Oasis Bingo Hall at the old Palatial Theater. He didn't quite know what he was looking for, but he felt that somehow, in some way, the account numbers were connected to the Bingo Hall.

He rapped on the door with his knuckles and after a moment the Cossack with the missile-shaped head opened up. He looked as if he had just been roused from a deep sleep. Surprisingly, he recognized Stone from his previous visit.

"Your friend no come work. I have to stay in this fucking place." He spoke with a thick Russian accent. "Tell your friend he's fucking shit of a fucking mother." The Russian's blue eyes were bloodshot, the whites almost entirely red.

"I'm just here to play," Stone said.

The Russian stepped aside, his barrel chest as wide and broad as the hood of a Cadillac. "Please, play then."

"Thank you," Stone said.

"Yes. Thank me."

Stone purchased ten cards at the counter, chips, a dauber and a small green-haired troll for good luck. He entered the dim auditorium and smelled what he could only describe as desperation. Women mostly, searched their cards with a frantic jerking of the head, placing chips here and there, or marking their cards with the colored daubers.

The caller this time was a woman in her 70s with a thick helmet of purple-rinsed hair. She wore large rounded glasses and from the distance of mid auditorium where Stone took a seat, he could tell her fingernails were at least two inches long. She was fast, with her low cancerous voice, wrecked from countless cigarettes, calling, "Cup of Tea, Debbie Mc-Gee; 23, The Lord's my Shepherd; Droopy Drawers, all the Fours—"

Stone spread the cards in front of him knowing now with absolute certainty that he was not here to play. He looked behind him to the dark overhang of the balcony, but he saw nothing, no shifting shapes, no glinting glasses, no hint of movement in the shadows. Someone to Stone's right called out "Bingo!" and a sigh went up from the crowd, followed by a heavy dragging of chairs.

Seligman had been there, but now he was gone. He felt closer than ever before to solving the riddle of the missing account numbers, and he had half-hoped that Seligman, his father's emissary, would be there in the darkness of the balcony to receive them. Stone knew he was close and a vein pulsed in his head.

"All right, ladies. Eyes down."

The ten cards spread in front of him encroached on his neighbor's space, a small, pale housewife, with thin straight, formless hair. She pushed aside the offending cards without even turning her attention toward Stone. But the cards were as mysterious to Stone as the crazy calls of the purple-haired woman. "Devil's Number," she called, followed by, "Royal Salute; Christmas Cake; Heinz 57, All the Beans; 76 Trombones," in quick succession.

The Judge had meant something when he had cryptically written Bingo in the front of the paperback on Gematria, the Hebrew numerology of the Kabbalah. He knew with absolute certainty that his father had written this for him to discover, a riddle to be solved, one final hurdle that could vindicate him in the Judge's eyes forever.

"Monkey's Cousin," the caller coughed into the microphone.

Perhaps there was some pattern encrypted into the Bingo cards, some slight puzzle that hid the account numbers. It was so simple that Stone nearly laughed out loud.

"Jump and Jive, 35."

Stone noticed that all the cards showed 15 or less in the B column and 30 or less in the I column, 45 or less in the N column, 60 or less in the G column and 75 or less in the O column. There was a pattern for sure, but this was not his father's doing. Stone discovered, as a wash of red-faced shame dulled his excitement, that the very nature of Bingo required the numbers to be organized in such a fashion.

"Queen Bee," the woman called.

Only three of the cards had a seven in the first column, two had 15s, four had threes and four had 14s. But, there was not enough to find a pattern. Stone moved through the other columns, working through I, N, G, O, working his brain in a way he had not done since 12th-grade calculus.

"Valentines Day," the caller called, and Stone thought he heard a note of flirtation in her voice.

The account numbers lay in Bingo. Stone was more sure of it the harder he tried, and he briefly thought of a short parable by Franz Kafka, that he had always read as emblematic of his relationship with his father.

In "Before the Law," a man spent his entire life trying to enter a door to the Law, but the doorman would never allow him entry. Other, more imposing doors and doormen lay beyond, but the man was never able to enter even the first door to the antechamber of the Law. Finally at the end of his life, the man says to the doorkeeper that surely others must want to reach the Law, so why has only he come begging to be let in? The doorkeeper responded that no one else could ever be let in because the door was made just for him. And he closed the door forever.

Stone knew that the door to the account numbers was waiting just for him and that if he could only find them he would stand before the Law, the Judge, bathed at last in his Heavenly light.

ᴏ 18 ᴏ

Dr. Cohen was seated at the foot of the table opposite Dovid Grunhut, their voices raised in hot debate. The aged doctor had risen out of his chair and his pants leg had slid up revealing a network of black varicose veins.

"What kind of beast walks into a hotel banquet hall, full of people, strapped with explosives and nails and detonates himself?"

"An animal," Dovid said.

"No animal could do this. Tables laid out for the Yom Kippur break fast; a massacre."

"Then tell me, Irving."

"Some *thing* that hates Jews more than it loves life."

A radio played loudly in the kitchen, the Hebrew voice of the announcer speaking hurriedly. Stone could make out the word Netanya, a city by the sea between Tel Aviv and Haifa.

"Every time there is a suicide bombing, I read the list of the dead and look for myself."

"Irving, you live in America."

"America," he laughed. "They will kill Jews wherever they can."

"I disagree," Dovid said. "It's about the Land. The Arabs are making a fallacious claim to the Land we were promised."

"It's not about the Land, it's about blood, Jewish blood." Dr. Cohen pulled his necktie loose and adjusted the clip on his *kippah*.

"Everything is about the Land," a youngish-looking man beside Yossi said. "Remove the Arabs from the Land, and you remove the problems."

Gabby interrupted, "Can you take a break from your hairsplitting for a moment? We have a guest."

Dovid raised his eyes to the entryway and noticed Stone standing awkwardly.

"Look at your history. It is nothing but a roll call of death. Killing Jews is the oldest sport known to man."

"Irving, relax. Yom Kippur is over and you have been written into the Book of Life for another year."

Stone apologized for being late, and Dr. Cohen crossed his arms on his chest.

"Now Yom Kippur is just another day," he added. His eyes were pink and raw.

Finally, Esther said, "You must be hungry," beckoning Stone to sit down opposite Gabby.

Stone was not hungry. He had spent the day immersed in the pages of his father's books and snacking on Pinky's leftover food in the refrigerator, and the talk of the suicide bombing and its subsequent carnage did little to stir his hunger.

Gabby smiled and winked at Stone, her eyes firmly fixed on him.

She looked beautiful, her hair pulled back tight from her forehead and tied at the back with a burgundy ribbon. She wore a black dress and her bronze neck shone in contrast to the dark fabric. The Roman glass pendant glowed like a beacon. She twisted her lips and rolled her eyes in Dr. Cohen's direction, then sipped her wine.

"Yes, the doctor is spoiling everyone's time, again," Dr. Cohen said bitterly, and reverted to Yiddish to continue his conversation with Dovid in relative private.

Stone realized that there were fewer guests present; a wooden leaf had been removed from the dining-room table, lending a more intimate atmosphere than there had been at the Rosh HaShana meal. Dov was absent of course, laid-up in the hospital. And Eli, who had known the Judge at Kiryat Arba all those years ago, was also absent. Two yeshiva boys to Yossi's left talked amongst themselves. Yossi sat beside Malka balancing a sleeping Arieh on his knee in a gesture that belied the brutality Stone had seen in his eyes the night he had brought Pinky to the basement of the warehouse. Stone realized with surprise that Seligman was missing from the table. He asked where he was and one of the yeshiva boys answered, "The Rav's gone back to the *Eretz*."

As Dr. Cohen spoke, reverting back to English, he seemed subconsciously to be referring to Stone, the only nonobservant Jew at the table. "When a Jew loses his faith, he is worse than a goy. If we're not careful we'll finish Hitler's job for him." His body tilted toward Stone when he lashed out at the assimilationists; he leaned away when he spoke of religious matters, as if guarding a secret. But Stone had been saying *Kaddish* for his father the last few mornings and had attended the Kol Nidre service the night before, and he had realized, as he recited the "*Al Chet*," prayer that acknowledges the mistakes Jews had made in the past year, that he was not alone in his guilt, and others had committed the sin of immorality, speaking harshly, wronging a friend, having a hard heart, desecrating God's name. Others had degraded parents, used vulgar speech, committed *lashon harah,* rushed headlong into evil. And as he read along to the Hebrew acrostic, matching up the words with their English equivalent on the opposite page, he saw that the worshippers beat their chests with closed fists as they recited the 44 statements of guilt. And seeing this communal act of repentance, Stone felt that he was part of a community of sinners, and he would be absolved.

"Did you have an easy fast?" Gabby asked Stone beneath the leaden words of Dr. Cohen. Stone shrugged his shoulders as if to say, I can't fool you.

"How many dead?" Stone asked, disturbed, the thought that a celebratory meal could end in the bloodshed of so many was difficult to grasp.

"Thirty-two, so far." Gabby furrowed her brow. "But life goes on, you steel yourself, or you go crazy."

"How was your fast?"

"My figure agrees, but my stomach gets cranky. Hey, I cut the bagels myself. You're going to want to try one."

"I detest any Jew who turns his back on his people," Dr. Cohen said, slamming his hand onto the table.

Stone nearly knocked over his glass of wine as he reached for a bagel. Gabby rolled her eyes.

"They're not turning their backs, Irving, out of malice. They're oblivious to history."

"If you forget your history, then you will die because of it. Do you think the anti-Semites forget their history?"

Stone saw in the sad faces of the sepia photographs that they had become part of that history.

"Esther, you know as well as I do what they can take from you."

"Irving, don't stir up the dead tonight," Dovid said.

"Kids," Esther said. "Why don't you finish dinner down-stairs? We'll call you when it's time to *bentsch*."

Gabby stood up as if she had been waiting to be freed, and stretched her arms skyward. She reminded him of a fountain about to spout water into the sky.

"Matthew, you haven't eaten anything yet," Esther said with concern in her voice. "You must be starving. Shmuel, help him get some food. He's shy."

A man with a large round face and a tentative beard, who had sat with his back turned awkwardly away from Stone, leaned over the table and haphazardly piled the cold runny salads onto his plastic plate with all the care of a san-itation worker. "Here," he said.

From the basement, they could hear Dr. Cohen's voice breaking above Dovid's jovial coaxing retort. "But the Holo-caust is never over, chapter and verse. That book remains open."

"He's going to drop dead up there," Yossi said, reclining into an orange armchair with a glass of wine. Malka had gone into a spare bedroom to feed Arieh and only Gabby and the yeshiva boys remained with Stone.

"It's been difficult for him since his wife died," Gabby said.

"Then he should go meet her," Yossi said.

"Not nice," Gabby said.

"When did she die?" Stone asked.

"Last spring."

"Springtime for Hitler," Yossi said.

"Shut up, all right?" Gabby snapped.

Her face was flushed from wine and Stone felt warmth in his belly. They sat side-by-side on a hard orange couch that had gone out of style 30 years earlier. The black and white tile floor was arranged in a checkerboard pattern, and the surrounding walls were covered with Judaica, artifacts from a lost world: menorahs, Russian samovars, twisting *shofars* that held the call of the desert within, spice boxes, bronze Sabbath lamps.

"Welcome to the Israel Museum," Gabby said, slipping off her shoes.

Yossi and his friends now stood smoking cigarettes quietly by the open screen door that led to a small backyard. They casually passed a bottle of wine amongst themselves and laughed as if amused by something that only they could see.

"The floor is cool. Feel it," Gabby said, sliding her sheer stockinged feet over the smooth tiles. "It feels like ice after standing in those shoes in *shul* all day."

The sight of her feet slipping across the floor stirred something in Stone.

"You don't need yours," she said.

Stone removed his shoes.

"Gabby!" One of Yossi's friends called from a cloud of gray smoke. "Tsk, tsk."

"Aw, close the door. You're letting in the bugs."

"Is that supposed to be an insult?"

"Maybe, Itzy. Now stop bugging me, you bug."

Itzy laughed and the screen door swung shut.

Their feet brushed up against each other briefly on the floor. "You know what?" Gabby said suddenly, turning her face to Stone. Her twisted incisor was prominent from this angle. "I've never invited anyone to have dinner with my family. I've never had a man to my house."

Stone smiled. "Really?"

"No, I'm making it up to seduce you. Matty, I'm serious. I can tell you anything."

"Go ahead."

"You first," she said.

"No, you."

"Don't you feel the same way?"

"I do."

"Then tell me something you never told anyone before."

The side of her left foot pressed against his. He felt her warmth passing into him. Stone took a long sip of wine.

"Something I'm ashamed of?"

"Just something that belongs only to you."

"I never thought I'd make it to my 30th birthday."

"And now?"

"Now, I don't feel that way."

Gabby smiled a bittersweet smile.

"Your turn," Stone said.

Gabby took a deep breath, her chest rising and falling with the effort. "I hope this isn't too forward, but I want to be with you." Gabby looked relieved, her big eyes taking in Stone and he saw himself reflected in her eyes, and saw that he was happy. The doorbell rang upstairs and Stone was suddenly aware that Dr. Cohen had been quiet for some time and that Dovid Grunhut had been singing in a deep hypnotic baritone.

"The door!" Yossi called from the backyard.

The bell rang again.

Stone heard chairs scraping against the floor and footsteps above, the door swinging open.

"*Oy-va-voy,*" Esther called. "It's Dov."

Gabby's face dropped, telegraphing a mixture of fear and joy and confusion. She had been elated after she had spoken her last words to Stone, basking in the silent afterglow, the wine buzzing through her veins. But now, as she stood up, Stone could tell that she was tense again.

Yossi ran past muttering, "Fuckin' A," under his breath. He was followed by his two friends.

Dov was surrounded by his coterie, the group that had held vigil at the hospital that day. The rat-faced one wore a Yankee hat jauntily tilted on his head and proclaimed, "*Hashem* has written him into the Book of Life." The others laughed and Stone noticed that the pear-shaped coward who had been afraid to call Dov's mother was staring at Gabby with intense watery eyes.

Dov stood in the middle of the circle propped up by an aluminum crutch. He wore a patch over his left eye and had salmon-colored burns on his face and neck. He had no eyebrow over his right eye. He wore a backwards Yankee cap on his head and a loose hooded sweatshirt from which his fringed *tzitzes* hung out raggedly. He looked tough and rakish and full of the unwarranted braggadocio of one who has survived a tragedy. "No hugs," he said, as Yossi pressed in. "The doc said my skin will come off like paper if you touch it."

"He's lucky he didn't burn his lungs."

"*Baruch Hashem,*" someone echoed.

"It's a miracle," Dovid Grunhut called from the table. "You see, Irving, Jews know how to do more than just die."

"They find who did this to you?" Itzy asked.

Stone felt himself being pushed into a corner. He was strangely excited by the burns on Dov's skin and wanted to get a better look.

"Where's Gab?" Dov said. "Where's Gab?"

"So impatient," she said, stepping past Itzy.

"I wanted to thank you for coming to see me. It meant a lot."

"Dov," she said. "Of course."

"When I was out, unconscious, I swear I could sense your presence over me. And it made me want to get better. But you only came to me once."

"Dov. Come on."

Stone pushed past Itzy and stepped before Dov, who was almost exactly the same height as Stone.

"Who's this?" Dov said.

"Matty, don't."

"Matty. Who's Matty?"

"All right, boys," Esther said. "It feels like Grand Central in here. Why don't you all go down the basement so we can finish dinner?"

Dov's friends had brought bottles of wine and vodka. And as they milled about in the low-ceilinged basement, bursting with tarnished artifacts of the past, drinking from clear bottles, Stone realized that this was Dov's going-away party. He was flying back to Israel the next day for rehabilitation. And, though he was confident that Dov could not drive a wedge between him and Gabby, he was relieved that he would be out of the picture.

"His nerves are messed up," a short Israeli named Boaz said, turning to Stone. "He's fucked up good."

"What happened?"

"Should've died," Boaz said. "Trust me. He should've."

Dov sat on the couch beside Gabby, surrounded by three of his friends. He looked unhappy, sulky, as if he were disappointed by his reception from her. Gabby seemed to be listening intently to one of the friends, her delicate neck craning slightly in his direction.

"She's very beautiful," Boaz said.

"She is," Stone said.

"You think he fucks her?" he said, pointing to Dov, slouched on the orange couch. The Israeli's eyes flashed with mischief. His hair was cropped short and a pale white scar ran along the side of his cheek.

"No. I don't think so," Stone said, after a moment.

Boaz handed him a bottle and Stone drank.

"Okay," he laughed. "You know he's engaged to her to be married?"

"Really," Stone said.

"Yeah, in his mind she already said yes and they are standing under the wedding canopy."

"What about her mind?"

"That's the problem. She has her own mind."

Stone noticed that Gabby had slipped her shoes back on and that Dov had moved closer on the couch.

"You want her," Boaz said, more a statement, than a question. "Don't bother. She's suicide. You might as well fall in love with the moon."

The basement was warm despite the fact that the door was open and a breeze blew in carrying gray filaments of cigarette smoke. Most of the others spoke of the bombing in Netanya and railed against the weakness of the Israeli government.

The pear-shaped one said something full of bravado that Stone could not make out.

"The only thing you will ever take is a piss," Boaz said in response.

The others laughed and tilted their bottles.

Stone noticed that Gabby was trying to gain his attention, her head craning around the shoulders of Dov's kneeling friend. Stone winked at her and she smiled.

Dov was silent and brooding, his right eye heavy-lidded and dark. His kneeling friend was talking up Dov's bravery, recounting an encounter he had had with an Arab in the Hebron casbah. ". . . and then he shoved him into a pile of tomatoes and made him apologize in Hebrew." The friend laughed, but Gabby did not.

As the alcohol rose from Stone's stomach to his brain, he sat on the hard arm of the couch to Gabby's immediate left and said, "What? And no medal to show for it?"

"What's that?" Dov said, staring straight ahead.

"I said—" Stone began.

"I heard what you said."

Gabby brushed her hand lightly along Stone's thigh, as a signal to lay off.

"What did you ever do?"

Stone tried to laugh it off.

"That's right, laugh."

"Dov. Come on," Gabby said.

"No, Gab, I'm not going to come on. The schmuck insulted me."

"Ooh," one of the friends said.

"Now, tell me, what did you ever do? Huh?" he said. "Huh, huh?"

Gabby grimaced in disgust. "What are you, a schoolboy? Dov, enough."

"Quiet, Gab," Dov said, pulling himself to his feet, swivelling the aluminum crutch to balance under one arm. The friends moved back and Stone felt a surge of cool air take their place.

"Have another drink, Dov," Yossi said.

"Yes, that's what he needs," Boaz said. "Another drink."

Stone felt Gabby pulling on his shirt as he stood up and met Dov face-to-face. He carried the medicinal smell of salve and unguent on his skin. Stone stood, arms crossed, facing down Dov, who adjusted the eyepatch and narrowed his good eye.

"You live in your father's shadow. Son of the Judge, big fuckin' deal. I knew him and you're nothing like the Judge. You're nothing."

Stone was about to respond when Dov said, "Pussy." A spray of saliva coated Stone's face.

"Aw, man," Yossi groaned.

"Dov? What did you do that for?" Gabby said, her voice rising. "Always the tough guy."

Stone felt the warm saliva on his face. He heard Esther's voice up above offering dessert to Dr. Cohen, and Arieh crying in an upstairs bedroom.

"Party's over," Yossi said. "Let's go."

"All right, Dov, are you happy?" Gabby said, taking Stone by the arm. "Let's get you cleaned up."

"Even now he doesn't do anything."

Stone heard Dov being lightly admonished by the pear-shaped friend. "Yeah, yeah, yeah," Dov said, "whatever."

Gabby locked the bathroom door, turned on the sink and wiped Stone's face off with a damp towel.

"I'm so sorry," she said. "He's always had such an intense temper."

Stone inhaled a hint of her breath. Her pursed lips looked like a pink bow. Gabby's forehead was creased with concern, her freckles glowed in the white light. "But I'm no saint either."

"He's jealous," Stone said.

"Well, you stole my heart."

She leaned in to kiss him, softly at first, and then hungrily as if she were biting into a ripe plum, her lips firm and pliant. Stone felt her tongue in his mouth and he closed his eyes and kissed her. She pulled him closer, her hands gripping his hips, pressing herself up and down against him. They breathed together, exhaling slowly.

"Wow," she said after a moment, turning off the running water. Her eyes sparkled as if lit from behind. Stone leaned in to kiss her again, but she placed her index finger over his lips. He playfully bit it.

Dov called, "Where's Gab?"

Someone responded, "Chill out."

They heard feet shuffling on the tile floor and the screen door swinging shut.

"I want to be alone with you," she said.

"So do I," Stone said.

"Take me to your place next time." He was still kissing her silver-ringed fingers.

"Do you know where I live?"

"I don't care where you live. I don't care if you live in a cardboard box," she said, pressing herself closer to Stone. Her voice shook as she spoke. "I don't care. I just want to be alone with you."

Someone was banging on the door with his fist. "Come on, we're going."

Dov was planted on the couch, arms crossed. His crutch lay at his feet and the pear-shaped friend tripped over it as he passed.

"Where's Malka?" Yossi said. "We're going. Someone tell her we're going."

Stone wondered if his flushed skin would give him away, but he realized that most of them had gone upstairs, had said their goodbyes and were waiting impatiently on the porch.

Dovid Grunhut called out, "Who's driving? Drive safe."

Gabby's dress was wrinkled at her hips where Stone had grabbed her; he'd felt her sheer panties pulling away from her skin as they had kissed, and he saw her hips shift as she walked, trying to work them back into place.

"Dov!" she said. "What are you doing?"

"How's your new love, huh? As good as the last one?"

Gabby's shoulders tensed. "Dov. Enough."

"What does it matter? I'm leaving tomorrow. You'll do what you want anyway."

"What do you want?" Gabby said.

"You know what I want."

The pear-shaped friend gestured toward Stone, beckoning him to go upstairs with him. Stone cleared his throat.

"What are you looking at?" Dov said. "This is none of your business."

"Matty, you'd better go. I have to talk to Dov."

"You don't have to do anything," Dov said, pulling himself to his feet. "I don't care if I ever see you again."

"Stop it, Dov, stop it. You're being childish."

"Get out," Dov shouted at Stone. "Okay?" He was crying and looked strangely awkward, his Adam's apple jutting out gawkily from his thin neck. "I wanted to speak to you, not your latest boyfriend."

"Gabby," Dovid Grunhut called, "is everything all right?"

"Yes," she called back, stamping a foot on the tile floor in frustration. "Matty. I'm sorry. You'd better go."

The doorbell rang and Stone could hear Boaz apologize through the screen door, "Sorry. I leaned on it."

Gabby's eyes were full of pain. She turned to Stone, her lips that he had just been kissing, downturned and thin. "I'll call you."

The pear-shaped friend ushered Stone out by the shoulders and he could make out Dov's pleading words as he climbed the stairs. "I'm not going to beg you. I'm not going to beg you—"

ᘒ 19 ᘒ

"He's at it again," Itzy said, kicking a flattened soda can into the street.

"Well, if it works," someone replied.

"Who said it works?" Yossi said. "Gabby's no fool."

"I say it works, or she wouldn't keep seeing him."

"Seeing him? She's tolerating him," Yossi said.

"Maybe she's sadistic," Boaz said. "Likes to see a man cry."

"What do you know?" Itzy said.

"Many, many women," Boaz said, lighting a cigarette. "More than you'll ever know."

They stood in front of the house. The air was cool and damp and Stone noticed that their faces were raw and pink like slabs of uncooked meat, with the exception of Boaz, whose skin was as slick as damp leather. The pear-shaped one's eyes were too small for his face; his beard barely covered his cheeks. "Gabby doesn't treat him right," he said, his chin doubling up as he cast his eyes downward.

"This is bullshit," Boaz said. "You sensitive Americans." He moved in and out of the streetlight, playfully jumping back and forth from darkness to light

Stone was overcome by weariness. The whole conversation sickened him. She had asked him to leave, not Dov, and she sat alone with him in the basement while he stood out in the cold. He was suddenly aware that all eyes were turned to him.

"What do you have to say about our friend's fit?"

"I don't like him very much."

"There's an honest man," Boaz said. "And, take note, women love honest men."

"Don't worry about him," Yossi said. "He's like that, but he's leaving tomorrow."

"He screws everything up," Itzy said in disgust. "What are we going to do now?"

It started to rain. From the darkness of the street Stone could see Dovid Grunhut through the illuminated window. He stood up from the table with a wide yawn. "Does anyone need a ride anywhere?"

Stone drove, crossing Avenue M, the alphabet unwinding itself in reverse order as the car passed under the sulfurous street lamps of Ocean Parkway. He mused upon the ugliness of Brooklyn in the rain, its low brick buildings squat, mundane, dingy, steam rising from their roofs. This was the same street that stirred such hopeful feelings within him as he walked it with Gabby earlier that week.

"Go," Itzy shouted with irritation from the back seat. "It's green."

Stone opened his eyes and through the swiping windshield wiper he could see the tail lights of Yossi's car fade into the darkness.

"*Boker tov*," Boaz said. "Wake up."

"What's the matter?" Itzy said.

"He's just sleeping," Boaz said.

"I'm fine," Stone said, pressing his foot to the accelerator. "Where are we going?"

"Just drive," Boaz said, flipping on the radio.

As the letters continued to flash on the street signs, L, K, J appearing and disappearing through the silver needles of rain in descending order, Stone thought of his father's book on Gematria, and his failed attempt to decipher the account numbers at the Bingo Hall. In Gematria every letter has a numerical value and by converting Hebrew letters into numbers and then adding the numbers together, another number arises, which is in turn converted back into the Hebrew word, and through this system, the mystics felt the secrets of the universe could be revealed. Stone could not figure out what the Judge had meant. Could it be that the puzzle was simpler than he thought? Could Bingo or its Hebrew equivalent hold the missing account numbers?

Boaz had found a techno station that blasted out electronic dance beats through the Judge's crackling speakers, and Stone returned from his meditations. The thumping beat made his eyes hurt.

"Israelis invented techno," Boaz shouted, as he swayed in the passenger seat.

"Turn it down," Itzy called, as the car sloped down onto a narrow highway. Stone obliged.

"You don't like trance?" Boaz said.

"No," Stone said, turning the station. He could see Yossi's car speed around a shining curve.

The radio announcer said the Yankees had won again and stated that their magic number to clinch the pennant had shrunk by two.

Another magic number, Stone thought.

"I'm sorry about Dov," Itzy said. "He can be a jerk."

Stone was silent.

"And he was always respectful to your father."

Stone was bothered that Dov had had a relationship with his father.

"We're not all a bunch of jerks," Itzy said. "I've seen you around the *beis*."

"The base?"

"The *beis midrash*," Boaz chimed in. "The study house."

"I've been saying *Kaddish* for my father."

"I know."

"Yes, Itzy knows everything," Boaz said.

Itzy made a face in the rearview mirror. "My father died too," he said after a moment. "A few years back, when the so-called peace process began. His car was sprayed with bullets on his way home from Jerusalem. They got him on a bypass road five minutes from home. Fucking Arabs."

"I'm sorry," Stone said.

"I couldn't even go to the funeral."

"Why not?"

"I'm a Cohen."

Stone was silent. He could see Itzy's thin face prominent in the rearview mirror, his skin ghastly and fishlike in the damp light.

"That means he can't go into cemeteries," Boaz said, blowing smoke out a crack in the window. "In case the Messiah comes and he is called to rebuild the Temple – there is no time to wash up."

"You make it sound ridiculous," Itzy said.

"It is," Boaz said.

"No, it isn't."

"Yes, it is."

"Did you say *Kaddish*?" Stone interjected.

"Of course."

"Look," Boaz said, as the highway began its rise above Brooklyn.

The Statue of Liberty stood tall in the distance, her torch raised high above her head. The water was black around her.

Manhattan appeared suddenly in the misty rain before them, strikingly close, as if its towers and spires would block their passage. Stone stepped hard on the accelerator. To his right he could see Brooklyn spread out below, with steeples and smoke stacks and houses piled up into the hills. In the distance, he saw the glowing face of the clock on the Williamsburg Savings Bank Tower, the building itself obscured by a gray smoky mist.

The radio announcer reported from the crime blotter that a headless body had been found in the Gowanus Canal. *Had Pinky been decapitated and dumped in the canal?*

"The victim was a black male, 250 pounds with tattoos on his arms and back . . ."

"Is that with the head or without?" Boaz laughed.

"Enough," Itzy said, shaking his head.

"Life in the big city," Boaz said.

After turning off the highway and driving for a while beneath the overpass, Stone realized that he was approaching his own neighborhood. It had come as a surprise to him because he was not accustomed to that route; he usually drove past the park on his way to Midwood, driving through a cross-section of Brooklyn's varied neighborhoods. The Navy Yard appeared on his left through the slanting rain,

Manhattan materializing and dematerializing beyond. He should have known; they were returning to the *beis*.

Stone pulled up in front of the warehouse. A drunken couple stumbled out of the Catbird Seat, slipping on the slick sidewalk.

"Okay," Stone said. "You're home."

"Ha," Boaz said. "Now we go to work."

"Come with us," Itzy asked, and Stone turned around so as not to have to talk to his partial reflection in the rearview mirror. He was a lot more handsome than Stone had thought previously and he spoke with true sincerity.

"Why not?" Boaz said, languidly lighting up another cigarette.

"Without Dov—" Itzy said.

"Yes, yes," Boaz said, "are you coming?"

The basement of the warehouse was still as cold as a meat locker, and in the dim light Stone stepped past three steel tanks and a pile of crates. He saw a figure approaching through the gray light, his footsteps echoing off the walls of the barren warehouse. "You're late."

Boaz and Itzy were silent. For a moment Stone wondered whether the words were directed at him. Brilliant was tall and slim with a high forehead and a sharp arrogant face with angular cheekbones that looked like they had been hewn with an ax. He wore his beard cropped short and his green eyes sparkled. "Where are the rest of those jokers?"

"Coming," Itzy said.

"Where the hell are they?" Then his tone switched to more a solicitous one as he noticed Stone standing beside Boaz. "Hello, Matthew. How are you?"

"Fine," Stone said absently.

"Good to see you again."

They heard footsteps up above and on the stairs. Yossi and the pear-shaped friend appeared followed by three others. They were laughing.

"You're late," Brilliant said. "Drinking again?"

"No, no," Yossi said. "We were just saying goodbye to Dov."

"Forget Dov. He's dead to us now. He almost blew the whole thing."

"He's going back to Israel tomorrow," the pear-shaped friend added.

"May he die and be well," Brilliant said, before stalking off. Their demeanor changed in the presence of Brilliant who was clearly in charge. The group followed him silently through a steel door into a smaller room with a low ceiling and banks of fluorescent lights. Moshe waited at the doorway with his arms crossed. After the last one entered, he closed the door and slid the latch.

Brilliant stood before the group, surveying them in silence. Stone could hear Itzy wheezing behind him; he reached into his pocket and sprayed his asthma medication into his mouth. Stone could see Boaz beside Itzy, standing straight and still, a hint of irony playing across his face. They stood for a long time in silence until Stone's legs began to cramp. The cold floor seemed to be drawing Stone's body heat out through the soles of his feet.

"Self-discipline," Brilliant said at last, "is more important than grand ideas, passion, righteousness. Self-discipline is everything, in fact. And when you show up late, with alcohol on your breath, everything crumbles."

Yossi began to speak, but Brilliant cut him off.

"I know what you're going to say. But that is no excuse. You are giving in to the evil inclination, distractions that will destroy all of us in the end. Yes, self-discipline is difficult with the daily obstacle of life getting in the way, but self-discipline is the only way. You may find it difficult to shower every day, eat three meals, but you do find a way. If you find it difficult to do what you have pledged, then you must force yourself with an iron will." Brilliant spoke with a profound inner conviction, staring hard at each face as he spoke. "You're still learning your ABCs, and time is short. Now tell me, what do I mean when I say ABCs?"

"Learn to shoot," the group shouted in unison.

"Good," Brilliant said evenly. "And why?"

The pear-shaped one took a step forward, "Because we cannot rely on the goyim to protect us, because blood will be shed as we reclaim our land."

"Good," Brilliant said. "Every day like clockwork. Discipline."

Stone suddenly realized that they were standing in front of a shooting range with low cinder-block walls and human silhouette targets hanging at the end of long alleys. The walls of the room were lined with a layer of cork for soundproofing. Beige sandbags were piled against the wall.

Even with the muffling headphones on, Stone thought that the sound of gunfire was deafening. He stood beside Itzy with a pistol in his hand staring down the long alleys. He had never held a gun before, but Gabby, she . . . Boaz came up behind him, "Don't worry. I'll teach you."

He showed him the proper way to stand and how to hold and aim a gun. "Never point it at anything unless you plan to kill it." He fired a shot at the target and hit it dead middle of the forehead. "Don't worry about the head. A shot to the chest will still kill a man nine times out of ten."

Stone fired and was he surprised by the kickback that wrenched into his shoulder. He imagined Gabby's strong, squared shoulders.

"Hurts, yeah? Try easy, loose – but firm." Boaz shook out Stone's arm for him, lightly massaging his muscles. "Now do it again. The pistol is part of your flesh."

He fired and the recoil was less severe with his shoulder relaxed. The bullet did not hit the target. He fired three more times and missed.

"Okay, think about the psychology of shooting. You have to want to shoot a gun with the same passion you feel about fucking a woman. If you are not turned on by her, you can't get it up. The same is for shooting. You must long to shoot the way you long to make love to Gabby."

Stone smiled.

"Do you want to shoot?"

"Yes," Stone said, between a volley of shots fired along the row.

"Then shoot." He fired again and hit the target. Stone felt that, yes, the pistol was an extension of himself, and if he visualized Dov as the target, or Zohar, his arrogant face smashed, or the drug dealer, or the homeboys from the Whitman Houses, or R.R. Nation with his false preaching, and fired the gun, he had the satisfaction of killing them again and again as each tattered target was replaced. He felt a strength now that he had never felt before, a strength full of possibility, that he could overcome his own physical limitations and be equal or better than those around him. He suddenly desired to kill. It could be so easy now.

Boaz moved up and down along the row and barked instructions. Stone turned around wondering where Brilliant had gone.

"Watch it," Itzy shouted. "Your gun."

Stone's pistol was pointing directly at Itzy's feet. "Don't let Boaz see."

Stone righted his pistol and aimed it towards the target. He didn't fire. "Who is Boaz?"

"He is a sharpshooter from Israel. Expert marksman."

"What is he doing here?"

"Teaching us to shoot," Itzy said, firing off a round. The acrid smell of burnt gunpowder hung in the air and a smoking shell-casing rolled to Stone's feet. Itzy continued, "He's the best hired-gun money can buy."

Boaz was shouting at the pear-shaped one, their faces pressed so close together that the pear-shaped one's *kippah* fell from his head as he angled his neck back for space.

"We're lucky you could step in in Dov's place."

Stone briefly imagined Dov in his place with Gabby, their bodies pressed close on the orange basement couch.

"Otherwise we'd be shorthanded for the plan."

"What's the plan?" Stone said.

Itzy lifted up his goggles and wiped them on his shirt, "You don't know?"

"No," Stone said. "I don't."

"The Rav said we had to be so careful. But I saw you at the *beis*."

Boaz signaled everyone to stop shooting. It was time to train with the M-16s. Stone removed his headphones and heard a crashing sea of white noise above the ringing in his ears.

"If you were in Munich in 1923 at the Beer Hall where Hitler tried to seize power for the first time, wouldn't you shoot him, put a bullet between his eyes? Think about history. Everything would have been different; no war, no *Shoah*, six million Jews, rest their souls, would've lived out their natural lives."

"But the plan?" Stone said.

"The Rally for Palestine. There'll be all sorts of Arab big-wigs from around the world. A State Assemblyman from Brooklyn who is a friend of Arafat, R.R. Nation with his Brown and Black Unity B.S. That's one thing we've learned from the Muslim Brotherhood; the way they shot down Sadat when he wasn't expecting it. It was perfection. Only, we'll come out of nowhere, we'll pop out of the manholes beneath the street and shoot them onstage for the world to see. This is a chance to get them all at once. Show them that there will be no Palestine beside or in place of Israel and any Arab who facilitates it will not be safe anywhere."

Stone's head spun. He reflected on Itzy's words about his own father being killed in an attack by Arabs. It all began to make sense now. It was his version of an eye-for-an-eye. Stone wasn't hot, but he was sweating. The thought of Nation made his blood boil. He had believed that his father would still be alive today if it had not been for the hectoring and harassment of R.R. Nation in his speeches to the media, always hungry to anoint the latest villain.

"How is that going to work?"

"That's the brilliant part. There's an old train tunnel under Atlantic Avenue. We've got it all mapped out. All we have to do is pop out and it's Whack-a-Mole." He laughed a high wheezing laugh.

Stone suddenly realized at the mention of the tunnel that this was a plan that had been hatched by his father before he had died and that the completion of this plan would be a fulfillment of his unstated wishes. The books whispered to him again. And Stone thought back to his recent marathon reading sessions in which he had come across underlined passages on tunnels and their relation to the Jewish struggle for nationhood again and again. Zedekiah, the last king of Judah, had escaped through tunnels running from Jerusalem to Jericho when the city was conquered by the Babylonian king Nebuchadnezzar. During the Bar Kochba Revolt against the Romans 600 years later, the Jews had hidden in underground tunnels until their ultimate defeat at Betar. During the Spanish Inquisition, Marranos living as Jews in secret, conducted Passover seders and other religious rituals in underground tunnels. The Judge had marked all these passages in his books, including articles in which weapons had been smuggled from Egypt to the Gaza Strip both during the 1948 War of Independence and recently during the conflict with the Palestinians. Stone had even found a newspaper clipping from a few years earlier written when rioting exploded in Jerusalem after the Israeli government opened a passage to a long-sealed Hasmonean tunnel that ran beneath the Dome of the Rock. Over 80 people died in the fighting that ensued. But, what really struck Stone and connected his father's seemingly random markings together was a quote found in an article on the defunct Long Island Railroad tunnel that ran under Atlantic Avenue from Columbia Street to Boerum Street in the pages of a book of Walt Whitman's non-fiction. He had planned on giving the book to Gabby as a gift, but he had held onto it when he noticed that his father had underlined the quote, "The old tunnel, that used to lie there underground . . . now all closed up and filled in, and soon to be utterly forgotten . . . the tunnel dark as the grave, cold, damp and silent." The Judge had written the single word *Yes* in the margin.

"You're going to use the tunnel as a means to murder?" Stone practically shouted. He could see Moshe walking down the line, handing M-16s out to Yossi and his pear-shaped friend. Stone put down the pistol on the narrow ledge before him.

"Nice shooting," Brilliant said behind him. "Careful not to shoot your mouth."

Had Brilliant been behind him the whole time?

"Matthew, let's talk." He beckoned Stone to join him in a corner. Brilliant's eyes were cold, but not unfriendly. He put his hand on Stone's shoulder. "I want to thank you again for bringing the *gonif* to us. You are part of this now. So you should know that what happens here, stays here."

"All right," Stone said. He felt his forehead breaking out into sweat.

"I hope you understand that killing one's enemy is not murder, but a Commandment of God. Do you understand me?" He tightened his grip on Stone's shoulder. "Your father may have saved my skin after the riot, but if you talk to anyone about this, I'll kill you. And I'd be doing it with your father's blessing."

❧

Zohar was sitting in the window of the Burger King. He was the first white face Stone had seen since he had entered the streets of the Fulton Mall, passing cheap clothing shops, furniture outlets and jewelry stores that advertised their selection of gold teeth. A constant bass beat accompanied Stone's footsteps as he moved through the crowds of people. He had chosen the Fulton Mall as a safe place to meet, because it was the least likely spot he would ever imagine running across someone from the *beis*, and he was especially afraid of being discovered by Brilliant, but looking at Zohar in the window, in his rumpled suit, Stone realized that he stood out like a white lamb in a sea of black and he felt a wave of panic wash over him. Stone momentarily questioned his judgment and was about to turn away when Zohar waved him over with the flick of a finger.

"Never out of uniform," Stone said. "Let's go sit in the back."

Zohar smiled and led the way. They sat by a swinging door that emitted a smell of burnt grease.

"Thanks for calling," Zohar said. "You are an important resource considering the bureau's reluctance to provide the manpower I've requested."

"You have the money?" Stone said.

"Under the table." Zohar slipped him a thin envelope. Stone had imagined something somehow weightier; the envelope may as well have been empty.

"It's all there. You can check it later."

Stone pocketed the envelope. Zohar leaned forward, "So, what have you got for me?"

"I hope this is helpful," Stone said. "I've been with them inside the warehouse. There's just a *shul* and a yeshiva inside. A bunch of men go there to study everyday. Everything seems pretty normal. It's difficult to tell what is going on because no one is saying much of anything, except for prayers."

"Okay," Zohar said. "What about any messages being passed?"

"Interesting," Stone said. "I did find something out. Someone whispered to me during prayer."

"Okay," Zohar said. "What is it?"

"You know there is a lot of travel back and forth between Israel and New York. They only pass information between each other in person. No phone calls."

"Yes, yes," Zohar said. "Anything about Seligman?"

"No," Stone said.

"You've got nothing on the Rav?"

"No, but this might be helpful. Now, I'm not sure of the exact date. Maybe tomorrow, or the next day, or maybe the next. But an important urgent message is going to be passed along to someone in Israel. They're using a married couple with a baby as their messenger, since they are the least likely to come under suspicion."

Zohar wrote furiously in a small black notebook. He looked up. "JFK?"

"Yes," Stone said.

"El Al?"

Stone nodded.

"This is quite valuable intelligence. Now, what are their names?"

"Michael and Rachel Zinaburg. He also goes by the name Mickey, Mickey Zin."

"Got it," Zohar said. "Thank you."

Stone arrived, breathless at the Chase Bank on Montague Street, which beckoned gloriously beneath the blue-blooded mahogany-and-leather law offices of Holland and McKim. In the vestibule by the elevator bank, Stone removed the warm envelope from his pocket and counted $5,000; fifty one-hundred dollar bills. He had never held so much money in his hands at once and he trembled with excitement. He figured that the least suspicious thing to do would be to make a deposit. Simply inquiring about the balance and then leaving was bound to raise some eyebrows, especially if there was as much money in the account as he had figured. But he was sure he had the number correct, of that he had no doubt, and as he picked up the deposit slip, he saw that there was exactly enough space for the seven digits he had committed to memory.

As Stone had read through the pages of *Hidden Worlds* he realized that he had been correct in assuming his father had encrypted the account numbers in Bingo, the numbers were buried in the word BINGO, or at least in its Hebrew equivalent. The letters had appeared in his mind's eye burning against the black background of the Judge's robe, *Bet, Yod, Nun, Gimel, Vav* and like a whisper, the matching numbers he had studied from Gematria slipped into his head, each letter matching its alphabetical equivalent: 2, 10, 50, 3, 6. And he knew with absolute certainty that those numbers were the missing account numbers, the numbers his father had hoped he would find, a life-affirming act that bound him to his father in a way he had never been connected in life.

His feet echoed off the marble floor as he moved through the line, and then he was at the teller. He slid the deposit slip under the glass. The teller studied it with a bored expression on her face, counted the money, ran something through a machine and stamped it, and asked if he needed anything else. Stone's throat was dry and he croaked, "Just the receipt."

He did not look at the balance until he was back out in the street. A group of schoolkids from Beecher Academy brushed past him laughing. He turned the slip over and discovered there was almost $3 million in the account.

When Stone arrived at his apartment, he found a note from Abi saying that she would be staying in Manhattan and she wanted to get together with him soon, "if that was all right." Her script was smooth and flowing, he did not remember his mother's writing, slightly tilting as if it were being blown by a heavy breeze, and there was an arrow drawn above the word "over." He turned the page and saw that Gabby had called. His mother had drawn a hopeful happy face beside Gabby's name much like the one he had seen in one of the Judge's books, when he agreed with a statement.

The painting of Pinky leaned against a wall. He was more vivid, more alive now with color in his face, hints of stubble appearing on his cheeks. And in the same way that the toenails and hair of the dead continue to grow after the heart has stopped, Pinky continued as well to persist stubbornly. Stone turned the painting to the wall and picked up the telephone.

He dialed information in Israel, and a Bezeq operator picked up after half-a-dozen rings. It would be late in the evening in Israel, but Stone figured it was not too late yet. He found Seligman's home number at Giv'at Barzel and he dialed. A woman answered in Hebrew with a heavy Brooklyn accent.

"Is Rabbi Seligman there?" Stone's hands shook and he pressed the receiver between his ear and shoulder.

"Is this America?" an irritated female voice asked.

"Yes," Stone said.

The line went dead.

20

Gabby's voice was animated on the phone. She invited Stone over to her aunt's house to help her build a *sukkah* in the backyard for the upcoming Sukkot holiday.

"Come on. It will be fun."

"Dov gone?"

"Oh," Gabby said. "Yes, he's gone. But Itzy and Yossi will be here."

"How about a rain check?"

"What's the matter? Itzy said you guys had a good time together after the break fast. You two could be friends."

"Gabby," he said at last. "You said we would be alone next time, just me and you."

"Yes," she said. "I know I did. And I want to be, very badly. But I have to do this tonight. Tradition. Family."

"Tomorrow, then."

"Absolutely," Gabby said. "And I owe you one."

"Can I hold you to that?"

"You can hold me however you want."

Just after midnight, Stone returned to the *beis*. Moshe let him in and led him to the firing range where Itzy, Yossi and the others were gathered in conversation.

"One dunam equals one tenth of an acre," the rat-faced one said with authority.

"You're wrong, Federman," Yossi responded, "because one dunam equals a thousand square meters."

"It's the same thing," Federman responded with irritation.

"No," Itzy said solicitously. "I think a dunam of land is equal to one tenth of a hectare."

"Are you sure?" Yossi said.

"I thought it was a quarter hectare and one tenth of an acre," the pear-shaped one added.

Boaz, who had been sitting off to the side picking at his teeth with a toothpick, interrupted, "No, no, no. You are all wrong. One dunam is equal to one quarter acre which is the same as a thousand square meters, which the same as one tenth of a hectare. Four dunams equals one acre."

Stone eased his way into the conversation, "And how many dunams are there?"

"As many as we need," Federman answered, not looking at Stone.

"The mathematics lesson is over," Boaz said. "Are you ready to shoot?"

"Hey, you feeling better?" Itzy asked Stone, as the group lined up before the firing range. "Gabby said you had a bit of a cold. She missed you."

"I'm okay now."

"*Baruch Hashem.*"

Stone was placing the headphones onto his head when Brilliant tapped him on the shoulder from behind. He had the uncanny ability to appear seemingly out of nowhere. "Matthew, let's talk."

The gunshots were loud in Stone's ears and he covered them with his hands as he was led away by Brilliant. He saw Itzy turn his head and wink.

Brilliant led Stone to the small room where the group had sat the night he had brought Pinky to them.

"The blue is the land we've already acquired for Greater Israel," Brilliant said, taking note of Stone's studied stare. "The green is the land we have yet to acquire."

Stone nodded his head. He was transfixed by the maps.

"Take a seat, Matthew," Brilliant said, gesturing bluntly to a wooden chair nearby. His eyes looked cold and unforgiving and Stone wished that he was back in the range with Itzy and Boaz firing his pistol at the targets. Brilliant stood, looming above Stone. "I want you to understand something so there is no mistake."

An electrical shot of horror shot through Stone's chest as Brilliant dropped a leaden hand onto his shoulder. Had he seen him talking with Zohar? Impossible. The Fulton Mall was the habitat of the homeboy and hip-hop and gold teeth. A brand of clothing using the acronym FUBU, meaning For Us By Us, hung loosely on funked-out mannequins in the shop windows. Neither Stone nor Brilliant were any part of "Us." The shoppers of the Fulton Mall wore du-rags or tilted baseball caps on their heads, not *kippahs* or black felt hats. Stone had been the only white face he had seen aside from Zohar's. Maybe it was because of these dark faces that Stone had stood out the same way a homeboy would stand out in synagogue. But, who had followed him?

He felt Brilliant's grip tighten, the thumb pressing close to the concave spot beneath his Adam's apple, his windpipe tightening. And as he looked into Brilliant's hard, impassive eyes, he remembered suddenly that these hands had killed before. Yes, he had been found not guilty by judge and jury, his own father, in fact, but he had killed, of that there was no doubt. The epileptic Arab, Nasser Al-Bassam, had been smashed in the head with a piece of brick, pummeled out of this world by the young Brilliant, his bare hands covered with the Arab's blood. He had killed then and he had promised to kill again the night that Pinky had died. Stone could feel hot sweat pooling in his armpits, dripping down his torso, his heart pounded in his chest. If Brilliant could hear it, he wasn't letting on. Stone tried to speak, but Brilliant squeezed harder.

"No, no," he said. "I called you here for me to speak." He relaxed his grip, but kept his hand in place. He breathed evenly, slowly and said firmly. "Never, never speak about our business on the telephone."

For a moment, Stone thought he was talking about his phone call with Gabby.

"What goes on here, never leaves here. Nothing is ever said. Nothing."

"I didn't say anything."

"Did you call the Rav's home in the *Eretz*?"

"Yes, but . . ."

Brilliant slapped Stone hard on the side of the head. He must have been wearing a ring on his finger, because he felt a sharp pain amid the dull sting that radiated throughout his throbbing skull.

"Don't be stupid."

"I don't think that Rav Seligman would approve of this." Stone rubbed his head.

"You still have to earn my trust. The Judge had his doubts about you. I know all about that."

Stone felt wounded and shook off Brilliant's hand.

"Seligman will vouch for me."

"I'm in charge now."

Stone's blood went cold. "What happened?"

"The Rav has been detained."

Stone felt momentarily adrift. He had so anticipated Seligman's approving smile, as if he were a direct pipeline to his father. He had cajoled him to say *Kaddish*, he had pointed him on the road to redemption, he had guided him back towards his father, but now he realized that providing the numbers to Brilliant would have their own palliative effect. He could earn his trust in an instant and prove that he truly was the Judge's avatar, ready, prepared, and willing to complete his life's work in his name.

"What happened?"

"He's been detained," Brilliant repeated.

"What about Pinky?" Stone said at last.

"I think you know what happened to him."

"You killed him," Stone said. He could see Brilliant smile for the first time, his hard eyes mollified, bottomless.

"Sometimes, one life saves many. One is sacrificed so the rest can continue."

"But Seligman?"

"I am not the Rav's keeper," Brilliant said flatly.

"Is he all right?"

"The Rav is very capable. He knows what to do."

"Pinky's dead, now Seligman's gone," Stone muttered.

"You are giving equal value to a lion of Judah as you are to an alley cat."

"What is it like?" Stone said. "To kill?"

"You can answer that yourself, you are as responsible for his death as I am."

Stone felt a fleeting unity with Brilliant, but he quickly realized that his inclusiveness was not strictly benign. Brilliant was saying "We've got you now. You are one of us, like it or not."

"It feels right," Stone said. "There was only one end for him."

"Yes. What he did endangered everything we stand for," Brilliant said. "You see, no thunderbolt from the Heavens struck you down. Life goes on."

"But the first time, the Arab," Stone pressed.

"I was young, Matthew, quick to anger. I honestly didn't know what I was doing when I killed the Arab. It was almost instinct and seemed to happen so fast and so slow, both at the same time, as if it were my destiny, or if I were entering history for the first time. It was wonderful, Matthew, and I came to the attention of the Judge, your father, may his memory be blessed. He saved me. He saved me because he knew that Jews stick together and damn the rest of them. I love him like a father."

"My father was a good man."

Brilliant pulled a chair before Stone and said, "You're not like the Judge. I worry about you."

"My grandfather," Stone said, "he knew Jabotinsky, gave him money."

"I know all about your lineage. But I don't see—"

"I didn't understand—"

"Would you kill again?" Brilliant interrupted. "If a Jew was in need, or the spilling of enemy blood helped the

Jewish cause?" Brilliant's bottomless eyes sparkled from their depths.

Stone was silent.

"You know your father saved me. But do you know how far he went to save my life? They were calling for the death penalty up in Albany, political anti-Semitism at its best. But your father would not see Jewish blood cheapened. *Ladam hu-matar*, the permitted blood, so cheap for so long. He had had enough."

"It cost him his career," Stone said.

And here Brilliant laughed again. "His career on the bench, maybe, enforcing their laws. But the Judge never gave up on his beliefs."

Brilliant ran a hand under his beard and paused as if to measure his words. "Do you know the name Emile Alcalai?"

"One of the jurors," Stone said.

"Yes," Brilliant said. "The state subpoenaed him and scared him with all sorts of threats; his mother, from Morocco, was not a naturalized U.S. citizen. He was going to talk eventually."

"He died in a hit-and-run," Stone said.

"Yes," Brilliant said. "That was when I realized that I owed your father my life."

Stone was not surprised. Everything he had learned about his father since his death pointed in this direction. The dent in the Volvo. Be ruthless, the marginal notes had told him. Be ruthless, or become nothing.

"And his reputation? Did he kill to protect his reputation?"

"Forget reputation with the anti-Semites and yellow journalists. He is a giant among the Jewish people. A great powerful mind, a visionary. He could have been prime minister, anything. Jabotinsky to Begin to Stone, just connect the dots."

"I have the account numbers," Stone stuttered.

Brilliant's expression did not change. "Where are they?" he said softly.

"I have them," Stone said, tapping the side of his head.

"So you had them all along."

"No, no," Stone said. "They were encrypted in one of his books. I figured them out."

"What are the numbers?"

"You need the numbers," Stone said. "So you need me."

"I see," Brilliant said. "You know the plan could go off without the numbers?"

"And then what?" Stone said.

"Then, we are dried up. Out of cash. But, you must understand that if you don't give us the numbers, you are not worth anything. We both want the same thing, don't we?"

"Yes," Stone said. "But, I control the numbers."

"All right," Brilliant said. "How is this going to work?"

"What do you need the money for?"

"I'm not asking for your permission."

"Good," Stone said. "What is the money for specifically? It is my father's account."

"It is the movement's account," Brilliant said.

"Then why didn't he leave the numbers with you or Rabbi Seligman?"

"The digging is almost done," Brilliant said. "We've tunneled all the way to Atlantic and have breached the old train tunnel wall. It's the city inspectors, they think we're building a bomb shelter in case the Russians attack," he laughed dryly. "But it costs a lot of money to dig up New York City and keep quiet about it. A lot of money."

"How much?"

Brilliant told him.

Stone shuddered. "How many people will die?"

"Just the dogs on the stage. Maybe the three or four who carry out the attack. Matthew, this plan is an absolute good. You know that nowhere in the world is a Jew safe. We are killed as if there is no prohibition against the killing of a Jew. I'm not just talking about the Holocaust. Eleven Israeli athletes murdered at the Munich Olympics, a Jewish community center blown up in Buenos Aires, Leon Klinghoffer, a Jew in a wheelchair, tossed from the deck of the *Achille Lauro* into the Mediterranean, as if he were a sack of garbage, while his wife watched in horror. Ari Halberstam, not much younger than you are now, shot and killed by an Arab gunman on the Brooklyn Bridge entry ramp, right here in America! His friends in the van traveling to Manhattan were maimed; one, losing part of his intestines, another, deaf in one ear survived a gunshot wound to the head. And the killer, a Lebanese national, shouted 'Kill the Jews,' as he made his escape. A one hundred and forty-one-year sentence will not bring back one second of Ari's life. Even the great Rav Grunhut, forceful and fearless to the end, sits in Heaven today, murdered by an Arab assassin. The list goes on and on and on. Why should Jews fear for their lives wherever they go, knowing that their murderers will not be prosecuted with the same vigor as those who kill the goyim? Why should an Arab who pledges the destruction of the State of Israel and Jews everywhere be free to walk the streets of

Brooklyn with no fear for his life? The entire world runs through Brooklyn eventually, Matthew. If they know we can hit them here, we can hit them anywhere. This is a balancing of the scales. The Land of Israel belongs to us, to the Jews. This rally on Atlantic Avenue is no more than a farce and an insult."

Brilliant's breathing was heavy, he leaned in close to Stone and put his hand in Stone's. "We need more people like your father, like Rav Grunhut, and like Dr. Goldstein, the saint from Brooklyn who had seen enough Jewish bloodshed as a doctor in Kiryat Arba."

"We were the victims," Stone said, echoing the Judge's written words.

"But not anymore," Brilliant said. "There was a Holocaust in the middle of the 20th century, a time of progress that surpassed in scope any that preceded it in the history of the world. And what did it take to stoke the ancient fires of hatred in the middle of Europe in the middle of the 20th century? Matthew, it will happen again if we are not strong, if we don't take the land that belongs to us. The Arabs have twenty-two countries and yet they cannot even see fit to grant the Jews a tiny homeland, a sliver really, along the Mediterranean. Why? Because they hate us. Because they want us to be annihilated. Jabotinsky saw the Holocaust coming long before the cattle cars rolled and he did everything he could to organize a Jewish army to instill physical courage in the Jew, after centuries of abuse, murder and persecution at the hands of the Gentile. He did everything he could to acquire land in Israel for the Jew and to settle that land as our own. He wrote that 'Judaea fell in blood and fire, and in blood and fire Judaea will rise again.' He taught us that as long as we can shoot a gun, there is hope. Your father is Jabotinsky's spiritual heir and he too saw the coming Holocaust, the disaster of assimilation, the ascendancy of the acceptance of a Palestinian terror state, a resurgence of European anti-Semitism, United Nations favoritism, the increase of weapons of mass destruction and ease with which they can now be acquired since the breakup of the Soviet Empire. Your father wanted to save the Jews, by reminding the world that we control our own destiny and that the popular political ideas of the day calling for a terrorist state on Israel's borders is nothing more than appeasement, thinly veiled anti-Semitism aimed at the very heart of Judaism. Your father started the work, and we will finish it."

"Who?" Stone asked.

Brilliant told him:

Jordan Issa, a State Assemblyman from Brooklyn, who had visited Yasir Arafat in Ramallah and stood smiling for photos as Arafat, in Arabic, praised the perpetrators of suicide bus bombings in the cities and towns of Israel.

U.S. Senator Joe Salem, who had called for a Palestinian state as well as a war crimes tribunal in The Hague to prosecute Ariel Sharon, Yitzhak Shamir, Shimon Peres and two dozen other Israeli leaders with crimes of genocide.

Edwin Daoud, Columbia professor and writer, who had written the landmark book *Irgunism: The Terror State of Israel*, required reading on liberal university campuses around the country.

Imam Walid Taibe of the Farooq Mosque on Atlantic Avenue who had preached that every Muslim should draw his sword and drive it through the heart of Jews everywhere to liberate Palestine.

Sheik Iyad al-Shuhada, author of a well-circulated *fatwa*, declaring that the killing of Jews is an ennobling act to be celebrated in Heaven and on earth, and was responsible for the campaign which sent hundreds of thousands of dollars to families of suicide bombers in Israel.

Hana al-Husseini, Chairman of the Land Day Committee, who on the eve of peace talks in Oslo encouraged Arabs throughout the West Bank, Gaza and Jordan to descend on the neighborhoods of Jewish Jerusalem, Jaffa and other communities with papers they claimed were deeds that proved their ownership of Jewish homes. A class-action lawsuit was also undertaken at the World Court to sue for compensation from Israeli Jews.

Yasser Ramadi, Palestinian Authority representative who had been exiled to Tunis along with Arafat and his PLO cronies, and had Jewish blood on his hands going back almost 50 years.

Jerry Steinberg, head of the ultra-liberal Upper West-Side-based Free Palestine Movement that purchased Jewish land to be "returned" to Arabs who had fled after the 1948 and 1967 wars. He spoke regularly on CNN about Jewish crimes of appropriation and once compared the State of Israel to the Nazi regime.

Reverend Randall Roebling Nation, founder and head of the Brotherhood Ministries, spokesman for the Black and Brown Coalition and former candidate for the head of the National Democratic Party, who had promised if elected president to withdraw American financial support for Israel in order to "balance the scales of equality."

He had also harangued Judge Walter Stone to an early death. Stone remembered the speeches before the courthouse, the oratory, the television interviews, everything aimed at destroying his father, his carefully built reputation. And Roebling had the charisma to match his righteous indignation. It was about more than simply speaking up for the underdog, the weakling, Stone realized. There was a visceral, high-handed, holier-than-thou righteousness when Roebling spoke, it was so transparent that Stone could not believe that he was not challenged with equal vigor. But who would speak up for the Judge? Seligman, the radical West Bank rabbi? Brilliant, the accused? Abi, the embittered ex-wife who was only too happy to gloat over his misfortune? Stone knew it was his responsibility to stand up for his father, that Roebling had committed *lashon harah* against his father, not simply because it was an opportunity to advance his own career at the Judge's expense, but also because he saw in his darkly shaded crosshairs the "man" incarnate, who had locked up nearly forty percent of young black males in the country. He was not simply attacking Walter Stone, a privileged Jew with power, but all Jews who rose at the expense of blacks, who succeeded on the backs of black failure. What could be better than to take down the Jew, publicly humiliate him in the heart of Hymietown?

Stone had failed his father then. He would not fail him now.

"And what about the Arabs shot in the head on Atlantic Avenue and Bay Ridge? How does that fit in?"

"The executions?" Brilliant laughed as if he had heard a hilarious joke. "Yes. What about them? These Arabs were killed by their own, with Israeli weapons sold to them by the traitor whose name I will not mention. More Arab propaganda. Another blood libel that Jews are murderers and

Arabs are the victims. The mainstream newspapers never picked up on it, though."

"But why?" Stone said. "Why did Arabs kill Arabs?"

"Because they were selling land to Jews in *Eretz Israel.*"

He agreed with Brilliant to transfer the funds to the appropriate accounts; it would look like nothing more than a payment for improvements to various Brooklyn neighborhoods, perhaps even the very neighborhoods where the Arabs had been murdered. Stone shook with excitement at the prospect of avenging his father, carrying out his plan and finding peace within himself at last.

◎ 21 ◎

The homeboys hooted and hollered outside of Stone's bedroom window with unusual vigor; they whistled, cursed and shouted, overturning the milk crates they had been sitting on.

Stone wondered what could be so fascinating about the outside of his bedroom wall that they literally clung to its faded brick like sea barnacles. They rarely returned to the Whitman Houses or they kept watch in shifts as if they were afraid to miss any of the happenings in the corner of the universe where Myrtle and Waverly intersected.

Stone's buzzer rang. Gabby was 45 minutes early, the sun having just set across the river, and Stone rushed to let her in.

He could still hear the homeboys calling after her as she approached through the faux marble entry hall. She looked beautiful in a dark fitted dress, elasticized at the seam from mid-thigh to just above her ankles. Her hair was down, and hung across the left side of her face. Her pendant glowed like celestial sea water against her chest. She wore a light sweater over her shoulders and a pair of calf-high leather boots.

"Hi," she said, spreading her arms in anticipation of an embrace. Her heavy book bag fell to the floor.

Stone held her and apologized for the homeboys' insults.

"It's nothing," she said. "Sticks and stones. And I know all about stones."

At first Stone thought she was referring slyly to him and his father, but then he realized that she was referring to the Palestinian stone throwers on the West Bank roads.

"It's okay. Hey, I'm thirsty."

"How's wine?"

"Is it cold?"

"With ice."

"Sure."

Inside the apartment she said, "This is a big place. Do you live here alone?"

"My roommate ran off to join the circus."

She laughed and said, "Who answered the phone when I called?"

"Would you believe I had a cleaning woman in here? Always trying to impress."

"You didn't!"

"I did."

"Matty, I'm sure it was fine before."

"Trust me. It wasn't."

She ran her hands up and down the red brick wall. "I love exposed brick."

Stone poured a glass of wine into a tumbler and dropped an ice cube in; he did the same for himself. Gabby surveyed the apartment. She found the picture of Pinky facing the wall and pulled it away. "Who's this?"

"*L'chaim*," Stone said, lifting her hair and pressing the cool glass to the back of her neck.

She took the glass, clicked his and said, "Yes, *L'chaim* and *Li'vriut*." They both drank, eyes on each other.

Stone felt his nerves gathering in his belly and he finished the wine in two gulps. He felt warm, brave, and he leaned forward to kiss her. Her lips were soft, her breath smelled sweet from the wine. Her tongue was cool, then warm. They kissed and fell back onto the couch. Stone's hand found her breast and they continued kissing. After a few minutes he reached for the zipper at the back of her dress. Gabby's breathing was heavy. She shot up and sat back against a cushion. "I'm glad I came here," she said.

Stone leaned in to kiss her and she bit his finger playfully. "It's nice to be alone. Isn't it?" he said.

"I don't want to make a mess of things by bringing it up, but I thought I should mention that nothing happened with Dov. He gets ideas in his head, crazy ideas. I'm sorry about the other night."

"I am too," Stone said.

"We'll make it worth the wait."

"But, Dov . . ." Stone said.

"That was a long time ago. Now, he's like a brother or cousin. That's all."

"I want to confess something," Stone said, gliding closer to her on the couch. Gabby looked nervous. "I don't speak Aramaic and I never sent poetry to the *Paris Review*."

"Your father loved you. That's all."

"In his own way," Stone said.

"Hey, what do you think my uncle and your father, best friends in the world, would think about this?"

"What?" Stone said playfully.

"This!" She laughed, running her hand softly over his chest.

"My father would be happy. I finally met a Jewish girl."

"Oh, come on. Am I just that – a Jewish girl?"

"No," he said.

"What then?"

"You're perfect."

"Now, I know you're drunk," she smiled, exposing her twisted incisor.

"What about your uncle? Would I cut it with the feared Rabbi Grunhut?"

She was quiet. "Yes. Of course. My uncle wasn't just about anger; 'a .45 to stay alive,' and all that. He cared deeply about the Jewish people, and he cared about me. You know what he called me? He called me his little girl. His. He loved me like I was his own, and I believe he worked so hard to defend Israel because he saw all Jews as being part of his family. His family."

They found their way to the bedroom after their third glass of wine. A police car's siren whirred past outside.

"Matthew," she laughed, bouncing onto his bed. "All these books."

"My father's."

"Did you read them all?"

"A lot."

"I'm impressed," she said, picking up a copy of *Don Quixote* off a nearby shelf. "Let's read to each other."

Stone kicked off his shoes.

Gabby read, "'The Delightful History of the Most Ingenious Knight: There lived not long since, in a certain village of the Mancha, the name whereof I purposely omit, a gentleman . . .""'

Stone unbuttoned his shirt and removed Gabby's shoes, as she flipped to another page of the book. He squeezed her feet softly. "Here's one," she laughed. "Is this you? '. . . he plunged himself so deeply in his reading of these books . . . whole days and nights; and in the end through his little sleep and much reading, he dried up his brains in such sort as he lost wholly his judgment.'"

"My judgment has never been better," he said reaching for the book. Her hands were soft and strong and he clasped his hand in hers. She balanced the book in the other . . .

"'His fantasy was filled with those things that he read, of enchantments, quarrels, battles, challenges, wounds, wooings, loves, tempests and other impossible follies.'"

"Put the book down," Stone said.

"Is that an order?"

"Yes," he said, and he climbed onto her. Her lips pressed against his and away and again they pressed. She slipped her tongue into his mouth. He could feel its soft contours exploring, discovering his tongue with hers. He opened his eyes and discovered that she had been kissing with her eyes wide open. They both burst out into laughter. He touched her cheek and then reached for the zipper of her dress. Her breasts were firm against the fabric and he was anxious to taste them, to take her pink nipples between his teeth. Her hand moved up his thigh.

"Matthew. I want to let you know that I've done it before. But, not tonight."

She directed his hand back to the zipper. "Just as long as you know. But we can do other things."

She slipped out of her dress and lay on the heaving bed in her bra and panties. Her thighs were toned, muscular and he could see the soft triangle of hair through the thin sheen of her panties. Her stomach was smooth and soft. She was not thin like Emmanuelle had been or even Fairuza. Her breasts were larger, fuller than he had thought, freed from their outer constraining layer. They sat firm, nicely rounded, and rose and fell with her breath. Her nipples were erect. He smelled her neck and kissed it with a handful of her hair tightly gathered in his fist. She kissed back aggressively, lightly biting his lips, his chin. He could hear her sigh as his hand slid to the wet place between her legs.

"Now you," she said. "Your turn."

Stone pulled his T-shirt off and tossed it onto the floor, he unbuttoned his fly and slid out of his pants, he kicked his socks off. He wore just his boxer shorts and breathed heavily. He did not know what she could see in the near darkness of the bedroom lit only by the streetlights outside. She touched his stomach, her hand grazing the head of his erection.

"You're thin," she said. "Beautiful."

He fell on top of her and their hands explored each other in the darkness. She ran her hand up his thigh and moved it carefully, as if she were studying the topography of his skin.

"What's this?" she said. "Your skin feels different here."

"Nothing," Stone said. "Just old war wounds."

She pulled herself out from under him in an instant, spun around and flipped on the bedside lamp. The glaring light burned his eyes.

"Let me see," she said.

Stone lay back against the wall. She ran her fingers over his scars with fascination. The scars were clumped together roughly assembled in the size and shape of an open hand. They were varying shades of purple, brown, beige, translucent white. There was one new wound that still hurt to touch. Gabby pressed her finger to the edge of the recent cigarette burn. "This is new. What happened?"

Stone was silent. He could see concern etched across Gabby's face.

"Nothing," Stone said. "They're just little burns."

"From what?"

Stone was silent again.

"Do they hurt?"

"No," Stone said. "They never hurt."

"You shouldn't do this, Matthew."

"It's better than a drug habit."

"I'm serious. Why would you do this to yourself?"

"It's a long story."

"I'm in no hurry."

"Not tonight. Let's not spoil tonight."

"Matty, it's just that I really care about you and it hurts me to know that you are hurting."

"We all hurt."

"I know."

"Trust me when I say it's all right. Like a hobby, or tattooing yourself or piercing."

"I hate tattoos."

"So do I."

Gabby's expression changed and she leaned in to kiss his bare chest. "You are a complicated man. Full of secrets."

"I have others, over here," he raised his left arm, and under the armpit there was another constellation of burns. There were fewer on his bicep.

"Promise me you won't do this anymore. Promise me if you feel like hurting yourself that you will call me."

"But it doesn't hurt."

"Promise me, Matthew, that you will call."

"I promise."

She kissed him and they explored each other's bodies once again. Gabby kissed his skin slowly, up and down, from his stomach to his neck. She swirled her fingers lightly over his ribs, pausing again at the scars. Stone could smell perspiration forming on her skin, salty, clean, and he ran his tongue down the line of her cleavage. He pushed the pendant aside so that it swung around behind her neck. Her bra unsnapped with ease and he tossed it to the floor. He felt himself trembling before her breasts. Her breasts were firm and smooth, and she sighed "Yes, yes" as he kissed them. Her hand found his penis through the opening of his boxers. She began to stroke lightly.

An unwelcome thought entered Stone's mind as she stroked him; had she done the same with Dov? Had she been in bed with him and opened herself completely to him? They had been together and Dov had felt he had possession over her; that could only mean one thing, that they had had sex. Stone felt a nauseating wave of jealousy wash over him, but Gabby's hand quickened on the shaft of his penis, gripping tighter, stroking harder. But the thoughts would not go away. Had Dov kissed her skin, bit it playfully, explored her mouth with his tongue? Stone wondered whether he was simply a replacement for Dov, in Gabby's heart, at the *beis* with Brilliant and Itzy and Boaz? Stone heard himself call out, "Oh my God!" as he came into Gabby's hand. He rolled over on the bed, so that he was lying up beside her. He could tell she was smiling.

"I wouldn't expect you to be thinking about God at the moment of release."

"I wasn't," Stone said. "What should I be thinking about?"

"Me." After a moment she added, "Hey, why do people call out for God at that moment? Are you making an offering to God? By the way," she indicated her sticky hand. Stone handed her some tissues.

"Ha, ha," Stone said.

"I'm serious. What do you think about God? How do you feel about God?"

Stone kissed her dry lips. "You first."

Gabby was silent for a moment and her breathing was heavy. Her face glowed in the dim light. She did not smile or frown. Stone figured that he was witnessing her pensive expression for the first time.

"God makes me want to be a good person, because if I'm not, I'm not the best person I can be, what does that say about God?"

"Are you afraid of God?"

"Of course not. No lightning bolt is going to shoot down out of the sky if I should kiss a boy before I am married." She smiled and kissed Stone. "It makes sense to me. That's all."

He wanted to talk to her about the *beis* and about the plan and about her time in the army. He had never served, of course, but now, he had the chance to make up for that. But, Stone knew that he should not say anything, and that Gabby would understand without words.

Gabby was so quiet that he was afraid for a moment she had fallen asleep.

She raised her head, "And what is God to you?"

Her warm ankle was draped across his thigh, he felt a light pulse there.

"We each create our own gods."

"Matthew!"

"I believe that God imprinted a set of rules, laws if you will, on our DNA, to keep us in line. That explains guilt. We police ourselves, overseen by our own guilt, which is God."

"Are you guilty?"

"Nope."

He climbed on top of her and her skin was clammy from perspiration. He spoke into her mouth, "I really, really—" and he smothered his declaration with a kiss.

"Me too," she said. "Where's your bathroom? I want to clean up a bit."

He told her, and she jumped out of bed with a stunning athleticism, bouncing to the floor as if she were a gymnast landing square.

She seemed to be gone an inordinately long time, and Stone had started to drift off.

"I have good news." Her voice roused him. He could not see in the dark, but he could tell that she stood across the room, near the bedroom door. "I told my aunt that I'm studying late at Butler Library and am staying with friends in the city. So I can stay the night."

"That's great," Stone said.

She approached in the dark, but something was different about her. She seemed to take up more space against the darkness. She was a black mass moving towards him like a cloud. A car passed by in the street and its lights played through his high windows, slashing light across Gabby's form. She was wearing the Judge's robe.

"What are you doing?"

"I was cold," she said.

"That's my father's. Nobody wears it."

"I want to wear it," she said, turning a pirouette in the middle of his room. "I won't hurt it."

"It's my father's," he repeated, sitting up on the bed.

"He was very strong, wasn't he? Very powerful. I'm drowning in it."

"Take it off."

"I can smell him in the fabric, that masculine tobacco smell."

"Take it off," Stone said.

"Can I wear it?"

"Take it off," Stone said.

"Do you wear it?" she said.

"When I want to be close to him. When I read his books. When I'm sad." Gabby stepped forward and a bare leg protruded. "Think of me when you wear it." She stepped up to the bed and kissed him on the lips. He reached for her breasts and felt her hard nipples. He could smell the briny scent of Gabby's sex and his father's stale-smelling Nat Shermans on the fabric. She dropped the robe to the floor, pooling it at her feet. She stood completely naked before him, no bra, no panties.

She made him come again later and Stone felt Gabby shudder and writhe against his hand pressed between her legs. Soon, she fell asleep.

Shortly after midnight, Stone dressed and went to the *beis.*

When he returned some hours later, Gabby was awake, worried. "Where were you? I woke up and you were gone."

"I went for a walk," Stone said.

"Out there?" she said, gesturing to Myrtle Avenue.

"Yes," he said. "Out there."

"It's dangerous," she said.

ꙮ 22 ꙮ

The last of the holidays came to an end with Stone being
called up to the *bima* to read the first lines of *Bereshit*, the
book of Genesis. Itzy had preceded him by reciting the last
lines of Deuteronomy, which ended with the death of Moses
and his burial in an unmarked grave. The words slipped easily from Stone's tongue, the Hebrew letters unfolding before him with increasing clarity. He read of the Creation of
the Universe, of unending renewal in the face of death:
from nothing, light was separated from the darkness and
the earth swarmed with living creatures. The Torah scrolls
were paraded around the small sanctuary in a swirling,
joyful celebration of the completion of the reading of the
Torah. Boaz danced a wild Goa-influenced trance-dance,
and Yossi and the pear-shaped one shuffled behind the
Torah, awkwardly kicking out their arms and legs. Moshe
hobbled behind, with uneven shoes, a silent golem waiting
to be called into action. Even Brilliant, always in control,
momentarily lost himself, his head thrown back with
laughter, eyes rolled to the whites as he danced beside the
Groom of Creation.

Stone had continued to recite *Kaddish* for the Judge every morning, becoming more and more familiar with the denizens of the *beis*. There may have been as many as 50 or 60 different men who prayed there, about a quarter of whom he saw again in the shadowy basement after midnight. Most of them were Seligman's former students.

It was during those midnight sessions that Stone felt truly self-possessed, the way he imagined the Judge had felt, striding through the world. With the pistol in his hand, first the practice .22, then the powerful 9 mm., Stone felt none of the apathy, depression or self-negation he had felt for years. It had been Boaz's steady instruction and his blue humor, "just pretend there's hair around it, and shoot your load," that had instilled Stone with the aim of a sharpshooter in short order. But something else was at play as well. The plan, hatched in the mind of his father, birthed by Seligman, and guided by Brilliant to be carried out by Stone and the others in the *beis*, was for something. He had never believed in anything before, but now he realized that he was answering the call of his blood that reached all the way back to Julius, his grandfather. He had been instrumental in the formation of the State of Israel, his assistance had led to death as well, and had shed blood, but it was for something bigger, a homeland for the persecuted, harassed, murdered Jews, of whom Stone realized increasingly he was entirely a part of. He understood that he was the descendant of kings.

Jabotinsky had written of a race that was proud, generous and fierce, who would rise again in all their strength and glory. Stone was a part of that renewal.

He trained nightly with the discipline that was required by the spirit of *Hadar*. And when Federman turned to him once at the shooting range and sneered, "Where did you learn to shoot like that? The FBI?" Stone held his tongue because the spirit of *Hadar* required nobility, chivalry and tact.

Gabby visited Stone three or four times a week after finishing her classes, sleeping over every second visit. They kissed and discovered each other's bodies.

Gabby whispered, "You are my man," as she drifted off to sleep one night.

She slept heavily and never again questioned where he had been when he returned from the *beis*. And upon waking in the morning, she never smelled the mix of chemicals clinging to his hair and skin, because he quietly showered before she awoke, and the acrid stink of the ferric oxide, nitric acid, phenol and methylamine was washed down the drain without a trace.

Boaz and another dark man, who seemed had no name and spoke no English, taught Stone how to fashion a small bomb out of a nine-volt battery and liquid nitrogen, which was held in an empty film canister. He was taught how to assemble the bomb using a simple wristwatch as a timer.

"It may be small," Boaz said, "but so was David."

The bomb could kill; it was strong enough to rip a man to shreds if placed under the seat of his car, but it could also blow a manhole cover, or knock a door down. "But this is still child's play," Boaz added.

Brilliant announced that they would draw lots to determine who would take part in the operation in which four men would enter the tunnel through the Henry Street house, emerge before the stage through the loosened manhole cover, fire their shots and disappear back into the hole.

Moshe would be waiting on Columbia Street with the escape vehicle.

"Only four?" Federman said.

"With four, you'll have enough firepower to kill a hundred men."

A bearded student named Miller said, "What about innocent bystanders? They could be killed too."

Brilliant appeared quickly in his face. He was nearly a head taller than the student and he stared down into Miller's shrinking face and said, "You have to be as strong as iron. Forget about bystanders. Nobody is innocent."

"But what about—"

"What? The children?" Brilliant laughed and said, "If you want to be good, then let yourself be killed. Give up everything that means anything to you." He shook his head and sarcastically added. "Die like a good Jew. Jewish blood has always been cheap."

"But I don't want to die."

"Good," Brilliant said. "Then you'll stay home."

"What?"

"You can leave now. Out," Brilliant said evenly. "Moshe."

Miller sheepishly walked away, glancing back once at Moshe's approaching figure. After he was gone, Brilliant said, "Make sure someone keeps an eye on him."

"This operation sounds like suicide," Boaz said.

"Not with a smoke screen. Nobody will see a thing, except the aftermath."

"It is still suicide," Boaz added.

Brilliant motioned again to Moshe who appeared with a fistful of straw from a corn broom. He held his massive fist out in silence.

"I have confidence in each and every one of you that you are capable of doing what needs to be done. But only four can carry out the operation without increasing the risk. The four who draw the longer straws are in. The rest are reserves, ready as needed."

Stone felt his heart quicken.

"Now I want to reiterate, you are all soldiers and I'm proud of each of you. The work that we have done and are doing and will do, brings Redemption closer—"

Itzy was called forward and he drew a straw. The pear-shaped one followed, then Federman, then Meir, and then Stone. Stone pulled, and the straw loosened from Moshe's sweaty grip was barely two inches long. He could see Federman pump his fist and shout "Yes!" And as the straws disappeared into the hands of the others, Stone realized he was out. *It can't be,* he thought. But it was. Federman, Meir, Yossi and another student, who Stone did not know, held their straws before them and Brilliant smiled a rare smile. "So it's set." They would carry out the Judge's plan.

The pear-shaped student with the watery eyes, who had groaned audibly when he had pulled a short straw, stepped forward and began to sing the Betar Anthem, and before long they were all singing, "*From the pit of decay and dust / With blood and sweat / Will rise a race, proud, generous and fierce / Captured Betar, Yodefet and Masada / Shall rise again in all their strength and glory.*"

When Gabby awoke in the morning, she kissed Stone on the lips and rested her head on his chest.

"Did I wake you?" Stone said.

"No," Gabby yawned. "My brain is so exhausted from studying it's getting that Bretton-Woods and Cape Breton are starting to sound alike to me. Sometimes I think I could sleep forever."

"You don't want to do that," Stone said.

"Not without breakfast," Gabby said, running her fingers over Stone's scarred thigh.

"Wait," Stone said, as Gabby froze in a wide-eyed comic tableau, dressed in her panties and one of Stone's old sweatshirts, the morning sun sifting down onto her golden body. "I just want to look at you."

It was the end of the first week of October and an early frost threatened. The Yankees had played up in the Bronx the night before in nearly 40-degree weather, and had won the game on a broken bat ninth-inning single. Yossi rang Stone's buzzer and called him out to the street. He had been reading steadily since he had awoken that morning and had lost himself inside his head. He had forgotten to go to the *beis* to say *Kaddish*.

Federman sat scowling in the passenger seat, and Stone was glad to see that Itzy was in the back seat. He got into the car.

"Didn't see you this morning," Federman said, lifting his Yankees cap off his head and wiping his brow. "You still with us?"

The car turned onto Myrtle Avenue, the windows fogging.

"Aw, leave him alone," Yossi said. "He forgot."

"That's why he's out and we're in." Federman punched the dashboard. "Where's your fucking defrost?"

Itzy looked tired and he smiled at Stone. The car stopped at a red light, and Stone could tell that Federman was nervous every time a black passed close to the idling car. On the sidewalk, a makeshift shrine of candles and flowers lay before a gaudy portrait of a young man painted on a red brick wall with the words "We'll never forget you T. Peace."

They drove on and soon the Williamsburg Savings Bank Tower was behind them receding in the rearview mirror, and they were driving down the broad industrial stretch of 4th Avenue, passing used tire shops, gas stations and dark squalid doorways.

"Don't worry about this morning," Yossi said. "You can say *Kaddish* tonight."

Federman tugged on his wispy beard. "This place is a hell-hole. Who could live like this?"

"Then why don't you go back to the *Eretz*?" Itzy said, speaking at last.

"When I've done what I have to do," Federman said.

They passed through Sunset Park and reached the fringes of Bay Ridge. In another few blocks Stone anticipated the Verrazano Bridge coming into view against the slate sky. The car came to a stop before an intersection. An 'R' train stop was on the corner and schoolkids bustled past.

Federman rolled his window down and crisp autumn air was fresh on Stone's face.

"Here they come," Federman said, leaning out the window. Stone could see a clutch of about a dozen schoolgirls, probably middle schoolers, dressed in their dark winter coats, white head scarves bright against their brown faces. They laughed and moved as one, as if each girl were connected to the same nervous system of a central body.

"Hey," Federman called out the window. "Going home to fuck your fathers, or your brothers?"

The girls laughed and stopped.

"You, with the mustache. They let you out without a leash?"

Several of the girls gave Federman the finger and moved on.

Federman jumped out of the car; so did Yossi. They were two heads taller than most of the girls. Yossi said something in Arabic.

"Bitch cunts," Federman called, as a few of the girls disappeared down into the 'R' train station. "Run, you monkeys."

"This is crazy," Itzy said. "I thought we were—" and he popped out of the car.

In an instant he was restraining Federman who pushed him away.

One of the girls shouted back, "Fucking Jew."

Federman threw a piece of garbage he had found on the ground and she called out, "Nice throw, asshole," and disappeared with the rest of the girls into the subway station.

"I'm going to get her," Federman said.

"Enough," Itzy said.

"You heard what that Arab called me."

"Leave her alone."

Stone stepped out of the car and helped Itzy direct Yossi and Federman back into the car. Inside, Federman turned to Itzy, "What are you, some kind of fucking goy? An Arab?"

"They're just girls."

"One day they'll be mothers," Yossi said. "And their sons will be martyrs of their genocidal fight."

"Oh, come on."

"Do you want Jewish blood to be on your hands?" Yossi said. "An Arab killed your father."

"No," Itzy said. "No. But this is not how we do it."

"You're a fucking goy, a weak and *converso* goy, who's ashamed to be—"

"I'm ashamed of you."

"Oh, are you," Federman said. "Then go convert to their gutter religion and get it over with."

Stone looked into Federman's hard eyes and saw blind conviction.

"Itzy's right, you know," he interjected.

"Shut up," Federman said.

"Hey," Yossi said. "Lay off him. He didn't do anything."

"That's right. He didn't do anything. He'll never do anything."

An NYPD cruiser slowed near their car and Yossi pressed his foot to the accelerator and turned right when the light changed.

"I know he's the Judge's son," Federman said, "but where has he been all this time? He's not like us. He doesn't know Torah, yet he's called up to read at Simchat Torah. He didn't study with the Rav. I don't know who he is. I don't trust him." And now he turned to Stone. "I'm keeping my eye on you. You'll fuck the whole plan up. You'll blab your mouth."

Stone knew the Judge would want him eliminated. Thucydides had written about the importance of discipline; so had Jabotinsky, Clausewitz and others. The Judge had marked those passages. "I don't care if you don't trust me. This was small-time thuggery, nothing more. I have two witnesses here that can attest to your reckless behavior today. You are a threat to the plan. My father's plan. You are a danger to us all. What do you think Brilliant would say if he knew that you were out on 4th Avenue calling attention to yourself? What do you think would happen?"

"You're going to tell on me?"

"No. You're going to tell Brilliant what you did."

"Over my dead body. You're not taking my place."

Stone ignored him. "You're going to tell him what you did today."

Itzy nodded approval.

Federman was silent in the front seat, arms crossed. His eyes were glazed with a film of tears.

Yossi looked into the rearview mirror, raised his eyebrows. After moment he tried to lighten the mood with a joke. "Who won the Arab beauty contest?"

The car was silent and for a long time Yossi held his tongue then finally said, "No one!" But nobody laughed.

~ 23 ~

Stone met Gabby beneath the glowing green globe that marked the entryway to the 'G' train station. She climbed the steep stairs that smelled of urine and other human waste, her school bag humped on her back as she called out, "Sorry I'm late." She wore a pair of studious-looking round, steel-rimmed glasses.

He looked down at his watch and smiled. "You're right on time."

She threw herself into his arms. "It took forever and I thought I'd never get here. Three trains, standing on the first two. It gives me the creeps, being packed into a small space like that. So helpless. I missed you," she said. "How do you like my Emma Goldman glasses?"

"More like the lascivious librarian," Stone replied.

"I was reading on the train."

"Anything good?"

"Yeah, real page turner on the International Monetary Fund."

They kissed. "Let's go home," she said, taking his hand.

Stone hesitated; they were outside. He had never held her hand in public.

"Who's going to see us?" she said. "My uncle Dovid?"

They walked down the crooked slate sidewalks of Waverly Avenue, giggling and joking around. Gabby blew a misshapen pink bubble that Stone popped with his finger.

"What did you learn at school today?"

She laughed. "So that's it. You love me for my mind." Her smile dropped in horror. "I mean you—"

"It's okay," Stone said. He was seized by an uncontrollable joy. "It's okay. I do."

"I'm stupid," Gabby said. "I'm sorry. I honestly didn't want to make you say that. I'm not a manipulator."

"But I wanted to," Stone said.

A streetlight flickered as they passed a newly renovated carriage house, bedecked with autumn wreaths and cornstalks. It was incongruous for the city and Stone pointed it out.

"It's just, I don't want things to change between us," Gabby said.

"They won't," he said.

The windows of the neighboring carriage house were dark, and Stone slowed to catch his reflection in the glass. He saw a face he barely recognized and stopped short before the image. Gabby continued down the sidewalk, humming lightly. He had noticed a gradual alteration in his features since he had returned to Brooklyn; his face, gaunt, sharp, intense, his eyes smoldering. And as time passed he realized that he looked more and more like his grandfather, Papa Julius. He was beginning to see the same confidence etched into his face that he had seen in all those old photographs. But now, the face staring back at him, this phantasm, this broad-faced dybbuk seemed to be mocking him with its idiot smile. He realized with a jolt that he was not seeing his reflection at all, he was in fact looking through the glass into the face of a young Chinese boy, who stuck out his tongue. Stone stared back studying the face, and then Gabby called after him. "Come on, slowpoke."

When they arrived at his apartment, Stone was surprised to see that the homeboys had gone, leaving their milk crates tipped over in the middle of the sidewalk. Stone was relieved.

As he fumbled for his key, an impossibly tall, thin man approached from the corner of his eye. He was white and wore chinos and a light windbreaker. "Excuse me," the man said. "Got a minute?"

"No," Stone said brusquely.

"Matthew, just a minute," the stranger pressed.

Stone turned to Gabby and her eyes said to give the guy a break.

"Why don't you go inside?" Stone said to Gabby. "I'll buzz you when I'm ready."

The door swung shut behind Gabby.

"Matthew Stone. I'm Agent Gargiulio of the JTTF." He had a long, thin face with deep worn creases in it.

"What happened to Zohar?" Stone laughed. "He get fired?"

"He wants to speak with you, but figured he'd be doing you a favor if he sent me. You don't want to be seen with agent Zohar by certain persons. Correct?"

"Maybe I don't want to see his person," Stone said.

"I have authority to take you in right now for passing false information. Now, you either agree to speak with him or I take you in."

Stone felt suddenly afraid. Maybe he wasn't FBI at all, but sent by Brilliant to test him, or someone else altogether. "How do I know who you are?"

"I performed the cavity search on Michael Zinaburg. Would you like me to describe his birthmarks or the length of his dick?"

Agent Gargiulio was more tightly wound than Zohar. His jaw was tightly clenched.

"I guess you're too tall for undercover, so you get stuck with the dirty work."

"Matty, are you all right?" Gabby's voice appeared over the crackling intercom.

"I'll be right in."

"Hurry," she said.

"I can take you in right now," Agent Gargiulio said, indicating the intercom. "Leave her to worry. Now what's it going to be?"

"Okay," Stone said. "Okay. When and where?"

"Tomorrow. First thing."

"But," Stone said, "I have to say *Kaddish*."

"I don't give a shit about cottage. Nine a.m. in the Greenwood Cemetery Chapel." And with that, Gargiulio stalked off, his long shadow stretching up the brick wall of Stone's apartment and around the corner.

"What did he want?" Gabby said, when he swung in through the door of his apartment. She had already slipped out of her clothes and into the Judge's robe and was eating a yogurt with a plastic spoon.

"He wanted to know how to get back to Long Island."

The answer seemed to satisfy Gabby. She kissed him and dropped onto the couch, pulling her hair back in a ponytail.

"Hey. How come we never go out? We always stay in here."

"Can you wear the robe at your aunt's house?"

"Matty, I'm serious."

"Where do you want to go around here? You said yourself it's not safe."

"I know," she said. "But I feel kept."

"Okay," Stone said. "So let's go out. I'll buy you dinner."

"No, no," Gabby said. "I don't care about expensive dinners. I like staying here with you. I do. Sit next to me."

Stone sat, could feel the warmth of her body against his.

"It's just, all we do is come here and—"

"You don't like it?"

"I do. Very much. But we should have a date. Be with people in public. I don't want to hide."

"Is your aunt ready for this?"

"That's not what I mean. There's a luncheon next Wednesday up at Columbia, and my professor is being honored. I want you to come. I want you to meet him. You'd like him."

Wednesday was the day of the Rally for Palestine. Stone was silent, then said "Wednesday?"

"Oh, come on," Gabby said in a harsh tone. "Are you afraid to cross the river into Manhattan? This is really important to me."

"Wednesday? You're kidding, right?"

"No. I'm not kidding. This means a lot to me."

She knew, she had to know. The fact that she wore his father's robe was signal enough. She was saying that she identified with the Judge, and by saying that, she was silently acknowledging the plan, the Judge's legacy.

"All right," Stone said, winking at Gabby. "I'd love to go. We'll go to Columbia next Wednesday for lunch."

⚮

The elaborately spired Gothic gate beckoned and Stone drove beneath the arch to the noisy squawking of the electric green parakeets that roosted in the nooks of the ornate spires. Stone felt his blood calm as he entered the gate, surrounded by the turning autumn trees and peaceful statuary depicting winged children, mourning women, and angels. He saw the black car that had followed him turn off Fifth Avenue and he pressed his foot to the gas, racing through the honeycomb streets of the cemetery, winding up and down hills, passing narrow footpaths, great obelisks, hunched stone tombs, majestic family crypts. He knew that many of Brooklyn's famous and infamous had been buried here: Samuel Morse, inventor of the telegraph; FAO Schwartz; Louis Comfort Tiffany; Charles Ebbets, owner of the Brooklyn Dodgers; Henry Ward Beecher, the abolitionist, who had founded Beecher Academy; the composer Leonard Bernstein, who had been buried there just after Stone had left for college; even Albert Anastasia, former mob boss, and Crazy Joe Gallo, hitman for the Gambinos had been buried there.

Stone thought briefly of Papa Julius and was saddened that he was buried so far from home, among strangers in a well-ordered verdant Florida cemetery, far from the majesty of Greenwood. He thought of the Judge, buried in the holy soil of Jerusalem, so far away, and Stone felt loneliness enshroud him. He would never be buried alongside his family, scattered throughout the world as they were.

316

He wound his way through the cemetery and finally parked his car near the statue of Athena that overlooked New York Harbor. The car that had been tailing him was gone, and Stone took off by foot through the graves towards the chapel.

The heavy wooden door to the chapel was closed, but not locked, and he entered the marble and glass sanctuary with trepidation. Zohar was sitting alone on the front bench before the altar. He seemed to be musing on the stained-glass tableau of Jesus, pensively stroking his trimmed goatee. He did not turn his head when he said, "Matthew. Sit down."

His voice was dry and flinty, absent of emotion, as if he were trying to hold back a torrent of rage. His words echoed off the high decorous ceiling and fell hard on Stone's ears. "You know how stupid you are?" Zohar said, staring straight ahead; it seemed as if he were chastising the mute representation of the Son of God. "You lied to a federal agent. You gave me false information."

"Do you want an explanation?" Stone said.

"What's to explain? You lied to me. And I was foolish enough to believe that I had gotten through to you."

"I saw you with my mother on DeKalb Avenue."

Zohar laughed. "So that's it. Playing childish games. What, to get back at your mother?"

"No," Stone said. "After 14 years without seeing my mother, she calls me after the death of my father. Why? Because she wants a relationship with her only child? No. It's because she was paid by the FBI to spy on me, to provide you with information to satisfy your quixotic fantasies."

"She cares deeply about you," Zohar said. "Any mother would try and keep her son out of trouble if she had the chance."

"Yeah," Stone said. "For a minute, I actually thought she came back to see me."

"I never paid her a cent," Zohar said.

"Then you got fair value. Because there's nothing to tell."

"What goes on inside that warehouse?" Zohar said.

"Oh, get off that," Stone said. "I'm saying *Kaddish* for my father."

"At two in the morning?"

"I'm studying Torah. Is that hard for you to understand? Why are we in a Christian chapel? If you want to know what goes on inside the warehouse, get a search warrant and look for yourself. I'm sure the Anti-Defamation League will appreciate that."

Zohar jumped to his feet, and, as if on cue, a soundtrack of angelic choral music flooded out of speakers hidden on high.

He looked tired, his face raw, his eyes wild. "I chose this place for your safety. This is the last place any of those fanatics would look for you."

"Why do you care so much about me?" Stone said.

"You know they would kill you if they saw you with me." Zohar paused a moment for effect. "NYPD found a wallet covered in blood in Wallabout Bay, then a body – your roommate."

Stone did not blanch.

"Matthew. He sold five pounds of military grade C-4 explosives to an undercover agent and the next day he was off our radar, gone. You could be next."

"I haven't done anything wrong."

"Just tell me what goes on in that warehouse. We don't want to have another Waco."

"It's a synagogue," Stone said.

"I'll bet it's an armed camp."

"Just leave me alone."

"You are not like them," Zohar said. "You are not part of that world."

Stone was silent. He watched Zohar crack his neck from jerking side to side. "As we move into the 21st century, it is us against them, the extremist against civil society. The biggest threat to our society is ideologically motivated groups armed with—"

"This is laughable," Stone said. "Admit you have your own agenda."

Zohar ignored him and continued, "You are part of this society with your liberal education, your urbane upbringing, your values."

"Is this what your thumbnail sketch says?"

Zohar rubbed his forehead. "There's going to be a catastrophic terrorist attack in Brooklyn. You can help me, or you can not help me, but I'm going to stop it. I'm appealing to your sense of right and wrong for the last time. Don't let yourself become an accessory to murder. People's lives are at stake."

"How do you know there's going to be an attack?"

"I'm connecting the dots."

"The assassinations, in Brooklyn, Jersey and Dearborn? Are those all dots?"

"Part of the big picture," Zohar said.

The morning light flared behind stained glass.

"What do you want from me? To help you arrest a bunch of yeshiva students, because you believe that they are a group of dangerous terrorists? I know and you know that the killing of those Arabs was carried out by other Arabs, not Jews. It's true isn't it?"

"It's true," Zohar said after a moment.

"Blame the Jews for everything," Stone said. "Another blood libel. You are a fucking liar. And you expect me to help you." Stone stood up, and the bench slid back, scraping on the marble floor. "Am I free to go?"

"Matthew, listen," Zohar said. "When I spoke to you, all the evidence pointed towards—"

"The Jews," Stone said. "Just like you tried to pin the World Trade Center bombing on the Jews."

"You don't understand. Two days after I spoke to you about it, an Arab man, a Palestinian in his mid-20s, reported his rental car stolen and was foolish enough to provide his real identification. We found gunpowder on his clothes, and he broke down, admitted to everything."

"And yet you point your finger at the Jews. Why are you always looking for Jews to be the villains?"

"Matthew, you know I'm not."

"Blue-blooded G-man in a suit. Do you think that becoming like them will save you?"

"Do you?" Zohar said.

"I'm not ashamed of being Jewish," Stone said.

"You've come a long way," Zohar said, chuckling.

"Fuck you."

"Do you want to know what happened to Fairuza Freij?"

"You've got it all wrong," Stone said. "The past is past."

"The past is never the past for a Jew. The past lives on perpetually, its weight and burden heavy on his shoulders. The Jew lives forever in the past even as time moves forward. Why do you think the Jew is so possessive of his past?"

"Why?" Stone said.

"Because, it grants him a power, a strength that is bigger than the individual. He is empowered by the bookish, pious, martyred history that connects him personally to God. How vain is it that the Jews believe that God chose them out of all the people of the world to be his Chosen?"

The door creaked open behind Stone and a white spear of sunlight slashed across the cool marble floor. An elderly couple stood in the sunshine smiling, as if waiting to be invited in.

"You hate yourself," Stone said. "And you hate yourself because you are a Jew and there's nothing you can do about it."

The door swung shut behind Stone and the couple was gone.

"I'm Jewish," Zohar said. "But I will not be ruined by history."

Stone laughed now. Everything was so clear to him. He thought of Jonathan Pollard, the U.S. Naval Intelligence analyst who had been arrested by the FBI for selling top-secret military intelligence to the Israeli government. He had been given a life sentence and his plea for clemency had recently been denied by President Clinton. But this was not the first time, Stone recalled, that Jews had been accused of split loyalties, of being a nation within a nation. He remembered the nightmare tales the Judge had told him about Alfred Dreyfus, the 19th-century French artillery officer, who had been accused of passing secrets along to Germany simply because he was Jewish, and of his exile to Devil's Island. Stone thought of the Rosenbergs, Ethel and Julius, who had been executed for passing nuclear secrets along to the Soviets. But it was Pollard, Stone knew, who had driven Zohar to seek out Jews as his target, as if wearing blinders to the reality before him, anything other than that would be suspect in the eyes of the conservative FBI establishment. Zohar had found a way to adapt, carved out his niche and saved his skin. But at what cost?

"If the future of Israel was at stake," Stone questioned, "and you had the ability to help her, at the expense of the United States, would you?"

"No," Zohar said. "I'm an American first."

"Do you remember that Senator, Joe Kennedy, the anti-Semite, and his work for the State Department during the war?"

Zohar stood up and slapped his thigh with the palm of his hand. "You've drunk the Kool Aid," Zohar said, walking to the door. "They got to you."

"Nobody got to me," Stone said. "*You* drunk the Kool Aid, swallowed the whole fucking pitcher. They'll never trust you. You can turn your back on your people, you can give up Israel, but to them you will always be a Jew."

"Matthew. What happened to you?"

"I woke up. It took a long time, but I finally opened my eyes to the world."

"You're sick. You need help."

"I've never felt better in my life."

Zohar crossed his arms. "What do you think happens to an unmarried pregnant woman in Beit Jala?"

"It's not my problem," Stone said.

"What if it was your friend, Fairuza Freij? Would that make a difference? Would it matter that she had to rush into marriage with a man she barely knew, someone her parents had picked out, just because she would not be able to explain away the growing bulge in her belly?"

"That's not my concern," Stone said.

"And how do you think Gabby Grunhut would feel about this, her boyfriend, father of an Arab child?"

"Keep her out of this," Stone shouted.

Stone stared with hard eyes. Mention of Gabby's name made his heart jump. He felt his arms shaking, his muscles electric beneath his skin. He would kill Zohar if he had to, since only he had the power to expose this awful secret to Gabby.

"Keep Gabby out of this. She hasn't done anything and neither have I."

"Matthew. There's going to be an attack at the Rally for Palestine on Wednesday. I don't know how, but I know there's going to be an attack."

"Stick up for anyone but the Jews, is that it?"

"These are human lives," he said. "Information I've gathered says that human lives are at risk. That is all that matters."

"Well, good luck then," Stone said, moving towards the door.

"His name is Salem," Zohar said. "Peace."

Stone paused in the doorway. He was a father just as Julius and the Judge had been fathers, neither perfect, both estranged from their sons, intense, distant, but deeply connected. And the sons had made it, Stone knew, both the Judge and he had survived and made their way through the world. One day his son would come looking for him, and Stone knew he would face him as an enemy.

"Thanks," Stone said.

"Do you want to contribute to this hundred-year conflict? Help create a more violent and divided world for your son to grow up in?"

"I don't want to do anything," Stone said flatly. "Put out your snipers and barbed wire and Jersey barriers. You won't find anything."

"Oh, I will," Zohar said. "I'll be there with my eyes wide open."

The door swung open, and Stone stepped out into the crisp autumn air. He was met by Gargiulio who grabbed him by roughly by the shoulders and pressed him face first into the stone wall of the chapel. He had been following Stone, after all. "Lying to a federal agent is a jailable offense," he said flatly. He pulled Stone's arms behind him and snapped on a pair of handcuffs.

"Let him go," Zohar said with disgust. He slipped on a pair of sunglasses as he closed the door behind him. "Forget him. This piece of shit's not worth the time."

❧ 24 ❧

On Monday morning, just two days away from the Rally for Palestine and the execution of the Judge's plan, Stone woke to find that he was alone, that Gabby was not in the bed beside him. In fact, the pillow was not even marked from the weight of her head.

He sat up in bed. "Gabby," he called. But then, shaking off the last remnants of a dream, he realized that they had fought the night before.

Gabby had returned from the library where she had been studying, and Stone was irritated that she had not called. In some dark part of his mind he knew that she was with another man; he had never studied so hard when he was at school. During his time at Wesleyan, whenever Emmanuelle had called, he had rushed over to her immediately, dropping everything related to his studies, just to press himself into her lean body, to sweat in the darkness with her. Even Fairuza had skipped class at the Hebrew University to be with Stone. She had given herself entirely to him, cried out his name as he came into her. But Gabby had remained reluctant to sleep with Stone, and he had

tired of her spit-slicked hand jobs. The one time she had
taken him into her mouth, after several days of cajoling, her
teeth had scraped up and down along the shaft of his penis
and left him feeling raw and bitter.

"Are you mad?"

"No," Stone said. "It's just—"

"It's just what?"

"Nothing," Stone said.

"It's not easy for me, you know. I'm trying, okay?"

The night before, when she was late arriving from the
library, things had been worse. Stone had drunk a bottle of
wine while he waited for her in the Judge's robe. When she
did arrive, he tore off her clothes, pulling her skirt and
panties down around her ankles.

"I want you," he had said. "I need you."

"Not now."

"When? When?"

"I don't know."

"You're not being fair," Stone said.

Gabby bit her lip. "I told you I'm not ready."

"When?"

"Matthew, don't."

"I've got protection."

"No."

"There's nothing to worry about."

He kissed her hard on the mouth and tasted cherry-fla-
vored chewing gum. She had kissed Dov with that mouth,
and others too.

"Let's go in the bedroom."

Gabby stepped back, bent over and pulled up her skirt.
She moved slowly, gingerly, her sad eyes on Stone.

"What?" He looked at her.

"We have to talk."

He turned, found a cigarette on the counter, and lit it.

"My aunt thinks I've been staying out too much."

"And?"

"I think I shouldn't stay over for a while. She's starting to wonder."

"You're a grown-up," Stone said.

"I know," Gabby said. "But, she's my aunt."

"And what am I?"

"Don't do that."

"Do you care about me?"

"Yes I do," Gabby said. "But I'm living in my aunt's house and have to respect her rules."

"You're twenty-three. You're not a child anymore."

"She's helping me out a lot by letting me stay with her while I am in school."

Stone leapt forward. "Stay with me. Move in here. I've got plenty of room. We can make you an office out of the second bedroom in back. You can study in peace."

Gabby began to laugh.

"What's so funny?"

"Nothing. I can see your erection poking out of the robe."

He closed the robe. "We're near the subway. Rent is cheap—"

"Be patient," Gabby said. "We're not in a hurry."

"Have a drink," Stone said.

"No. I'd better go."

"Now?" Stone took her hand and gently pulled her towards his room.

"Not tonight," Gabby said. "Come on."

"What about what I want? Doesn't it matter that I want you to stay? Or is it always about you?"

"Me?" Gabby said, pulling away. "Don't be ridiculous. Let go of me."

She twisted her arm and wrenched herself free.

"Don't you care about me?"

"I do," Gabby said. "But things are complicated. I don't always know what I want. It's scary."

"Don't go."

"I have to."

"Don't."

And then Stone fell back on the old habit he had drawn on in times of helplessness, loss and pain. He took a deep drag of the cigarette, pulled open the robe and pressed the cigarette into his skin, just above his heart. And he felt a jolt of pain like he had never felt before, an elemental shock that made the valves of his heart constrict as if he were being choked from within.

"What are you doing?" Gabby screamed. "Stop it!"

He pressed the cigarette into his skin again. He could smell the acrid odor of his own flesh burning, and a sense of power and control gathering itself within his chest. She would have to stay now.

"Stop it. Stop it. Stop it," Gabby cried, fat tears rolling down her face.

"I just want to be with you," Stone said through glazed eyes.

"So do I," Gabby said. "Drop it, please."

"Stay tonight?"

"I can't. Matthew, please put the cigarette down."

"You're leaving."

"Matty. I have to go."

He took a long drag on his cigarette, reigniting its pulsing tip. He held it between his thumb and forefinger in a casual backwards motion so the filter faced Gabby and the tip, his bare skin.

"Run away then."

"I'm not running. I care about you."

"You don't care."

"I do. I, please—"

"Then why won't you let me— ?"

"Stop it."

"You and Dov did it."

"Matthew. If you have to know, Dov and I never had sex."

"But you said—"

"It was a long time ago. I was too young, fifteen, with a soldier from Be'er Sheva who was guarding our school bus. I don't even know how it happened. I did it once and it was a mistake. There was nothing sexy or erotic about it, okay? Now you know everything. I'm not holding back because of you. It's not you. You have to trust me when I say that I want to. It's just that I can't yet. I have to be sure because you can never take it back."

He butted the cigarette out on the counter and moved forward to embrace her.

"I've got to go," she said, moving towards the door. "Promise me you won't do anything stupid. Please don't hurt yourself."

"I'm sorry, Gabby."

"I am too," she said, and was gone.

After Gabby had left, Stone rushed to the *beis* and found Brilliant in conference at a round table with Moshe. He looked surprised to see Stone.

"We're finished training," he said. "Go home, Matthew."

Stone shivered in the frigid warehouse, his chest burning beneath his thin shirt.

"Federman's gone?" Stone questioned.

"Yes," Brilliant said.

"Let me take his place on Wednesday. I'm ready to die if you need me to."

Brilliant laughed. "Spoken like a true soldier."

"I need to be part of this," Stone said.

"You are a part of this," Brilliant said, standing up from the round table. He approached Stone and opened a bright smile that almost made him look handsome.

"Please," Stone said. "Please. I need to be part of this. I need to be the one."

"You want to shoot Amalek? You want to fire the gun?"

"Yes."

"Matthew, I just want you to understand that we are all part of this. We are all brave Maccabees. But everyone has a role to play and you have done so well in yours."

"But I haven't done anything."

"Yes, you have."

Stone felt his eyes film over. His chest burned.

"My father would have wanted—"

"Your father would be proud. You are a quick study. And there will be other opportunities."

"No," Stone shouted. Moshe looked up from the table, blank-eyed. "I have to be part of this. Federman's out. Put me in."

"It's too late," Brilliant said in a soothing tone. "They've already had a test run down in the tunnel. They know the landscape. You've done your part."

"Please," Stone said. "You don't understand."

Brilliant took Stone by the shoulders and gave him a soft shaking. "Matthew. It's going to happen. You have done your part and you should be proud. Now go home, get some sleep and on Wednesday, sit back in front of the television and watch as the fruits of your labor bloom for the whole world to see."

Stone opened his mouth to speak, but Brilliant said, "Goodnight," and returned to Moshe at the table.

∞

Stone heard footsteps and the soft creaking of the floorboards in his living room.

"Gab," he called.

Nobody answered and Stone went pale. He had made a point of double locking the door after returning from the *beis*. His voice trembled as he called, "Gabby!"

"It's me," a voice that was not Gabby's returned. "I've been calling you all week."

For a time, Stone said nothing. A weak morning light sifted down through the windows as the garbage men out in the street tossed empty cans clattering back to the sidewalk. The pneumatic brakes of a city bus sighed loudly out on Myrtle Avenue.

He heard Abi's feet moving closer. "Have you been avoiding me?" She appeared in the doorway wearing fitted black leather pants and boots. Her hair hung loosely around her face, and even from the distance of ten feet he could see stray gray hairs against the black background.

"What time is it?"

"Twenty after six. I wanted to make sure I got here before you left for the day."

"How did you get in?"

"Michael gave me a key."

"Give me the key," Stone said, sitting up. He pulled a T-shirt on and jumped out of bed.

"What happened to your chest?"

"Nothing," Stone said.

"Did you burn yourself?"

"Why don't you ask Agent Zohar?"

She threw up her hands and said, "What should I have done then? He said you were in trouble. Any mother would have done what I did."

"I'm not in trouble and you are not a mother." He stared with scrutinizing eyes at her in the shining leather pants, her white shirt untucked, open at the neck to reveal a line of cleavage. "Look at you."

They stood in silence while Stone pulled the covers back over his bed.

"If you're going to stay, I'm going out."

"I want to talk to you, that's all."

"I'm listening."

She sighed deeply. Her face seemed suddenly to be worn by age and worry.

"I had hoped you would have given me another chance. Maybe it was too much for me to force myself onto you. It wasn't fair to stay here. It was just that I felt we had the opportunity to make up for lost time all at once. It was a mistake. But I thought we had a chance for a fresh start without the Judge to get in between us. I wanted—"

"And you always get what you want, don't you?"

"This is not what I wanted."

"You didn't want to be a renowned artist?"

"I did. But I wanted more. I wanted a family. I want to be with my son. Do you know how hard it's been all these years?"

"Don't tell me about hard."

Her dark face had turned pale and seemed to be transforming itself right before Stone's eyes into that of an old woman, gaunt and drawn. Her outfit seemed slightly vulgar to Stone.

"Why do you show up here dressed like that?"

"Oh, Matthew," she said. "What happened to my little boy? You know I used to take you everywhere, the park, the galleries, Coney Island, and everywhere we went, you held my hand so tight, you wouldn't let go. We went to the Botanic Garden and looked at the trees and the flowers and you asked so many questions. You loved me. Do you remember?"

"And then you left."

"I don't want to sound like a martyr."

"Then don't."

"I did it for you. I could have spoken to a lawyer about bringing you to live with me. I could have spoken to dozens of lawyers, gone to the papers. But it would never have worked out. Your father smeared me, made me look like an unfit mother. He had it all figured out, that cynical bastard. But I was just the opposite. He was connected, he was a judge with a steady income, and I was a hand-to-mouth artist, always on the move. What else could I have done to change that?"

"You could have stayed if you really wanted. You're not a weak person."

"I had to leave. I had no choice."

Stone stared at her. He saw her eyes filled with tears. "Is this supposed to be some display of maternal compassion?"

"You hate me."

"I don't know who you are."

She wiped away a tear. "And I don't know who you are. But you are my only son."

"I have to go say *Kaddish*," Stone said, pulling on a sweater. "Lock the door on your way out and slide the key under the door."

"Matthew," Abi's lips trembled. "I'm going out to California. I have been offered a position at Berkeley."

"Congratulations," Stone said flatly. "You see, things do work out for you."

"I've got a cab waiting outside and two plane tickets. I want you to come with me, live with me. I have a room set aside just for you. You don't need to be angry anymore."

"I'm not angry," Stone said. "I've never felt better. I feel completely at peace with myself and the world."

"Come on. Brooklyn is a complete cesspool, it always was. Matthew, there's nothing here for you."

"There's everything I need. I have my books. I have a woman. I have a synagogue where I say *Kaddish*."

"So you've become a full-time penitent. Make peace with your father in the next world, that bastard. He fucked up your head. I know. I lived with him too. I know how he can make you feel inferior. Well, Matthew, I have news for you, nobody in this world could ever please Judge Walter Joseph Stone."

Her eyes flickered as she caught sight of the Judge's robe hanging on the wall behind Stone. She leapt past him before he could react and grabbed the robe and began tearing at it with her hands. "If you're going to burn something, burn this. Your father is nothing but a cult of murder and lies."

Stone grabbed the robe back from her. He could smell Gabby intermingled with the Judge on the fabric.

"Stop your moralizing. The way I see it, what you did to me was worse than anything the Judge could ever have done to anyone. I inherit my father. You can crawl away and die."

"Matthew, you're sick. Your contempt is frightening."

"Then leave."

She stepped into the hallway, her gait stern and confident as if she were trying to force strength into herself through her steps alone. She turned around at the door, her black eyes hard again.

"I'm afraid for you, Matthew. Not of you, but for you."

"Goodbye," Stone said.

∽ 25 ⊲

A cheery female voice intoned, "Security is tight at today's Rally for Palestine, described by organizers as a gathering of hope, in support of self-determination and equal rights for the disaffected around the world and in Palestine. And it seems that they *have* come from around the world *and* around the city by the thousands, New Yorkers and visitors alike."

Stone found the rally televised on a local cable station, the one that aired *City Hall This Week* and *Close-Up on Broadway*. He sat on the couch in jeans and short sleeves, though the day outside was crisp and clear, with an autumn chill in the air. He lit a joint and inhaled deeply. The streets outside his apartment were unusually quiet and Stone sat still before the set, his eyes narrowed to focus on the small screen. He dragged on his joint and felt his body relax into itself. He felt the wound at his chest, thought of Gabby and imagined that part of his heart had been ripped away. He stretched his hand out before him and studied the back of it, the blue tributaries of veins, his pale skin, nails chewed short. Had this hand done all it could? What if he were the one to fire the gun? His life as he knew it would be forever changed. But now, he had to sit back and wait.

"Traffic is snarled throughout downtown Brooklyn as the NYPD has closed off numerous streets with concrete Jersey barriers along Atlantic Avenue and 4th Avenue where the procession will make its way to the recently completed Al Salaam Mosque in Bay Ridge. Tension is high in the wake of twin suicide bombings in Tel Aviv Sunday morning and Jewish leaders have pledged to demonstrate against the rally."

The camera cut to a previously taped interview with a silver-bearded man in his early fifties who wore a large *kippah* on his head. "Blood is on their hands. I just don't think it's time to party when people are dying."

Next, a young woman with a pimply complexion spoke. She was dressed in the colors of the local Quaker school that nominally competed for students with Beecher Academy and St. Anne's. She spoke with a passion and sincerity that irritated Stone. "The colonial occupation of Arab lands must end. As long as there is one Arab child living in squalid refugee camps, the resistance is justified."

The female newscaster picked up where she had left off before the producers had cut to video, "The Mayor's office issued an eleventh hour appeal to organizers to postpone the rally until the political situation abroad has stabilized, even threatening to issue an injunction, but organizers cited the annual Salute to Israel rally that runs down Manhattan's Fifth Avenue as precedent that gatherings such as these have not been canceled in the past despite political turmoil."

Stone thought of his father, buried in the earth on the Mount of Olives. He had marched in the Israel parade for years. If only he were alive to see this. Today would be the final legacy of the Judge's great life. Stone rushed to his room and found his father's Judge's robe beneath the bed where Abi had tossed it in anger. He laid it out on the bed, ironed out the wrinkles with the palm of his hand and closed his eyes. He imagined the Judge materializing before him, rising from the bed, his bulk incredible as he towered over Stone. His broad chest heaved as he breathed in and out, his eyes like burning coals, his head like a sculpted block of marble. His sheer physical presence was dizzying. He reached his hand out, large as a first baseman's mitt and touched Stone on the chest, above the heart where he had burned himself. He felt a rush of blood to the spot where his father touched him and words like failure, disgrace, worthless, vermin, contrary and disappointment were excised from his body like a tumor being cut away. His father's hand cauterized the wound. When he opened his eyes, his father was gone and the robe lay as it had, flat on the bed. He draped it over himself and returned to the television.

A podium was set up amidst the crowds of people, many chanted and some held banners above their heads. A photo of the Israeli prime minister shared a placard with Adolf Hitler. A lectern draped with the Palestinian colors stood at the front of the stage; a row of chairs lined in the back. Stone could see stern-faced plainclothes men and regular officers holding back the crowd, and people hanging out of their apartment windows for the best view.

"Quite a crowd today," a male voice said. "There's almost a circus atmosphere here in Brooklyn."

"Wait till next week and the Yankees parade down the Canyon of Heroes which we will carry live from Broadway."

"Not so fast," the male voice laughed. "We still have to win one more game."

"Well, I have confidence that the Bronx Bombers will bring home another championship for this great city."

A solitary fly buzzed past Stone's ear and rested on the screen. The banter was nauseating.

"And here they come now," the female voice said, rising in excitement as the speakers took their places on the stage. "There's State Assemblyman Jordan Issa, followed by U.S. Senator Joe Salem. And there's Edwin Daoud, writer and Columbia professor." He nodded his head solemnly to the crowd.

"Who didn't read Mr. Daoud in college?" the male voice broke in.

"And now, Brooklyn's own Reverend Randall Roebling Nation, today's master of ceremonies is ascending to the lectern."

The crowd cheered as Nation, dressed in a finely tailored gray suit, clasped his hands together above his head and shook them in a gesture of friendship. He wore stylish sunglasses and a thick gold chain around his neck. His hair was brushed back on his head and shone in the sun. He was about the same age as the Judge had been. He stood in silence, smiling a straight-toothed smile as the crowd cheered. He calmed them down with a gesture of his flattened hands horizontally pressing down on air.

"Thank you, my friends. Thank you." His voice was rich and sonorous. "I stand before you today not far from the spot where a nine-year-old boy was carelessly run down by a speeding truck, his life taken from him before its time. I stand on the very epicenter of the awful riot that took the life of one man, injured dozens and stained the very soul of this peaceful neighborhood. I stand before you on the spot that has marked division and hatred ever since. But I'm not here to speak about rage or hatred. No. I have seen enough to last me ten lifetimes, a thousand. I come to you with a message of hope."

The crowd cheered on the television.

"As many of you know, I grew up in Jim Crow's South, where a black man was considered a fraction of a man, less than human. We were slaves and remained so, long after Emancipation. Black men and women were raped, lynched, terrorized, denied their God-given rights during one of the most ignominious and ignoble periods in human history.

"My mother, God rest her soul, was chosen. When I was nine years old she took my brother and me and our two sisters on a bus ride that would change our lives forever. My mother was chosen, and we went to the Promised Land, to New York City, to a place with the stately sounding name of Bedford Stuyvesant, right here in Brooklyn."

The crowd let up a cheer.

"We went to a city where a man could fly as far as his hard work would carry him, freed from the stinging yoke of history. My mother was chosen, and I was chosen. But wait, let's not stop there. We are all chosen by the Almighty, each and every living soul. No one is a favorite child, not the whites who work on Wall Street and live in their glass towers, or the poor blacks of East St. Louis, Bushwick or Watts, not the Serbs or the Croats, not the Japanese or the Germans, not the Pakistanis or the Indians who aim their missiles at each other's hearts, not the Hutus or the Tutsis who have massacred each other in God's name. The Sons of

Abraham, both Isaac and Ishmael, sit side-by-side in Heaven. There is no favorite child. We are all God's children. We are all chosen.

"You might ask me, Reverend, if we are all chosen, then why does one suffer while another does not, why does one drink the wine while the other is parched? I'll tell you it's because one must choose one's fate. You are the chosen, but you must choose. If my mother had not chosen action over defeat, if she had not chosen to be brave, if she had not chosen to be chosen, all those years ago, would I be standing here before you today, a reverend with ministries in every borough of the greatest city in the world, former Democratic candidate for the President of the United States—"

And here the crowd roared again.

Pure hypocrisy, Stone thought. This was the man who had harangued his father to death. Everything in Nation's public life was strategic, political, working the angle. He had co-opted the mantle of Chosen People from the Jews, not to bring peace and harmony to the world, but to bring the Jews down, to strip them of their rights to a land of their own.

Nation stood on the dais, smiling, calming the crowd with his well-practiced gestures. He didn't know it, but this would be the final speech of his life, as death, the great equalizer lay just beneath, in the old train tunnel under Atlantic Avenue. He would see his God sooner than he knew. The boys from the *beis* would see to that.

Stone's buzzer rang and he dropped the robe to the couch as he stood.

"It's me."

He buzzed Gabby in and stood in the open doorway to greet her. She sheepishly walked down the hall, dressed in warm fall colors, her hair tied back in a ponytail, her high boots clacking on the tiles.

"How are you?" she said, with genuine warmth. "I was worried." She kissed him softly on the lips and entered the apartment. "You're not dressed."

"Yes, I am," Stone said.

"Ha, ha. Get dressed."

"I am," Stone said.

"Matty. Come on. You can't go to the luncheon dressed like that. I want you to meet my professor."

Nation continued speaking on the television set: "And when our brothers and sisters over in Palestine find themselves imprisoned, shot in the streets of their towns and cities, their land taken from them, their homes demolished by bulldozers of hate . . ."

"Will you turn this down?" Gabby said. "I can't hear myself think."

"Wait," Stone said. "Listen to him incite the crowd."

Nation continued: "And if only dark days seem to lie ahead, we must always remember that we must choose to be chosen. We must rise up and choose to be free, we must rise up and choose our destiny, we must rise up and choose to be strong, we must rise up and choose to be chosen. Rise up and choose to be chosen, rise up and choose . . ."

Gabby clicked off the set. "This isn't fair. We're going to be late. Now, please get dressed."

Nation's words still rung in Stone's ear.

"But, the rally," Stone said.

Gabby looked at him uncomprehendingly. "What do you mean?"

"The rally. We've got to watch until it happens."

"Matthew. I don't know what you are talking about." A deep vertical line formed between her eyebrows. "Matthew. What's going on?"

"You don't know?"

"Don't know what?" she said.

"I thought you knew."

"Matthew, you're scaring me."

"You really don't know?"

She looked beautiful to Stone for what would be the last time, as she chewed on her lower lip, her left eye screwed shut to hold back a tear. He wanted to hold her and he went to her, but she held her arms out between them, stopping him short.

"Tell me, Matty. Tell me what you've gotten into."

He told her everything from Seligman to Brilliant, to the account numbers and shooting range at the *beis*. He told her about the Judge's books and the narrative he had pieced together from his marginal notes and underlinings. He told her he had never felt more strong and in control his entire life. He said he was fulfilling his father's final wish, completing his legacy and laying the groundwork for a new generation.

"My father would be proud," Stone said. "He thought I was weak, incompetent. I could never do right by him. But, now—"

"But now, what?" Gabby said. She wore a face that Stone did not recognize, stricken, blanched of all color and definition. "You're just going to sit here in front of the television and watch people die?"

"They're our enemies. You should know. You were in the army."

"But, I never killed anyone. I only shot in practice."

"Gabby, the entire world is against the Jews. We have to show the world that we are strong and that there is no permitted blood. You said yourself that you hated Daoud. And what about Nation, how he smeared my father, tried to destroy him? These are the same people who murdered your uncle. There are known terrorists and enemies of Israel on that podium."

"Matthew. This is crazy. Don't tell me that you have bought into the paranoid delusions of the Diaspora Jew. This is crazy. What are you going to do? What are you going to do?"

"This is what my father planned. This is what he wanted. It can't be stopped."

"Don't touch me."

"This is my last chance to obey his wishes. And nobody innocent will die."

"And who gave you that power to decide?"

"The Judge."

"You're crazy," she said, stepping away in horror. "How can you talk like that? I spoke to your father last Tu B'Shvat when he knew he was dying of cancer. Matthew, he was a broken man. You know how devastated he was, how embarrassed he was that he had to step down as a judge after the Riot trial. He was humiliated. He was dying and he was so afraid that he would be remembered for that after all of the good work he had done, after working so hard to make a name for himself that was not connected to Julius Stone, the gangster. Matthew, your father could never have agreed to this plan, knowing that it would tarnish his reputation. Yes, he had strong feelings about the Arabs. But he had stronger feelings about his name, his reputation. Do you know what he was reading when he came to visit? *Othello* by William Shakespeare. He said he wanted to reread all of his plays one last time. And I remember him reading me Cassio's pitiful lines after he was punished by Othello, stripped of his honorable position."

"'Reputation, reputation, reputation.'" Stone murmured.

"Yes," she said. "'And all that remains is bestial.' Your father was deeply concerned with his legacy after the disaster of the trial." She ran her fingers through her hair. "Who put you up to this? Was it Rabbi Seligman?"

Stone nodded his head.

"You trusted him? You know he's an ideologue and an extremist, Matthew, just like my uncle was before he was killed. Neither of them made it a secret that they wanted the Arabs transferred out of Israel."

"He seemed softer, somehow," Stone said. "I thought he'd changed."

"Nobody ever changes," Gabby said.

"There was something soothing about his presence, as if he had a special connection to my father, as if through him I found a facsimile of my father. They were best friends, after all."

"A long time ago, Matthew."

"What do you mean?"

"You didn't know your father and Rabbi Seligman had a falling out? They had barely spoken in years. They had a terrible fight."

His father's dying words started to make sense now. When he had mentioned Seligman's name he was not directing Stone towards him, but warning him to stay away from him. When he had mentioned numbers, he had wanted Matthew to keep them out of Seligman's hands. His stubborn father, the Judge, had kept that vital information to himself until the very end, held back from his incompetent son in case he should live. And then, when it became clear he would die, it was too late, his voice was gone, the death rattle ticking lightly in his throat.

A great cry tore through Stone's belly. "Oh my God," Stone said. "I've made a mistake. I've made a terrible mistake."

Gabby stood before him, tears streaming down her face. "How could I have ever thought that I could give myself to you?"

Stone was silent. He imagined the palm of his father's massive hand slapping him across the face again and again, forever.

"What have you got to say?"

"I'm sorry," Stone said. "I thought I was doing the right thing. This was my chance to give something back."

Gabby kicked at him with her high boots, beating on his face and chest with her clenched fists. "Stupid! Stupid! Do something. There has to be some way to stop it. How did you ever get such a crazy idea in your head? Did you think I would love you for this? I'm sick," she said. "I'm going to throw up."

She vomited hard into the sink. For a moment Stone felt more pain for Gabby and her suffering than he did for all those people on the podium on Atlantic Avenue. Then he realized he would drag the bodies of the dead with him for the rest of his life. He began moaning and cried out something beastly and unintelligible.

Gabby turned to him, her wet eyes full of hate. "Get out of here," she screamed. "Get out! I'm calling the police. Maybe there's still time . . ."

He felt a stabbing pain shoot through his chest, and his legs buckled, but he found the strength to run. He sprang out of the door in his socks, burst out onto Waverly Avenue and ran as fast as he could towards the *beis*. His heart beat hard in his ears. Maybe it's not too late, he thought. He ran through broken glass and tripped on the median under the BQE.

A shining black car sat idling in front of the warehouse, its trunk open. Moshe appeared in the doorway of the warehouse carrying two suitcases. Brilliant appeared behind him with his beard neatly trimmed on his long arrogant face. He wore a freshly pressed black suit that gave him a grave, funereal air.

"Matthew. I'm surprised to see you here."

Stone pushed Brilliant back into the warehouse as hard as he could, his vision blurred by tears. Brilliant fell to the floor. Stone felt Moshe's heavy hand on his shoulder.

"Let him go," Brilliant said, getting to his feet.

Stone breathed heavily, and felt his throat and sinuses burning. "You've got to stop this."

"What?" Brilliant laughed. "It's too late for cold feet."

"You're a murderer."

"Suddenly you have a social conscience, Matthew. I'll have you know that you are a murderer too."

The warehouse was barren, cleared out of all signs of habitation. The floors were swept clean and a chemical smell of industrial cleaner hung in the air.

"What's going on?" Stone said.

"We have a plane to catch in an hour."

"A plane? I don't understand."

"We'll be safe on the runway, ready to take off for home. It'll be over soon. You didn't think we were going to stay as Atlantic Avenue is blown up beneath their feet? We have to get to Israel before the investigation starts. You understand, don't you?"

Stone nodded his head.

"A remote-controlled detonator that can be set off from a timer will ignite four drums of compressed hydrogen to be used as accelerant for seventy-five pounds of C-4. There will be a massive explosion, the likes of which this country has never seen."

Stone stared blank-faced at Brilliant's sparkling eyes. He could hear Moshe slam the trunk shut behind him. Stone could see Moshe's shadow lengthen across the floor as he filled the doorway.

"No," Stone muttered. "No, no, no, no, no."

"I know you've done a lot of reading, school, your father's books. But, did you ever come across anything about Israel's extradition treaty with the U.S.? Let me explain: Israeli law prohibits extraditing Israeli citizens when they're accused of a crime in a second country."

Stone felt himself go cold. "What does that mean?"

"If one understands, then one has everything," Brilliant laughed. "Matthew, we're dual citizens. Citizens of both Israel and the U.S. Moshe's Israeli, I'm Israeli, Yossi, Itzy, everyone from the *beis* is Israeli. Except you."

"This will be the worst terrorist attack in U.S. history."

"You knew what you signed up for."

"No, I didn't."

"You knew people would die. What's the difference?"

"They'll come looking for you."

"Why would anyone cause an international mess like that when they have a suspect right here in America? Is Washington going to withhold aid packages and loan guarantees when they have you to blame?"

"Nobody will ever believe I did this by myself."

Brilliant laughed again and so did Moshe. "The only thing to do with an idiot and a thorn is to get rid of them both. Remember, you transferred the money from your father's account. No one else had access to it. And you were quite a capable shot at the range. I'm sure the police will find it interesting that a gun with your fingerprints all over it is the same gun that killed your foolish roommate."

"No," Stone gasped.

"Yes," Brilliant said. "Moshe dropped it in a mailbox just this morning. It'll be found in the afternoon pickup."

"This is impossible."

Brilliant continued, "Just as your grandfather smuggled weapons from New York to Tel Aviv, you and your roommate smuggled weapons from Tel Aviv to New York. It's a perfect circle."

Stone fell to his knees. "Why did you do this to me?"

"Your father just died. We knew you were in mourning. We knew you were weak. An apple waiting to be plucked. That's the trick of the evil impulse, it's sweet in the beginning and bitter in the end. You would have believed anything to take the pain away."

"Didn't my father save you when you killed Bassam?"

The sun streamed in through the open door, which Moshe had vacated and merged with the artificial lights overhead to form a disorienting hazy screen between him and Brilliant. Moshe grabbed Stone under the armpits and lifted him up. "We have to go," Moshe said.

Stone did not want them to leave. He wanted them to stay forever as they were, just the three of them alone in the warehouse, outside of time, just the three of them.

"Plane's leaving," Moshe added.

Stone went cold.

"Matthew, when history is written people will remember one name when they think of this attack, this horrible attack that maimed and killed Arabs so far from their corrupt terrorist states. People will remember the name: Stone."

"No," Stone cried.

"You are just the end of this story. But it began a long time ago, with your grandfather strangling his victims to line his pockets, his midnight hits and shakedowns. He's a great anti-hero. People are fascinated with him. Yes, he helped with the establishment of the State of Israel, but he will always be remembered as a killer, and your father, the Judge, who fixed a jury to save a killer, a Jew, me. He always lived with the taint of your grandfather hanging over him. And now that his son has released such horrible carnage on the streets of Brooklyn, and on the very anniversary of the riot, to avenge his father. What do you think people will remember? They will remember the blood that the Stone family shed across more than half a century."

"I'm not a killer," Stone cried.

"When you are called before the Throne of Judgment, tell that to the Heavenly Father. Here on earth you and your father are and will remain killers in the great collective memory, the worst in the history of this country. Goodbye, Matthew."

Brilliant turned to walk away, and Stone rushed at him, flailing his arms wildly.

Moshe grabbed Stone by the hair and pulled him off Brilliant, lifting Stone up from the ground with incredible force. He flew through the air and crashed head first into a brick wall.

When he woke, Stone was alone in the darkness. He wondered briefly whether he was dead, but then smelled the cleaning solution and heard the muttered voices of students at prayer sifting down from the third-floor study house. His head ached and his tongue screamed where he had nearly bitten it in half. *Did it really happen*, he thought? He looked at his watch, but it had stopped when he had hit the concrete wall. Lying on the cool floor, he felt everything had turned upside down, that he had in fact not understood anything in his life and all the wisdom in the world from here on would be of no use. He stood up with difficulty and felt each and every bone in his body – bruised, misaligned from the force of his fall. He found his way to the door in the darkness, feeling his way with hands reaching before him. He unlatched the door and pulled it open. The day was bright and blue, the sky deep, expanding, seemingly forever. He stepped out into the cool air and saw the city beyond, its buildings and towers sparkling, each one created with man's ingenuity, strength and will. They rose up into the sky and fit seamlessly into the space created for them.

A group of pigeons loitered nearby and Stone called to them. They flapped their wings and ascended into the sky, circling as one in the sunshine. Stone knew it was a stupid thought, but he felt as if he too were rising up, up, up. They rose higher and circled, the entire city spread out beneath them, the dazzling waters of the East River catching the sun just right. The lazy sound of the waves filled his ears and soothed his throbbing head. The birds were beautiful to watch, moving as one synchronized body through the air. And it occurred to Stone that perhaps the day had stood still, caught in the languid web of the warming sun. Then, as the birds circled above for a second time, something shattered the still of the day, something distant, but distinct, and they dipped, looped and seemed to drop dizzily from the sky, scattering in all directions like a fractured dream, to be lost forever.